ANATOMY

OF THE

TRUTH

ANATOMY

OF THE

TRUTH

a novel

W. D. McCOMB

TreaShore
PRESS

ANATOMY OF THE TRUTH
Copyright © 2020 by W. D. McComb.

wdmccomb.com

All rights reserved. Published by TreaShore Press.

ISBN 978-1-7340904-7-5 (hardcover)
ISBN: 978-1-7340904-8-2 (paperback)
ISBN: 978-1-7340904-9-9 (ebook)
First edition.

Printed in the United States of America

DEDICATION

First, I would like to remind readers that this is a work of fiction. The characters, events, and procedures herein are entirely my creation and serve only the purpose of bringing a story to life. The contents of this book should in no way be viewed as disparaging, critical, or representative of real people or places. The professors and instructors who trained me, while they were tough and demanding—as well they should have been—were top-notch. If medical training was a competition, and perhaps it is in many ways, I would put them up against anyone, anywhere. I owe them all many thanks.

Second, my deepest gratitude goes out to all those patients and their families who have chosen to participate in whole-body or organ and tissue donation programs. Both types allow for one of the most beautiful paradoxes known to mankind. Whether in the minds and hands of healthcare providers who learn the mysteries of the human body in a Gross Anatomy course, or in a more literal way within the body of a recipient of an organ or tissue donation, those whose souls have left this world are able to not only live on within it but also extend the lives and enhance the quality of life of those left behind.

Finally, a clarification is necessary. One portion of this novel is actually inspired entirely by truth. My Gross Anatomy cadaver did indeed have a gunshot wound through the chest, and my partners and I did nickname him Lucky. As far as I know, though, he was not part of a plot to kill us or ruin any of our lives. His nickname was meant to be ironic, assigned in a stressful time when levity was a valuable commodity often hard to come by. In hindsight, I think we chose the name in part because we knew we were the lucky ones. Thank you, Lucky, for all you taught us. I will never forget you.

Also by W.D. McComb

<u>Short stories</u>

"The Recruit"

"They Roam Those Hills"

<u>A Novel</u>

THE TRUTH THAT LIES BETWEEN

PROLOGUE

JET Townsend's friends asked him many times over the years if he had seen the light, back when he had camped at Death's door for over a week. Jack and I probably posed the question a dozen times between us, like being almost dead somehow carried an obligation to have a sort of supernatural epiphany, and Jet was holding out on us. But his answer was always a similar version of the same story. He wanted to say yes, that he had seen and felt the warm, inviting sun of the afterlife calling him. That he had resisted the urge to let go of the pain of this world and bask in the glow of something better. That he turned back because he knew there were adventures to be had, loves to love, lives to save.

The truth was he didn't remember much about being in a coma. One second he was catching a glimpse of a black Camaro crashing into him, and the next he was in a haze of excruciating pain in a hospital bed with a tube down his throat, trying to make sense of it all while doctors pinched his toes and asked him to blink once for yes or twice for no. Yes, he was certain he had visited Death back then, but as far as he knew, he hadn't been invited in.

The haunting question later became why he had been spared an invitation, but as best he could tell, his brother got forced through the door.

It was a question without an answer, of course, at least not a satisfactory one. But that didn't stop Jet from asking it, and Jack and I came to fear that its mere existence might change everything for our friend. How could he expect to become a physician, to realize his lifelong dream of healing the sick and wounded, if he couldn't accept the fact that death, in all its ugly unpredictability, would sometimes be an inevitable part of that process? But Jet insisted those doubts were wasted on him. He had no reservations whatsoever about whether he could handle it. He had overcome too much not to. A medical degree was his for the taking, and he planned to stride through the doors of the Jackson University School of Medicine and seize the moment like none who had come before him. Yes, he would meet Death face to face in Gross Anatomy, his very first class, but he would conquer it and march on until victory was his.

That was his plan, anyway.

PART ONE

"Shut off the past! Let the dead past bury its dead. So easy to say, so hard to realize! The truth is, the past haunts us like a shadow."

— Sir William Osler

ONE

1993 — Biloxi, Mississippi

THE fifteen-foot Boston Whaler skiff slid easily off the trailer into the murky water of the Old Fort Bayou. At this time of the morning, it was the only boat launching. Adam Townsend figured the hardcore fishermen had probably pulled out two hours earlier, and the recreational boaters hadn't quite rolled out of bed. He was neither, but he wished he had pried himself from under the covers a bit earlier with the fishermen. The early September sun would climb quick and hot and fierce, spreading the last burns of summer before fall softened it.

A shove with his foot to ease the boat away from the water's edge, a pull of the choke and two turns of the starter, and Adam had the outboard motor roaring to life. As usual, he felt a twinge of guilt for the exhilaration that came with the inevitable puff of gasoline fumes whenever he cranked the 88-horsepower Evinrude. The smell signaled either pending adventure or work, sometimes both, and while it was unnatural and briefly covered the pungent, unadulterated, marsh aroma he relished even more, it was a necessary means to an end.

A slow push of the throttle had him heading west, toward Biloxi Bay. Adam studied the foamy roll of water against the starboard side absently, his mind wandering. Then a flash of cinnamon and black and white caught his attention as a flock of American avocets passed low in front of him. Wouldn't be long before they headed on south.

Redirecting his thoughts to the task at hand, he continued west around Fort Point, then turned the skiff toward Biloxi's Back Bay. He waved politely at one fisherman who acknowledged him and ignored another who was concentrating on his own efforts and paid Adam no attention. He cruised between Big Island and Little Island before turning back south, finally killing the engine about one hundred yards offshore, due north of the Double Luck Casino. No one stirred onshore, surprising since this was a cooler part of the day, if one could call it that. The place would be abuzz with activity inside though, even at nine in the morning.

Adam surveyed the waters around him for a moment. More out of curiosity than anything. He was a people watcher, but there was nothing to see here. The few boats moored nearby sat quietly. He contemplated wetting a hook but really wasn't in the mood. Besides, this really wasn't where he'd fish even if he wanted to. He slipped five empty vials out of his backpack and moved to the bow, away from the stern and the motor that might contaminate things. He leaned forward, careful not to fall overboard, filling each one. He sealed and labeled them before placing the vials carefully back in his bag, then readied to head out again.

"Whatcha doing there, boy?"

The voice startled him, closer than he thought anyone could possibly be. Adam was a little embarrassed and hoped whomever it was had not seen him jump. He turned to see a man wearing a Stetson and aviators standing at the bow of a luxury cruising yacht that looked to be in the forty-five-foot range. It wasn't as close as he'd thought, though. Sound was carrying surprisingly well across the morning's unusually calm water.

"Excuse me?" was the only response he could think of.

"I wanna know what you lookin' for. I've seen you around. You must be one of them DEQ guys."

Even Adam's brother Jet had assumed he was working for the Department of Environmental Quality when he told him he was doing water quality surveys. Everyone seemed to know who they were and what they did. But no one was supposed to know about this. "Not DEQ. Just routine water sampling," Adam called across as he cranked the motor. He nonchalantly eased the boat in a wide arc at idle speed to get a better look at the yacht and its owner. Now he could see the boat's lettering clearly. *Double Trouble.*

"Funny how your routine sampling always needs to be done right here." The man lowered his voice as Adam cruised by. "We know what you're doing, Mr. Townsend. Here and elsewhere."

Adam was really unnerved now. The man had feigned uncertainty as to who Adam was at first but obviously did know him. And wanted Adam to know it. How could that be? Adam said nothing, just nodded his head and moved on. Nothing to be gained by an argument with this redneck. Rich redneck, actually, from the looks of the yacht. If it even belonged to the man. Did the man really know what he was doing? And if so, how? And who was *we?*

No matter. Just get finished with the other samples, get some lunch, and get back home.

———————

Adam had no other altercations while he took another set of samples from the Back Bay and two out in the main Gulf, but the whole time he couldn't help wondering how many others were watching him. He tried to put the encounter out of his mind as he loaded his skiff and secured it to the trailer. It might be a joke, maybe a friend of his boss. But that would be a problem, too, since his boss didn't know about this project. Or at least Adam thought he didn't.

Whatever. He was essentially done with his assignment anyway. Just had to run the samples through the lab. As best he could tell, this was just somebody's useless crusade that didn't look like it was going to turn up anything. Which was, in most ways, a good thing. There were worse things than not being hated by everyone on the whole Mississippi Gulf Coast.

Adam turned his truck into the place that had occupied his thoughts for much of the morning, at least until he'd met his coastal cowboy friend. Billey's on the Bayou, read the royal blue, hand-painted letters on the restaurant's façade. It wasn't much to look at, with white paint chipping off the wooden siding and a roof sagging slightly on one corner, but it was less than half a mile from where he launched his boat for these monthly outings, and as far as Adam was concerned, it had the best seafood in Ocean Springs or Biloxi. He pulled around back to park so as not to obstruct the small gravel lot.

The blast of cool air that greeted Adam when he opened the door was a welcome relief. The room was small as most restaurants go, sparsely furnished with eight or ten tables with white Formica tops and mismatched wooden chairs. The wood slat walls displayed a few dozen faded fishing photos with no frames and curling edges. All the tables were empty. *Good, I beat the crowd.* Adam picked a spot and was quickly approached by a cute, sandy-blonde waitress.

"Man, this air feels goood! Biggest sweet tea you got, and an order of fried green tomatoes," he told her. "With the remoulade. And could you bring me a menu and a wine list?"

"Sir, I'm sorry but we don't have menus or a—"

"I know, I'm just messing with you." Adam pointed to the menu written in chalk on the wall behind the counter. "I just need a minute to study what you've got." She nodded and turned away to wipe off an adjacent table, which suited him just fine. What he really wanted to study was her, since he already knew what was written on the wall. The fact that he didn't know who she was surprised him at first, but the more he thought about it, maybe not. He only stopped in once a month, on the days he collected samples. On his meager income, he couldn't afford to come here or to any other restaurant often, so new faces on occasion were inevitable. This new face might be one to remember.

"Sir?" She spoke as she whirled and caught him staring.

Adam didn't look away and was thrilled that she held his gaze, seemingly unfazed by it. Her eyes were hazel, guarded by dark eyebrows that were slightly bushy where they came together. Not in an ungroomed way, but in a Brooke Shields kind of way. She possessed a natural look, where you weren't sure if she had makeup on or not but hoped she didn't. Her teeth were almost perfect. Just close enough for her parents to maybe talk themselves out of the expense of braces when she was a teenager.

"Sir? Would you care for a beer?" She stood erect and waited on his answer.

He smiled. "Ma'am, before we go any further, I need one thing from you."

"Yessir?"

"I need you to quit calling me sir. I can't be that much older than you."

She blushed, and her posture softened. "I'm sorry, my boss insists on it, no matter what age the customer is. But if I'm going to quit calling you sir, you're going to have to quit calling me ma'am."

Her accent wasn't thick, but it was clearly from somewhere north of the Mason-Dixon line. "Well, ma'am, I'm sorry but that's not going to be possible. See, whereas sir can be a formality that often interferes with making casual conversation and intimacy …" Adam paused ever so slightly for effect and to see how she reacted to the last word. "Here in the south, ma'am is a sign of respect for a lady of any age, from six to ninety-six. And you certainly do seem to fit the definition of lady as best I can tell."

Her blush faded, replaced by the natural smile he had seen earlier. "Well, I don't know about that, but thank you."

"What's your name?"

"Anniston. Anniston Lewis."

"Like the city in Alabama?"

"That's the one. How do you know where Anniston is?"

"But you're not from Alabama." She frowned at him suspiciously. "The accent," he continued. "I'm not sure where it's from, but it ain't Alabama."

She smiled again. "My Dad grew up there. I was born in Kansas, believe it or not. Got an aunt that lives here, so I'm just working down here for the summer. Don't see her much, though. Either working or gambling at the Golden Pearl."

"Well, I'm Adam Townsend, and I'm from Amberton, Mississippi, and I'm starving." Adam extended his hand to shake that of his new friend. Her hand was warm despite the coolness of the room. "How about a bowl of the gumbo? I'll share it with you."

Anniston raised one eyebrow. "Now, I've had some pickup lines used on me before, but never that one. I'll share my gumbo with you?"

Adam laughed. It was his turn to blush. "Guess I'm just hungry. Yeah, that one was pretty bad. How about this one? Would you have dinner with me sometime?"

She flashed her perfectly imperfect smile. "Much better. I get off at three today. Supposed to be off to go to the eye doctor, but I think that appointment just got cancelled." She winked and lowered her voice to a whisper. "Shhh, don't tell." Anniston twirled and sauntered back toward the kitchen.

Look back over your shoulder. Look back! Anniston's pace slowed, she rotated her head slightly, then stopped, as if trying to decide. Then she peeked back. Ever so slightly, but there was no doubt about it. Adam locked his gaze on hers.

Bingo!

———————

"Holy roux, this is some good gumbo." Adam gestured with his spoon toward Anniston sitting in the booth across from him. "If you weren't here, I think I'd slurp it up then lick the bowl."

She laughed. "Holy roux? You really know how to win a girl over, what with your clever gumbo pickup lines and idioms."

Adam swallowed hard and raised both eyebrows. "Did you say idiom? You sound like my brother Jet, always using words most folks don't include in casual conversation."

"Well, dangnabbit, *exkee-uuuse* me for being edumacated." Anniston gave an exaggerated imitation of a southern backwoods word-butchering drawl.

"Not bad for a Kansas girl." Adam smiled. He slid out of the booth and stood. "Hey, I'll be right back. Gotta hit the men's room, then I'll pay out."

Adam studied himself in the bathroom mirror. *My lucky day.* He considered himself something of a lady's man, but it wasn't every day that he walked into a hole-in-the-wall restaurant and walked out with a date with a bombshell. And a smart one with a sense of humor to boot. He brushed his fingers through his hair, washed his hands and arms and face in case he smelled sweaty, then dried himself thoroughly so he didn't look sweaty.

Just as he threw the paper towel into the trash, he heard Anniston shout. Then a crash and a cry of pain.

TWO

ADAM burst through the door, throwing it open with both hands hard enough that it bounced off the doorstop. He only caught a glimpse of a man scuttling out the front door. Khaki pants, white shirt. Boots, maybe. A navy baseball cap was pulled low on his head, impossible to see the logo from the back.

Anniston was lying on the floor beneath one of the tables near the door, groaning. Two chairs were overturned.

"Call 911!" Adam yelled to whoever might be on the other side of the kitchen door, as he ran to Anniston's side. "What happened?"

She was breathing heavily, holding the back of her head, struggling to stand. "I'm okay, I'm okay." She brushed Adam back as he tried to help her.

"What happened?" he asked again.

"A man came in, I went over to take his order, but he just ignored me." She grimaced, rubbing the back of her head as she pulled out a chair to sit. She pointed to where Adam had been eating. "You need to look at your table. He did something to your food. Like he was poisoning it or something. I yelled at him, but he pushed me down and ran out."

"What's going on out here?" An obese man with no neck, a three-day beard, and a stained white apron lumbered into the room.

Adam pointed behind him at Anniston as he strode across the room, back toward the table where he'd been sitting. "She's been assaulted, and someone tried to poison me. Call the police!" He stopped and stared at his gumbo bowl. Empty only minutes before, it was full of what appeared to be dingy water now. The contents of several glass vials had been emptied into it. A few were scattered on the table. Two were stuffed in his tea glass. He didn't have to walk outside to his truck to know where the vials had come from.

"The police are on their way," the sweating fat man with the apron said. "S.O.B. comes up in my place bustin' up my customers and employees, gonna be hell to pay."

"What was he doing over there?" Anniston asked.

"I'm not sure, but I'm gonna find out." Adam shrugged as if he didn't know. "Maybe just a friend playing a prank."

"Your friends always knock women around?" the fat man asked.

Adam ignored him, his mind racing. "Anniston, I need to go check on a few things." He turned to the man he presumed to be the owner. "Sir, I didn't see anything, and I'm not sure why the guy poured stuff into my food, so I don't think I'll be much help to the police. I've gotta go. Make sure Anniston gets taken care of." He moved toward the door.

"Adam?" Her voice stopped him in his tracks, and he turned back. "Can you drop me off at the ER on your way to wherever you're going? I don't feel so well, and it's just up the road." Her face bore a pleading look, but the sparkle in her eyes told a different story than her words. She winked at him.

"Sure, I can do that."

"You can't leave!" the fat man said. "Police will need your statement."

She ignored him and helped Adam gather up the glass vials around his table. "I'm sure you can tell them what they need to know."

"Leave here now, and you're fired! You need to wait on the police and ambulance."

"No sir, I need medical attention immediately. They can find me at the ER."

Adam gave the man a raised-eyebrow, what-do-you-expect-me-to-do-about-it look as he escorted her out the front door. He found his empty backpack lying in the gravel just outside the restaurant.

Anniston waved Adam off and refused his offer to help her get into his truck.

He slid into his seat and closed his truck door, tossing the bag into the extended cab behind him. "So I guess you're not hurt too bad?"

"No, I'm okay. Hated working there anyway. Food's good, but the owner's a jerk. And if you didn't see a need to talk to the cops, then neither did I. The guy just pushed me down. I've had worse on the school playground."

"Well, we'll get you checked out anyway."

"No!" Her voice was abrupt and harsh, then it softened. "Sorry, didn't mean it like that. I'm fine, don't waste your time is all I meant. Where we headed?"

"We? Where is your car? Where do you live?"

"Aunt lives about a mile from here. She dropped me off this morning. I usually walk home. But I don't want to go there now." Anniston bit her bottom lip teasingly. "Just take me wherever you're going."

"You don't even know me."

"I know you well enough. It's in the eyes. You're a good guy. At least in the ways that matter. But I do wonder if you're a bad boy in the ways that matter, too."

Adam glanced sideways and confirmed her eyes were locked on him, but he said nothing. His heart and mind raced, and he thought both might get away from him. His instincts told him he needed to take her to the ER, go to his office immediately to check on things, or both—but he supposed that could wait. It looked like she wanted to go back to his place, and if she wouldn't go to see a doctor, then who was he to disagree?

"Aren't you gonna ask me what those samples were?" Adam finally asked.

"I figured you'd tell me when you were ready. You'll find I'm not a nosy person. But I could tell you knew what was poured in your bowl. That's what was in that bag, huh?" She motioned to the dusty backpack lying out of sight behind them.

"Yeah, it was some of my stuff. Just a, uh, research project I've been working on. Kind of a side job. I have no idea why someone would want to sabotage it, though. Probably just some misunderstanding. Weird. I'm sorry you got involved."

"I'm not. If it hadn't happened, I wouldn't be in your truck right now, and I'd be having trouble concentrating on my job, wondering if you were really gonna show back up to take me to dinner."

Adam turned into a parking lot, weaved between several buildings, and parked. His building was just a narrow duplex, small but fairly new, with a kitchen and living room downstairs, a single bedroom upstairs. He nodded toward the door to his apartment as he slid out of the truck. "Come on." He could already see what was about to happen. Pretend to gently check the place where she hit her head, lean in slowly for the inevitable kiss if she didn't beat him to it, and then who knows …

The door was unlocked. He turned the key but could feel it wasn't necessary. He hoped she didn't notice—he didn't want her to think he was irresponsible. Still, it was unusual for him to forget, and he thought he remembered checking it like he always did, but it had been a strange day.

He opened the door and immediately knew why the door was unlocked. The place was a complete mess. Tables overturned, drawers opened, papers strewn everywhere.

Anniston gasped, her hand automatically over her mouth.

"Go get back in the truck."

She didn't move.

"Go get in the truck!" he repeated more vehemently. "Get in the driver's side and crank it and be ready to leave as soon as someone comes out that door, whether it's me or someone else! Hurry!" Adam put the keys in her hand and squeezed it.

He swept the downstairs to make sure no one was there. He grabbed a butcher knife from the kitchen but wished that he kept his pistol in his truck. He wasn't exactly a handgun expert, but he kept one for self-defense and was confident in using it if needed. The problem was, his .357 S&W revolver, two 12-gauge shotguns, and a .270 rifle were under his bed. Upstairs. Where the intruder who had ransacked his apartment might very well be.

"Hey!" he shouted. "Just so you know, I'm not gonna walk up there and let you ambush me, and the police are on their way.

So you're trapped!" Adam spotted his aluminum softball bat lying on the floor by the couch. From the looks of his shattered lamp, the intruder had spotted it too.

Adam studied the knife in his hand, then stuck it in his back pocket and picked up the bat. Thank goodness for church softball. He stepped behind the wall of the stairwell where he could not be seen by anyone coming down, lifted the bat in a loaded position to swing, and listened.

Nothing.

He waited for a couple of minutes that seemed like an hour, his heart pounding in his throat. How and why this was suddenly happening to him? Like he was some spy in a James Bond movie. Was Anniston waiting outside, or had she driven away to get help? He wouldn't blame her if she had raced out of the county and left behind all the trouble that came with Adam Townsend.

Still nothing.

Adam peeked around the corner to look up the stairs, half expecting a bullet to come screaming by him. He had heard Jet say that if a bullet hits you just right, you never hear the report from the gun because the speed of the bullet exceeds the speed of sound. He had never done the math, but if Jet said it, you could mark it down as truth. Adam didn't want to find out.

No bullets came. He crept up the stairs. Why hadn't he just called the police? It wasn't like he was hiding anything criminal. But could there be something going on that the police were best left out of altogether? On any other day, he would have just figured it was a routine break-in, somebody looking for jewelry or money or guns or electronics to pawn. But the events on the water and then at Billey's on the Bayou told him this was something else.

Adam paused and took a deep breath at the top of the stairs, fighting the urge to race back down and out the front door. Totally unsure of what was around the corner. He darted his head around for a quick look like he'd seen done in movies. Heart still pounding in his throat, he thought his voice box might coil up and burst out of his neck at any second.

Again, nothing happened.

Then, he was standing in his bedroom. The scene was similar to that of the downstairs. Nothing was where it should be. Someone clearly had been searching for something. Adam doubted they had found it, for two reasons. One, his guns were the only thing of value he owned, and although they had been pulled out from under the bed, they had not been taken. Two, if they were searching for something related to his activities on the water this morning, that data was not in his apartment. Never had been.

Adam's heart sank when he turned and looked at his dresser. He was not surprised to see the mirror was cracked, but it was something else that bothered him more. A photo of his family, taken at his college graduation—him in cap and gown, smiling with his parents and his brother Jet—had been ripped from its frame. One of his hunting knives was stabbed through the center of the photo, impaling it into the wood of his dresser. And into the wood a single word had been carved. The word and its message were both unmistakable.

STOP!

THREE

One week later — Amberton, Mississippi

STIMPY Riggins jumped at the sound of the phone ringing. He hated calls at this time of the night. For one thing, it was never anything good. And for another, it usually woke his wife, who would realize he wasn't in the bed and wander up to the kitchen to find him, asking questions about what he was doing. And then they would fight. Always a fight. He reached to turn the computer off as he hastily picked up the phone, hoping she hadn't heard it.

"Yeah?"

"Stimpy, you up? It's Ernie."

"I wasn't, but I am now," he lied. "I know who you are. Lord knows you call me enough. What you got?"

"Some old coot down at the rail yard. Hobo or something. Come see what you think."

See what I think. That's what they always said. As if he was a real medical examiner or something, instead of just a guy who worked at a funeral home and got elected coroner twenty years back. Oh well, it helped pay the bills, so if they thought he was more qualified than he was, he'd let them keep right on thinking it. "Foul play?"

"Naw, don't really look like it. But like I said, see what you think. See you in a minute, Stimpy."

Stimpy hated his nickname. It hadn't been that bad at first. He knew he was a little bit stumpy, and his middle name was Stimpson, so it didn't bother him when, as a kid, one of his clever friends fused the two into Stimpy, and it stuck. That's what everyone had called him for thirty years. But now there was that cartoon show with the dumb cat named Stimpy, and everyone got a big kick out of suggesting how alike the two were—physically and mentally. Stumpy *and* stupid. It wasn't funny.

Oh, the irony—wasn't that the word? Some people thought he had some kind of medical degree, and others believed he was a dimwit. Whatever. Unlike a lot of folks, he had a computer and was smart enough to figure out how to work it. Or, at least smart enough to learn how to use it the way *she* had shown him. He wasn't exactly sure what to make of this thing called The Internet, but he liked it. He could find some of the naked pictures he liked and websites where people talked about sex in ways he'd never heard before. But his favorite was the photos she scanned and gave him on the little floppy disks. Even though it wouldn't hold but fifteen at a time, it was better than the actual photos, since his wife didn't even know how to turn on the computer. He checked again to make sure the computer was all the way off and turned to leave.

"On that stupid computer again, I see?" His wife was standing in the door to the hallway in her bathrobe.

"Couldn't sleep."

"Ain't nothing good happening with you on that machine, Stimp. I know it."

"It ain't nothin', I swear it. Just killin' time. Go back to bed, honey. Got a call to go check out." Stimpy blew her a kiss and walked out the door, closing it gently behind him.

———————

The Amberton rail yard of which Ernie Leaks spoke wasn't exactly a bustling hub of activity, but Stimpy knew the place. It consisted of a three-rail junction, but he thought only one of the lines was used these days. A few rail cars were parked there at any given time, but other than that, not much happened. The old train depot was nothing but a crumbling ghost of a building. The Walsh Coal and Ice building was still standing nearby, but just barely. In the daylight, if you looked closely, you could see the white lettering across the front of the weathered red stain of the wood. The thing probably needed to be torn down, but maybe it was one of those historic landmarks, or whatever they called them.

Stimpy found the deputy standing erect in front of the Walsh building, arms crossed and sentry-like, peering down the railroad track like he was awaiting a new arrival. "What you got, Ernie? Did you notify medical?"

"Naw, I was only a quarter mile away when I got the call. Some kids called it in from a pay phone the other side of town. Said there was a dead guy on the tracks. And he was definitely dead when I got here. Didn't see no need for an ambulance. You didn't hear on the scanner?"

Stimpy frowned. "Told you I was asleep." He figured there was no need for Deputy Leaks to know he had turned his scanner off. A fellow had to if he ever wanted some peace and quiet.

"Found him here just like that." Ernie nodded to a spot behind him and to his right.

Stimpy could barely make out a long horizontal shadow on the ground beneath a scraggly pine sapling, about forty feet off the tracks. As he drew closer, he could see it was indeed a man, lying on his left side. His legs were bent, and his hands were tucked under his head, resting on a ragged backpack like he was in a peaceful sleep. "Got a light?"

Ernie produced a flashlight. "Looks like he went to sleep and that was it. Heart attack or OD or something."

The man's hair was disheveled, a mix of dirty blond and gray, and two-week-old patches of facial hair covered bronzed skin with deep wrinkles. Late forties, maybe early fifties, but hard to tell. It was the face of a hard life. "Odd place for a nap. Got an ID?"

"Naw, I ain't touched him. Told you I found him just like that."

"Some investigator you are. What about the sheriff?"

"No again," Leaks said. "Sheriff don't wanna be bothered with a call about some guy dying in his sleep."

Stimpy had never known Sheriff Rex Reynolds to tolerate his staff leaving him out of the loop of the goings-on in McKinley County, but whatever. That would be the deputy's problem tomorrow.

He knelt by the body to examine it. He wasn't a forensics expert—not by a long shot—but he had learned a few things over the years. He touched the skin of the dead man's face with the back of his hand. Felt like he'd been dead an hour or two, although it was hard to tell—the Mississippi September night was so warm, it didn't take much cooling for a body to reach ambient temperature. There was no rigor mortis yet, so that fit too; the death had happened in the last three to four hours. He directed Ernie on where to shine the light and rolled the body just slightly, pulling up the shirt to examine the skin on the left side, closest to the ground. It was a bluish purple, with a well-demarcated margin extending up and down the torso, clearly distinguishing the discolored from the normal, pale skin. "Livor mortis." With his free hand, Stimpy touched his fingertips to the discolored area. "Where the blood pools by gravity after death. Sets in within twenty minutes or so. Looks to me more than likely he died in this position right here."

"Mmm hmm." Ernie nodded. "So, like I said, a heart attack or something. Died in his sleep. Nothing to wake the sheriff over."

"I didn't say that. Waking him or not is your call." Stimpy patted the dead man's pockets and found a shabby, faux leather wallet. "Gimme some light back here again." The deputy obliged, and Stimpy fished through the wallet, searching for some identification. He found four dollars, a McDonald's coupon, an expired driver's license, and another plastic card.

"Well, who is he?" Leaks said.

"Fellow by the name of Randy Belue. Says here he's from Rolling Fork. And whaddaya know, lookee here." Stimpy held the card up for Leaks to see. "You don't see this every day from a hobo."

Leaks squinted, then shook his head. "Just tell me. Ain't got my reading glasses."

"It's a donor card. He's donating his body to science."

———————

Stimpy stood outside Restor and Sons Funeral Home and watched Ernie's patrol car pull away. It wouldn't be long before the deputy eased into some parking lot and napped while pretending to watch the road. Stimpy smiled. He would do the same thing if he had to cruise McKinley County's dark roads all night long. A little on the lazy side or not, at least Ernie had been willing to help him get the body inside before whining that funeral homes gave him the creeps and making a hasty exit.

Stimpy went back inside, back to the body for a once-over in better light. He saw nothing out of the ordinary—heart attack or stroke from a hard life, or maybe a drug overdose. He predicted this guy, whoever he turned out to be, would have a rap sheet and rehab record a mile long.

He thought about ordering an autopsy, but what was the point? The guy was dead from his own doing either way, and Stimpy had been told before that bodies subjected to autopsy were disqualified from being medical donors. Stimpy didn't know a lot about medicine—nothing, in fact—but he knew he wanted his doctor to have been well-trained in human anatomy, however they did it. So who was he to stand in the way of science? Stimpy smiled at his own wisdom and insight into how to serve the greater good. *They didn't elect me for nothin'. I do know a thing or two.*

It wasn't the first time Stimpy had dealt with a medical donor, so he knew the drill. Call the 1-800 number on the card, they tell you leave the body alone, they'll be there within two hours. It would be up to the sheriff's department to notify next of kin and work out any problems or protests to the decedent's wishes. Meanwhile, it made no sense to let the body start decomposing. They'd take it over to the university, freeze it in the morgue, and await official word.

Stimpy wanted to go home and go to bed, but no sense in trying now. Might as well sit and wait, or else about the time he got home and dozed off, he'd have to come back. He wished he had his computer, but he didn't even have a good magazine. He walked out on the porch to smoke while he decided whether or not to try for a nap on the faded leather couch in the office. He liked how Amberton was quiet this time of night. Stimpy broke the hush with the click of his lighter, then strained to hear anything else of interest, but there was nothing. Not even the hum of a distant car. For a moment, it seemed even the crickets were taking the night off.

The voice came from behind him. "If you turn around, Stimpy, I swear on your mother's grave, I'll blow your head off."

Stimpy Riggins wet his pants. Not a shoe-soaking bladder evacuation, but enough of a slip that he knew it showed in the front. He didn't move a muscle or say a word. The voice was unfamiliar to him. It sounded disguised, but he wasn't sure.

"What you got in there, Stimpy?"

"F—f—found a man down at the tracks."

"Who is it?"

"Don't know. Some guy not from around here."

"What happened to him?"

"I—I'm not supposed to tell that kind of stuff."

"Does that include when you have a nine-millimeter pointed at your head? You better start yapping."

Stimpy turned his head slightly, to better hear the voice directly behind him.

"If you turn around, I'll be the last thing you ever see."

Stimpy jerked his head forward and down, straining to help his bladder hang on. He stared at his cigarette, burning helplessly on the ground where he had accidentally spit it out. He dared not move to pick it up, but if he could get a pull or two, it might help him think. He froze like a praying statue instead, trying to make some sense of what was happening.

Earlier, it seemed pointless to examine the body very closely, it appeared so straightforward. Now he felt foolish. Maybe the University Body Donor Program wasn't where the body of Mr. Randy Belue from Rolling Fork needed to go, after all. "It looked like natural causes," Stimpy finally said, "but I could be wrong."

"Oh no, you're exactly right. Natural causes is exactly right. You know how I know, Stimpy?"

"I'm afraid to ask."

"Because you like the sound of five hundred dollars cash sitting on the front seat of your car right now. There'll be five more show up in six months if you do your part."

"Well, uh, sure, yeah." Stimpy gulped. "What makes you think I can be bought?"

"Because you're a greedy little rat. And because your life as you know it depends on it."

"On what?"

"On that person in there being dead from natural causes. You write it up that way."

"It's not, not, entirely up to me. I mean, if it gets questioned—"

"Shut up, Stimpy. Figure it out. Just write it up and get that body embalmed or whatever you call it, and make whoever needs to believe it, believe it. No autopsy. Otherwise, your wife and the newspaper and the police will know about your little underage girlfriend down there at Movie Magic, about the pictures and everything else she gives you, you sicko. You'll lose your wife and that fat inheritance you're waiting on. Lose your job, too. And, oh yeah—you'll be somebody else's little girlfriend for a few years in the clink. And that's if I let you live."

Bile rose in Stimpy's throat. *This is a bad dream. Maybe I'm really just taking that nap on the couch.* "You can't be s-s-serious."

The sound of a hammer being pulled back filled Stimpy's ears. "Does that sound like I'm joking?"

A warm stream flowed down Stimpy's leg and into one shoe.

FOUR

Eleven months later — Jackson, Mississippi

JET was snoring. Not the deep, rhythmic snore of a man tucked comfortably in his bed at home, but a restless one. Unsettled and erratic, it was the fitful breathing of a shallow, unfulfilling sleep, the kind induced by a sedative that had failed to remove a deeper pain—either physical or emotional. Or both.

His mother had greeted me with a hug in the hall outside the treatment room. "He had a bad fall. But it's more than that. He's really having a hard time, Case. With everything." She had looked tired, but there was more there than the sudden worry that comes with a son's accident. The new gray in her short hair and deepening of the crow's feet at the corners of sunken eyes told me the months since I'd last seen her had been hard. "I've never seen him like this. Ranting and raving, making no sense."

Maggie Townsend's voice had quivered and broken off, and she took a moment to gather herself before continuing. What she had told me next was incomprehensible. It wasn't like Jet Townsend, the most intelligent and resilient person I'd ever known, to go off the deep end. But that was precisely what she had suggested before patting me on the back and walking away. "Go on in and talk to him, see what you think. I'm gonna take a walk and try to clear my head."

I paused just inside the door, watching Jet's erratic snoring, unsure what to expect. The monitor above his hospital bed showed some multicolored numbers and squiggly lines that meant nothing to me, but I heard only the rattles of his breathing—no beeping alarms. That was a good sign. The bandage around his sandy brown head also covered one eye, though. Maybe his injuries were worse than I'd been told.

Jet stirred and opened the exposed eye. He squinted and pushed up the edge of the dressing where it had slipped down, revealing his other eye socket, whole and intact. Then he grimaced and reached to touch the back of his head.

I gestured for him to stop. "Leave that alone, dude. Took a pretty good lick, I hear. Lucky you didn't crack that thick skull of yours."

I was no doctor, but there might be a simple explanation for Jet's behavior. I had seen plenty of concussions, and Jet must have a bad one. Not your entry-level, run-of-the-mill concussion with a brief blackout and bad headache, but the deluxe package, complete with confusion and delusions. Plus a scalp laceration requiring eight sutures to close.

He opened both eyes wide. "Hey, Case. What are you doing here?"

"Word travels fast. Your mom was worried about you, so she called me."

Jet fiddled with the IV in his arm and glanced at the bag of fluids hanging over him. "Yeah, it's been a pretty bad day."

"So medical school hasn't started off the way you hoped?" I smiled teasingly, hoping to lighten the mood.

"Passing out in the middle of Gross Anatomy lab on the second day, hitting my head, bleeding all over the floor. No, you could say it has fallen short of what I had envisioned." I could tell he wanted to say more, so I said nothing. I wanted him to initiate what would come next. He appeared to mull over his thoughts for several seconds. "There's something else, Case. Did Mom tell you what happened?"

"Yeah, she told me."

"I know it sounds illogical. Crazy, even. I know it does. It just seemed so real." He touched the bandage on his head again, but the way he shook his head as he spoke suggested the grimace on his face was from more than just a headache. "What you think?"

I desperately wanted to avoid the question. I reached in my pocket and pulled out a set of keys. "What I think is that I've got something for you. A pretty redhead gave them to me as I was coming in. Said they fell out of your coat. She told me she'd check on you later."

His frown softened. "Gracie. One of my lab partners. But you didn't answer my question. I want to know what you think."

I inhaled deeply and decided to try once more to evade the answer he sought. "Okay. I think you've had a rough time, man. Concussions will mess you up sometimes The CT scan was fine, so they say you'll be back to yourself in no time."

His expression changed, and he glared at me, hard. "I saw what I saw *before* I fell, Case." His tone matched his eyes— brimming with indignation. He had been measuring me before to see if I would believe him unconditionally. Now he was mad, but it didn't matter. If he insisted on an answer, I would give it to him. He needed to hear the truth.

"I know what you *think* you saw, Jet. But *you* know as well as I do that's impossible. I think you've just been under too much stress. Your mom. Your brother Adam. Starting med school. And Abi, too."

Jet looked away, cut his eyes back to me, then looked away again. Weighing my words against his thoughts, I supposed, waiting for one to tip the balance against the other. "Did you ever finish your book?" he said finally.

"I did, if you can call it that. A pile of pages in a box under my bed. Maybe one day I'll have time to edit it and try to get it published."

"Well, do me a favor, will you? Consider writing another. About this."

"About you? Wanna be famous when I get a movie deal, huh?"

Jet frowned and waved a hand at me. Not in the mood for jokes. "I'm serious. Just record what I tell you—today and over the next few weeks or months—and we'll see where it goes. Maybe it will be a book about a crazy med student. Maybe it will be something else."

I raised an eyebrow. "Why don't you just write it yourself? Seems like eliminating the middleman would be easier."

"I'm not a writer. Don't care anything about it. But you do. And I'm giving you an opportunity at another story to tell. The first one was really good. This one may be even better."

I wasn't sure what the story was, but it didn't matter. "Jet, the thing is, I can't write a book right now. You know I'm starting my new job." I jabbed my thumb against my chest. "You're looking at the newest English teacher and football coach for South Rankin High. Coach Reynolds—can you believe it? It has a certain ring to it." It was my first job out of college, at a small school just up the road. Technically, I would just be coaching junior high for now, but still, I had worked hard for the position and was proud of it. The last thing I needed was a distraction.

Jet smiled and sat up a little in the bed. "I know. But that's good because South Rankin is close." He was missing the point entirely—and intentionally, I was certain. "You don't have to write the book now. Just listen to me and take notes. Look, there's some things you don't know, things nobody else knows. Things I didn't think mattered anymore. But maybe they do. And I trust you like nobody else. Worst case, you get nothing worth writing, but at least listening to me will help me work through this. Best case, you help me *plus* you either wind up with a compelling memoir about the travails of a troubled first-year medical student or a mystery novel with a sinister, twisted plot that you embellish however you see fit. I don't care which. Just help me."

I shook my head, trying to make sense of it. But I could only think of one logical thing to do. I stood up and headed toward the door.

"Wait," Jet stopped me. "Where are you going?"

"To find a pen and some paper."

FIVE

One day earlier — Jackson University School of Medicine

JET arrived at the auditorium early and took a seat halfway back, only slightly surprised that he wasn't the first one there. He figured the others were there to get the best seat or hoping to impress an equally punctual professor. Jet was there because he wanted to watch, to size up the other members of the class.

He was not intimidated by the prospect of beginning medical school. Apprehensive, perhaps—how could a normal person not be? But not intimidated. In college, Jet had seldom met a fellow student of intellect comparable to his, but he had no way to know what to expect from the 106 students matriculating into the Jackson University School of Medicine. He had to assume that, like him, each had graduated college near the top of the class, with exemplary MCAT scores. And he knew that medical school could be cutthroat. Not just a challenge to absorb an exorbitant amount of material in a short time, often likened to attempting to sip water from a fire hydrant, but also a race to the finish line four years away. A competition for class rank and favor from professors in order to one day be admitted to the best post-graduate residency training programs.

"Let the competition begin!" A voice rang out as if reading Jet's mind. A tall, broad-shouldered man made the proclamation as he sauntered down the aisle past Jet. He scanned the room to confirm he had been heard by all present before giving a smug smile and taking a seat on the second row.

"Sterling Virchow." Someone tapped Jet on his shoulder from behind. He turned to see a striking redhead nodding over his shoulder toward the man named Sterling. Her green eyes were narrowed and scornful. "Pompous jerk. Steer clear of him if you can. Haven't seen him in a few years. He went to Dartmouth, I think, but we went to high school together."

Jet smiled and extended his hand as he introduced himself. "Well, I'm glad to know somebody who at least knows *somebody*. I went to Vanderbilt, and I doubt I'll know anyone in the class."

"Gracie Tollison." Her grip was firm but not aggressive. Confident without pretense. "Hey, I bet we'll be in the same Gross Anatomy group." She smiled, proud of her deduction.

Jet had no idea how she knew that, and his expression must have betrayed his lack of understanding. Before he could fully utter his "Huh?" she interjected.

"Townsend and Tollison. Our names both start with T. They always group you alphabetically for Gross. I suppose we could fall into different groups, but I doubt it, don't you?"

He shrugged. "If you say so." He turned back to see the action. Students were pouring into the auditorium now. Sterling Virchow knew many by name, calling out to them like a one-man welcoming committee. Jet twisted back around in his seat toward Gracie. "How does he know so many folks?"

She picked up her backpack and stepped over the back of the seat in front of her, dropping nimbly into the seat next to Jet. "His father. Stuart Virchow. Professor of Surgery and a Vice-Chancellor, or something. I think he's on the Medical

School Admissions Committee, too. They're quite the pair. Pompous One and Pompous Two, if you ask me."

Jet chuckled. "Well, don't hold back. Tell me how you really feel."

She patted his arm. "Don't you worry, honey, I will."

Within minutes, the room had filled with other students. Jet watched quietly while his newfound friend identified those she knew and guessed at the life story of those she didn't. Jet stole glances at her while she remained preoccupied with her survey of the room and its occupants. Average build, scattered freckles, round cheeks, the slightest hints of dimples just below the corners of her mouth that appeared and disappeared as she talked.

The room grew quiet as a rotund, bearded man with round glasses stepped onto the low stage and tapped the microphone. The top button on his white lab coat strained to keep his belly from bursting forth. Jet was afraid if the man laughed or coughed the button might pop off and take out someone's eye. He didn't know Sterling Virchow but secretly hoped it might hit him.

"As some of you know," the man spoke in a deep baritone that resonated even more through the microphone, "I am Dr. Sylvester Cronin, Chairman of the Department of Anatomy. Many of you probably expected a welcome from Dr. Virchow, the man who oversaw your selection for this class, or Dr. Turing, the Dean of the School of Medicine. You'll hear from them and several others in a moment. But first, you get me. Why? Because I insisted. Because I am the person who, more than any other human being or god in the universe, stands between you and becoming a second-year medical student.

"Shortly, you will go upstairs, pull back the sheet on your cadaver, and begin your odyssey through Gross Anatomy. Get ready for the ride of your life. We will not slow down, and we will stop for no one. It will be the most miserable, exhilarating, beautiful, dark, frustrating, and rewarding thing you've ever done. And that's if you pass it. If you don't, it will be the most disappointing failure of your life. That is, of course, if you care as much as you should. If you don't, then I didn't want you in my medical school anyway."

Professor Cronin paused and strummed his plump fingers together across his ample belly. Jet watched the button, afraid that a misplaced tap might cause it to blow. "Before we go any further, let me say one thing about the most important contributor to your entire medical career. Look around the room and guess who it may be." Most of the students glanced around the room with uncertainty. "Don't see him or her? That's right, you don't, because that person is dead. That person is lying in a tank of formaldehyde right now up on the sixth floor, waiting on you and your clumsy lab partners to destroy the flesh that held their souls for their short time on this earth. Remember, they each gave themselves to you, so give them the respect they deserve in return. Anything less will be an injustice. Now, unlike me, you will never know their stories, how they lived or how they died. Yet you should treat them with the dignity you would give a family member. Because you have an opportunity for a part of them to live on and even save lives one day through you. What you learn over the next year through your interaction with them will shape your entire career. Make it count."

The professor clapped his hands together and paused, scanning the crowd, eyeing each individual student for a millisecond before continuing in a low rumble that crescendoed to a thundering boom by the finish. "Now, let me tell you this. Unless you cheated your way to get here—and I promise I'll find you if you did—you are all sufficiently intelligent to pass Gross Anatomy. What will determine whether or not you pass is your intestinal fortitude. Your grit, as I like to call it. You either have it, or you don't. If you're not sure where yours is, then by God in heaven you better dig deep and find it quickly. Get ready for Gross Anatomy. You will never forget it."

SIX

"EVERYONE, and I mean everyone, listen closely while I call your names and give your table assignments," Dr. Cronin bellowed while studying the information on his clipboard. The nervous energy in the room was suddenly palpable, the rumble of anxious, lowered voices rippling through the students like far away thunder. After listening to several boring and largely uninformative speeches from various professors, then sitting through their first Biochemistry lecture, the hour the medical class had been waiting for was finally at hand. "If I have to repeat myself," he continued, his voice even louder now, "that's an ominous sign that your listening and/or retention skills may be inadequate to pass this class."

"Wonder if he knows it's an ominous sign that his belly is the size of a spare tire?" Gracie whispered to Jet. He smiled.

"Alford, Ambuja, Banks, Bethel. Table number one." Dr. Cronin continued down the list alphabetically. Jet watched as those whose names were called searched to identify the others with whom they'd be spending more time than their family, friends, and pets for the next eight months. A few who obviously knew each other high-fived or fist-pumped when they heard their names grouped together, apparently confirming what they'd hoped for.

Jet was indifferent about the whole group-matching process. He didn't know a soul other than Gracie Tollison, and who knew what to make of her? It suited him just fine to fly under the radar, anyway. Maybe people like Sterling Virchow thrived on drawing attention to themselves, but Jet had no desire to do so. He planned to let his grades alone say what needed saying. The scores he planned to make might be enough by themselves to get a target on his back from classmates clamoring for class rank. No point in pinning one on sooner for students and professors alike to aim at.

"Tekowski, Tollison, Townsend, Tucker. Table twenty-four." Dr. Cronin quickly finished the list, but as the students stood to leave, a high-pitched voice rang out from somewhere in the back.

"You didn't call my name, sir."

The professor sighed with exasperation and eyed the source of the comment. "I'm sure that is not the case. Perhaps you are here on the wrong day. Dental hygiene classes don't start until next week. What is your name, oh deaf waster of my time?"

Jet cringed. *Speaking of putting a target on your back....*

"Oliver."

"Oliver Twist, Oliver Stone, Oliver Wendell Holmes, what?"

By now everyone had frozen in place and strained to see which unfortunate soul was inviting such ire from Professor Sylvester Cronin. It was difficult to see him, but as best Jet could tell, the perpetrator was wearing a black Motley Crue T-shirt and sporting a mop of bleached blond hair that wasn't sure in which direction it was supposed to go.

"Tucker Oliver, sir. You called out a Tucker but no Oliver."

Cronin sighed again and checked his watch impatiently. "So what is the problem? You just said I called out your name."

"Tucker is my first name. Oliver is my last name."

The hefty professor stared silently at his clipboard for several seconds, clenching his jaw and turning crimson. Then he looked up and glared at his antagonist like he would strangle the small man if he could figure out how to reach all the way to the back of the room.

Tucker Oliver, or whatever his name was, just stared back, unfazed, with his head cocked slightly to the side, waiting patiently on an answer while the entire class held their breath.

Finally, the professor spoke. "Your name is Oliver Tucker. Table twenty-four."

———

"I'm confused. Is your name Oliver Tucker or Tucker Oliver?" Gracie asked as she and Jet edged alongside the young man while walking to the elevator.

"And who might you be?"

"Gracie Tollison. And this is Jet Townsend."

"Ah, two of my three illustrious Gross partners. You can call me whatever you want. I really just wanted to mess with Humpty Dumpty a little bit."

"You wanted to get on his bad side before you even got going?" Jet asked, incredulous.

"Nah." He smiled. "Just wanted to have a little fun. Figure there won't be enough of that once we get started."

Jet eyed Tucker with uncertainty. At five-foot-ten, Jet considered himself average height, but this man was a full six inches shorter. With the girth of a soup can. No wonder it had been hard to see him at the back of the class. He seemed likable enough so far, but no doubt his stature, demeanor, and dress did not fit what Jet had envisioned as the typical medical student profile. Not by a long shot. What would Tekowski, the fourth member of their group, be like?

The line waiting for the elevator was long, so Gracie suggested the three take the stairs. Jet did not relish the idea of walking up six flights, but he didn't want to wait all day either. The words of Professor Cronin echoed in his head. *We will not slow down, and we stop for no one.*

"Jet, is it?" Tucker asked over his shoulder as he pivoted around the handrail to turn up the second column of steps. He moved like a jitterbug. "Not your given name, I suppose? Are you super fast or something?" He looked back and saw Jet limping up behind him. "Oops, sorry about that."

"Unfortunately," Jet said, unfazed, "if our med class has to go outside for Field Day, you won't want me for the three-legged race. An accident in junior high. I used to be velocity-challenged, now I'm just plain slow. John Edward Townsend is my name. Jet was sort of a combo oxymoron-acronym that my friends got a kick out of."

"Well that's not very nice," Gracie said. "Especially after what you went through."

"Nah, they called me Jet way before this happened. No big deal. My friends are okay folks."

"Well, lucky for you," Tucker called down from two flights further up the stairwell, "I doubt we'll be doing any egg tosses or three-legged races. Question is, is your brain faster than your legs?"

Gracie was hanging back with Jet. "He made a perfect score on his MCAT," she volunteered.

Tucker whistled loudly. "No kiddin'? Well, didn't I just hit the jackpot with my anatomy partner! That's what I'm talking about!"

Jet stopped in his tracks and stared at Gracie while he caught his breath. "How did you know that?"

"Word gets around." She shrugged matter-of-factly and started climbing again. "C'mon, we gotta find this Tekowski and get to work."

The hallway outside the Gross Anatomy lab on the sixth floor was as crowded as the area in front of the elevators had been on the first. Students were already standing shoulder to shoulder, wrestling with the combinations to their lockers and hurriedly trying to cram their belongings into them so they could get inside to their assigned dissection table. A few were already scuttling through one of the two entry doors.

Gracie gave Jet a one-eyed, crooked half-grin. "So much for taking the stairs to beat the crowd."

"Should've warned you I'm not a big fan of the Stairmaster."

Her grin blossomed into a laugh. "Yeah, give me a heads-up next time!"

"So, this is the infamous Jet Townsend." They turned to see Sterling Virchow approaching. His voice was rich and smooth, the timbre of a sports broadcaster. He stood four inches taller than Jet but seemed to strain to get there, like he wished it were more. He was already in his lab coat, stark white and smooth and stiff, as if it had been starched and pressed. Virchow's name was monogrammed in a flamboyant cursive font above the left breast pocket.

Jet peeked at his own wrinkled lab coat, just recently re-moved from the plastic wrapping it came in, but thoughts about discrepancies in coat quality were quickly replaced with irritation that his ideas about remaining incognito were not going to be the reality.

Gracie intervened before Jet could gather himself to speak. "Nice coat," she said. "If one didn't know better, they'd think you were already a doctor." She traced her finger over the letters of Virchow's name in a way that could be interpreted as either flirting or mocking, depending on one's bias.

Virchow chose flirting. He reached out to place a hand on her cheek. "Never too early to project the image of a professional, my dear."

Gracie withdrew and rolled her eyes, and Jet suppressed a smile. He wanted to probe further to see how much of a tool Virchow really was, but he wanted to know something else even more. "How do you know who I am?"

"Well, I do, uh, have a few connections," Virchow gave a patronizing smile. "In my experience, it's not every day that we see students with entry scores like yours. Or a story like yours." He scanned Jet up and down before his eyes settled on his lower half.

Jet fought an urge to punch the guy. Clearly this arrogant loser had read his file, including his transcripts and application essay, where he had described his lifelong dream to become a doctor, and how it was nearly derailed by a terrible accident before he even got to high school. "The leg is fine, thanks for asking," he said.

"Oh, yes, the leg. True, that was inspiring, how you recovered from your accident. But I was referring to the other thing. I hope it's not hard to focus on your studies this soon after." He held the back of his hand to his mouth and spoke in an apologetic half-whisper, "Especially, you know, interacting with the dead like we'll be doing." His voice changed again, brassy and upbeat. "Anyway, enough lamenting. I'm sure you'll do fine. See you inside, eh? By the way, I'm sure we'll be collaborating quite a bit. My table is right next to yours, I believe."

It dawned on Jet that yes, V was essentially right after T, alphabetically speaking—not many names started with U. He imagined spitting at the back of Virchow's head as he sauntered away.

"Eoughhh! I can't stand that guy!" Gracie huffed. "But what was—"

"Aw, don't worry about him." Jet tried to deflect both the impending question as well as his thoughts. "He'll keep us entertained, if nothing else. Hey, where did Tucker go?"

As if on cue, sprigs of blond hair bobbed through the crowd in their direction, accompanied by the characteristic voice they'd heard call out from the back of the auditorium earlier. "Guys, look what I found!" Tucker had another man in front of him, prodding him along from behind by intermittently grabbing his elbow like a herding dog nipping at the heels of a sheep. Jet recalled a photo he'd once seen of an Australian Kelpie actually walking on the backs of sheep in a pen and smiled at the thought of Tucker doing the same to the white-coated crowd filling the hall. "I bring you the one, the only, Craig Tekowski!"

Tekowski had dark brown hair, parted precisely on top and closely cropped above the ears, with a hint of gray at the edges. He wore gold wire-rimmed glasses, a blue button-down dress shirt, brown slacks, and a deep frown compressing what were already very thin lips. He was apparently none too happy about the delay of his entrance to the Gross Anatomy lab. "Yes, that is my name. Could we not have introduced ourselves inside?"

"Well, we could, dude, but we gotta get to know each other ASAP since we're gonna be, like, family for a while!" Tucker said.

"I doubt that, but, fine, let's get this over with."

Gracie clapped her hands together then gestured toward Jet. "I'm Gracie Tollison, and this is—"

"Jet Townsend. Nice to meet you."

Gracie gave Jet a sly, maternal grin as if she was proud of him for introducing himself.

"Likewise. Now let's get to work. Our cadaver isn't going to dissect himself."

"Let's hope not," Tucker chuckled. "That would be weird."

"Himself? How do you know it's a him?" Gracie put her hands on her hips.

"Or herself. Whatever! I don't mean to be rude, but I'll see you guys inside." Tekowski nodded at the group awkwardly, as if to indicate that his abruptness was an unpleasant yet unavoidable consequence of the situation, then turned and walked away.

"Stuff some coal in his butt and I do believe he'll crap a diamond by this time tomorrow." Tucker laughed as the three ambled down the hall.

They paused at the entrance to the Gross lab, and Gracie tugged at Jet's coat sleeve. "Jet, what was Sterling talking about before? Your other thing?"

Jet hesitated. Was she perplexed at how whatever it was could be afoot without her knowledge, or was she genuinely concerned? If she was concerned, was it as a new friend, lab partner, or both? Instead of answering, he focused on the door's combination lock and punched in the code. At the moment he touched the last number and reached for the door, a starched white coat whisked by him.

Sterling Virchow pushed the door open with a dramatic flair and gestured toward the open room filled with steel tanks beyond it. "I am firmly convinced that the best book in medicine is the book of Anatomy, as written in the bodies of men."

Jet almost succeeded in walking past Virchow while ignoring his smirk, but he just couldn't let it go. He stopped, backed up two steps, and paused in front of Virchow without turning around. "I think Osler's words were, 'the book of *Nature*, as *writ large* in the bodies of men.'" Jet walked away without waiting on a response.

Gracie giggled behind him, and Jet imagined her sticking her tongue out at Virchow as she passed by. She tugged at Jet's coat and came up beside him. "What was that?"

Jet shrugged. "He brought it on himself. He was trying to quote an article Sir William Osler wrote a hundred years or so ago about teaching medicine. He recounted an eighteenth-century surgeon named Hunter—I believe he was Irish, no, maybe Scottish—who pointed to the dissecting room when asked what books the medical students should read."

"I think Sterling may need a bandage for his chin, it hit the floor so hard."

Jet scanned the room and nodded toward a table near the back. "You know, Tekowski did have a point—our cadaver isn't going to dissect him—or, uh, herself."

SEVEN

THE lab buzzed with activity as each group pulled back the sheets covering their cadavers and prepared to begin the dissection assignment. A few irreverent wisecracks filtered through the room.

"Smells like my girlfriend's vomit after too much vodka."

"This guy needs two tanks instead of one."

"Oh, look, our lady's already missing one leg. Maybe Cronin will give us a discount."

For the most part, though, the conversations were quiet and respectful and usually about dissection logistics. Who would start the first cut, whose dissection manual they would follow, who had studied the night before to know the overall plan.

Jet knew the moment of truth—the unveiling of their own cadaver—would be a shock, despite his best efforts to prepare himself ahead of time. But what they found defied anything he could have imagined.

The initial dissection assignment was the neck and upper back, so the man was facedown with a small towel over his head when they pulled back the yellowing protective sheet, moist with formaldehyde. The sallow, leathery skin was not unexpected, and while the limbs were contorted— not grotesquely, but subtly, unnaturally, in a way that sparked an urge within the group to reposition them just a bit—that didn't strike him as surprising. Nor did the unfamiliar, overwhelming, acrid odor of preservative, nauseating at first until it finally overpowered and extinguished all sense of smell.

What shocked him and his partners was the cause of death.

Prone position or not, there was nothing left to the imagination. The bullet had entered just to the left of the upper spine, between it and the left shoulder blade. The hole was round and perfect, as if a giant leather awl had punched through the skin. No doubt the exit wound would be somewhere near the center of the chest.

No one in the group spoke for a time—probably just a few seconds, but it seemed much longer—they just looked uneasily at each other and around the room. Whatever images of the moment they might have envisioned ahead of time individually, their collective expressions suggested this scene was not among them. For Jet, rather than an old man who had lived a long life and perhaps faded away peacefully while his loving family prayed at his bedside, he was staring at someone who had obviously suffered a brutal, horrible, premature death. And it was as if they all had somehow been thrust in the midst of his violent end without even knowing what the conflict was.

Tucker spoke first. "This guy has a bullet hole. That's crazy!"

"You wouldn't think they'd let murder victims be dissected," Gracie said.

Tekowski leaned over and peered at the hole, holding his glasses in place with the tip of an index finger. "Do you think he's had an autopsy? That could mess up the anatomical landmarks for us. Might make things more difficult. Do you think Professor Cronin will allow some leeway for that?"

"Bodies that have been autopsied are disqualified," Tucker said.

"And how do you know that?" Gracie asked.

Tucker shrugged. "Heard it. Worked in the surgery department back in the summer, tagged along in here a few times with one of them. They come in here to practice sometimes."

Beyond being shocked, Jet found himself disappointed. The cause of death was supposed to be something they stumbled on in the middle of a dissection, perhaps during class, or maybe in the middle of the night in a frantic catch-up session. "Hey, look at this, his coronaries are occluded," or "Wow, I feel a mass in the pancreas the size of a baseball." If he was going to have to suffer through a nightmare semester in the anatomy lab soaked in formaldehyde, at least he should be able to look forward to solving his first "case" while he was in there. Instead, there it was, on day one—a bullet hole. His very first medical mystery solved within three seconds of pulling the sheet back. Before he even got to know the person, so to speak. It seemed inappropriate somehow, but it was more than that. Like he had been gypped.

At least as disturbing was one other salient difference between their cadaver and those atop the other twenty-six stainless steel tanks in the room. Elsewhere it appeared that wrinkles and sagging skin, muscle wasting, and age spots of the elderly were the norm, but the man on their table had taut skin and seemingly no imperfections. In life he had possessed the muscular frame of a person familiar with exercise, hard work, weightlifting, or all of the above.

He just seemed too young to be here. Much too young.

Gracie seemed to be reading his mind. "He's young." She touched the bullet hole gingerly with an index finger then abruptly pulled back. "Maybe it was a suicide. Sometimes they don't do autopsies for those if it's cut and dry."

It wasn't a bad idea, for more reasons than just the age. Certainly, the thought of suicide is always unpleasant, but one could at least imagine the patient had some sort of terminal illness, that maybe the suicide was the quickest end to what would otherwise become a living nightmare. But that was not the case here. Jet shook his head. "Not a suicide. This person was shot in the back. That looks like an entry wound there that—what are you doing?"

Tucker had followed Gracie's lead but gone a step further, with a gloved finger inserted into the hole, probing. "Feeling for a bullet," he said.

"Stop. You won't find it," Jet said. "It looks like at least a .35 caliber. It goes deeper and likely exited the other side."

Gracie stared at Jet incredulously. "You're saying this was a murder? How do you know so much about this? You a cop or something in a former life?"

Jet paused for a time. "I didn't say it was a murder. Maybe an accident, I don't know. But to answer your other question, for one, I've shot guns and hunted practically my whole life. So I have an idea about what size hole the bullets make, give or take. Plus, my ex—she took a lot of forensics classes, so I picked up a thing or two. And third, I had to do a little research on this type thing before. A long story from a long time ago that I don't have time to tell."

"Nor do we have time to listen," Tekowski chimed in. Irritated. He already had his dissection kit out, ready for action. Small beads of sweat erupted on his forehead, and he removed his glasses to clean the moisture condensing on them. "I'm sure that however this particular individual got here, the cause of his demise has been carefully sorted out by the proper authorities. Now, can we please get to work?"

"Knock yourself out." Tucker gestured like a model on a game show toward the body before them on the table. "Wait— hang on." He extended his foot beneath the table and slid a step stool out. He stepped up, now eye to eye or slightly higher than the other group members. "Okay, now I'm ready. But if you find a bullet, I want it."

"Okay, Teacakes," Gracie said, "you start the incision, I'll take notes, and Jet can read the instructions from the manual and help identify landmarks. Tucker, you supervise from your crow's nest there. And keep an eye out for the bullet, I guess."

"Teacakes—I like that." Tucker chuckled.

"Speak for yourself," Tekowski spewed. "At least folks know which of my names is the last one."

Tucker smiled. "Touché. Lighten up and just cut, please." He wrinkled his nose and scowled. "Man, that formaldehyde smell is awful!"

Jet had been silent, still studying the back of the cadaver. This was going to be harder for him than he'd feared. "The odor could be worse," he said, nonchalantly, hoping to talk his way through the dread. "You know, before air conditioning and modern embalming practices, they only taught anatomy classes during the winter months. The smell was too bad during the summer. Not to mention there was a shortage of bodies to dissect. Had to dig them up."

"Could we please get going?" Tekowski said.

"No, wait, I gotta hear this," Tucker said. "Dig 'em up?"

"Yeah, it was very common in England. Nobody donated their bodies to science, so medical schools actually employed body snatchers. Off the record, of course. Happened here in the States, too. One guy, who was a founder of George Washington University Medical School—Thomas Sewell—he was convicted of exhuming a woman's body for the purposes of dissecting her in the early 1800s. That was before he became the personal physician to three U.S. presidents."

"Okaayyy." Gracie eyed Jet with more than a little uncertainty. "That you know that is just weird, darlin'. And you look a little bit pale. You just relax. I'll read." She put her notebook aside, grabbed the spiral-bound manual Jet was holding, and pointed her finger at a line of text. "Incise along a line beginning at the external occipital protuberance and extending down the midline of the back to the coccyx."

Tekowski studied the diagram in the manual then turned his attention to the cadaver, grasping a scalpel. "Hey, get a load of this." He pointed to the skin in the midline, between the upper buttocks. It was vertical scar approximately the length of a man's thumb.

"Dude had a crack right above his crack," Tucker snickered.

"Now that's what I call a crack attack," Tekowski said.

Tucker laughed. "Tea! You made a joke!" He tried to high-five Tekowski but got no reciprocation. He shrugged and dropped his hand. "Fine, leave me hanging. I still think that means there's hope for the world. I'll have to buy you a drink for that one."

"I believe that's called the intergluteal fold." Jet smiled despite himself. "But crack works too."

"C'mon guys, let's move on." Gracie scratched something in her notebook. "He has a scar. So noted."

Tekowski fingered the scalpel again. Holding it just above the skin surface, he followed the line of the cut he planned to make, simulating an incision from the top of the neck all the way down to the tailbone. He was sweating more now than before, the pinpoint drops of moisture on his forehead coalescing into large beads.

"Remind me not to let you operate on me," Tucker said. "You're a bit shaky there, Tea."

"It's not like I've done this before, you know. At least, not on a human. Somehow the time spent dissecting worms and frogs and cats for college anatomy seems immensely irrelevant."

"Hey, stop philosophizing and let's do this," Tucker said. "You haven't even broken the skin yet."

Tekowski pointed the scalpel at Jet without looking up. "I'm not the philosopher." He took a deep breath and began a vertical incision along the path Gracie had recited.

"Seems like there should be some blood even though we know it's all been sucked out, huh?" Tucker said.

Tekowski gave an exasperated sigh. "Why don't you help me instead of just standing there yapping? I'll use forceps on one end and bluntly dissect with scissors, and you do the same on the other."

Gracie held up a hand. "Hold on, there, guys, there's more." She pointed at the text of the dissection manual. "Incise the skin from the spine of the seventh cervical vertebra to the acromion process of each shoulder. Then reflect the skin laterally to reveal the borders of the trapezius and the latissimus dorsi muscles."

"That's a very nice recitation of the text, Ms. Tollison." The full, deep voice was unmistakable—and unwelcome. "But I'm wondering, first of all, why only two of you are participating, and second of all, what is taking so bloody long at this table? You four are lagging behind everyone else in the room." Professor Cronin stood at the end of their table like a bouncer at the entrance to an elite club, arms crossed and scowling, his job to decide who would be admitted and who would be turned away. And to be intimidating, of course.

"Professor, I've been trying to get them to get started, but they'd rather talk than work," Tekowski said. "My colleague, Mr. Townsend here, wants to give us all a history lesson."

Jet was only vaguely aware of the accusation. Something just wasn't quite right, and he didn't know why. A sense of foreboding suddenly pressed upon him as if the walls were closing in and the oxygen was somehow being sucked from the very air filling his lungs. He had expected this day to be difficult, but this was impossible. He was suffocating.

"Oh, is that right?" Cronin said. "Mr. Townsend?"

"Professor," Gracie interrupted. "I can vouch for Jet. He's had a stomach virus or something. Just now recovering from it. That's why he's sitting back a bit."

Cronin ignored her lie. "Mr. Townsend, did I miss the part where you already passed this class? Where you are an instructor here? Because unless that is the case, then I expect your full participation. There are no free rides. I don't care what you made on the MCAT or your rudimentary college anatomy class. You can throw those irrelevancies out the window as far as I'm concerned."

Jet barely heard him. His face was on fire. No, not just that. The entire room was aflame, with churning clouds of black smoke and burning bodies and an overwhelming odor of gasoline. Or was that formaldehyde? *That's where the oxygen is going. Consumed by the fires! No wonder I can't breathe! Where are the screams? Why is it so quiet?* He felt locked in place for a moment. Confined by imaginary restraints. Or wait—was it his lab coat? Like a straitjacket that would melt to him if he didn't get out of it. *I've got to get out of here!*

Jet staggered out of the room, oblivious to the quiet stares all around and the sneers of Sterling Virchow and the voice of Gracie telling him not to worry, she'd get his lab coat for him.

EIGHT

Ten months earlier — Amberton, Mississippi

HEY, Case, what's up?"

It was the first time I'd spoken to Jet in several weeks, but I knew why he must be calling. I glanced down at my desk to a framed, four-year-old photo of me and a half dozen other sweat-soaked teens in football pads, laughing and yelling and holding a trophy. "Hey, man. I need to be studying for mid-terms, but you know how it is. Senior year is taking its toll on my motivation."

"I can relate. You gonna be there for the football ceremony Friday night?"

"You know it. It'll be good to see the guys. What about you? Haven't seen you back home many weekends lately."

"Well, I stay busy with school, you know. Trying to cram an engineering degree and med school prerequisites into four years. Plus, it's a four-hour drive."

"Aw, come on! You know you want to."

Jet laughed. "Yeah, of course I'll be there. You hear from Jack?"

"You know Jack's ego wouldn't let him miss it."

"They're gonna let me go down on the field, too."

"Why wouldn't they? You *were* a part of the team. Could have been a bigger part, if, well, you know...."

Jet ignored the second part. "Uh huh, you wouldn't have scored all those touchdowns without my astounding videographer skills."

"Wasn't me scoring. That was Jack. I just threw it or handed off to him."

"Some truth to that, but you were pretty dang good yourself, Case." The line went silent and I questioned whether our connection had been lost for a second. "Hey look, I got something to tell you." What had been an excited edge in his voice had disappeared.

I frowned into the phone. "What is it?"

"It's just something I need to explain. I wanna tell you and Jack together. This weekend. You know, like old times. Adam's coming home, too."

"Okay, sure. What about Abi?"

Jet paused on the other end. I dreaded the answer yet wasn't sure what I hoped it would be. "Yeah, I think she'll be there," he said after a time.

———————————

As is the case for a lot of small towns in the deep South, most everyone in Amberton, Mississippi has long considered Friday nights in October to be synonymous with one thing— high school football. It's certainly been that way as long as I can remember.

What sets my hometown apart, though, is that unlike a lot of small towns in the deep South, Amberton's enthusiasm for its high school team seemed to remain uninhibited despite it languishing in mediocrity for the better part of a generation. That was, until 1988, when what seemed like an impossible dream became a reality—my junior year, we won a state championship. It turned out to be the first of three in a five-year span, and thus, the usual fever of Friday nights was replaced by unadulterated fanaticism.

So when I got the call that my school wanted to invite players and coaches back for a halftime ceremony commemorating the five-year anniversary of the first of those three championships, the sudden surge of adrenalin I felt had been intoxicating, immediately and vividly taking me back to so many games past. Sweat and blood and tears, shed for pride and glory and impassioned coaches, in front of screaming fans in packed stadiums under brilliant lights on crisp autumn nights. Before the phone call was even over, I had found myself inadvertently perspiring and gritting my teeth and fighting palpitations as if I was in the locker room again. Just one of Pavlov's dogs. No, scratch that. One of Coach Marchianti's Cougars. Same principle.

The locker room was packed. Between the entire football team, the assortment of coaches, and the twenty-seven former players who were willing and able to be in there for the pregame speech, there wasn't much breathing room left. Truthfully though, while the pervasive aromas of stale sweat and body odor might be nauseating to an outsider, on this night they were invigorating to those who had fought the fights that helped create them. Or at least it was that way for me. Made me want to put on a helmet and crash through a wall. That, and Coach Marchianti.

"Boys, you are part of the select few who are privileged enough to wear the scarlet and gray of the Amberton Cougars! Part of the select few who have the passion, the desire, the toughness, the *cojones* to be a part of this program. Each of you will have friends sitting in the stands tonight who wish they were down there playing but don't have the guts to do what it takes. But you do! You do! You boys are a team! A family! A family of soldiers that goes to war for your school, your pride, your teammates!"

He took a breath, either for effect or because he needed one, or both. Coach Marchianti paced the room like a caged animal, head down and fists clenched, red-faced to match his scarlet shirt, veins bulging at his temples. Black curly hair, bushy eyebrows, square chin. Short, but built like a chunk of granite.

"Let me tell you about what it means to go to war with your brothers, boys. My father fought in World War Two. He was an infantryman in France in 1944. He and three of his buddies made a pact to leave no man behind, no matter what. While they were advancing on a target one bitterly cold January day, a mine exploded, seriously wounding my father. His unit was ordered to press on, and most thought he was dead. It got down to five degrees that night. Five degrees!

"When the battle was over, his friends asked for permission to go back and get him, but their commander refused to let them, saying that it was too dangerous in the dark and anyone left would be dead from the cold anyway.

"But my father's buddies would have none of it. They snuck out before dawn and went looking for him, hiking miles in the dark, risking land mines and enemies and court martials. But guess what?"

"They found him!" A burly lineman in front piped up.

"You're dang right they found him, and he was alive. He had crawled under two dead soldiers to stay warm, and he still got frostbite. And if his buddies, his *brothers*, hadn't gone back, I wouldn't be standing here today because I would've never been born.

"Now, you boys look up here at this group of brothers that came back tonight because they care about you, about their school, about Amberton pride! These brothers fought their war, they stuck together, they left no man behind. And they won, just like we did in World War Two! The first-ever state championship for Amberton High School, five years ago."

Coach Marchianti pointed at me and the other former players. "Guys like Case Reynolds, a kid with average talent who refused to give up and who made himself into an All-Area quarterback.

"Jose Medina, a linebacker who played the championship game with a broken wrist and didn't tell anyone. Jack Masterson, a gifted athlete who made All-State but refused to give the newspaper a quote unless they promised to include a quote from another player who hadn't ever been quoted before.

"Jim Earl Huddleston, who blocked what would've been a game-winning field goal with his chin cuz the man blocking him was holding one arm down and he couldn't lift the other cuz of a separated shoulder. Sam "Bigs" Staten, the scrawniest offensive linemen in the history of football, who went a whole season without letting his man lay so much as a finger on the quarterback."

The coach focused his attention back on his players in uniform. "All these men in front of you are warriors. If I had time, I could tell you the same kind of stories about each and every one of them. But we have a game to win. The next step to our championship." Coach Marchianti craned his neck, peering toward the back of the room. "Slim?"

A short, round, pimple-faced kid with a blond, peach-fuzz mustache strode into the small open space in the middle of the room where Coach had been pacing back and forth. He took a can of red spray paint and painted a circle on the floor.

"Now, who is with me?" Coach Marchianti yelled.

"We are!" the team shouted back in unison.

"Who is with me?"

"We are!" Louder now.

"Who is ready to go to war?"

"We are!" Now the players were on their feet, hopping up and down, the beat of their cleats on the concrete floor like a war drum, in perfect rhythm.

"Don't leave anyone behind! Don't let your brother down! If you are willing to fight for your school, your pride, your friends and brothers, then get in this circle with me right now!"

The shout was deafening. The red circle could not have been more than fifteen feet in diameter. And I believe each and every coach, manager, and player—both current and former—got in it.

As I jumped and stomped and pounded the backs of my friends, Coach's words reverberated within me, growing in volume so as to first supersede, then supplant, the thunderous shouts of the frenzied throng. War. Pride. Friendship. *Brother.* Words—no, ideals—that football certainly cultivated, but for Jack and Jet and me, words that were rooted much deeper than just being on the same team once upon a time. Together, we had fought and suffered and succeeded and fought some more, in ways that others in the room couldn't fathom, both before and after we worked together for a football state championship. And by those struggles we were each bound forever to never leave another of us behind. Both Jack and Jet caught my eye as we joined in the clamor, and I knew they both felt it, too.

NINE

ADAM Townsend closed the door behind him, nodded, and smiled at Jet and me sitting at his family's kitchen table—just like we had so many other Friday nights over the years.

"So, Adam, did you drive all the way up from the coast just to watch your brother go out on the field tonight? Or did you just want to remind yourself what a real football team looked like, since your teams always sucked?"

Adam pretended to ignore my chiding as he walked by, but then he stopped abruptly and punched me in the arm. "Case, I might expect a sorry comment like that from your boy Jack, but not from you." He tried to get me in a chokehold from behind, but I resisted and spun out of my chair.

"You messing with the wrong man, now!" I lunged at him, only partially succeeding in getting my arms wrapped around his stout chest before he brought the full force of his strength to bear and got me off balance. We both gave up the fight when we accidentally knocked over a picture frame on a side table.

Adam ran his fingers through his hair to straighten it as he caught his breath. "Dang, boy, you're not as scrawny as you were last time we locked up!"

"Well that was three or four years ago. And I never was scrawny."

It was true. As a kid, I had always been above average size for my age and fairly muscular. But to Adam, our senior by four years, I probably had always been scrawny. Whereas Jet might have at one time been considered pudgy, especially when he was younger, to my recollection, Adam was always what I called solid—thick, muscular, and strong as a bull. Nothing had changed.

I gave him a playful push and sat back down. "What are you doing here, seriously? Tired of teaching Flipper new tricks?"

"Adam is a marine biologist, not a dolphin trainer, you meathead," Jet chimed in. "He's been studying the causes of harmful algal blooms in the Gulf of Mexico that lead to high concentrations of brevetoxin in the water. It's a neurotoxin from certain dinoflagellates that interferes with normal function of sodium channels in the neurons, causing fish to die."

Science never was my thing, and Jet knew it. I stared at him blankly, squinting as if I was trying to interpret Mandarin Chinese. "First of all, you can't call me a meathead just because I'm gonna be a football coach. The best football coaches are brilliant. Second, I'm an English major, which disqualifies me from meathead status." I turned to Adam, who was leaning cross-armed against the wall, and held up three fingers. "And third, please tell me your job is really to train dolphins, or to free Willys or something. Otherwise, I'm going to think you're just as big a nerd as Jet is."

Adam laughed, but a new voice interrupted before he could respond.

"Nobody, and I mean nobody, is as big a nerd as Jet Townsend!" Jack had let himself in. No knock required, just like always.

"Hey!" Jet pushed himself up and limped over to meet his old friend halfway across the room. "Didn't really get to talk to you at the game. But don't forget. Nerds rule the world!"

Jet reached out to give Jack a high five, but Jack grabbed his hand and embraced him instead. "I don't doubt you'll rule the world someday." He laughed. "But you'll still be a nerd."

Jack Masterson was our oldest friend. Known for being a free spirit and for his "Master" plans, which, when we were younger, often succeeded only in getting us into trouble. Played a little college baseball, had to drop out to sort out some personal and legal issues, tried the minor leagues for a year, then gave that up to start his own landscape contracting business. To hear him tell, he was doing well for himself down in Jackson, or at least was earning a living. "So Adam," he continued, "you were saying? Something about being a normal person with a real job?"

"I was saying that I came home to hunt a little, but yeah, I thought I'd watch you hometown hero wannabes revel in your glory one last time before I headed to the deer camp." Adam stopped and watched Jet settle back into his chair. "Speaking of which, brother, I need to trade trucks for the weekend. Four-wheel drive on mine is acting up, and my four-wheeler is back at Ocean Springs."

Jet gave him a thumbs-up without looking up. "Told you, you should've bought a Ford."

"Adam, back to your job." Jack hopped backward onto the counter and slapped a few open-palmed drumbeats on his thighs. "What Jet said—is that really what you do? Sounds like that might set the record for most boring job in history."

Adam and Jet shared a look that suggested there was more to the story, but I didn't ask. No need to be nosy. "Sometimes it gets boring, but, uh, sometimes there's some excitement."

"Yeah, I'll bet that's a thrill a minute," Jack said.

"Okay, Jet," I said. "You wanted us all here to discuss something. So here we are. Give it to us."

"Can't yet. Abi isn't here. I want her to hear it too."

Abi Rossini. I'll just say it's complicated. My first love, if one can call it that, though of course it's hard to know what love is at age fourteen. Still, you remember it. She was Jet's first love, too, though it took him having a terrible accident and Abi helping nurse him back to health for him to recognize it, or at least to admit it.

The question burning within me was on the verge of bursting forth, but Jack beat me to it. "What's the deal with y'all now anyway, Jet?"

"What do you mean?"

"You know what I mean! You may be a science genius in the body of a social retard, but even you know what I'm talking about. I mean, what's the deal with y'all?"

"We broke up, but we're still close," was all he said.

My heart skipped a beat, and I wasn't sure why. "Wait," I said, "you guys date for four years, break up, and you're still close?"

"Yeah, Abi and I will always be close. I could never not be friends with her."

"So, little brother, why the breakup?" Adam was interested now. "I thought you guys were soul mates or something."

"Well, it was hard with us being at different schools, you know. Me at Vanderbilt, her at Middle Tennessee."

"Hey, bud, I'm sorry, I didn't know." Jack had jumped back in the conversation, his tone softer now. "But there's got to be more to it. I mean, y'all knew going into it you'd be at different schools, huh?" Jet had picked Vanderbilt because he thought he wanted to go to medical school there, and Abi had gone to MTSU for their criminal justice program.

"I don't want to talk about it, okay?" Jet's sharp tone was reinforced by the hand he held up to signal the end of the interrogation, as far as he was concerned. Clearly, it pained Jet to even discuss it. But he had invited Abi tonight as well, for whatever it was he wanted to tell us, which meant they must be on some semblance of good terms. Strange, to say the least.

The doorbell rang, and my heart rolled again. I had not seen Abi in over two years. That interaction had not gone well, and I hoped she had either forgotten it or would now pretend that she had. We had happened into the same restaurant one weekend, and I was in a foul mood after a recent breakup, not because I was particularly fond of the girl, but because I was even less fond of the fact she had dumped me for another guy.

"Who you got here with you tonight, Abi?" I had said when I spotted her and walked over to her booth.

Abi looked up and pushed a dangling spiral of hair behind one ear. Her smile was quick and broad. "Hey, Case!" She gestured to a girl sitting across from her. "This is Samantha, my roommate. Sam, this is Case Reynolds, one of my oldest friends. We used to date a little back in the day, if you could call it that." She laughed. "Before we even had a driver's license, huh? Lots of water under the bridge since then!"

"Yeah, you could say that," I said. "Mind if I slide in?" I pushed in beside Samantha, who frowned and wriggled over to accommodate me as best she could. Why I chose her side instead of Abi's is anyone's guess, but that's what I did.

"Just make yourself at home, then." Abi enunciated each word slowly, as if she was deciding how much to be annoyed.

I ignored Abi's comment. "Samantha, tell me about yourself." I turned toward her, as much to get a better look as to better hear her response in the loud restaurant. Unlike Abi's intense blue eyes and dark curls, Samantha possessed light brown eyes, and her hair was straight and blond, at shoulder's length. She wasn't in Abi's league, but she was cute enough.

"Sam."

"Huh?"

"You can call me Sam."

"As in Uncle?"

Her frown was immediate. She'd heard that one before and didn't like it. "Do I look like an uncle? No, as in short for Samantha."

"Don't make me answer that. The uncle part. Ha! Just kidding."

Abi patted the table twice to get my attention. "Case, what's the matter with you? Have you been drinking?"

"Not enough, clearly. Samantha—sorry, Sam—did you know that Abi was my first kiss?"

"Can't say that she's talked about that particular event."

"I'm not surprised, I guess. She and Jet are the thing now. Just carry on, like nothing evvvver happened between us."

"Case, come on, now, that's not fair. We had already broken up, and you know it."

"Yeah, yeah. I know, I knooow. I love Jet. You got a winner right there. Sho' did." I turned to look at her roommate.

"Samantha … Uh oh, no, it's Sam. Why do I always forget that?" I pounded the table with my fist and stared at Abi. "Sam, it was nice to meet you. If you ever want to go out, you let me know. I'm a good date. Abi used to woulda vouched for me."

"I'll be sure to look you up," Sam had said, not trying to hide the roll of her eyes.

I now shuddered at the memory. Many sleepless nights had followed that encounter. I had called Abi a week or two later to apologize and stress that I most definitely did not still have feelings for her, other than as a good friend. She assured me it was fine, no big deal, but I'm not sure she believed me. We hadn't talked or seen each other since, and Jet had never once mentioned it. Had she ever even told him?

I had convinced myself that Abi's hold on me had passed on through, that the meltdown at the restaurant had been just an isolated thunderstorm, a temporary turbulence in the weather that did not define the climate. My conscious reassurances to myself did nothing, though, to calm my trepidation at the prospect of seeing her again, like maybe I anticipated seeing a tornado whose path I couldn't resist walking right into. My upper lip began to perspire, and it frustrated me.

I had told myself many times just to forget Abi. The problem with that: Abi Rossini is unforgettable in every way. Her playful, mischievous side was what attracted me to her in the first place so many years before. Her compassion and generosity was what led her to nurse Jet back to health after he was almost killed by a car in a hit and run—and what made me love her even more, albeit from a distance, when we grew apart as she and Jet grew closer.

Beyond that, she is the type of person who commands the attention in the room, like the only person with a flashlight on a black night when the electricity goes out. You can't help but look.

This night was no different. Adam answered the door, but all eyes locked on the beautiful brunette who appeared at the threshold. Perfect posture made her look taller than she was, and there was no question that she was a classic beauty—high cheekbones, strong chin, rich, warm complexion consistent with her Italian heritage—but it was her air of confidence, conveyed by penetrating, electric blue eyes seeming at once to see everyone and everything around her, that always caused men and women alike to take notice.

"Hey, Abi," I said, as indifferently as possible. "Long time, no see."

Abi smiled at no one in particular, pausing in the doorway. Then her eyes settled on mine, and she grinned. Just barely. "You could say that, I guess. Has it been that long? Seems like just a few weeks ago."

Was it possible for a smile to be both smug and playful? Clearly, she recalled our last encounter as vividly as I did. Unfortunately.

"Glad you could come!" Jet said. "Come on in and have a seat! I know everyone has places to go. This won't take long."

Abi did not come on in. Her mouth opened to speak but she hesitated. She whispered something over her shoulder, then turned back toward us. "I brought someone with me."

Jet had risen to greet her but stopped suddenly. Frozen in place. A hand grasped Abi's shoulder from behind, then a man stepped into the room beside her.

My mouth dropped open.

"Aw, you gotta be kidding me!" Jack dropped from his elevated perch on the counter edge. "I'm outta here!"

Jet reached out and grabbed his arm. "Please don't leave."

Jack jerked away and leaned back against the counter, arms folded across his chest. He nodded but didn't speak, eyes fixed on the doorway.

I wasn't sure if I wanted to follow Jack out the door or stay to find out how this had happened. I just couldn't believe my eyes. Surely Abi was not coming in the door with Lane Buckley. The same Lane Buckley who had been in that street fight with Jack seven years before, the fight during which Lane's friend and our nemesis, VJ MacIntosh, had tried to run Jack over, and Jet had pushed him out of the way. VJ had gone to jail or juvie or somewhere for attempted murder, Jet had gone to death's door, and Lane had moved out of town. We had scarcely seen him since. Until now.

"Abi," I said, "is there something you need to tell us?"

Abi opened her mouth to speak, but Lane beat her to it. "Yes, Abi and I are dating." He looked around nervously. He was more slender than I remembered him. Lanky would be the word for it. Probably not pumping iron like he did in high school, when he had been the quarterback while I was still in junior high, before he moved away. "But look, guys, I'm not here to cause trouble. Abi was invited, so I met her here. That's all."

"It's complicated," Abi said.

"That doesn't even begin to describe it." Jack's gaze fixed on Lane, who appeared to be making a conscious effort to avoid the hard stare. "Jet, I'll stay for you, but you better get this show on the road before this room clears out. I'm just wondering if VJ is coming, too. Because that will send me over the edge."

A hundred questions bounced around in my mind. I wanted to hear what Jet had to say but doubted it was more important than grilling Abi—and Jet—about what had happened that led her to be with Lane. His buddy VJ was the vilest person I knew, and even though I hadn't seen VJ in years, in my mind, he and Lane were inextricably linked. Maybe Lane was a decent guy now. I had to believe he was, or Abi wouldn't be with him. But VJ—never. I didn't want to put Abi on the spot, so I kept my mouth shut and listened.

"VJ isn't coming," Lane said.

"Good enough," Adam piped up. "Because I might have to hurt him. So, little brother, you got us here, and you got our attention. What's the story?"

Jet took a deep breath, buried his hands in his pockets, and stared at the floor. "Okay, here goes. I don't know how to tell this, so I'll just do it." His shoulders rolled forward, and he seemed to shrink an inch or two. "You guys know I always wanted to go to medical school, right?"

Nods and questioning looks all around.

He sighed deeply and did not look up. "And you know I said I was going to either Harvard, Stanford, Johns Hopkins, or Vandy, and nothing else would do. Right?"

We all nodded again, frowns deepening.

"Well, I've got some good news." Jet raised his head, revealing a broad smile. "I changed my mind. Decided I'm gonna practice medicine right here in good ole Mississippi, and we have a good school here, so why not start my training here, too?

So I applied to Jackson University School of Medicine. The early entry program. I got accepted, and that's where I'm going!"

Jack broke out of his sulk with a whoop and strode over to pound Jet on the back. "That's my boy! Dang, Jet, I'll bet they did let you right in. Begging you to come, I guarantee, smart as you are! That's awesome. Just awesome. Hey, I'll be right there in Jackson with you!"

"And so will I," Abi said softly. She walked slowly toward Jet. Her eyes were misty wet, which was a bit confusing to me under the circumstances. She reached out and embraced Jet tightly, affectionately, holding it for several seconds. "I'm so proud of you. I know that was hard for you."

"No it wasn't," Jet said. "Easiest decision I've ever made."

Abi pulled back and their eyes met, again in a way I didn't understand. Were they broken up or not?

I stepped in and pushed him playfully with an open palm. "You sorry joker. Had us all thinking you'd decided to drop out and sell books door-to-door or something."

Jet pointed an index finger at me. "Gotcha."

Something in Jet's expression told me it wasn't that simple, but Adam stepped in with a bear hug before I could say more. His smile stretched from ear to ear, and as soon as one hug ended, he came right back with another. Between squeezes, he quizzed Jet on whether he had told their parents, what made him decide to go to med school near home, what specialties he was considering, when he would start, and where he thought he'd live, among other things. Big brother looking out for little brother as much as he could, even though he knew, as did we all, that Jet was perfectly capable of making his own way, much more than most.

As Abi stepped out of the conversation, I did, too, and gently grabbed her elbow. "What did you mean, 'So will I'?"

"I took a job with the Mississippi Crime Lab. Jackson office. Crazy how we all are going to be in the same place, huh?" A look of realization came over her. "Well, most of us. I guess you don't know where you'll be yet, huh?"

"No, but it'll be fine. I'm glad you can look out for each other. Just like old times."

Another voice broke into the conversation, and Lane had his hand on Abi's shoulder again. "I hope *everything* isn't just like old times." He smiled.

I stiffened and studied his face in a futile effort to gauge his sincerity. I just didn't know him well enough to get a read.

"I'd like us all to be friends. Might as well let bygones be bygones." Lane reached out his hand, and I shook it reluctantly.

"We'll see," was all I said.

The sound of metal hitting glass interrupted the conversation that I was determined not to continue with Lane. "Don't leave! I'd like to say a few words," Adam called loudly, tapping a glass with a spoon. "I didn't know this was going to be a celebration, or I'd have provided some more appropriate refreshments."

He gathered up six glasses and a pitcher and started pouring. "But it is what it is, and I can't let folks leave without proposing a toast first. So sweet tea will have to do. Anyway, I just want to put it on the record how proud I am. You guys know, John Edward is smart. A dang genius, if you ask me. And he has the courage of a lion. We learned all that when he saved Jack and almost died and missed most of his freshman year of school but still graduated valedictorian, on schedule with his class."

He glanced at Lane, looked away, and quickly continued. "But those things aren't what makes Jet special. He has a heart of gold. A heart of gold. You guys know it. If I had a brain like his, I figure I'd brag so much that nobody'd wanna be around me. But he doesn't. Never has. And he'd give you his shirt off his back if you needed it. Any of you. I'm just proud to call him my little brother. And I know y'all are proud to call him your friend." Adam's gaze settled on Abi this time, but he didn't look away. They both were tearful.

"Yeah, but he ain't worth a crap in a footrace." Jack's insult brought a laugh from everyone in the room. Maybe he was trying as hard as I was not to cry, maybe he was just being Jack. Either way, I appreciated the levity. Laughter trumps tears any day in my book.

"To Jet!" Abi said.

"To Jet!"

TEN

THE harsh, screaming wail of the siren startled me. Was it an ambulance, or law enforcement? And how did they find us, way out here?

A sudden awareness of feline eyes penetrating the darkness of the dilapidated barn, and a long, serpentine tail flicking to and fro in its shadows, transformed my speculation to alarm. The siren was not a siren at all.

"It's looking for him." I jumped a full six inches in the air, startled by the voice behind me. Jack frowned forbiddingly and nodded his head toward the ground at my feet. Jet was lying in a heap, motionless, his body contorted unnaturally. Blood stained his clothes and smeared his face.

The big cat made its awful scream again and erupted from the gloom.

"Case!" Jack grabbed my shoulder.

"Case!" Mom's voice now. Where did she come from? The dark scene of the barn and predators and injured friends dissolved into a groggy daylight stupor, and I awoke in my old room. At home. She shook me again. "Wake up, son, it's okay."

"What's going on?" I rubbed my eyes and rolled over to find the clock on my bedside table. 8:21 a.m. So much for sleeping late on a Saturday morning.

"You were having a nightmare again. I thought those had disappeared."

The nightmare had not visited me the last couple of years at college, and I had hoped it was gone forever. But apparently it had never been very far away. "I'm fine, Mom. I'm going back to sleep."

I had left Jet's house only a few short hours earlier. Celebrating his admission to medical school, reliving football glory days, and catching up on old times with him and Jack had lingered on deep into the morning hours, and the late night had grown even later when Jet shared what was riding heavy on his heart.

He had decided to stay close for medical school in large part because his mother had recently been diagnosed with breast cancer. They thought they had caught it early, but she would still need surgery and chemo, and Jet wasn't going to let himself be very far away. Not wanting his mother to ever think she had in some way held him back, he had made Jack and me swear never to tell a soul the reason for his decision. Abi was the only other person he had told.

But now Mom had woken me much earlier than I intended, and she was shaking her head. Late night with my friends or not, restless nightmare-laden sleep or not, closing my eyes again was not going to be an option. Then I understood why. She was holding the telephone, covering the mouthpiece with her palm. "Talk to Jet." It dawned on me then that the phone had been ringing—a sound sometimes as ominous in the middle of a deep sleep as sirens and screaming cougars. She thrust the phone toward me. "He needs you, Case." The look on her face told me it was bad.

It turned out to be much, much worse than that.

Adam was dead.

Killed on his way to deer camp. He had said his goodbyes and left sometime well before midnight. The call had come in several hours later. His truck had been found smoldering in a ravine about five miles short of his destination in Willow Springs, about halfway between Amberton and Jackson. Unfortunately, it was off a rural county road, unlikely to have much traffic in the early morning hours, and no one had spotted the smoke until after sunrise.

The Stanford County sheriff said it looked cut and dry, just an unfortunate but nonetheless ghastly accident. Adam had somehow lost control, probably going too fast, and the truck had run off the road and dived into the brushy ravine. A full five-gallon can of gasoline in the bed of the truck had crashed into the cab, a projectile of pure combustible destruction. It was hard to tell what had ignited it, but the inferno had consumed everything. The coroner told the family they could take some consolation that Adam was unconscious when the fire started. He was sitting right where he'd been buckled, with no signs of struggle. The seat belt itself had melted and burned away, but the metal buckle was still firmly latched.

The huge, yellow and black wasp darted around us like a low-flying attack helicopter, scanning for targets in the grass beneath it, suspended by a blur of ruddy wings. It hovered briefly, as if anticipating a kill, then shot away around the corner of the funeral home as if called on a different mission.

"You remember Murphy McElwain?" Jet fiddled with the top buttonhole on his charcoal gray suit, sliding the button through it, then back out again.

"Yeah. Big, scary-looking kid," Jack said. "What, five or six years older than us? Always hung around the country club pool in the summers, even though he was older than everyone else."

I had been watching the insect, too, and already knew what Jet was thinking. "A legend in his own mind. Murph will long be remembered as the idiot who said he'd show what a real hole-in-one looked like. Then got his junk stung by a gigantic cicada killer wasp. What was it, on the number eight or nine green?"

Even Jet laughed out loud. "Number eight. You read my mind. What an idiot. Got on his belly, stuck it in the hole, and got hammered. I'd give anything to have heard that scream."

"I think Steeple Starns was with him. Said he thought it had gotten cut off or something when he hollered," I said. "That cicada killer must have thought he had him an itty-bitty cicada snack coming at him!"

"She," Jet said. Jack and I just looked at him and waited on the explanation. "You said he. Males don't have stingers, so it was a she."

Jack punched him in the arm playfully. "Whatever, brainiac! Anyway, I heard it swelled up so big it almost busted." He slapped his thigh and wiped tears from his eyes.

"I think he had to wear his granny's panties for a week just to have room for it," I added, finishing off the much-needed laugh while we caught our breath.

The chuckles faded, and Jet's expression darkened, automatically extinguishing the last vestiges of our smiles with his. "When I was six or seven, we were swimming at the country club." He nodded in the general direction of the country club, across town, due north of our position near the side door of Restor and Sons Funeral Home. "Adam and me. Adam was supposed to be watching me, but he had wandered off. I knew not to swim with him gone, so I sat on the edge of the pool splashing my feet. I wasn't even supposed to be that close to the pool."

"Jet, don't—" Jack started. He knew the story.

I frowned at him and shook my head. *Let him talk.*

Jet continued as if Jack had not spoken. "I was the only one at the pool for a bit. I'm not sure where everybody else had gone, but Murphy walked up. Asked where Adam was. Told me he'd watch me while Adam was gone. Said he'd heard I may be fat but that I sure was smart. Rumor was, the size of my brain matched the size of my belly, or something like that. Said he wanted to learn something from me, but I'd have to learn something from him, too—how to be tough. So he started asking me math problems. Simple at first, but then he got harder and harder, multiplying three-digit numbers or something. I think I actually got some of them right, and I doubt he knew much more than two times two himself, but he started telling me I'd missed 'em. Each time he claimed I missed one, I'd have to swim to the opposite ladder and back. It was probably only fifteen feet, but heck, I couldn't swim much anyway. After four or five trips, I was spent.

"'I thought whales could swim,' I remember him saying, over and over. Laughing at me. Adam showed up and asked what was going on. I was struggling to stay afloat, and Murphy at first stopped Adam from helping me, said I needed to learn how to survive on my own. Adam pulled away from him and dove in to pull me out.

"I'll never forget it. Murphy was just laughing, laughing. And Adam walked straight up to him and slugged him. Hit him as hard as he could. Murphy never flinched. He stopped laughing and just smiled an evil smile. Adam suddenly looked afraid, and I thought he might grab me and run, but then Murphy told Adam he could run but he couldn't hide. Whether that day or the next, he promised he'd beat Adam first, and then he'd get me. I remember standing there crying like a little girl."

"You were six, Jet," I said.

"The look on Adam's face changed to something I'd never seen. As soon as Murphy said he'd get me, everything changed. Adam told me to run, but I couldn't. I was frozen. He walked back up to Murphy and hit him again. Murphy was a lot bigger and a lot stronger, but this time it was like Adam was possessed. I thought he was going to kill Murphy McElwain. It took three people to get him off. Murphy never messed with either of us again."

"Adam was one tough dude," Jack said.

"I don't know," Jet said. "Maybe. But I knew then that my big brother had my back. No matter what." Tears welled and flowed freely, a spring of emotion suddenly uncapped. "That's a once-in-a-lifetime kind of backup."

I didn't know what to say, and Jack didn't either. We just hugged him and told him he'd get through it, and we'd always have his back, too.

At the funeral, Abi hovered around Jet like a protective mother. I overheard Jet tease her at one point that he had one mother, and while he was quite fond of her, he certainly didn't need two. Abi told him she didn't care, she was going to be there if he needed her.

I spotted Lane Buckley lurking around the periphery of the crowd, watching Abi, seeming to be on guard himself. He didn't look as lean in his gray suit as he had a few nights before. I was glad Jack hadn't spotted him—things might get ugly—but I walked over to talk to him anyway. If Abi thought he was worthy of her time, then maybe I should, too. Maybe.

"Did you know Adam?"

Lane turned and raised both eyebrows. Not surprised that I was at the funeral, of course, but that I was talking to him. "Yeah, I knew him. Great guy. Played football with him a little. He was a senior when I was a sophomore, before I moved away."

I nodded. "Pretty terrible, how it happened."

"Yeah. Freak deal. I guess it was just his time."

Just his time. My grandmother had often said the same thing regarding untimely deaths. What did that even mean? I shrugged. "I guess. Just doesn't seem possible."

"Metal gas cans are pretty hard. Had a lot of momentum, maybe. Deep ravine."

I turned to look at Lane. "You know the place it happened?"

"Naw, not exactly. Been through that area before, though. Heard the truck was down in one of those deep ones."

I didn't want to talk about Adam anymore. "Lane, what's the story with you and Abi? And Jet, for that matter."

Lane cut his eyes toward me, followed by his head a millisecond later. He held it there briefly, head cocked slightly to the side, then turned to track Abi again. "She's a great girl," was all he said.

I agreed with that. I couldn't believe I was standing there having this conversation with him. Eight years earlier, Abi had broken up with Lane to date me, and he and I had essentially become enemies. Then Jet had gotten hurt and everything changed. Sure, we were just kids then, but the emotions born of first love are forged strong and deep and indelible. Forgetting is hard to come by, and forgiveness is even harder. I couldn't for the life of me imagine why Abi had gotten hooked up with him again. "You didn't answer my question."

He stared straight ahead. "Didn't know I had to report to you."

I stiffened, but Lane mitigated my adrenaline surge before I could say something I regretted.

He turned and grabbed my shoulder, gently and apologetically. "I'm sorry, that was rude. Forgive me. The stress of all this is just wearing me thin. Abi clearly cares for Jet quite a lot, and her worries become my worries." He dropped the one hand from my shoulder and placed both in his pants pockets, rocking forward then back from the balls of his feet to his heels. "We're going to get married."

Luckily, my tongue is and always has been attached to the floor of my mouth or I would have choked on it. "Get married? How? Nobody's seen you for years, and now all of a sudden you and Abi are getting married?"

"Abi's been seeing me. Quite a bit of me, actually." He smiled at his own joke, but I didn't reciprocate. "I guess she just didn't mention it. I transferred to MTSU, we had some classes together, she and Jet broke up a while back, and the rest is history. Look, Case, I just want to be friends with everybody. You know I had nothing to do with Jet getting hurt. That was VJ. We were all just stupid kids. We're all different now, me included."

I knew he was right, and there'd be a time for full reconciliation later, especially if he and Abi really got married. But, for the time being, I chose to ignore what I interpreted as a thinly veiled apology. The truth was it really hadn't been his fault. But it was his friend driving the car. And my friend who nearly got killed. "Jet never told me why he and Abi broke up," I said.

"People just grow apart sometimes. You know that. Plus, Jet was figuring to go to med school way across the country. Abi's just a Mississippi girl. She didn't really want to do that."

"But Jet's not going way across the country. He's going to be right here in Mississippi."

Lane turned and gave me a hard look. A penetrating look, the kind where you're not sure if the person is searching for something deep within you or just seeing right through you, like Superman's x-ray vision. His gaze diverted toward our feet. He sighed heavily. "I am all too aware of that."

ELEVEN

Gross Anatomy, Day One

THAT *stupid doorbell! I don't wanna buy any cookies or whatever they're selling!* Jet pulled the covers over his head and tried to blot out the sound. He just wanted to stay in bed. Possibly forever. He wasn't sure what had happened in the Gross Anatomy lab, but he was pretty sure he wouldn't—couldn't—go back. It was so incredibly disappointing! He'd worked his whole life to get into medical school, and now his plans were disintegrating after barely getting off the ground. He remembered sitting in his eighth-grade science class watching eagerly as the Space Shuttle *Challenger* launched. Then without warning, it exploded. Anticipation turned to anguish in the blink of an eye. That summed up his day—maybe on a lesser scale, but medical school meant everything to him. *Quit ringing the doorbell!*

Resigned to the obvious fact that this Girl Scout or book salesman wasn't going to give up, Jet threw the sheets back and stormed up the hall. Still wearing the same clothes he'd put on that morning. He didn't even bother to look out the window before jerking open the door. "Whatever you're selling, we're not buy—"

Gracie Tollison stood on the front steps, holding his white lab coat.

"Gracie, what are you doing here?"

"Honey, I'd say I need to ask what you are doing here."

Jet realized she was looking at his rumpled clothes. Then her eyes diverted to his head, and he knew without reaching up to touch it that his hair must be a mess as well. "I—I was just resting."

She held up the coat. "I brought this."

"I see that. You could have just put it in your locker, and I'd get it later."

"Really? You were mumbling something about being done when you walked out. I wasn't sure you were coming back. So maybe I used the coat as an excuse, because I think you need to talk to someone. Are you going to invite me in, darlin', or leave me standing out here all night?"

Jet stepped back to open the door wider, not sure if he was annoyed or enamored with the way she threw terms of endearment out like pronouns. He tried to pat his hair back into place behind her as she walked past. "Have a seat." He pointed to the sparsely furnished living room. Two recliners, a set of TV trays, a frayed couch, and a television on a rickety wooden shelf defined the space. Gracie glanced at his hair, then took a seat on the couch.

"Quite a bachelor pad you have here."

"How did you find me?"

"Talked to your roommate."

"My roommate? He hasn't been here all day."

"Didn't say I called him today, baby," she smiled. "Sammy Clark and I are old friends."

So, she knew Sammy. Jet didn't even want to ask how. It wasn't important. "Guess I made quite a scene today, huh?"

"Well, I've never had a first day of Gross Anatomy before, so maybe that is just par for the course, who knows? What happened in there?"

The room felt too warm all of a sudden. Stifling. Jet stood and adjusted the thermostat to a lower setting. "I don't know. Let's not talk about it. Maybe I'm just not cut out for this."

Gracie snorted. "Not cut out for this? Bull! You're more cut out for this than anybody in there, I'd say."

"How do you know?" Jet recalled what she'd said earlier in the day about his test scores. "How did you know my MCAT score? You and Sterling Virchow and everybody else, I guess?"

"I used to date Sammy a little bit. So he's told me some about you. But he and Sterling are friends, have a few beers on occasion, Sterling's father is admissions chairman. You get the picture."

"You and Sammy, huh?" Jet forced a smile, although for reasons he couldn't pinpoint, he somehow felt betrayed.

"Nah, we're just friends now. Enough about that." A wave of her hand to brush it off. "You dodged my question. What's going on with you?"

Jet wondered why she was so interested. Nosiness or genuine concern? She seemed to show tendencies toward both, as best he could tell, but he could not deny he felt drawn to the latter. "It's a long story."

"I've got all night, darlin'. I brought my books so we can study. You like pizza?"

Gracie closed the Netter's *Atlas of Human Anatomy* over her hand to keep her spot marked. "The dorsal roots of spinal nerves contain skeletal motor and autonomic fibers, whereas the ventral roots contain only sensory fibers." She nodded decisively. "Got it."

Jet smiled, shook his head, and grabbed a piece of pepperoni and jalapeño pizza, unfazed by the fact it was now cold and chewy. "No, it's the opposite. You have it backwards."

Gracie pulled her hand out of the book, staring at a blank wall across the room. "Okay, so let me get this straight. I can't get it off my mind. You got run over by some teenage maniac when you were fourteen because you and your friends found a dead body on some guy's farm, and in the process of figuring out who the dead guy was, you figured out that the father of the guy who hit you was a criminal."

"Something like that, yeah. VJ MacIntosh was his name. Truly a vile human being. Sub-human, actually. He went to jail, I guess. But I got over that a long time ago."

"Did you? You said this VJ guy, his best friend is dating your ex-girlfriend."

"Lane. He was. Or is—maybe. I don't know. Abi and I are still friends, though. It doesn't matter."

"Abi, huh?" Gracie paused and let that hang in the air a moment. Jet chose to let it stay there. "And then your mother came down with breast cancer, so you decided to stay close for medical school."

"Yeah, she went through a rough patch. But it's better. In remission. But we still worry, you know?"

"Jet, that's more than enough for anybody. And then—"

"And then that happened to Adam," he finished her sentence.

"That must have been horrible." Gracie touched Jet's arm for the second time that night, only a brief pat compared to the tearful clench she had held while he told the story the first time. She had listened in stunned silence, letting him get it out before he had shut it down and suggested they study awhile. She had done most of the studying, while he had pretended not to be distracted. "You and Adam were close?"

"He was four years older than me. But yeah. I idolized him. I guess we complemented each other. He was the athlete, the lady's man, the All-American type. But he was smart, too. Sneaky smart—he didn't really want folks to know it. I was always the smart kid who couldn't be anything else. Adam had a way of making me feel good about myself, though." He brought his palms together in front of his mouth and paused before dropping them down into a double fist and continuing. "You know the worst thing about his death?"

Gracie shook her head and waited for the answer.

"I never got to say goodbye. His body was burned so badly the coroner said there was nothing recognizable. I didn't want to see him like that."

Gracie shuddered. "So that's really what got to you today? Thinking about him?"

"I guess. Something about that cadaver. He looked so young. And I started thinking about what Adam would have looked like, if I could have seen him. It was just too much. I know, it's weird."

"Don't you say that! It's not weird. Nobody can tell you how to feel!" Gracie's tone was emphatic, but she raised an index finger and lowered her voice, nearly to a whisper. "I do know one thing, though."

Now it was Jet's turn to wait for her to finish.

"I never met him, but I've heard enough to know this: Adam would want you to go back tomorrow. He would be very unhappy if he knew that somehow he kept you from realizing your dream."

Jet's eyes moistened, but he said nothing. He couldn't. Soon the tears broke free, and he wiped them with the back of his hand until Gracie handed him a napkin and kept one for herself.

"Why do you care so much?" he asked. "You just met me today."

She winked. "Because I need help with Gross Anatomy, and I hear you're pretty smart."

TWELVE

Gross Anatomy, Day Two

A S Tucker and Gracie each grasped a handle and opened the hinged cover to the stainless steel tank, Jet noticed that their lab jackets, pristine white like his the previous day, were now dotted with pale amber stains from preservative and scattered flecks of tissue that had survived attempts to brush them all away.

It occurred to him for the first time that the dissection had proceeded right along after his abrupt departure. Of course it had. He wasn't sure why he would have expected anything different, as if everyone else's world froze in time as his had the afternoon before. What was the phrase? Time and tide wait for no man. He wasn't sure who said it, maybe Dickens, maybe someone before him. No matter. Time marched on, and he planned to march with it. Thanks in large part to Gracie.

Tekowski cranked the lever to lift the body out of the cloudy, yellow pool of preservative, a recipe of formaldehyde, phenol, methanol, glycerin, and who-knew-what else—the stock for what was becoming a soup of floating fat globules and other tissue particles.

As Tea turned the last rotation of the crank, Jet reached to pull back the wet sheet covering the body and realized they were all looking at him skeptically. "What? Why so quiet? I'm fine."

Tucker shrugged, an if-he's-good-with-it-then-so-am-I gesture. "You missed the good part yesterday. We got to see some of where the bullet went." He stepped up onto the stool to better demonstrate. "Look—it blasted right through the left latissimus dorsi muscle."

Jet eyed the anatomic location and nodded. "Full metal jacket."

"Never liked war movies," Tucker muttered.

"It's a bullet type. Look how clean the hole is. The bullet shot through in one piece, so must've been a full metal jacket. They don't mushroom and disintegrate. They're cheaper, so a lot of people use them for target loads. Military uses them sometimes because they often don't kill as quickly. Takes more resources to tend to a wounded soldier than a dead one. Of course, this guy probably took it straight through the heart, so I doubt it mattered what kind of bullet it was."

"Okay, whatever," Tekowski said. "Anyway, it was ridiculous yesterday. Tucker wouldn't quit looking for the bullet. We dissected down, and he didn't find it, just like you told him he wouldn't. Then he started reaching under it, feeling around, trying to find whether it exited or not. Look at his coat sleeve. Soaked in formaldehyde up to the elbow."

Indeed, his right sleeve was a dingy yellow compared to the left. "That's gross. You need to wash that thing. What did you find out?"

"Wouldn't shut up until we helped him lift it and look," Gracie said. "Bullet came right through just like you said it probably did. And you're right, the hole was perfect, just a little bigger."

"Then Cronin chewed us all out for not following proper procedure." Tekowski frowned at Tucker.

"But on a lighter note, we did pick out a name," Gracie said. Jet raised his eyebrows, puzzled, and she answered his question before he could ask it. "It's customary to name the cadaver. Wouldn't be right to spend that much time with someone and not even know their name."

"Lucky," Tekowski said.

"Lucky?"

"Yeah, Lucky," Tucker said. "We're lucky to be here, and he, obviously was not so lucky. So we chose the positive. A fitting tribute, don't you think?"

"You could have just named him Diametric," Jet said. "Has a nice ring to it."

Gracie smiled and shook her head. Apparently glad his sense of humor was intact, odd as it was.

A familiar baritone voice interjected. "Well, well! I saw you sitting in the lecture downstairs earlier but wasn't at all sure you'd make it back up here to the lab. I knew we'd see some attrition eventually, but on the first day? Not from the mighty Jet Townsend."

"He had a bad day, Sterling," Gracie said. "Cut him some slack and go back to your table."

Virchow smiled. "Oh, I'm not being critical. Quite the contrary. I would have been disappointed had he not come back. So much promise. Still a long way to go, though. Gross Anatomy is full of surprises so far, eh? I wouldn't be surprised if there aren't more to come. Might be entertaining."

Jet smiled stiffly. What was this guy's problem? Virchow appeared to have a brand-new lab jacket on today. Jet wondered if he might have two or three hundred of them monogrammed and starched, ready for action, a new one each day. "I'm glad I'm here, too, Sterling. Thanks for the pep talk."

Virchow circled their table, inspecting their progress like a vulture sizing up fresh roadkill. "So, tell me. How are things coming here with Mr. Lucky? Looks like you guys are dragging a little. We have already dissected down to the spinal accessory nerve."

Jet started to tell Virchow he'd soon be a candidate for having his own body donated to science if he didn't shut up and go away but held his tongue when Professor Cronin approached Virchow from behind.

The course director spoke at the same time he grasped Sterling's shoulder, eliciting a wide-eyed lurch that Jet vowed to imitate later. "Mr. Virchow, crown jewel of the offspring of our medical staff, since you have advanced so far with your dissection that you have extra time to confabulate with the students around you, let me ask you, do you feel lucky?"

Virchow furrowed his brow then smiled. "Sir, I'd have to say yes, I feel very fortunate for the opportunity to be here."

"Ahh, so you ascribe to Seneca's definition of luck."

"Seneca, sir? I'm not sure I know her. Is she one of the professors?"

"Good grief, I thought we were on a higher plane of dialogue here, but apparently not. Forget that. Perhaps your preparation is functioning on a higher plane. Can you tell me what forms the triangle of auscultation?"

Sterling clasped his hands in front at waist level and then separated them, nervously tapping his fingertips together. "I believe that is the, uh, teres major muscle, and the—"

"Stop!" Cronin interrupted. "Definitely not lucky today." Cronin turned to the others at the table. "Anybody else?"

No one spoke for several seconds. Cronin's glower made it seem like minutes. "That's what I figured. I would have thought more of you, Mr. Townsend. Perhaps you should try staying through the whole dissection today and see if you become enlightened." He turned to walk away, and Virchow moved to walk with him, evidently intent on explaining how he would be sure to know all the answers from now on.

Gracie elbowed Jet in the ribs.

Jet coughed, gave her a sideways frown, and then spoke quietly. "Seneca the Younger, sir."

Cronin stopped mid-stride and turned back. "Excuse me?"

"The Roman philosopher. He said that luck happens when opportunity meets preparation." Virchow glared at Jet over Cronin's shoulder. Jet ignored it. *If he can be a pompous jerk, then I suppose I can too.*

Cronin looked for a millisecond as if he might give Jet some credit for knowing the trivia, but if he softened at all, it was only fleeting. "Unfortunately, Mr. Townsend, this is not a history or philosophy class. I was interested in the answer to my anatomy question."

Jet nodded and spoke without hesitation. "The triangle of auscultation is the triangle formed by the convergence of the scapula, the trapezius muscle and the latissimus dorsi muscle. At that location there is less tissue intervening between the skin and the lung, making it an ideal place to listen, or auscultate, with the stethoscope."

"Bingo," Gracie said under her breath, beaming.

"Did you have something to add, Ms. Tollison?"

"No sir, nothing at all."

Professor Cronin pushed his glasses up and frowned. "Hmmph. Get to work. You're way behind. And help your lab partners stick to the assignment. Yesterday they decided to skip ahead and dissect the anterior." He glared at Tucker. "Anterior means the front, Mr. Tucker—or Oliver—or whatever moniker you're going by today." The professor shook his head and moved on to another table, searching for other victims.

"Don't worry about him. He comes across like a rabid old grizzly, but that's not the case at all." The four turned to confront a new face. She was smiling. "I am certain he does not have rabies." The name on the white coat read *Marta Winscote, PhD*. Jet had seen her in the lab the day before. One of several assistant professors who assisted with the teaching, as well as the dissections when needed. She was tall, able to look eye to eye with Jet, with thick, black-rimmed glasses, long brown hair with a hint of curl, parted in the middle. A pinch of a nose rested inconspicuously over full lips. She was pale and wore no makeup. Jet couldn't decide if she was naturally homely or just needed a stylist. She was pleasant, though, and under the circumstances, that counted for a lot. "Are you guys coming along okay? I can help you if you're behind." Without waiting for an answer, Dr. Winscote proceeded to inspect the group's progress. "Ooh, looks like you guys do need some help. What have y'all been doing?"

"Talking, that's what," Tekowski said sarcastically, glaring at his group members.

"We were one short yesterday, you know," Tucker said. "No offense, Jet."

"Uh oh, looks like you cut the insertion of the serratus posterior inferior muscle on the right, where it attaches to the ribs. It's a common mistake when you reflect the latissimus dorsi muscle—you think they're the same muscle, but if you're careful, you'll see that the fibers separate." She paused while she briefly examined the body further. "Hmmm, the landmarks on the left are distorted by the bullet hole, so you need to be very careful on the right. No matter, I'll sew it back so you can see where it's supposed to be. You guys use your manual and follow each step very closely, though, okay?" The professor deftly reattached one end of the small muscle back in place with two loops of silk suture.

Then, in half the time it would have taken the whole group combined to do it alone, she helped them expose a few other important anatomical structures. Satisfied with the quick progress they'd achieved, she stepped away to another table.

"Jet, honey, are you okay?" Gracie asked. "You've got that look again."

Jet had stepped back a few feet, staring at the cadaver. He was most definitely not okay. The consuming feeling of suffocation from the day before had not returned, nor had the visions of burning corpses. But the dead man nicknamed Lucky had taken on an eerily familiar appearance. Jet wasn't sure why. Nothing had really changed.

But as he had watched Dr. Winscote demonstrate and dissect, it was as if a spotlight had suddenly shined on the cadaver, penetrating a veil of darkness he hadn't even recognized was there, giving way to perfect clarity. Horrible, unspeakable clarity. Yet it was preposterous, wasn't it? Wasn't his imagination playing cruel tricks on him? He told himself it was unequivocally impossible, yet he had never more certain of anything in his life.

Jet's heart raced as he stepped toward the embalmed remains of a man who ostensibly had volunteered for this, for his body to be here in this place, subjected to display and exploration on a stainless steel table, his back splayed open, in a grotesque yet wholly justifiable way—the way thousands before him had done in order to save millions of others. But he was suddenly convinced this man had not volunteered.

Jet's hand trembled violently as he reached for the thin towel covering the head of the cadaver. The roar in his ears from a thousand tempestuous thoughts drowned out the concerned inquiries from his lab partners as to what was going on. He wanted to run away. Forget this whole thing and save his sanity. But he couldn't do it any more than he could travel through time and reshape the past. This must be what mental illness felt like: the mind seething with uncontrollable, irrational theories which the body seeks to organize and reconcile through inexplicable compulsions. And now he was compelled to look. Not in four weeks when they were scheduled to flip the body over and begin the anterior dissections, but right now. Before he could take another breath. He had to see.

He pulled the soaked towel back and turned the head toward him slightly with both hands. To reveal the face.

The face of his brother.

The face of Adam.

Jet gasped and stepped back. He reached into his pocket and pulled out his keys. He could think of only one thing. Get away! Drive! Race out of the building, get in the truck, and drive. Somewhere. Anywhere but here. Suddenly, his legs went numb.

He staggered and fell backward as his surroundings became blurry and dissolved into darkness.

In the instant before the blackness was complete, Jet Townsend did not care if the light never returned.

THIRTEEN

stared at the notebook in my lap, scrambling to make sense of some modicum of Jet's story. He had talked for an hour in the treatment room at the emergency department, then insisted I drive him home. Admonitions from his mother and me that he just needed rest, both mental and physical, had proven futile.

Realizing that his claims were about to send his mother over the edge, Jet had backed off and told her he knew he was just too stressed—easily cured with a Valium or two and some rest and a few visits with a counselor like the ER doctor suggested. No, he didn't need to go back to Amberton, but he'd call her in the morning.

But he didn't get the Valium prescription filled, he threw away the counselor's phone number, and instead of resting, he had rambled with both his mouth and his feet for at least another hour when we got to his house. Jet paced and talked, intent on telling me everything that had happened his first two days of medical school, fearful of leaving something out that would prove to be important at some later date. More to pacify him than because I had any faith it would serve a useful purpose, I scribbled ten pages of notes, with Jet frequently pausing to verify what I had recorded with a "read that back to me" or "did you get that?"

Shortly thereafter, Jet had kicked me out of his house.

It just didn't make sense, and I couldn't lie to him and say otherwise. Adam had died ten months earlier, in a horrible accident. He had died instantly, then been burned beyond recognition. I was there in the immediate aftermath, had seen the wrecker pull Jet's truck from the ravine, had watched Jet languish over whether or not the fact Adam was driving an unfamiliar vehicle had anything to do with him running off the road. I had consoled Jet that day and several more, all the way through the funeral. I had seen the casket perched atop the scaffold over the six-foot hole, and I had visited Adam's grave with Jet just a few weeks later, when the tombstone was placed.

"Jet, it's impossible," I had said. "You have to know that."

"I know what I saw, Case. I know what my brother looks—looked—like."

"Like you told your mom—you just need to get some rest. It's too much for you. Maybe not school—that's probably easy for you. Just all the changes. Adam, Abi, your Mom being sick. But maybe school, too."

He glared at me. "I told Mom that only because she was about to have a breakdown. That's the only reason. Look, I can't explain it. I know it makes no sense. But I'm not crazy. Adam was on that dissection table. They, they—dissected him." Jet shook his head, holding it between his hands, fingering his bandage. He looked up at me, eyes brimming with tears and a pleading stare. "You have to believe me, Case. Tell me you believe me. You're my best friend."

I studied him for a moment, unsure what to say. "I would love to, but—"

"Get out."

"Jet, c'mon."

"I said get out!"

So I sat in my truck, parked at the curb of the cul-de-sac opposite Jet's house, studying the papers in my lap and trying to decide what to do. I hated to leave Jet alone, what with the head injury and anguished—or was it delusional? —mental state. But he had been emphatic, and while I was no doctor, upsetting him more would surely be counterproductive to his recovery.

Reading my scribbles helped clarify very little, but there was one thing. Adam had confided to Jet a few weeks before his death that he might be in some kind of trouble. Something about a side job he was doing. Jet hadn't been given many details, and after Adam's accidental death he had thought it irrelevant. But maybe now that memory was feeding Jet's paranoia, at least in part. The most sensible thing I could come up with was that the cadaver was similar in age and appearance to Adam, and maybe Jet's recollection of his brother confiding that he was in some trouble before he died had fueled some type of delusional paranoia.

I had to talk to Jack. He had been friends with Jet even longer than me. I wasn't necessarily confident he would know what to do, but I had to talk to somebody. And I trusted no one more. If I had one of those cellular phones, I could've called to see if he was home. But I didn't, and I wasn't going back in to ask Jet, so there was nothing to do but drive to Jack's and hope he was there.

———————————

Jack tapped the button on his answering machine and crossed his arms while I listened to the message. "Jack, it's Maggie Townsend. Something terrible has happened. It's Jet. He's fine—well, he's not fine, but he's not hurt. Hurt a little but not bad. But that's not why I'm calling. Just thought you'd want to know he's had an accident. He's … He's … I'm worried about him. I'm on my way, but I'm two hours away. Thought you could get there before I can. He's at University. I called Case, too."

He took a deep breath and rapped his fist on the kitchen counter in frustration. "Wish I had gotten that. No good way to reach me when I'm out on a job." He gestured across his small kitchen: washer and dryer snuggled in a corner, one door opening into his bedroom, another into a small living room. "Can't afford more than this 900-square-foot house, much less a secretary, so I usually just have to call in to check it every couple of hours for calls from clients. For some reason I didn't this afternoon." Jack kicked his leather work shoes into a corner, revealing soil-stained socks laden with grass clippings. "You know I would have dropped everything and gone."

I hopped backward onto a narrow counter and watched Jack rummage through his dryer for a clean pair of socks. "They know that, Jack. Don't beat yourself up. Jet's okay. He's home now."

"You believe what he told you?"

"How can I believe it? He must be having a nervous breakdown or something."

"That don't sound like Jet," he said over his shoulder, removing his grimy shirt and tossing it in the vicinity of a plastic hamper as he walked into his bedroom. "He's a tough S.O.B. You know that. Remember what he went through to recover after he got run over?"

"I know, but how else can you explain it? He's convinced that his cadaver was Adam. Absolutely positive. But Adam's been in the ground for almost a year now. Besides, he was burnt up."

Jack emerged, pulled on a clean shirt, and reached for a pair of upturned shoes beneath his kitchen table. "We should give him the benefit of the doubt."

"Benefit of the doubt? In principle, maybe, but we're not gonna do him any favors by buying into that nonsense. You know I'll do anything for him, but he needs his friends to be real with him."

"I'd say what he needs is real friends." Jack hopped on one foot toward the door as he slipped the second shoe over his heel with a forefinger then stomped his foot to finish the job. "Come on, let's go."

It was well after 1:00 a.m. when Jack threw the gearshift lever of his GMC Sierra into park and killed the engine. We sat in silence for a time before Jet spoke. "I'm not so sure this is a good idea."

"Jet, we're here for you, man," Jack said. "You say you saw Adam, but nobody believes you. Ain't but one way to find out, best I can figure. If it ain't him, then you need to know that so you can move on and do what you gotta do. If somehow it is him, then you're gonna need some friends to help you figure out how to deal with that."

"If that's the case, he'll need help figuring out more than just that." My skepticism had not waned in the four hours we had rehashed the details with Jet before finally convincing him to take us to the anatomy lab to settle this once and for all.

Jack shot me an irritated look and gave Jet an encouraging backhand slap on the shoulder before getting out of the truck and closing the door with a decisive slam. "Looks like he's going with or without us," I said to Jet as I opened my door and climbed out. "You'd better c'mon and guide us, or this could get real interesting."

The Jackson University Medical Center was a sprawling complex occupying 145 acres in the center of the city and comprising the 458-bed hospital, medical library, medical school, dental school, and schools of nursing, pharmacy, and health-related professions.

Built in 1955, the hospital and affiliated institutions of education had grown exponentially over the years, eventually pushing the only parking of any substance off the campus to be shared with the city's football complex next door. Most students and employees had to walk almost a quarter mile both ways to get to and from the parking lot.

I expected the sidewalk to be desolate at such a late hour, but instead, it was abuzz with activity. I marveled at the eclectic collection of pedestrian action, from haggard nurses in scrubs trudging their way toward their cars after stressful ten-hour shifts that were supposed to have been eight, groups of students with backpacks and huge coffee mugs reciting facts from their notes to each other one last time before calling it a night, a worker late for a shift, jogging up the hill, checking his watch and cursing under his breath.

"Expected it to be a lot quieter than this." I nudged Jet. "Might be hard to sneak us into the lab with you. This is like Times Square."

"I know," Jet said. "Jack, I told you, there may be people in there all night. Dr. Cronin told us we could come in there and study any time, twenty-four/seven."

"Let me worry about that. It'll be fine." Jack's long, quick strides made it difficult for Jet to keep up, but Jack had a plan in mind. History had taught me that when that happened, there was no slowing him down.

Jet's right hand was trembling when we finally reached the medical school building and he punched the elevator's number 6. He grabbed it with his left and squeezed, trying to steady himself.

I put my hand on his shoulder. "We really don't have to do this."

Jet shook his head emphatically. "No, Jack was right. It has to be done. But I don't know how. I don't think I can see that again. What if it is him?" His voice cracked, and he bit his bottom lip. He was pale, like he might be sick.

"Don't worry about that. Let us handle it." Jack patted him on the back. "Just show us where it is."

The elevator door opened, and Jet hesitated, then pivoted to his left. "This way." A sharp turn around the corner revealed rows of brown lockers lining both sides of a long hall. Jet stopped in front of a set of double doors recessed in a gap between them. "No one is supposed to go in there other than students and professors. If we get caught, I'll be in some trouble."

"You're already in trouble," Jack said. "Either you've been hallucinating, or your brother Adam, who was buried almost a year ago, is in there in a metal tank. Either way...."

I heaved an exasperated sigh and rolled my eyes at Jack.

"What?" he said. "It's true, ain't it?"

"Well, I may be a skeptic," I said, "but at least I have tact. I'm sorry, Jet. Jack was raised by baboons. Now—what are the odds that someone is in there?" I looked at my watch and up and down the hallway. Ample fluorescent lighting should have made it brightly lit, but several bulbs were either out or flickering, the cinder block walls were painted dark gray, and the VCT floor tiles matched the drab décor of the walls. I saw no sign of activity, and we hadn't encountered a single soul since we entered the building. "It's 1:45 a.m., and this place is quiet as a cemeter—uhh, quiet as a church. Sorry."

"Baboons, huh?" Jack snickered.

"Shut up." I turned back to Jet. "What you think? Will someone be here?"

"I don't know, Case. Let me go in and look first." He entered a series of numbers on the keypad and paused briefly with his hand on the doors before pushing one of them open. The space was brightly lit and open, with several rows of stainless steel, coffin-sized vats. "The light stays on at all times," Jet whispered, answering my question before I could ask it. He eased into the room, and in just a few seconds, he stuck his head back out the door. "It's empty, come on."

My only experience seeing dead bodies had been a few funerals, after careful preparation by trained morticians to make the deceased look as natural as possible. That wasn't counting the time we found a skeleton when we were teenagers, but that was different—surreal somehow, since there had been only bones and no flesh. It suddenly dawned on me that we were about to descend upon a real human being—one who had been cut open and dissected, no less—without the benefit of a mortician's skill to soften the landing. Maybe not a big deal to a medical student who had worked his whole life toward that very moment, but I was no medical student. I was an English teacher and football coach. At least I wouldn't know the person. There was no way it could really be Adam, could it?

Jet crossed the room with a slow, reluctant pace and then backed slowly into the wall on the far side. He sat down with his back against the wall and crossed his arms over his knees. He said nothing and stared vacantly across the room.

"Tell us which one," Jack said.

"Right there, that one." Jet pointed at a tank on the second row toward the center of the room. "I'm not opening it."

"You sit right there, bud. We got it." I hoped my voice sounded more confident than I felt. I had no idea what we would see when we opened the tank. My heart beat wildly in my chest, and I half expected a sudden screeching of dissonant organ chords in a minor key to erupt just as the tanks doors were cast open to reveal its grisly contents. Of course, that didn't happen. And nothing else happened right away, either. It had never occurred to me that the body would be completely submerged in the murky preservative.

"You have to turn the crank to lift it," Jet said softly.

Jack nodded, grabbed the protruding handle on his end, and began to turn it slowly.

The surface of the stagnant fluid began to shiver and then parted as the cadaver emerged from its turbid bath. He was face down with a saturated cloth draped over and conforming to the shape of his head, just as Jet had described to me earlier at the hospital.

I fought a tinge of nausea and tried to avoid gawking at the incisions, exposed musculature, and bullet hole on the back.

Jack took a step back from the table and froze, wide-eyed and statuary. This had been his idea, but it was clear he had gone as far as he was willing or able to go. "You do it, Case."

I took a breath, grabbed the corner of the cloth, and lifted it carefully. My first thought was that I probably should have put on gloves before touching the chemical-laden drape. My second thought leapfrogged the first one.

I didn't know who that person was, but it was most definitely not Adam Townsend.

FOURTEEN

THE violent clangs of stainless steel collisions reverberated throughout the spacious anatomy room. Jet moved like a deranged lunatic, practically running station to station, slinging lids open, turning cranks and pressing lever bars to elevate the bodies for quick inspection. "Help me!" he pleaded. "They moved him! I know they did. They moved him to a different spot!"

What had been a bleak but orderly array of nondescript tanks had become, to my eyes, a scene appropriate for a B-list horror movie. Dead bodies popping up everywhere—male and female, obese and emaciated, dark brown and pale yellow and every color in between—erupting from aqueous coffins, resurrected by a mad scientist whose motives made sense only to him, for none of them rose to join him in his search.

"Jet, stop! Stop and think just a minute," I said. "The guy over there in your tank has a bullet hole. You said your cadaver had a bullet hole. It doesn't make sense that they could have switched one with a bullet wound for another in the exact same spot."

"I know what I saw!" Jet bellowed. "Y'all think I'm crazy like everybody else?"

Jack and I stood motionless, indecisive. "Just settle down," I coaxed in the calmest tone I could muster. "It's okay, man. Nobody could blame you after what you've been through."

"Yeah, dude. I'm sorry, this was a bad idea." Jack eased toward one of the opened tanks to see if he could gently return the body back to its proper place. "Let's get you home."

"I'm telling you it was Adam! He's got to be in here somewhere!" Jet began again, darting frantically from tank to tank.

By the time Jack and I had come behind him and managed to lower four or five of the bodies, he had raised and inspected all twenty-six. The body of his brother Adam was nowhere to be found. Jet strode back to the tank where it all had started and punched it with what must have been enough force to shatter bones. He didn't flinch. "He was in here! Right here! I swear it!"

"I know he was, Jet. We believe you." I watched Jack to make sure his thoughts were congruent with mine. Whether we believed him or not, Jet was about to have a breakdown, and if we didn't assuage his feelings of anguish and abandonment, who knows what he might do next?

Jack nodded. "We'll find him," he soothed. "We'll find him." He reached for Jet's arm, but Jet jerked it away and slid down to the floor, leaning against the leg of the tank.

A tear slid down his cheek. He wiped it with the back of his hand, then ignored the ones that followed.

I jumped at the sound of the door opening on the other side of the room.

"Somebody's coming!" Jack hissed. "Jet, get up!" He grabbed Jet's hand and yanked him to a standing position. Jet cooperated reluctantly, as if by reflex and not conscious intent.

The sound of wood hitting against wood announced that whomever had opened the door was still there, but no one emerged for a few seconds—long enough for me to foolishly wonder, albeit only briefly, if we should have tried to hide. With a quick scan of our surroundings, I determined there was no-where to go. Just then the figure of a man, stooped and dragging something, backed into the room. I realized it was a janitor, pull-ing a rolling mop bucket and having trouble keeping his mop handle from banging against the door frame. He didn't look up, either oblivious or indifferent to the fact that he was not alone.

I stood wide eyed, waiting for him to turn around. When he finally did, it was his turn to startle. "Sweet mother of Methuse-lah!" He took a step back and dropped his mop handle. "What in the Sam Hill is goin' on in he-ah?" He appeared to be every bit of eighty years old. He was bald on top, and the matching shocks of hair protruding from each side of his head were stark white. The contrast against his deep coffee-hued skin was strik-ing.

"We were just leaving, sir." Jack nudged Jet from behind, toward the door.

I joined in as we approached the man, who hadn't moved. He knew we had to go by him to leave. "Yessir, we were just leaving. Just reviewing a few things from class. You know, com-paring notes, er, I mean, bodies."

The old man's eyes narrowed suspiciously as he studied our faces and the room full of open cadaver tanks behind us. He took a step to his right as we tried to pass, gently blocking our exit, as if to suggest he only wanted to talk. "You ain't no anat-omy student," he said to Jack. Then he turned to me. "And you ain't, neither." My heart raced. *Busted.* I was concerned for Jet more than myself, since I doubted there would be meaningful repercussions for Jack and me. At worst, some minor trespass-ing charge not worth pursuing, especially since Jet obviously brought us into the lab.

Then the elderly janitor's face brightened, and he smiled. He was looking at Jet. The janitor struggled to stand as erect as possible, and I realized for the first time he had once been a tall man. "But you is a doctor student, Mr. Townsend."

Jet cocked his chin downward ever so slightly, with a dart of his eyes from me and to Jack before settling on the elderly man again.

"You know this man, Jet?" I asked.

He shook his head and opened his mouth to speak but was interrupted. "Naw, he don't know me, but I know him," the man said.

"How?" Jet asked.

"I knows all my doctor students. Professor Cronin gives me they pictures to study each year. Been learning them all since 1972. I likes to see what kind of doctors they turns into. I feels like I helps 'em in some little way. You know, by cleaning up after 'em."

My watch read 3:15 a.m. "You always clean this time of day?"

"Aw yeah, I clean other spots too. I be done by ten every day. Then I goes fishin'!" He gave us a crooked, snaggle-toothed smile.

"We, uh, we're sorry if I made a mess," Jet said. "They didn't have anything to do with this. Just gave me a ride."

"It's okay, Mr. Townsend," the janitor said. "I'll take care of it."

"I didn't catch your name." Jet extended his hand. "You know mine. I should know yours."

"Just call me Soap." He smiled again. "Started washing cars when I's a kid, been cleaning ever since."

We smiled back and moved on past the man, each anxious for different reasons to get out of the room and away from the place. "Oh, Mr. Townsend." Soap caught Jet by the back of his shoulder as he passed. "You hang in there. It all gon' be alright. I just believes it will be. You just gots to believe in yo'self like I do." He winked and gave Jet an assuring nod.

Jet nodded back but looked puzzled again. He said nothing and walked out the door with us.

"Odd fellow, there," Jack said after the door closed behind us.

"Must have heard what happened today," I said. "Nice of him to encourage you."

"Yeah, maybe." Jet shook his head with a preoccupied look. "Wish I shared his confidence. Let's get out of here."

"Soooo, he is alive."

I jumped at the sound of the deep voice behind us. What was with the people around here? It was three in the morning, for crying out loud. I turned to see a tall man I did not recognize standing in the hall with his arms crossed. Trying to appear authoritative.

Jet gave a heavy, rumbling sigh. "Sterling, I'm not in the mood."

"What are you doing, Townsend? Thought you quit anatomy, first of all, but if you came in to catch up on what you missed today, who are your friends?"

Jack stepped toward the man, extending his hand with a forced smile. Irritated but not intimidated by whoever this person was and trying to make the best of it. "Jack Masterson. And yes, Jet is an old friend of mine. Just came to get something from his locker."

"Yeah." I followed Jack's lead. "He has a concussion, so he can't drive, and things are a bit foggy for him. He just remembered which locker was his. It's, uh...."

"652," Jet said. "Sterling Virchow, meet Case Reynolds."

I nodded but made no move to shake hands. I didn't like his tone or his smug expression.

Sterling Virchow's eyes narrowed, and his gaze remained fixed on Jet. "Just came in to review with my group. I'd ask you to join us, Townsend, but I understand two breakdowns in one day would probably be enough to send anyone over the edge."

Jet trudged away from us and began to fiddle with the combination on his locker.

Heat rushed to my face as I squared my shoulders toward this Virchow person. "Do you have a problem with my friend that I need to know about? Because he's had a rough day, and if you aim to make it worse, then it's you and I who have the problem."

I expected him to cower or at least soften. We outnumbered him three to one, after all. I was sure that my demeanor was making it clear that I'd do whatever was necessary to take up for my friend and was perfectly capable of handling the job.

But whether it was because he knew the odds of us initiating a physical altercation that would jeopardize Jet's future were highly unlikely or because he had reinforcements on the way, or because somehow being on familiar turf made him supremely confident, he did not back down. Virchow only stiffened with a thin-lipped sneer. "There's no problem here, friend. Only problem Townsend there has is if he doesn't have what it takes. Sometimes brains just isn't enough."

"Hey, jackass," Jack chimed in. "You listen here—"

"Let it go!" Jet interrupted him. "I've got a headache, and y'all are making it worse. Take me home."

I took a deep breath to calm my nerves. He was right. Nothing good would come from continuing this standoff. "C'mon, Jack. He's right."

Jet slammed his locker, and without another word, the three of us headed down the corridor. I glanced back over my shoulder to see Virchow enter the code to open the anatomy lab door. He stopped in the doorway, wide-eyed. "What the—?" He stepped back and glared in our direction. "Hey! How do you explain this?"

I ignored him. Jack gave a middle finger salute over his shoulder as we walked away, and I smiled to myself. Jet never looked up or slowed down, and we followed him to the elevator.

FIFTEEN

Gross Anatomy, Day THREE

A*ctually not a bad seat.* Jet had never been too keen on claiming a place in the back row unless it was at church, certainly not the far back corner of a classroom, and definitely not five minutes after a lecture had started. Today was different, though. He dreaded the looks and the questions and the whispers that would inevitably come with his return. At least his scalp laceration was in the back, hidden by his hair. They had told him not to shower for twenty-four hours, but he'd done it anyway—no way he was coming back with blood-stained hair.

He had difficulty concentrating on the biochemistry lecture. Dr. Stefan Corovsky was doing his best to make oxidative phosphorylation sound exciting, but Jet wasn't really listening. His head pounded and his mind raced, still trying to make sense of what happened the day before and how to best navigate the day at hand.

The image of Adam's breathless face staring back at him was seared into his brain like a brand from a red-hot Kodachrome, and he fought to suppress it and the nausea it bore. He wasn't crazy. He was certain of what he'd seen—he just couldn't explain it. Somehow, the body he'd found in his group's tank during his after-hours return visit had not been Adam's. It was a male, and it had a bullet hole in the same location, but it was not

Adam. And neither were any of the other cadavers in the room. *I'm not crazy, am I?*

Suddenly, a familiar redhead on the end of a row about ten forward of Jet stood up and tiptoed up the outside aisle stairs. She eased into the seat directly in front of Jet but avoided his gaze.

Dr. Corovsky opened his mouth as if to comment but stopped when most of his students' heads turned to follow his stare. The professor cleared his throat, turned back to his notes, and began expounding the importance of understanding ATP synthesis with renewed vigor.

Jet felt a flush of warmth to his face and fought a sense of unease. What did his newest friend think of him? She obviously cared enough to do what she'd just done, but was it genuine concern or charitable pity? Or a more practical motive— expediency—getting a head start propping up the weak link of the anatomy group before it collapsed and dragged them all down. He desperately hoped it was the former as he studied the subtle waves of her auburn hair, heart fluttering slightly while he waited on her to turn around. He needed to see her face, read her eyes. Just then something tapped the side of his leg. Gracie was reaching back between the seats, holding a neatly folded note.

Are you okay?

Like junior high again. He smiled at the memories and the growing hope that her concern was real. He studied the note a moment and then scribbled a reply. *I'm fine, just a few stitches.*

I'm not talking about your head, I'm talking about YOU!

Jet's heart fluttered more furiously. *I'm fine - Thanks!*

What happened? Your mom said you weren't taking visitors.

Jet considered his response. He couldn't trust himself at this point, much less anyone else. To his knowledge, the only people who knew what he claimed to have seen were his mother, his two best friends, and the staff in the emergency department, who were bound to secrecy by principles of medical ethics and privacy laws. Perhaps it was best to keep it that way, at least until he figured out what was going on. The last thing he needed right now was for his only medical school friend to think he was crazy, not to mention his professors. *Same thing as the day before. I'm okay now. Taking some medicine.* He hated to lie, but she had to believe he was okay and had a newfound, valid reason to be.

Good. Was worried! I'll help you catch up.

———————

Dr. Sylvester Cronin sat in his leather chair with his fingers intertwined atop his desk. He motioned to a pair of chairs across from him. "Come in, Mr. Townsend. May I call you John?"

It wasn't hard for Jet to guess what had prompted the summons to the office of the chairman of the Department of Neurobiology and Anatomical Sciences, but dread of the possibilities weighed heavily on him. "Jet. Most people call me Jet."

The man lifted one eyebrow and held it there while Jet positioned himself, tense and uneasy, on the front edge of a chair. "Interesting. Jet, you appear to be struggling with the dissection part of my class."

"Yessir. That might be an understatement." He wasn't in a joking mood but thought it might somehow temper the tension of the moment.

"Yes, I guess it would." Cronin showed no hint of a smile, yet Jet detected no malice in his demeanor. "I understand you've experienced some family hardships?"

"I have. My mother had cancer. And my brother died."

"And your father?"

"He's been working overseas, since Mom went into remission. Government contractor in Saudi Arabia. Medical bills piled up, so he couldn't turn it down."

"Hmmm … I see." Cronin twirled a Montblanc pen in one hand while he caressed his beard with the other. "And you had a personal trauma of your own?"

"I was hit by a car when I was a teenager. But sir, that was a long time ago. I don't see what—"

"Gross Anatomy is not for the faint of heart, no matter the cause. No one would think less of you for dropping out, considering what you've been through."

Jet was already shaking his head. "That's not possible sir. I will not quit. Becoming a doctor is all I've ever wanted."

Cronin said nothing for a time while he studied a small stain or pen mark on the sleeve of his white coat. Then he pushed his glasses up on his nose and surveyed Jet like an animal on an auction block, trying to determine if he was bid worthy. "I'm not sure you're cut out for it. How do you plan to become a physician if you can't even make it through a single dissection lab? It doesn't get easier from here."

Jet wanted to scream. To tell Dr. Sylvester Cronin where he could shove his fancy pen. To pin him to the floor and force him to confess what he had done, to explain how Adam had wound up on that dissection table yesterday. But at the same time, Jet not only understood others' skepticism, a part of him shared it. How could it have been Adam? It was impossible, right?

Nothing made any sense at this point. One thing was certain, however. He could not quit now. There were two possible answers, and the path to both was the same. Either that person in his tank was Adam, in which case he had to stick around long enough to figure out how and why. Or it was not Adam, and Jet was suffering from some sort of mental illness or psychological breakdown, like some were hinting at if not blatantly suggesting. Either way, he had to stay until he could find out.

"Jet," Cronin said. "Are you hearing me? What do you have to say?"

Jet rubbed his face with both hands as if to wipe away a giant cobweb clouding his vision. "I'm sorry, sir. Just give me one more chance. I promise I'll be fine."

Cronin nodded. "Okay, but this is it. One more breakdown, and I'll be forced to dismiss you from the class, which will in effect dismiss you from the School of Medicine. We've had too many disruptions already, and as I'm sure you recall me saying, Gross Anatomy waits on no one."

It was Jet's turn to nod. "Yessir. Thank you, sir." He stood to leave, then paused and turned back. "Can you answer one question for me?"

"Go ahead."

"The body donor program. Are you in charge of that?"

Cronin's dark eyes flashed like the lightning of a Mississippi thunderstorm. "I'm in charge of everything." His eyes narrowed even further, causing the skin between his brows to wrinkle like corrugated metal. "Is there a problem with your cadaver, Mr. Townsend?"

Jet noticed the professor was using his surname again, but he didn't back down. He squared his shoulders, looked him the eye, and said, "No sir, my cadaver is just fine."

SIXTEEN

I swallowed hard, trying not to grimace against the bitterness of the espresso. The Corner Coffee, a quaint bar in the Fallon District, sandwiched between downtown Jackson and the Medical Center, had been Abi's idea. It was less than a mile away from her apartment and halfway between Jack's home and mine. The location made sense, but the nearby Chickasaw Diner with its iconically good burgers and fried cheese would have suited me better. No matter. This meeting wasn't about food. Or coffee, either.

Jack elbowed me in the ribs. "What's the matter, Case? Looks like you swallowed a rotten frog." His metaphor wasn't far from my opinion of it.

"I don't know how y'all drink that stuff. It smells good but tastes awful." I grimaced. "Sort of like cologne."

Abi shook her head, amused by what she and Jack both considered to be my juvenile palate. "You'll grow up one day. Go ahead and order you a Coke. I won't be offended. At least you gave it a shot."

Our smiles faded, and a thick silence wafted over our table, settling between us until I took a deep sigh and broke it. "So Abi, did Jack tell you what happened?"

Her eyes flashed like a blue flame. "He did. And I'm mad."

"Mad?"

"She's mad," Jack confirmed.

"Why did no one call me yesterday when all this happened? Of all people, someone should have called me!"

"Not sure how you figure that, Abi," I said. "After all, Jet is your ex. Ms. Maggie called me, couldn't get Jack on the phone. Not many mommas would call an ex-girlfriend. Especially one who's dating another guy."

"Don't bring him into this."

"So you and Lane are still dating?" I challenged.

"That's irrelevant, Case. The point is, I'm not just any ex."

"Oh, why didn't you just say so?" I chose to ignore her evasiveness about her love life. "I'll call Ms. Maggie right now and clear this right up." I simulated putting a phone to my ear. "Yes, Ms. Townsend, I know she and Jet aren't together anymore, but she wants to be informed of anything that happens. She's not just *any* ex."

Jack burst into a laugh, and I couldn't help but join him.

Abi slid her chair back from the table with a violent squeak and stood. "I don't have to sit here and take this, especially not from you." Her unwavering scowl was fixed firmly on me.

When I reached out and tried to gently grab her by the arm, she jerked away. "Don't leave. I'm sorry. That was uncalled for. We're just messin' around."

Jack pitched in with a wide-eyed, pursed-lip, pleading nod. Wanting her to stay, trying to suppress another laugh that would lessen the odds of it happening.

Abi stood there glaring at both of us for a moment until her expression softened and she chuckled softly. "Yeah, I guess that is pretty silly of me to think that. It's just that I do still care about him. We're still close friends, you know."

"We all know that," I said. "That's why we're here. Jet just wanted us to tell you. He's embarrassed about it. Plus, he's trying to study tonight to catch up on what he missed."

Abi sat back down. "Bless him. The brainiac is having trouble adjusting to dead bodies, huh?" She giggled, then stopped abruptly. "What?" she asked, reading our faces. "I know he's embarrassed about passing out, but you've gotta admit it's a little bit funny."

"There's more to it," Jack said.

"What is it?" She frowned at Jack then fixed her gaze on me.

I hated to even think it, much less say it. "He told everybody, that his ... his cadaver ... it was Adam."

Abi's jaw dropped. She shook her head in disbelief. "Oh my. What? Why would he say something like that?"

"Because he believes it." I shook my head. "I'm not sure how, but he does. Maybe it's a nervous breakdown."

Abi turned up her coffee and gulped the last sip before lightly smacking her mug down on the table. "I don't believe that."

"I don't either," I said. "You know, and we know, that's impossible. Adam's been dead almost a year. You saw him put in the ground in Amberton just like we did."

"That's not what I'm talking about. I'm talking about Jet. I don't believe he's having a nervous breakdown. He's too strong for that."

"Well that's fine and all," Jack said, "but Jet swears it was Adam. How else do you explain it? Formaldehyde fumes suddenly fried his vision?"

"Maybe it's Adam's, what is it called? His doppelganger."

Jack leaned forward and turned his ear toward Abi. "His doppel-what?"

"Doppelganger. It's basically an unrelated twin. Some people think everyone has one somewhere in the world. You know, like in *A Tale of Two Cities*."

It was my turn to elbow Jack in the ribs. "Yeah, Jack, you love Dickens, don't you?"

Jack chuckled. "Yeah, sure, my favorite."

Abi smiled. "It should be easy enough to figure out, guys. Just go up there and take another look."

"Did that already," I countered. "Last night. Adam wasn't in the tank—surprise, surprise. But it didn't change anything; Jet's as convinced as ever. He thinks somebody switched the bodies or some sort of craziness. He opened every tank to look. It was insane."

"So let me get this straight," Abi said. "The smartest person we know, who had enough mental toughness to survive a lifetime of pain and misery when he was hit by a car as a teenager, who helped his momma get through cancer from four hours away while his daddy was working overseas, all while finishing his degree at one of the best universities in the country with a 4.0, who has dreamed of nothing other than going to medical school his whole life and would do nothing to jeopardize his position there, is saying that his Gross Anatomy cadaver is actually his brother, who was incinerated in a car wreck a year ago?"

I noticed the barista standing beside our table, eyes wide, looking around absently and pretending she hadn't been listening to Abi. "Just, uhh, wanted to, umm, walk over and thank you guys for coming in, and uh, see if you needed anything." She fidgeted nervously with the strings on her brown apron.

"Working on a school project," I said. "English Comp."

Relief washed over the young woman's face, and she smiled. "Oh yes, of course. I read lots of fiction. Love John Grisham. He's from Mississippi, you know." She waited on us to pick up the dialogue but the three of us just inspected our coffee.

"We don't need any refills." Abi gave a dismissive smile. "But it's very good."

"Yeah, very good." I choked down another sip. I was determined to show Jack and Abi that my palate was perfectly mature.

"Just let me know if you need anything, including plot ideas." The barista smiled as she turned and walked away.

Jack patted the table between him and Abi. "Okay, I'd say you covered the gist of it. Jet is smart and tough. Your point?"

"My point is, have you two knuckleheads considered giving Jet the benefit of the doubt and taking his word for it?"

"Meaning?"

Abi met my gaze and didn't waver as she answered. "Meaning, maybe it's a gaslighting thing. Or some other scenario you just haven't figured out yet."

Jack snickered. "Gaslighting? Like that trick I used to do with a cigarette lighter and a fart?"

Abi laughed and sputtered on her sip of coffee. I frowned at Jack, fighting the urge to ask him and Abi both, for different reasons, if they'd lost their minds.

"I'm kidding," Jack said with a dismissive backhand wave. "I know what gaslighting is." He wrinkled his brow. "I think. But whatever it means, Jet's story can't be true. I'm on his side as much as anyone, but like Case said, that's craziness."

Abi shook her head. "All I know is that Jet deserves for someone to be on his side. The least we could do is go along with it for now. If Jet said it, somebody's gonna have to prove to me that it's not true."

"And how to you propose we do that?" I asked.

"I don't know. Surely two smart guys like you can figure that out." She winked at me and smiled. I hated when she did that. And loved it. Something about the way her azure eyes seemed to talk and the precise curl of her lips that always drove me crazy.

"Maybe," I said. "But you never answered my question."

"Are you changing the subject? What question?" A puzzled expression.

"Are you and Lane still dating?"

Jack coughed across the table, and I shot him a sideways, shut-up look.

"It's complicated," Abi said.

I remembered her telling me the same thing ten months earlier, when she had shown up at Jet's house with Lane in tow. "C'mon, what's complicated? Either you are or you aren't."

"Case, I don't have to explain my dating life to you. Or Jack, either."

Jack threw up his hands as if a gun was pointed at him. "Hey! Don't bring me into this. I don't have to say a word. You know how I feel about that guy, but I didn't ask the question." He picked up his cup and pretended to sip, clearly amused by the turn of the conversation. "I'm just drinkin' coffee."

Abi narrowed her eyes at me.

I said nothing, studying her, waiting for some sort of an answer and making no apologies for it.

"Remember that night we all came home last fall, for the football homecoming?" she said after a moment. "The weekend Adam was killed?"

Of course I remembered. Almost every detail, clear as crystal. A flood of good memories upon seeing her had washed into a gutter of bad when I realized who she was with. It only got worse when I received the call about Adam the next morning. "Yeah, you shocked us all when you showed up with Lane that night."

"Yeah, I guess I did. So, we had been dating a few months then. He transferred in to MTSU for his last year, about the time Jet and I broke up. He said it was for his degree, but I wondered if it had something to do with me. Not to be egocentric, but it seemed a little odd. I mean, not a lot of folks from Amberton wind up at Middle Tennessee State. Sure enough, he started calling me. I was wary at first, but he treated me great, a perfect gentleman. He helped me through a tough time. I didn't think it was all that serious, but then that weekend we came home, he had a ring."

A ring? Lane had told me at Adam's funeral he was planning to marry Abi. I had thought at the time it might be nothing more than empty gibberish, but apparently he had been telling the truth.

Jack coughed again and waved at the barista, pointing to his cup when she looked over.

"Not funny," Abi said.

"Just gonna need something to wash this down," Jack said.

I glanced at her left hand but saw no ring. "So?" I said.

"Would you two just listen for a minute, for crying out loud? No, Case, there's no ring there." She waved her left hand in front of me. "And we aren't engaged. Never were." Abi locked her eyes on mine. "I turned him down."

"Wow. How'd he take that?" I asked.

"Not well. We had a huge fight, and he left town. I think he would have left me in Amberton, but he felt bad and came back when he heard about Adam. We broke up a few weeks later."

"Abi." Jack reached toward her and tapped the table. "I don't want to get in your business, but we're friends, and we're here, and I've just got to ask—why did you say no?"

Abi shrugged. "Why does any girl say no? It wasn't right."

"Was it Jet?" I wasn't sure I wanted to hear the answer.

"In a way, yes." I tried to hide my disappointment. I'm not sure if Abi picked up on it or not, but she continued as if she was reading my mind. "But not in the way you might think. Jet and I sort of fell together when he was going through that rough patch, with his rehab and stuff. But we eventually figured out we stayed together out of convenience. Familiarity. We realized we were really just good friends. But I still had a tough time with it. I mean, we dated for what, three years? So Lane stepped in, helped me when I was down, but I wasn't ready to marry him. I wasn't even in love with him."

"Sucker doesn't deserve you," Jack said. "Or anyone else walking upright on two legs, for that matter."

"Jack!" Abi folded her arms and leaned back in her seat. "That's not fair. Lane's a really nice guy. I know y'all had that fight and all, but good grief, we were all just kids. Grow up and let it go."

Jack nodded. "I know. Not the only guy I ever got in a fight with. He's probably okay. But anyone who is friends with VJ MacIntosh has a screw loose, as far as I'm concerned." He gave Abi an inquiring tilt of his head. "Unless you tell me they ain't friends no more."

Abi hesitated before answering. "I'm not sure."

"Seriously, Abi?" I said. "VJ MacIntosh, who terrorized us back in the day, who tried to kill Jet? I assumed Lane had kicked him to the curb after he went to juvie, but you're telling me they're still friends? What, y'all been going out for drinks and double dating?"

Abi's face turned crimson. "Dang it, Case. Why do you have to always assume the worst? I haven't seen VJ in seven, eight years." She sighed and shook her head. "But I think maybe he and Lane talk on occasion. I don't know."

Jack made a swirling motion beside his head with one finger. "Like I said, loose screw."

"Stop it, Jack. I'm gonna leave if you keep it up."

"What difference does it make?" Jack said. "Y'all broke up."

Abi looked down and ran her finger around the rim of her coffee cup. "I told you, it's complicated."

I wanted to bang my fist on the table, but I didn't. I had picked up the phone to call Abi on multiple occasions over the past several months but assumed she and Lane were still together. I never had taken rejection very well, so my pride kept me from dialing the number. Now she had just told me she and Lane had broken up, only to come back in the next breath and tell me again it was complicated. "So what's the deal? Either you're dating, or you're not."

"We still talk. He's good to me. As a friend."

"You don't stay with somebody just because they're good to you," I said.

Abi's eyes became cobalt lasers. She locked them on mine and didn't flinch. "What do you care, Case? I haven't heard from you in months. Not sure you're the person who should be giving me relationship counseling."

I held her gaze for a moment before looking away. "I knew—I thought—you and Lane were … It's complicated."

She held up both hands and waved them to the side dismissively. "At least we can agree on that. Now can we get back to Jet? What are you two gonna do to help him?"

"We both have full time jobs, just like you," I said.

"Somebody needs to do something. He's in a bad spot. Whatever the truth turns out to be."

"We'll figure something out," Jack said. "I heard that medical students have to study forty hours a week on top of class and stuff. Jet ain't gonna have time for much else."

"Any ideas?" I asked.

"You know me." Jack gave a sly smile. "I can always come up with a plan. Let me talk to Jet again."

SEVENTEEN

JACK wanted to stop in Hattiesburg to see an old girl-friend—it was halfway between Jackson and Ocean Springs, so why not? Reminding him that we had limited time—it had to be a day trip, since I had to be back by one o'clock on Sunday for football film study—had no effect. Only when I threatened to turn around and forget the whole thing did he relent and agree to quit pestering me about it.

"I'm just saying, that's fine if you don't want to stop, but it's your loss, bud. If you ever saw her legs, you'd understand."

"Well, why aren't you still with her then?"

"What she has in leg buxomness, she loses in personality."

"Buxom means big boobs, not nice legs."

"I think you can use it for either. Her legs are buxom."

"That makes no sense, but whatever. And for all you know, she may be married by now."

"Possibly."

"So no personality, could be married, but you still wanted to stop and see her?"

"I'm not gonna try to explain it. You'd have to see the legs to understand."

I chuckled and shook my head. "If you say so." Jack certainly had his own way. Often like a leaf blowing in the wind, wondering where he'd land yet happy not to know, unconcerned when his wind seemed to be blowing a different direction than most.

"By the way, you been coaching 'em up?"

"Trying."

"First game in a couple weeks, huh?"

"High school is. For that, I'm still just a grunt. Run the camera from the press box and haul coolers and junk to the field house after the game."

"You mean Coach Marchianti won't let his old QB, the Great Case Reynolds, coach the high school?"

"Very funny. Coach is trying to win. You know, the pressure is on him, his first year and all after moving up from a small program like Amberton to a big 5A school like South Rankin. I'm just proud to be there."

"I hear ya. Won't take you long to move up."

"Yeah, go undefeated with my seventh graders, and I'll be a shoo-in for varsity."

Jack laughed and shook his head, then turned to gaze at the passing scenery.

We rode in silence for several miles as Hattiesburg shrunk to nothing behind us, the cracks of Highway 49 keeping tempo like a metronome as our tires popped them in rhythm. Soon the DeSoto National Forest flanked us on both sides, mile after mile of uninterrupted evergreen canopy held aloft by rows of erect brown timbers.

Normally, I would have contemplated the place's possibilities in vivid detail, imagining the wildlife roaming within its boundaries and wondering whether a hunting trip might be warranted in the future, but I was focused on the task at hand. Whether it was a good idea or a pointless whim. Whether it was even any of our business.

"And you said Jet's mom was okay with this?" I asked. "When you went to get the key?"

Jack cocked his head and raised an eyebrow. "Relax. I already told you. She was more than okay. Ecstatic."

I nodded. "Just seems a little weird. Going through Adam's stuff."

"It's not like we're doing anything with it, just looking through it. She's just glad for someone to be helping Jet."

"Can't really imagine how this will help, but if it will make him feel better, fine," I said. "Did she or Jet tell you why all Adam's stuff is in storage?"

"She got sick with the chemo and all. Heartbreak, too, I guess. So they hired some movers until they could sort through it all together later. Guess it's been easier just to leave it than sort through it."

"I guess. So why did Jet not mention this storage shed to me when he told me about everything else?"

Jack shrugged. "Prolly never got around to it since you made him mad when you didn't believe him. Or he knew I'd be the one to insist we check it out."

He was probably correct on both counts. "Yeah."

"Why aren't we talking to Stimpy Riggins, the coroner? Seems like that would be a good place to start, huh?"

"Because he might tell Dad. And you know how that would go."

"Yeah, save that for last," Jack said. "Sheriff Reynolds don't play around. So, what are we looking for? I got the key from Ms. Maggie like he asked me to, but Jet said you'd know why we needed to look."

"Jet didn't want her to worry, but Adam told him something right before he was killed. That he thought he might be in some trouble."

Jack whistled. "Now there's a fly in the soup. Trouble, huh?"

"You mean fly in the ointment?"

"No, that's dumb. I don't eat ointment. Do you?"

I just shook my head. "Anyway, he didn't tell Jet much about it. Just said he was working on a project for some tree hugger group, and some people were not too happy about it. Jet didn't think much about it. Until now."

"Some people not too happy? How much not happy?"

"Don't know. Jet just said Adam was upset about it. And there's something else. Adam had a girlfriend." I patted my front pocket "I've got her address."

"Yeah, Adam mentioned her to me. That weekend he was home. But you know, she wasn't at the funeral. Seems like she would have been there."

"Yeah, I asked Jet about that. He says they hadn't been dating long, but Adam liked her enough to tell him about her. You, too, I guess. Maybe she didn't think so highly of him."

"Or maybe she had a reason not to come."

"Aw, come on, Jack. You're not already concocting some conspiracy theory, are you?"

"No, not about the girl," Jack said. He looked up through the windshield and pretended to be scanning the sky. "UFOs, yes."

I chuckled. "Well, the sign up ahead says you got forty miles to figure out the best place to find these aliens."

The storage facility consisted of a collection of twenty-five or thirty gray metal buildings parked behind a dilapidated gas station. The mildew-stained sheds were randomly wedged between scattered live oaks shading the entire operation. A rusty, lopsided sign by the road identified Harry's Self-Serve and Storage, but Harry was nowhere in sight, and the antique gas pumps suggested there was nothing to serve.

"When he told you about the storage, did Jet give you any idea what we might be looking for?" I cruised at idle speed down the gravel drive searching for the match to the key in Jack's hand.

"There it is. Seventeen." Jack pointed to the left. "Like I said, he told me about the storage facility and that you'd know why we needed to look."

"Jet is convinced that whatever trouble Adam was mixed up in is the reason he wound up in an anatomy tank."

I pulled over to park, and Jack was out of the truck with key in hand before the wheels stopped rolling. "I don't know that he's convinced about anything. But maybe." He popped the lock and threw up the rolling door.

I wasn't sure what to expect, but whatever it was, I didn't get it. No tangles of cobwebs, no clouds of dust, no shadowy perpetrator knocking us down as he beat a hasty exit. And nothing out of place front and center to break the case. A set of box springs and a mattress turned on their side, propped against the wall. A cracked leather recliner. Two boxes filled with random kitchen utensils and small appliances, and several copy paper boxes. An empty, red plastic, five-gallon gas can. A climbing deer stand leaned on one corner, and a small kitchen tabletop nestled against a sofa, with its legs unscrewed and tucked beside the sofa's skirt. There was a computer monitor sitting on the floor. A squat, four-drawer chest perched near the back wall, drawers only partly closed, beside it a dresser with a cracked mirror.

A quick inspection of the chest revealed three drawers full of clothes, but the bottom one contained an assortment of gauze, tape, adhesive dressings and ointments. I stood up and slapped the dust off my jeans. "The usual stuff here, but I don't know what to make of the medical."

"Dunno, maybe he secretly wanted to be a doctor like his brother?" Jack turned his attention toward a milk crate resting on the floor. "Look, dude had good taste in music." He lifted it onto the dresser and removed several CDs, stacking them beside the crate. "Pearl Jam, Nirvana, Goo Goo Dolls, Blues Traveler. Even has Toad the Wet Sprocket. This is good stuff."

"I'd prefer Garth myself, but don't get distracted." I motioned across the front of the dresser. "Anything in these drawers?"

Jack rolled his eyes and placed the CDs back in the crate. "One man's distraction is another man's action." Just as I was about to ask him what in the world that nonsense was supposed to mean, Jack let out a low whistle. "Check this out. Shine a light."

It took me a minute to make it out, but the stain of the cherry dresser top had been altered, as if it had been damaged and only part of it refinished, a valiant but ill-fated effort to repair some type of insult without a complete refurbishment. "So Adam wasn't very good at furniture restoration. Big deal."

"Look closer." A touch of excitement suddenly tinged Jack's voice. "Feel it."

I ran my hand across the area in question and felt a distinct difference. With a more tangential light angle and the aid of my finger, I could make out the letters:

STOP!

"Uh huh, how's that for distraction, smart guy? What do you think it means?"

I shot him a you-got-lucky smirk. "Not sure, but I'm betting Adam didn't carve that into his dresser." I pulled out a 35 mm camera and snapped several photos. "Evidence."

"Oh, ok." Jack laughed. "You think you're Columbo now?"

"Hey, if we're gonna do this, we might as well do it right." I stepped back and took several photos of the storage room, making sure I captured every object in there. "Now, let's see what's in the boxes."

The first box contained a collection of college textbooks on ecology, marine biology, marine mammal physiology, organic chemistry. "And I thought Jet was the smart one," Jack said.

"Adam was no slouch himself. He just didn't want people to know. Thought it might interfere with his love life. At least that's what Jet always said." I smiled at the idea of it then shook my head in disgust at the injustice of a promising life cut short.

The next box was about half full, with a collection of empty photo frames, miscellaneous pens and pencils, and other odds and ends. I figured Adam's family had taken all his photos home—might be worth a look later, especially if we couldn't find this alleged girlfriend.

Then something caught my eye in the bottom of the box, adhering to the side of it. It was a photo of Adam's family, the day he graduated from college. Cap and gown and smiles all around. But it had a slit in the middle of it. "What do you make of this?" I said.

"Looks like it was stabbed with a knife."

Before he even opened his mouth, my attention was wandering back to the ominous message carved into the top of the dresser.

EIGHTEEN

JET was completely baffled. He had finished his first week of medical school, and Gross Anatomy had proceeded uneventfully since the accident, aside from his brief meeting with Cronin the following day. But that was the problem. Things were too normal. No good-natured wisecracks from Tucker, no snide comments from Tea about the group falling behind because Jet wasn't pulling his weight. Even Sterling Virchow steered clear of Jet and his group. Gracie had been tremendously helpful, spending extra time going over what he had missed, but something was odd there, too. Jet couldn't define it, but she was just different.

Meanwhile, Jet had participated dutifully, saying very little as he assisted in the dissections. He knew Cronin was watching him like a hawk. The others knew it too and seemed to be unnerved by it, as if maybe he was also watching them. Like a group of gazelles in the dry season who have no choice but to go to the watering hole knowing the lion is watching but hoping he's not hungry. So Jet walked the line, following instructions to the letter, while his mind sped through every possible scenario that would explain the events of the past week. And nothing made sense.

Either someone had switched cadavers, or he was completely insane. It wasn't just that he had recognized Adam and now had no familiarity whatsoever with the face of the man in his tank. It was more than that—everything was different. Different in subtle nuances of body habitus, skin markings, muscle mass, hair patterns and color; all the things that discern one individual from another independent of facial features. And beyond that, they were not even close to the same age. Adam had been at least ten, fifteen years younger. Maybe twenty.

But everyone acted as if nothing had happened. Nothing. It was as if he was living in some alternate universe. Or, after he hit his head, someone had traveled back in time to spare him by planting a different cadaver, but a malfunction in the time warp caused him to remember anyway. Or, maybe he was actually just a character in a computer program where a software glitch had inserted his brother into the cadaver slot, but the programmers had corrected it to prevent more mayhem and a system collapse.

Or maybe it was the simplest explanation—someone had switched the cadavers. In real time, in the real world. That would explain the what. The why would be a different animal altogether. If that was not the answer, then Jet feared he was incomprehensibly, irrefutably, and in his opinion, irreparably crazy.

Jet mulled it over all night Friday, distracted from his studies. He alternated between studying and racking his brain. Straining to remember every detail from the first two days of Gross Anatomy lab. Granted, there wasn't much to recall—he had checked out fairly quickly both days. But surely there was *something* that would help him. He stared at his biochemistry lecture notes, seeing pencil markings on the pages but processing very little.

Then suddenly it hit him. That's it. The notes. It was time to test his only friendship in the class. He called Gracie, and she agreed, reluctantly he thought, to meet him at the anatomy lab on Saturday afternoon.

Jet had the tank opened and was just raising the body when Gracie walked in. There were a few other students scattered throughout the room, studying or catching up on dissections. They all ignored him.

"Hey, hon." Gracie smiled. It seemed genuine. "What's up? Thinking about reviewing the extrinsic and intrinsic muscles of the back? You probably know it already, but I do need to review their innervations."

"Actually, I don't know it already. Haven't been paying much attention the past few days. You bring your notes?"

"Well that's a silly question. Of course I did."

"Can I see them?"

She answered his question by reaching into her backpack and withdrawing a spiral-bound notebook.

"Show me the notes you took on the second day."

Gracie's expression changed to one of concern. "Jet, don't."

"Show me, Gracie." He said it louder than he meant to.

Heads turned in the room, but no one said anything, and all quickly resumed their work.

She flipped several pages, then stopped and handed him the open book.

"What are you looking for?" The question was almost a whisper.

"Just give me a second." It took him a minute to acclimate to her handwriting, but he quickly found what he was looking for. "Gracie, read this." He pointed to a specific line in the text.

She took the notebook and scanned it in silence.

"No, read it aloud."

Gracie didn't look up. She shook her head slightly, sighed deeply, and obliged in a subdued voice. "Note: SPI and LD same origin but separate at insertion. Error: cut right SPI at insertion."

"You see it right there, huh? Remember that? I'm not sure who did it, but don't you remember? One of us cut the serratus posterior inferior—the SPI as you noted, and Dr. Winscote had to show us how it was separate from the latissimus dorsi—the LD." Jet's voice was tremulous with excitement now. He wasn't sure what had happened, but he would now have irrefutable evidence that the body in the tank was not the same one from the first two days. He pulled back the preservative-soaked sheet and called Gracie over. "Now. Come look at this and tell me what you see."

Jet stepped back so Gracie could examine the area in question. He crossed his arms triumphantly, awaiting her explanation of the discrepancy between the findings documented in her notes and the actual body before them.

She hesitated. "Jet, honey, just drop it, okay? Don't do this."

"C'mon, Gracie. Humor me. You see what you wrote in your notes. Now show me what it looks like."

Gracie didn't move. She shook her head. "I'm not going to do this with you. You told me what Cronin said. One more strike and you're out."

"Well, he's not here right now, is he?"

"Just drop it, for your own good."

"For my own good? For my own good? Really? Forget it, I'll show you myself." Jet snapped on a pair of disposable rubber gloves. He snatched a pair of forceps and started peeling back the superficial layers of skin and fascia to reveal the target of his inquiry—the proof he was looking for. The bullet hole was there as always, on the left side. He and Gracie had been working around it the past two days, with Tucker and Tea on the right. He still thought there was something strange about the bullet wound, but he couldn't quite decide what it was, not yet. No matter. He was concerned about the right side today. The latissimus dorsi muscle was set perfectly back in place where it had been severed from its origination at the lower spine and pelvis. He peeled it superior and lateral—up and out—to show the serratus posterior inferior. The SPI from Gracie's notes. Jet looked up at Gracie, eyes wide and mouth open. "No. This can't be," he exclaimed.

"Jet, baby, I told you, leave it alone." Her tone was muted, withdrawing. A glisten of moisture shined in her eyes.

"I know I'm not crazy. That muscle has been cut just like we did that day. The same mistake. And sutured back in place, just like Dr. Winscote did that day." He was flabbergasted that he had not noticed it the previous two days, but then again, he had been preoccupied with other thoughts and had been focused on dissecting the left side. And he hadn't been looking for it—not until the memory of the error suddenly popped into his head the day before. "Gracie, tell me right now what's going on. I need someone on my side."

Tears streamed down her face now. "I'm sorry, Jet. I'm sorry."

"Sorry for what? Tell me what's happening!"

"I'm sorry for you. I'm sorry this is happening to you."

Jet frowned and stepped back from the table, head cocked slightly to one side. "Are you saying you think I'm insane? This is somehow all in my mind? Is that what you're sorry for?"

"I didn't say that. It's just a big mess, and I don't understand it. And I want to help you, but I don't know how. I'm sorry." Gracie grabbed her belongings and strode out of the room, wiping tears from her both cheeks as she went.

Jet turned to watch her leave and realized that Tekowski had come in and had been standing behind them. "How 'bout you, Tea? Gonna tell me what's going on?" Jet said.

Tekowski dropped his chin and stared at the floor. "Let it go," he mumbled.

Jet could sense the stares from all in the room. He wanted to turn and glare at them and scream an obscenity or suggest they take a picture so it would last longer, but he didn't. He turned around and methodically covered the body, lowered it back into the tank, and trudged out of the room the same way Gracie had gone.

NINETEEN

"YOU said Adam mentioned her, so what's the skinny on this girl?" I spun the steering wheel and aimed my truck in the direction Jack was pointing.

Jack smiled and used his hands to simulate the outline of a woman's figure "I have no idea if she's skinny or not, but knowing the way Adam was, I'll bet she's just about right."

"Yeah, yeah. Nothing else?"

"Adam just said she was a hottie. What you got?"

"I told you. Not much. They'd been seeing each other a month or so, but he liked her. All I've got is that address."

"No phone number?"

"Yeah, but whoever answered the other day told me she didn't live there."

Jack motioned at our destination coming up on the right. "So this is all we've got."

The doublewide mobile home sat on a half-acre, give or take, that hadn't been mowed in two weeks, give or take. The faux rock skirting had pulled loose on one corner, and its color, which was surely supposed to be brown, somehow exuded just enough of the wrong yellow to clash with the buttery hue of the trailer's exterior wall.

With Jack just behind me, I climbed the wooden stairs to the front door. The stairs didn't creak much, but our approach was not unnoticed. A small dog yapped furiously on the other side of the door. What must have rivaled the highest-pitched barking in the world went up another octave when I knocked.

"Coming! Coming!" a raspy voice called. "You don't have to keep pounding it."

I turned and shot Jack an amused grin and shrugged. After several seconds, the door opened a few inches, and a tall, slender woman peered around it suspiciously. A screen door that I presumed was still locked separated us. The woman's skin was like a brown paper bag that had been wadded up and spread back out. Oxygen tubing was attached to her nose and a cigarette to her nicotine stained fingers. A red sticker on the door warning all visitors of the flammability of oxygen suddenly stood out, whereas I'd barely noticed it before. I took a small step back.

"Boy, are you just gonna stand there, or can I help you?"

I decided to put my fears of being incinerated aside for a moment. She probably chain smoked and hadn't blown herself up so far, so it seemed unlikely that she'd suddenly do it now just because we showed up on her porch. "I'm sorry, ma'am. Forgive me. My friend and I—uh, my name is Case Reynolds, and this is Jack Masterson. We're looking for someone and wondered if you could help us."

Her gray eyes narrowed suspiciously. "Well, are you gonna tell me who it is, or you want me to guess? Jimmy Hoffa, maybe?"

Jack coughed back a laugh behind me.

"Yes ma'am. Her name is Anniston Lewis. She's a family friend."

"Must not be no good family friend. First off, cuz if'n she was, you wouldn't be here now not knowin' where she's at. And second, cuz I'm her family, and I don't know you."

This lady was sharp. "I, uh, understand, ma'am. You're correct, in a way. She's a friend of a friend. Or she was. Well, I mean, I hope she's doing well. Not that she was. He was. Our friend, I mean. He passed away. We're friends of his. Well, we were. We are his brother's friends. His brother wants to find Anniston."

"Good grief, boy, you trippin' over yo'self like a hobbled mule trying to skip rope." In my peripheral vision I could see Jack, who had eased up beside me, cover his eyes with his hands. "What do you need with Anniston?"

"We just want to talk to her. Promise."

"Why?" The dog had shut up, but now it was back, between her legs, snarling and barking at me. "Hush!" She swatted it with her foot, and it shut up again.

"Our friend's brother. Adam Townsend. He and Anniston were friends. He died a while back and the family never, uh, really got to talk to her about it."

"So why they send you? Why now? That was a long time ago."

I looked over at Jack. Now we were getting somewhere. She knew Adam.

"Yeah, I knew Adam. Don't be shooting each other looks like you done solved something, like you Miami Vice or something. No secret. They was friends. Dating, I guess. Don't know what else they was doin'."

"How are you related to Anniston, if you don't mind me asking?"

"I do mind you asking, but she's my niece. But she ain't here. We had a parting of the ways. Now, you still ain't told me why y'all need to talk to her."

"We have learned that Adam might have been in some trouble before he died. His family just wants to clear things up. Put it behind them and move on."

"I ain't interested in helping you or nobody else bring another family's trouble to mine."

"Oh no, ma'am. Your niece is not in any trouble. Can you tell me where she is?"

She smiled for the first time. "I can." I stood patiently but she said nothing, just stared at me. "Maybe you should have asked me if I *will* tell you where she is." The smile disappeared.

"Will you?"

"No, I will not."

Jack coughed again.

I turned to my friend, palms open and eyebrows raised. *You wanna pitch in and help here?*

Jack read my gesture and shook his head. Nope.

"Now, sirs, I have enjoyed our little visit, but I have a date shortly with the Golden Pearl, and I don't intend to miss it. Drive safe."

"Ma'am, I'm sorry, can you … er, will you, tell me your name?"

"I don't think I will today. Thanks for the invite, though."

"You and Sparky have a nice life," I grumbled as I turned to leave.

"Mr. Reynolds? One more thing." I stopped for her to finish. "Assuming yo' sidekick down there ain't deaf nor mute, tell him if'n he was a real friend, he woulda helped you explain yo'self instead of standing there snickerin' like a silly little schoolgirl while you looked like a fool with yo' tongue spinnin' yo' words into cotton balls. Have a nice day." She slammed the door.

Jack's jaw dropped, but he couldn't hold back a half-cocked smile.

It was my turn to snicker. "That's a good one, right there." I kicked him in the butt as we walked back to my truck. "Thanks for the help back there."

"Hey, I saw real quick I didn't want no part of that crocodile. She was tearing you up."

"Well, I hope if a real croc ever attacks me, you'll give a better effort."

"Depends on how big and nasty it is."

"She still got you, though. I'd rather be a hobbled mule than a silly schoolgirl any day."

Jack reached out and stopped me. He appeared to be enamored by the mailman parked at the old lady's mailbox. "Go ahead and get the truck." A familiar look of mischief lit his eyes. "Pick me up at the road. Might wanna roll your windows down."

As the white USPS Grumman LLV pulled away, Jack marched up to the mailbox, just like he owned the place.

The lady opened her door and began shouting at him before he even opened the mailbox. "Hey, you little punk! Mail theft is a federal offense!"

Jack waved a white envelope above his head. "Call the FBI then, Ms., uh …" He looked at the envelope again. "You gotta be kidding." He gave her a wide-eyed grin. "F. Liona Broom?"

"You put that back right now! I'm calling the cops!"

Jack didn't say another word. He just maintained his smile and shook his head as he replaced the envelope with exaggerated precision. "Fly on a broom. That explains a lot." He broke into a full laugh as he climbed into the truck.

I hit the gas and spun the back tires a half turn, uprooting some packed gravel as a parting shot, and aimed my truck for the main highway. "That was entertaining, at least.

"Watching you strike out has always been entertaining," Jack said. "Guess we can head back. You got a better idea?"

"Chicken-on-a-stick." I veered into the dusty, oil-stained lot of a truck stop. In addition to my favorite chicken-on-a-stick, the flashing arrow sign also recommended cheese sticks, corndogs, pizza, and tater logs. And twelve packs of soda for $3.99.

I wondered briefly why the 92 Truck Stop was on Highway 90, but not enough to dwell on it much. Probably an inside joke anyway. This wasn't a slick, bright-signed, national chain kind of trucker hangout but a modest operation that looked a couple generations old. The type of place where the elderly aunt of the owner came in at 3 a.m. to cook the biscuits just right, joke with the regulars who ran the local routes, and get lunch going before she limped back home, stooped and tired but too proud to have it any other way than the way it had always been done.

"Good call there, Case-o. I think better with a full stomach."

The glass door swung open easily, and a loud bell announced our entrance. Neither the man behind the counter, the three guys smoking at a back corner table, or the smattering of customers looked up. The smell of deep-fried everything hit me just as I'd hoped it would, making my mouth water and my gut rumble.

"You boys having a good day?" The man at the counter spoke without looking up as he calculated our damage a few minutes later. He looked to be about sixty, with white hair, a faded polo shirt, and a baseball cap. He seemed to be in slow motion, and my stomach growled in protest as I eyed my Mountain Dew and the food in the paper sack made translucent by the grease.

"It's been alright. Unique, at least." Jack turned to me and lowered his voice. "Not every day that you meet a witch." He elbowed me and chuckled.

"Fly on a Broom." I slid a twenty-dollar bill across the counter. "That was her name."

The man cocked his head and grinned. "You boys met F. Liona?"

Jack and I exchanged glances of disbelief.

"You know her?" Jack said.

He laughed. "Oh yeah. Most folks around here know her. Talk about a piece of work. Her husband was a regular here before he died a few years ago. She was always storming in here looking for him, putting us all through the shredder. Looking for his girlfriend."

"Hard to blame the guy," Jack said.

The man chuckled as he handed back my change. "Nah, Pete was harmless. No girlfriend as far as I knew. Just liked to smoke and drink coffee. And get out of that trailer." His eyes narrowed, and his smile stiffened. "So what business could you boys possibly have with that old piece of shoe leather?"

"Not with her," I said. "Not exactly. We just had the address. Actually looking for someone else."

"Ohhhh." The white-haired man's eyes measured us top to bottom. "Y'all are what, early twenties? A bit too young."

"Sir?" I said. "Too young?"

"Her niece. Thought y'all might be old friends of hers. But she's late twenties, I think."

Jack tapped the counter excitedly. "Are you talking about Anniston Lewis?"

"Isn't that who you're talking about?"

"Yessir, that's her. How do you know her?"

"Ole Pete loved that girl. She breezes through here now and then."

The man held up an index finger and nodded over my shoulder.

Jack grabbed me on my shoulder to nudge me aside for another customer to pay out. "Looks like yo' chicken-on-a-stick is turning out even better than you thought, bud," he whispered in my ear.

I had almost forgotten about my battered chicken-onion-potato-pickle-chicken kabob. My mouth started watering again. "My stomach is going to eat my backbone if we don't get this show on the road. But yeah, looks like we may luck out."

Jack and I stepped back to let the other patrons pass on their way toward the front door, but Jack wasted no time getting back to the counter. "So, can you tell us how to find Ms. Lewis? No, let me rephrase. *Will* you tell us how to find her?"

"You didn't tell me what you want her for."

"She is a friend," I said. "Sort of. We had a mutual friend who passed away last year. Truth is, we just wanted to say hi."

"Then the answer is yes and no." He plucked a pen from an old coffee cup and grabbed a scrap of paper. "Tell me your names." We did, and he stepped back, removed a cordless phone from its receiver in the corner, punched a number from memory, and turned his back to us. His head bobbed and shook as he talked, but I could hear only muffled sounds instead of words. After what was probably two or three sentences, he turned back to us. "Who's the friend?"

"Adam Townsend," we said in unison.

After several more seconds of mumbles and gestures, he clicked off the phone and turned around. "Here's the deal." He gazed out the front window with his arms crossed and phone still in hand. "You boys seem alright, but I don't know you. Could be a coupla psychos for all I know. So I called Anniston. I know where she works. She first said she didn't know you, but when I told her your friend's name, she said she'd see you. She don't get off for an hour, though."

"That's no problem," I said. "We can kill some time. But where do we find her?"

"You're not listening. I told you the answer was no, I would not tell you where to find her. But I did tell her where to find you."

"And where is that?" Jack asked.

"Right here, of course." He pointed to one of the booths in the smoky corner. "And I'll be watching."

TWENTY

"**B**UXOM."

I followed Jack's gaze to the front door where its now-familiar ding had just announced the latest arrival. She was about five-foot-three with sandy blonde hair pulled back in a ponytail. Her dark eyebrows were striking and seemed more exotic than the cuteness of her other features. She wore little, if any, makeup and appeared to be no more than two or three years older than us. And yes, as Jack so quickly pointed out, buxom was an apt descriptor. "I think you got the word right this time, Jack. But we need to focus on the business at hand."

Anniston Lewis stopped at the checkout counter and glanced our way while she exchanged words with our cashier friend, then turned and disappeared to the back of the store.

"Think she bailed?" Jack asked.

"If she took one look at your slobbering face, then I'd say she probably did."

Before we could wonder further, she reappeared with a bottle of soda. Mr. Cashier waved her away when she attempted to pay. She walked over and stood beside Jack for an awkward moment, until Jack caught her hint and my gesture for him to switch sides so she could slide in across from us. "So, what brings you boys to my neck of the south Mississippi woods?"

Before I could answer, she noticed me eyeing her drink. "Like root beer?"

"No, tastes like worm dirt if you ask me," I said.

She laughed and extended her hand. "Anniston Lewis. And I don't want to know how you know what worm dirt tastes like."

"No, you probably don't. Case Reynolds. And my friend here is—"

"Jack Masterson." Jack almost knocked the table over as he stood to shake her hand.

"Nice to meet you. Now, let's get down to business. You boys come all this way just to insult my choice of soda, or something else? Uncle Cal says you knew Adam."

"Uncle Cal?" I said.

She looked puzzled. "Isn't that why you came in here to my uncle's store? Looking for me?"

"Not exactly," I said. "That dude there is your uncle?" I nodded toward the checkout counter.

"He is. Mother's brother. He tries to keep an eye on me."

"Small world," Jack said. "We actually just happened in here looking for chicken-on-a-stick."

"Well, we started our search just down the road there. Got a tongue lashing from one of your other relatives."

"Oh, so you met Aunt Elfie." She nearly choked on a mouthful of root beer when she read our expressions. "Aw, c'mon. Couldn't have been that bad."

"Let's just say we ain't invited for Sunday dinner," I said. "Elfie?"

"She goes by F. Liona. Sounds silly if you ask me, but that's her. I had trouble pronouncing it when I was a kid, came out 'elfiona'. She's been Aunt Elfie ever since."

"So you live with her?"

"Lived. For a time. We didn't get along real well. For some obvious reasons. Plus, she had some bad habits. Got my own place now." She shrugged, and her expression became more serious. "But enough about soft drinks, nicknames, and family trouble. Why are you looking for me?"

"Funny you mentioned family trouble," Jack said. "It's Adam's little brother."

I nudged Jack's hip with the back of my hand, out of Anniston's view. This was going to take some diplomacy, not always Jack's strongest suit. He could be a smooth-talking persuader when he wanted to but was just as likely to be tactlessly blunt. "Jet," I said. "Jet is his name. He's in medical school, just started. But he's having a hard time coping with Adam's death."

She stared at her root beer and spun it between her palms on the table. "I'm sorry to hear that, but I'm not surprised. Adam was a great guy. Loved his brother. He's a whiz kid or something, huh?"

"He's a genius," Jack said.

"Very bright. But he's been through a lot. Adam's death was hard on him."

Anniston sighed. "Like I said, I'm sorry, but what does that have to do with me?" She tipped the amber bottle back to finish the last sip. It was difficult not to stare at the bulge across the front of her faded Saints T-shirt.

"Okay, here's the deal." I refocused, watching her reaction to what I said next. "Jet is our best friend. And he believes that Adam was in trouble when he died."

Anniston's confident air shifted slightly. A dance of her eyes, a tilt of her head. Her finger suddenly tapping the empty bottle ever so subtly. My father, the sheriff of McKinley County where we'd all grown up, had taught me a few things over the years. The first was how to defend myself, the second was how to read people. And so I knew that Anniston knew something.

"What kind of trouble?"

"We're not sure. Hoping you could tell us," I said. "How did you and Adam meet?"

She stiffened. "Am I on trial now? You gonna grill me on my personal life?"

"No, no," Jack said. "We just know Adam thought the world of you. And we figure anything you can help us learn about what was going on with him might help Jet to rest his mind. From what Adam told Jet about how great a person you are, we just knew you'd be willing to help." There it was. The silver-tongued Jack.

As if on cue, she grinned slightly. "Okay, sure. But why are you two here? Why not Jet himself?"

Jack nodded at me. He wanted me to take the lead.

"Busy with medical school. No other reason."

"Hmmm. Okay. Adam and I met when I was waitressing. He came in. We hit it off and started hanging out."

"Do you remember when that was?"

"A month or so before he got killed."

Got killed. Interesting choice of words. "So y'all were together a lot?"

"What do you want? A written record? Yeah, we were to-gether a lot." She gazed out the window. Either to remove her-self from the moment or better remember the past. "We were just, you know, getting to know each other." Her voice cracked.

"Adam told Jet the night before he, uh, died that he was in some trouble. Something about his job. Adam laughed it off, enough that even after the accident, Jet didn't think much of it. There didn't seem to be any connection, so he didn't see any point in worrying about it."

"And you think I might know what it was."

"Hoping."

"Why is it important now, when it wasn't then? Almost a year later?"

"Something came up. A new development." Jack said.

Don't run too far ahead, Jack. I've got an idea.

"A new development? What do you mean?"

"Did Adam have any bad habits?" I ignored her question for a moment. "Gambling, that type stuff?"

"No!" she said emphatically. "He gambled some, wasn't a choir boy, but he was pretty straight up. Nothing excessive. Worked hard, played hard. Normal guy."

"What about his job? Maybe something happened and he was worried about getting fired or something?"

"He worked for the DEQ. Government job. Not exactly a high-pressure position."

"DEQ?" Jack tapped on the shoulder with the back of his hand.

"Department of Environmental Quality," I said. "Okay. Last thing, then we gotta head back. Take a look at this." I spread a photo on the table between us. "One-hour photo is pretty handy. Took this a couple of hours ago."

Anniston glanced at the photo and shrugged. "Okay? A closeup of a dresser with a cracked mirror."

"True, we were curious why the mirror was cracked. But look closer. There was something carved into the wood."

She did not look at the photo. "Stop."

I tapped the photo. "We'll stop when you give us some answers. This is important."

She sighed. "Not you, the photo. The dresser. It said stop. S-T-O-P."

Jack leaned forward and put both elbows on the table. "Tell us what's going on. Please."

Anniston took a deep breath. "Okay, I'll tell you what I know. Adam worked for the DEQ. His day job. But he had something going on the side. He was working for a seafood group."

"What kind of seafood group?" I said.

"Gulf Seafood Company. Wait, no. Consortium. Something like that. I know the initials were GSC. He was doing some kind of water testing."

"Water testing?"

"Yeah. Taking samples from the Gulf. Testing for pollution or something."

"Pollutants that might be a hazard for marine life? Seafood?" I said.

"Maybe. Look, I've got some education, but I'm not a scientist. Adam didn't give a lot of details, and I wasn't interested enough to ask."

Jack flicked the photo toward her with a finger. "So what does that have to do with some bozo practicing his woodworking skills on Adam's furniture?"

Anniston went on to describe the day they met at Billey's on the Bayou, how Adam had collected the vials from the Gulf that morning only to see them destroyed by the man who attacked her in the restaurant. "We left there and went to Adam's place, and his apartment had been turned upside down. That word was carved into his dresser. Really freaked me out, lemme tell you. Adam wasn't too worried. Mad more than anything. He said someone wanted him to stop his testing. He just didn't know who it was."

"So did he stop?"

"He said it didn't matter. He was pretty much done anyway."

"And that was it?"

"That was it. Nothing else happened. That's all I know."

"There's one other thing we should tell you." I took a deep breath and paused for effect. Then I threw out another piece of bait to see what we'd catch. "We have reason to believe that Adam's death was not an accident."

I wasn't sure if we actually believed that or not. In fact, I wasn't sure what we believed at this point. But I wanted to see her reaction. I deliberately left out the part about Jet thinking he had seen Adam's body. For starters, I couldn't begin to wrap my brain around that idea or its implications, but I also thought we needed to keep a little something in the tackle box for later, if the need arose.

Anniston Lewis's reaction this time was completely different. It was visceral. Her mouth opened slightly, the skin paled around her lips, and her fingers began to tremble. She grasped the bottle on the table with both hands. Something different happened in her eyes, though. A nervous look formed, then faded, replaced with another, harder look, fleeting in its own way, melting into the growing redness of her face. The kind of deep crimson that can mean embarrassment, anxiety, or anger, and sometimes all three. But the flame in her eyes left no doubt. Anniston Lewis was suddenly angry

The muscles in her jaw bulged, and the tremor in her hand disappeared into a white-knuckled clutch of the bottle. She spoke through clenched teeth. "You want to know about Adam? Well that makes two of us. But I guess it's too late, ain't it?" She stood to leave.

Jack stood with her. "Wait! Please don't go."

Anniston slammed her empty bottle into a trash can behind her, and in the corner of my eye, I glimpsed our friendly cashier craning his neck to see what was going on. "I wish you boys the best. I got stuff to do," she said. Her angry flush had not abated.

"At least tell us how to reach you." I hastily slid a napkin toward her and gestured for Jack to retrieve a pen from the cash register.

Anniston Lewis stood with her hands on her hips while she waited, staring hard at me in a way that held me silent, thinking she was about to speak. She did not. She scribbled down a phone number and slapped the pen on the table.

I doubted whether it was even a real number. "Is that legit?"

She looked from me to Jack. "Guess you'll have to call to find out." And she marched out the front door.

"Boy, she did not like that." Jack watched the glass front door close behind her. "Mad at us?"

"Maybe. Not sure."

"What now?"

"Seems like only one thing to do." I was already digging in my pocket for my keys.

"You read my mind!"

TWENTY-ONE

"HURRY up! We're gonna lose her!" Jack slapped the dashboard two or three times.

"I ain't Bo Duke, you ain't Luke, and this ain't the General Lee. Not real good at high flyin' maneuvers!" I shouted. "Just keep your eyes on that car."

Anniston's head start of a several seconds hadn't seemed like much, but she had left in a rush. We followed the maroon Nissan that spun a cloud of dust leaving the lot, assuming it was hers. Wherever she was heading, she was doing so with a purpose. And we were having trouble keeping up. Luckily, she hadn't made many turns. Due west on Highway 90, weaving around traffic, double yellow line or not. We tried to stay several cars back without losing sight of her, but she gave no indication she suspected being followed. She was just in a hurry.

"Where is she heading?" Jack said.

"Maybe she's just driving. You know, blowing off some steam."

West across Biloxi Bay, then north on Oak Street.

"Seemed to be more than what she was telling us, though, huh? You hit a nerve with that about Adam's death being no accident. Where did that come from, anyway? Nobody ever said that."

"It's a logical conclusion. Well, not logical. Nothing about this is logical. But if we're gonna consider the lunacy that Adam was in Jet's anatomy tank, then it's not a stretch to ask whether there was something hokey about his death."

"Do you believe that?"

"I didn't. I was just throwing it on the wall to see what mess it made. Didn't expect it to stick."

She turned west onto Bayview.

Jack tapped the glove box to get my attention. "She's slowing down. Ease up, not too close."

"The Double Luck," I said. "That's one way to blow off steam. Blow some cash at the blackjack table."

"Runs in the family."

Anniston was out of the car as soon as it came to rest. She marched in the front door beneath the glowing golden letters flanked by double four-leaf clovers. Not her first trip through it. Jack and I almost had to run to keep up with her, fearful that she'd get away but worried she'd look back and see us. She never turned her head, though.

"We should slow up," I said. "We'll find her at a table or the slots, you know. Not like we don't know where she's going."

"Maybe." Jack didn't slow up, and I stayed with him.

We burst through the front door and stopped just inside to survey. I had never been much of a gambler, but I had been to the Silverstar Casino on the Choctaw Indian Reservation in Philadelphia, Mississippi, when I was in college. And tried the greyhound tracks a time or two across the state line in Eutaw, Alabama. But that was the extent of my visiting gambling establishments. Despite that, it was not an unfamiliar place. The smell of cigarettes, colored lights, the clangs and rings of the slots, muffled voices of dealers moving their games along, high-hipped waitresses satiating thirsts at every turn were all similar to what I'd seen in person and on TV.

"I don't see her," I said.

"There." Jack pointed.

Anniston was talking with a burly man in a black suit. He stood with hands crossed at his waist, feet shoulder-width apart, chest bulging behind his lapels. He nodded upward, toward a huge pane of one-way glass, presumably the window to a room overlooking the casino floor. The man frowned and shook his head, but she put both hands on her hips and continued to talk, unrelenting. She wagged a finger at the man, who was at least twelve inches and a hundred pounds her superior. He suddenly seemed amused. He checked his watch and shrugged, then pressed the button to a small elevator behind him. Within seconds Anniston disappeared behind the elevator doors.

"Where's she going?" I asked.

"Owner, manager, something," Jack said. "Whatever you wanna call him, I'm sure it's the boss. C'mon."

Jack was gone before I could protest. It dawned on me that we needed to get out of the center of the floor, no matter what. Assuming Anniston was admitted to the room above, she'd be able to see us if she looked. Jack walked straight past the man in the suit as if to call the elevator.

"Hang on, there, buddy," the man said. "Restricted access."

"Oh, I'm sorry. Just looking for the can. Beer runs straight through, you know."

"Well that ain't the can. Down there." He pointed to our right where the sign clearly said Restrooms.

"My bad," Jack said. "Hey, just curious. Who was the girl you just let in?" He nodded above us, similar to how the suit had done with Anniston earlier.

The man smiled. "Oh, I see what's happening. Chasing some leg?" He held up a ringed left hand. "I remember those single days. That girl is a pistol."

"Okay, you got me," Jack said. "Had my eye on her all night. Looks like she got away. Just when I was gonna make my move."

The man shook his head and gave me a sneer, as if remembering a third wheel that held him back, back in his heyday.

I said nothing, figuring Jack was having better luck with his solo act than I had earlier. But I'd take this suit over Fly on a Broom any day.

"She won't be long. Meeting with Bobby."

"Bobby?"

"Bobby Meyerling. Son of Mr. Robert Meyerling, the man who built this place. Turned most everything over to Bobby." The man looked both directions before speaking in a hushed tone from the corner of his mouth. "Ain't half the man his father is. But you want to know about the girl. I don't know her name. Used to come in here more. With some old wench sometimes. Ain't seen her in a while."

"Wench?" I asked.

The man looked back at me, annoyed. He turned to Jack. "Her aunt or grandmother or something, I think. Sun-dried string bean with the bite of a habanero."

Jack smiled. "Thanks for the warning. I'll stay away from her. What's the girl so worked up about?"

"What does everybody get worked up about around here? Losing money."

"Thanks, bro'," Jack said. "I'll catch her another time."

"Good luck. She might be worth waiting on."

I grabbed Jack after we had walked a few feet away and handed him a twenty-dollar bill. "Ask him this. Ask him if he ever saw Adam in here with her. And ask how long ago Anniston stopped coming by."

Jack paused and appeared to consider it. He turned and talked to the suit while I watched the proceedings of the nearest blackjack table between sneak peeks in their direction. The man turned to frown at me, but his look softened when Jack wrote something on the bill and handed it to him. He said a few more words before turning to speak with a waitress who wandered by.

Jack winked at me and smiled as he turned, and I led him around the edge of the casino, hoping to stay out of the immediate line of sight of whoever was in the room above. "Well, did you find out anything?"

"Adam never came in here with her that he saw. And today's the first time he's seen her in months."

"Ten months."

"Maybe."

"Hey, what'd you write on the twenty?"

"Told him you didn't know her but had seen her around town with a guy you had the hots for. Wanted to know if he was still around. He seemed to get excited, so I gave him your number. And the twenty, I guess."

I stopped in my tracks. "You're lying. He had a wedding ring."

"Hey, who knows what makes a man's cookie crumble?" Jack laughed so hard he started coughing and could barely get the words out. "You'll—you'll—wonder every time the phone rings for a while, won't you?

TWENTY-TWO

"I can't tell you how much I appreciate you guys going down there for me." Jet spread the photos across his kitchen table.

"So, what's happened since you went back to school?" I asked.

"Nothing. Absolutely nothing. That's what bothers me. They act like nothing happened." Jet studied the photos before him while Jack and I exchanged looks. "This is what I want to see. Did you guys notice anything unusual?"

Jack slid one photo to center view. "This one. It's hard to make out, but somebody carved a warning on his furniture." He slid the stabbed family photo alongside it. "Anniston confirmed both of these were done during a break-in of his apartment. Looks like Adam was in some trouble like you said."

Jet pushed his index finger through the slit in the family photo and held it up with a steely-eyed stare. "Told you something was fishy!" His triumph was short-lived, though, and his look turned contemplative. He pulled his finger out of the photo and tapped the one of the dresser. "Stop. Stop what?"

"Anniston said he was working for someone on the side," Jack said. "Some seafood company. Testing the water in the Gulf."

"Why would someone break in his apartment to give him a warning?"

I shrugged. "Depends on what he was finding, I guess."

"Or who had something to lose. Did he tell her what he was looking for? What the results were?"

Jack shook his head. "Negative. Said she had no idea. And we didn't find anything in storage."

"Well, he had to be keeping records somewhere. Maybe at work? Let me look at the other pics." Jet surveyed the photos closely for a moment. I had done so myself for at least an hour after getting home the night before and had come up with nothing new. "What about all these medical supplies? Gauze and tape and stuff?"

"You tell us," Jack said. "You're the doctor. Adam have any recent injuries?"

"Not that I know of, but I'll ask Mom. Look at this here." He slid a different photo to the forefront. "A computer monitor and keyboard. Where's the hard disk drive?"

"Not in there. Think they took it?"

"Maybe it wasn't just a warning. Maybe they were looking for data."

"Or maybe his drive crashed, and he chunked it but hadn't bought a new one yet," I said.

Jet stared across the room, absorbed in a thought of his own.

Jack eased into a chair and looked at me with a twist of his mouth that told me he thought this could take some time. "Jet, bud, what you thinking?"

I followed Jack's lead and took a seat myself while Jet ignored the question, leaning onto the table and studying the photo spread. "What you guys think about this?" He pointed at the image of the five-gallon gas can.

"Empty gas can," Jack said. "So?"

I suddenly understood Jet's reason for the question. *Of course!* "He had a gas can in his truck when he crashed. It's what started, or at least aided, the fire."

"Correction," Jet said. "He had a gas can in *my* truck when he crashed."

"In your truck?" Jack looked perplexed for a second then nodded. "Oh yeah, he had borrowed your truck. But again, so what?"

"So, Adam left his four-wheeler in Ocean Springs that weekend. Mom sold it and his boat after he died. And according to this photo, his gas can was back home with the four-wheeler."

"Or maybe he had two gas cans."

"Yeah," Jack said. "One for the boat, one for the four-wheeler. In case he had them in two different locations some-time."

I looked at Jet as I spoke to see if his line of thinking was the same as mine. "But, even if he had two, why bring a gas can back to Amberton that weekend if he didn't have the four-wheeler with him?"

"Some folks just keep a can in their truck," Jack said.

"But it was my truck," Jet said, "and I don't have a gas can."

Jack nodded and stood up. His tone became more excited. "So he'd have had to get it out of his and put it in yours before he left that night."

"Exactly." I stood and pushed Jack playfully. "And why would he do that if he didn't have his four-wheeler?"

Jet held up two hands. "Cool your jets, guys. There is at least one logical possibility. Maybe he was bringing it for one of his buddies at the hunting camp."

"Who was he meeting?" I asked.

"Rob Myles if I remember correctly. Maybe Tuba Hansen, too. College friends."

"Sounds like a phone call might clear that up," Jack said.

"Okay, moving on. Change the subject slightly. What about Anniston Lewis? She give you any other information?"

I told Jet about our conversation with her, how she was reluctant to tell us much, how she seemed to become angry, or at the least, alarmed, when we suggested Adam's death might not have been an accident.

"She jumped up and went straight to the casino." Jet recounted my description. "Why would she do that?"

"You know, I thought about something," Jack began pacing, the volume of his voice rising. "Something Anniston said, along with what the dude in the suit told me. Remember, Case? Anniston said she and her aunt had problems because of the witch's bad habits."

Jet held his hand up to stop us. "The witch?"

"She flies on a broom," I said. "Long story, I'll explain later."

Jet shrugged, and Jack continued. "So, I thought she was probably talking about chain smoking or smoking with her oxygen or whatever, but remember that guy at the Double Luck said she came in there raising Cain about losing money."

"Okay, so she ain't the most talented gambler," I said.

"When I opened her mailbox to find out her name." Jack stopped walking and cocked his head forward and sideways, replaying the examination of the mailbox as if we were playing charades. "I saw a bunch of the same type of envelopes. Big red letters on the outside, saying Past Due and Late Notice, stuff like that."

"Dude, you didn't think that was important to share with me? She obviously has a gambling problem. Remember she told us she had a date at the Golden Pearl. So she hasn't slowed up."

"So what does all that mean?" Jet popped his fist with the palm of his other hand.

"I don't know," Jack said. "I wouldn't think much about it if Anniston hadn't raced to the casino like she did when we told her about Adam. There has to be a connection."

Jet waved both hands in front of his chest. "Let me think on that. Just got to have time to process all of this."

"Okay, let's switch gears again." I said. "We're down there on the coast, trying to figure out what was going on with Adam, all because you believe you saw him here. But I'm still trying to process that. How it could even be remotely possible? Adam's body burned up in that fire, remember?"

"Somebody switched the bodies. We buried somebody other than Adam."

I shook my head and blinked, as if I was trying to shake off some cobwebs. "Okay, let's say that's true. Who would do that? And why?"

"Maybe whoever was harassing Adam killed him. And wanted to cover it up."

"But why this way? Why not just make him disappear?"

"Because it would be months before it was discovered, if ever. Maybe they didn't know I was going to be here to find him."

"And it's a coincidence that he wound up in your tank? What, a one in twenty-five chance?"

"Twenty-six."

"Okay, fine. Then who was the other guy? The one you buried?"

"All good questions. Case, I don't know the answers yet. I have the same questions."

"And to top that off, you see that it's Adam, come back later in the day, and he's nowhere to be found. Does that make sense?"

"None whatsoever."

I held my hands out, palms up, a helpless look. We were getting nowhere. Jack frowned at me and turned to Jet. "What was it about the cadaver that looked like Ad—"

"I told y'all, it was Adam."

"Okay, it was Adam. Surely there's something different about that body than the one you have now."

"Of course there is. The faces are different. Everything is different. I looked at the body once, could see it was different, and that's about it. I can barely look at it without getting sick. Speaking of which, before this happened, if your nose wasn't buried in the cadaver, Cronin was on you like slither on a snake. Now, I stand to the side and let everybody else work, and he barely notices. He's treating me like everybody else in the room does, pretending everything is normal, but it's not. It's almost like I'm not there. Or untouchable. Like a pariah."

"And you're not screaming to the roof about it all to everyone in the room?"

"I can't. They've told me they'll kick me out if I cause another disruption. Any little peep."

"Okay," Jack said. "What about something more objective? Something you can prove."

"Well, there was a dissection mistake we made on the second day. Gracie—one of my partners—made a note of it. So I went back up there yesterday to prove it. Just the two of us, so as not to cause a scene, and in case I got sick. But it didn't work. It was the same, on the new body. See, the latissimus dorsi muscle—"

"Whoa, whoa," Jack held his hand up. "Don't wanna know any Latin. What do you mean, it was the same?"

"Just that. We made a wrong cut on the first one. It's a subtle thing, so I had forgotten. But I remembered and met Gracie to prove it, but the same cut had been made on the new one."

"And what did Gracie say?"

"She freaked out and left."

"Jet, think about it," I said. "Is there a chance—"

"No! I know what I saw!" Jet's face reddened. "At least, I think I do. Crap, it makes no sense." He pounded the table, scattering the photos.

I flipped a couple of overturned photos and made a calming gesture. "Okay, let's think about this. We can shine a light on Adam's personal secrets and all that, yes." I tilted my head forward to make sure Jet met my gaze and tried to speak in a consolatory but firm tone. "But you know you need more than that. What you think, what Jack and I think—all irrelevant. You need some hardcore evidence to support your story."

Jet looked to Jack, who just shrugged. "He's right, Jet. We're here for you, but you need more than this."

"Okay. You're right. I'm working on it. Just don't quit believing in me. Not yet." Jet turned to me. "You still writing everything down?"

"Every detail you tell me and some in between."

He nodded slowly and eased into a subdued but assured smile. "Gonna be an amazing story. You just wait."

TWENTY-THREE

dreaded making the phone call. Not because we didn't have a good relationship, but because I knew what the answer would be. My father was a pragmatist. Things were mostly black or white to him, with very little shading in between. You were either in law enforcement or you weren't. Something was either a crime or it wasn't. The person is either telling the truth or is lying. By nature, his profession left very little room to accommodate the middle ground, and he extended that approach to most everything else in his life as well. But I had promised Jack that I would try, and so I would. It actually was a good idea. I just wished someone else was making the request.

"Been reading about South Rankin's team in the paper," Dad said after the customary hellos. "Haven't seen any quotes from you, though." He knew I hated not yet being a varsity coach and didn't mind teasing me about it.

I forced a laugh, not in a joking mood. "Very funny. Maybe you've been reading the wrong paper."

"Your time will come, son. Just work hard and be patient." Not the first time I'd heard those words.

"Speaking of reading the papers, how's your investigation going?"

"Which one? You know, we generally have a lot of investigations ongoing at any given time."

I gave an eyeroll into the phone. "Yeah, okay, Amberton is such a hotbed of high crimes. You know which one. The hitch-hiker murder case. The one that I know is keeping you up at night."

"What makes you say that?"

"Because I know you. It's not every day that there's a killing in McKinley County. And I've been hearing about the investigation a little, from my friends at *The Amberton Advocate*. From when I worked summers there in college."

"To answer your question, it's going okay. Not many leads just yet."

"Didn't I read it was up in Sandy Hollow?

"Between Amberton and Sandy Hollow is where they found him."

"Drugged and stabbed?"

"The first part of that has not been confirmed. Still waiting on autopsy reports. Where did you hear he might have been drugged, anyway? That's not in the press."

"I have my sources, Dad."

"Your mother has a big mouth sometimes." His words were sharper than his tone. He wasn't angry. Mom had shared things with me over the years that she probably shouldn't have, but Dad knew I could keep a secret.

"Has to if she wants to get a word in edgewise with you." We both knew that wasn't true. My father was nothing if not a proponent of the adage about it being better to keep your mouth shut and be thought a fool than to open it and remove all doubt.

He laughed. "Well, anyway, we'll see what turns out on that case. But I know you, and I know that's not why you called. What's on your mind?"

"Dad, there's a problem with Jet. He may need your help."

"My help? I heard he passed out or something, but what's he need from me?"

"You're not gonna believe me when I tell you."

"Try me."

"This is strictly confidential. Only a few folks know."

"Keeping secrets is kinda part of my job, you know. Lips are sealed. As long as it's not criminal."

"Well, it's not criminal. Not for him." I paused, not sure how to say it. I decided just to get on with it. "Jet thinks he saw Adam."

"Adam who?"

"His brother Adam."

"Son, you're not making any sense. Just spit it out."

"Jet thinks Adam's body was in the Gross Anatomy lab. That somehow the body in the crash wasn't Adam, and instead he wound up at the university. As a cadaver."

After Dad made me repeat myself, he was silent for several seconds. "Oh, wow. Bless his heart, Jet's such a good kid. He's been through a lot the past few years."

It was the reaction I expected. Same one I had, that I was fighting to suppress. "I know, Dad. I know. It makes no sense, but—"

"It should be easy enough to prove to him that it isn't Adam."

"It's not that easy. The cadaver—the one he thought was Adam—it disappeared."

"Disappeared? Wow, he's really messed up. You want me to talk to him? He has to know the truth, deep down, but maybe I can reassure him. Or, I can make some calls, see if I can help find a reputable psychologist there in Jackson?"

"Well, let me ask you this. How do you know it was Adam? In the accident."

"Let me think a second. It's been awhile." He paused. "Okay, it was Jet's truck, and we know Adam borrowed it. Maggie identified what was left of his belongings. Clothes burned up, but some of his wallet was left. He had a money clip, a watch. Adam's shoes didn't burn completely either."

"Did y'all run dental records, DNA?"

"No, son, we didn't. There was no sign of foul play. No reason to suspect anything other than him falling asleep at the wheel. We offered, but his family didn't see the need, and the coroner didn't require it."

"So you can't say for sure it was Adam."

"Case, what is going on here? You remember what happened last time you played detective."

I bristled at the insult. When we were teenagers, Jack's stepfather had disappeared, and Jack and I got in quite a bit of trouble trying to figure out what happened on our own. I had actually helped my father solve a cold murder case in the process, but he always chose to forget that part. "Yes, Dad, I remember. I'm not playing detective. Just helping a friend."

"What makes you think the help he needs isn't just some intense counseling?"

"Maybe it is, but I think I should give him the benefit of the doubt. I called you because there's one thing you can help him with that will settle it, once and for all."

"Case, I know what you're thinking, and the answer is no."

"C'mon, Dad. This is important. Jet is gonna flunk out of school if we don't help him settle this."

"I doubt that. Jet's never flunked anything in his life. But what are the school administrators saying?"

"They're pretending that Jet was hallucinating or something. That nothing happened."

"And don't you think that's telling? That Jet is the only person who believes it?"

Now I was getting mad. I was as skeptical as anyone, but for some reason, hearing my father disparage Jet's sanity made me want to defend my friend. Kind of like brothers. They can say whatever they want about each other, but someone else better not unless they want to get slugged. "Look, Dad. It's more than just what Jet says he saw. We found out Adam was in some kind of trouble. He had been threatened. Jack and I did some checking around, and—"

"Then you are playing detective again."

"Forget it. I'm just saying, if Jet says he saw a flying elephant with purple bat wings, then I think I should believe him until proven otherwise. Isn't that how you treat people in your job, Sheriff? Innocent until proven guilty?"

He huffed. "No, that's the attorneys. Everybody's guilty until I prove they're not or the D.A. says she can't make the case."

"Fine. Do it as a friend, then. You know Jet would do anything he could to help me. And you, too, for that matter." The line was silent for several seconds. "Dad?"

"I'll ask Judge Aycock about the chances for a court order to exhume the body. Only because Jet is your friend."

"Wow, Aycock is still there? He was old a long time ago."

"Still there. Ornery as ever. Listen, Case. No point in mentioning what I'm doing to Maggie yet. I'm assuming she knows? No point in getting a mother more upset than she already is."

"You think the judge is going to say no, don't you?"

"We'll see."

TWENTY-FOUR

J ET couldn't bear the thought of Gracie being mad at him. Was she angry at him or the situation, whatever that was? Either way, surely sleeping on it had cooled her down. He wondered if she might call, yet somehow knew that was a false hope. But he wasn't about to call her, either. He couldn't stand the thought of her not answering and him wondering if she was just avoiding him. That equivalent to rejection was too impersonal to him. If he was going to go down, he wanted to do it eye to eye. He had to go see Gracie, and he knew where she'd be.

The Palmer Ridge Tennis Park offered just what its name implied—eight tennis courts and a park complete with a playground and walking track. As far as Jet knew, Gracie didn't play tennis, but from hearing her talk, she loved that walking track. Every day, seven in the evening, a 4.8-mile wind-down before shower and supper and studying.

He'd only come with her once, two days before. She had encouraged him to join her, but he knew he couldn't keep up. Rapid bipedal movement was not among his arsenal of talents. He had always been a far cry from fast on his feet, and that was before he'd been run over by a car by VJ MacIntosh.

So he had leaned against a beech tree and watched her for the entire hour. He liked the way she held her head high, shoulders back, proud, with long, confident strides. And without a doubt, she looked good in the spandex shorts, too.

But that wasn't the best part. It was the understated smile she gave him each time she passed, shaking her head as if to say, "I'm glad you're here, but don't you have anything better to do?" He could watch that a hundred times.

Today he wasn't sure if he'd get the smile or not, but he settled against the same tree he'd partnered with before and waited. And hoped. He didn't have to wait long. Less than five minutes, and there she was, approaching from his right, two hundred feet away. He strained to read her expression, hoping to catch her reaction the moment she saw him in case she tried to mask her feelings afterward.

Her face was obscured by shadow, though, at first. The muted light from a cloudy day was even more scarce on that part of the track, where the live oaks were more prevalent and the canopy from their sprawling limbs and thick foliage blocked the seepage of light onto the earth below. That, and the way the tall privet hedge lining the park edge cast its own kind of natural shadow.

Jet thought she smiled. He wasn't sure. He tried to hold her gaze, but she looked away into the bushes for an instant, distracted, before turning back toward him. Yes, it was a definite smile. *I'm glad you're here, because we need to talk*, is what it seemed to say. She lifted her right hand to her chest and waved with a cupped wiggle of her fingers. Shy almost, as if she might be chastised for communicating with the spectators during the race.

Jet's spirits soared as she passed on by, now concentrating on the track scrolling beneath her feet, determined, focusing on the task ahead. He knew she wouldn't stop to talk until she had finished all four laps, and that suited him just fine. He would wait for her, and then they would talk.

Jet noted the others using the track. It wasn't as busy as it had had been before, but the clientele was similar. An elderly couple walking a dog of the poodle variety, a forty-something man sporting a pot belly and a grimace suggesting his first exercise in fifty pounds or so, a too-skinny girl who looked like she should be eating instead of trying to run a five-minute mile, two young mothers pushing strollers straight from the corner boutique.

No one paid him any attention, but nonetheless he tried to appear nonchalant, smiling as they passed or just looking away, preoccupied, not a stalker. But mostly he watched Gracie. The second time around the track, as she neared his position from the right, she turned her head slightly to peer into the bushes again, just as she had thirteen minutes before. It was hard to tell in the shadows, but it looked like her eyes widened, and maybe she opened her mouth to say something.

Then she disappeared.

She was literally there one instant, and the next she was not. Her path had carried her behind a tree, and instead of being obscured from view for only a split second, she never emerged from behind it. Vanished, like she'd fallen through a trap door.

Jet jumped to his feet, bewildered and frozen for a split second, trying to process what had happened. Then he ran, if one could call it that, toward the last place he'd seen Gracie. He couldn't believe what he was seeing. Or not seeing. No one was racing, as he was, toward her last location. There were no loud clamors of protest or concern. No shouts for someone to call 911. He quickly realized why. The other walkers and runners were either turned away from Gracie's position or shielded from view by the layout of the track.

No one else had seen a thing.

Then he smiled. Gracie was playing a trick on him. A little mischief, a game of cat and mouse. She must have hidden from him, changing course or maybe even just lurking behind the substantial trunk of the oak, poised to cackle and laugh when he overreacted to her feigned disappearance, chastising him to relax and have a little fun.

But just as quickly as the idea seemed reasonable, it didn't. Gracie knew what he was going through, and while he didn't know what role she was playing in his saga, he thought he could read her well enough to believe that she had ample compassion so as not to take advantage of his heightened sensitivity at this point in his life.

Jet thought his guts might explode through his chest before he got to the spot sixty or seventy yards away, both from the labor of the effort and the fear of what he would find. He wanted to tell himself he was overreacting, but the week's events thus far told him he probably was not. Something bad had happened.

He found Gracie's portable CD player lying on the bare earth to the left of the asphalt track, and his heart sank. The plastic casing was cracked, either from its fall or someone stepping on it. He looked frantically around to see where she might have gone. Then he saw her headphones hanging precariously among the branches of the hedge paralleling the walking surface.

"Hey buddy, you drop your headphones?"

Jet whirled to see the man with the belly stopped behind him on the track, hands on his knees, sucking air. Thick black hair, a dark beard, and dark skin contrasted against a light gray T-shirt with a red, white, and blue bald eagle, although perspiration darkened the shirt at the armpits, neck, and center of his substantial midsection.

Jet glanced at the pink CD player in his hand, then up at the headphones hanging on the bushes. "What? No, they're not mine. My friend. They're my friend's."

The man was fully upright now, heavy breaths slowing in frequency. He looked at the cracked CD player, then to Jet, and back down again. "Where is your friend? I saw you running over here. I was about a hundred yards back, but I saw you running."

"Did you see what happened? She was in front of you."

"Buddy, I ain't seen nothing but the asphalt under my feet. Jogging ain't exactly my thing. But I looked up and saw you running."

"Fine. Do you mind going to get help? She, uh, disappeared. Please hurry. I'm gonna stay here and look for her."

The sweaty man frowned but didn't move. "Where did she go?"

Jet heaved an exasperated sigh. "I don't know. That's what I'm saying. Please, go get some help. I'm telling you something bad has happened to her."

The man must have heard the sound at the same time Jet did. He abruptly spun his head to the left, glaring into the bushes, his frown deepening.

Jet didn't hesitate. He jumped through the hedge, swiping the limb holding the headphones to the side and fighting off a tangle of briars clawing at his arms and face and clothes. He saw nothing at first, but he followed the sound without a pause. The man with the eagle shirt was right behind him. A natural seam in the foliage led them right to Gracie, fifty feet in. The elation at the sight of her was quickly replaced by fear and dread at the sound of her feeble groaning.

"Gracie!" Jet cried, kneeling beside her. "Gracie!"

She was lying prone, face down in the leaves, moaning. Her arms and lower legs were covered in scratches and abrasions, blood mixing with dark earth to stain her cuts and intact skin alike. Her black spandex shorts were ripped on one thigh, and twigs and leaf particles peppered both the shorts and her shirt.

She was moving both her arms and legs, which told Jet she likely did not have a spinal cord injury. At least not so far. "Help me roll her over. She could have a neck injury. I'll hold her head and we're gonna roll her like rolling a log!"

The man hesitated, his uncertainty obvious by the way he started and stopped and scanned his surroundings like his head was on a swivel. After several seconds, he took a deep breath, dropped to his knees, and did as Jet instructed.

"Gracie!" Jet pulled off his own shirt and wiped her face, picking vegetation and other debris from her nose and mouth. "Can you hear me?"

Gracie blinked, then closed her eyes, then opened them. "Jet?"

"What happened, Gracie?"

"Jet, what did you do?"

Jet looked up at the man kneeling at Gracie's feet. "What's your name, sir?"

"Ridley. Amos Ridley."

"Mr. Ridley, will you please go and get some help? I'll stay right here with her."

The bearded man named Ridley stood slowly and turned as if he was heading back toward the park.

Gracie blinked hard, clearly having difficulty focusing as her gaze roamed wildly, occasionally pausing to look at Jet but mostly fixating on nothing. "What? What happened?"

Jet opened his mouth to answer but stopped short when he sensed they were not alone. Ridley had not gone for help. "Please, mister, I need you to go get—" Jet stopped midsentence when he realized why the man had not left.

Amos Ridley held a large stick in his right hand, about four feet long, picking it up and dropping it into the palm of his left hand rhythmically, methodically. Threateningly. "I'm sorry, but I'm not going anywhere, and you ain't, either."

TWENTY-FIVE

"LET me get this straight. You just happened to be there at the park where she was running?"

"No, not exactly. It wasn't an accident. I mean, I knew she would be there. She goes every day."

"So you patterned her behavior?"

Jet took a deep breath and exhaled slowly, studying his interrogator, measuring his words. The officer was shorter than Jet but every bit as thick, and his was from gym reps rather than table muscle. Jet thought maybe the arm holes on the uniform were somehow cut aberrantly small. He eyed the name on the badge as he spoke, to make sure he got the pronunciation correct. "No, Officer Gutierrez, not exactly. We are lab partners, spend a lot of time together."

The officer scribbled onto a notepad without looking up. "And you said you both are medical students?"

"Yes. First year. Started one week ago tomorrow. Listen, can I go in and check on her? I heard them say she had woken up." Jet glanced back anxiously over his shoulder toward the closed door behind him.

"She's with the doctor now. I may have to ask her some more questions myself later."

"Jet! Hey, my man!"

Jet turned back around just in time to catch the high five from a young man in green scrubs and a short white coat. His pockets were stuffed with an assortment of index cards and handbooks and pens, and he wore a gray stethoscope around his neck. His facial hair was long enough to imply he was trying to grow a beard but ungroomed enough to suggest he just hadn't had time to shave lately. Dark circles under his eyes helped make the case for the latter. "Can't get enough of us down here, huh?"

"Hey, Sammy. Just down here with a friend." Jet felt guilty for not telling his roommate about Gracie, since they were friends, too. But for reasons he couldn't explain, he didn't. Protecting her privacy, perhaps. Or, more likely, jealousy about the idea they had dated in the past. He changed the subject. "You look rough, man!"

"Fourth year is supposed to be easy, but these twelve-hour shifts are killing me!" Sammy smiled. "Gotta make time for my lady when I get off, too, ya know." Sammy's smile faded, and he glanced at Officer Gutierrez, who had stationed himself behind Jet and near the door to the examination room where Gracie was being evaluated. Sammy motioned to get the officer's attention, then he pointed at Jet. "This guy is sharp. Crazy smart. He'll be able to help you, whatever it is." Sammy winked at Jet before continuing on his way, asking loudly if anyone knew which nurse had room five because he was going to need some Haldol before things got out of hand.

Jet turned to face the policeman again, hoping to answer his questions before they were asked. "I did some volunteer work down here this summer. Sammy's a fourth-year med student. Showed me the ropes a little bit. You know, the university ER can be a jungle sometimes."

Gutierrez ignored Jet's explanation while he scratched something else on his notepad. He looked up. "Are you and Ms. Tollison romantically involved?" He winked and grinned. "You know—work a little, play a little?"

"No!" Jet exclaimed, more forcefully than he intended. He lowered his voice. "I mean, we just met. But we're friends."

"Okay, take it easy, buddy. Just trying to figure out what happened to your friend."

"I can tell you what happened. Someone yanked her in the bushes and knocked her unconscious."

The officer strained to read the words on a small notebook in the palm of his hand. "I got a statement at the scene from Mr. R—Rip—Rid—"

"Ridley. Amos Ridley."

"Yeah, that's it. Ridley. He says he saw you watching Ms. Tollison, then you took off running toward her. And Mr. Ridley says by the time he got to the spot where it happened, you were standing on the track picking up her broken CD player."

"Well, I guess that's about it, yeah, but you might want to take whatever else he said with a grain of salt. He threatened me with a club and wouldn't go get help."

"How did the CD player get broken?"

"How should I know? She was running, then she disappeared. When I got there, it was over."

"What was over?"

"The attack. Whatever happened. That's what I'd like to find out—what the doctors say happened, and who you say did it." Jet cocked his head to one side and frowned. "Are you thinking I had something to do with this?"

Gutierrez was stone-faced. "We are not thinking anything at this point, Mr. Townsend. Just trying to gather as much information as we can. Can you tell me how you got the blood and briars and scratches?"

Jet looked down at the bloodstains on the sleeve where he had tried to clean Gracie's wounds. He hadn't noticed the brown piece of a briar limb stuck to the lower edge of his shirt. "I tried to wipe Gracie's face when I found her." He carefully picked the briar off and held it between two fingers, looking around for a trashcan. "I ran through some thorns and stuff when I heard her moaning. I was clean before this happened. Ask Mr. Ridley."

"Mr. Ridley says he can't remember what your shirt looked like. He was distracted by the broken CD player you were picking up." He paused for effect. "And the moans of the victim."

"I don't understand—"

"You don't have to. That's my job. Now, just one more question."

Jet nodded.

"Any idea why Ms. Tollison would have said …" He looked at his notepad. "Why she would have said 'Jet, what did you do?' when she regained consciousness, after you arrived with Mr. Ridley?"

Jet's jaw dropped. She had asked that. He had barely even noticed what was surely nothing more than a symptom of the stupor caused by a blow to the head, or whatever had happened. But was there a chance that wasn't it? Why would Gracie have said that?

Gutierrez handed Jet a business card. "Call me if you think of anything else."

Jet regained his composure enough to hold the card up between his index and middle finger and saluted with it. "Will do, sir."

Just then, the door to Gracie's room opened, and a balding man with wisps of gray hair at the temples and black half-rim, brow-line glasses appeared. Jet noticed his white coat was longer than Sammy's had been, indicating he was a full-fledged physician. His age suggested he was the attending in charge.

"Excuse me." The doctor abruptly brushed past before Jet could make out the name on his badge, much less ask a question. He lightly touched the arm of Officer Gutierrez and nodded to the side. The two men took several steps down the corridor before stopping to talk, presumably to ensure they were out of Jet's earshot.

Jet waited until they were deep in conversation before easing open the door and sliding into the treatment room.

Gracie was lying on her back, eyes closed, hands clasped across her waist. The injuries to her face were less severe than they had first appeared, now that the grime and blood had been cleaned away. There was some bruising around her neck that he had not seen before.

"She's resting now." The voice behind and to his left startled him.

Jet turned and was surprised to see Professor Marta Winscote sitting in a vinyl chair in the corner. It took him a second to recognize her without her lab coat, but the round, black-rimmed glasses, tall slender frame, and long brown hair were instantly familiar.

"Doctor Winscote? Why, umm, what are you doing here?"

"Gracie's family lives three hours away and hasn't had time to get here yet. I was afraid she wouldn't have anyone. Didn't know you would be here."

"How did you know she was here, if you don't mind me asking?"

"I've been helping Gracie a little bit. She was supposed to come by the anatomy office but didn't show up. Heard through a friend who works down here that she had been attacked. Do you know what happened?"

"I'm not sure. Somebody attacked her. That's all I know."

"You didn't see it?"

"No, not exactly. I was across the park but couldn't see it. He pulled her into the bushes. I think I got there before he could really do some damage."

"Lucky you came along, then." The anatomy professor turned to Gracie who was mumbling and appeared to be awakening.

"Jet?" Gracie said past squinted, heavy eyelids. "What are you doing here?"

Jet frowned. "I found you, remember? I was there when it happened. You know I wouldn't not be here."

"Retrograde amnesia." Marta Winscote walked to the side of the bed and patted Gracie's arm. "That's what the doctor called it. She can't remember anything from the time she got in her car and left her house until about an hour after she arrived in this room."

Jet searched Gracie's eyes. "Gracie, remember? I was there at the park. Watching you walk. Remember? You smiled at me."

Gracie gave a somber smile then looked away, combing through her auburn hair with her fingers. "I'm sorry, Jet. I'm just blank on that." She pounded the mattress with her right fist and gave a frustrated sigh. She looked up at Jet again and gingerly touched the bruises about her neck. "Who could have done this? They say he choked me."

"It happened so fast. You were walking, and then you just disappeared into the bushes. I ran as fast as I could to get there."

Her eyes diverted to the door, and Jet turned to see two familiar faces in the threshold. "Tuck and Teacakes." Gracie's usual cheerful tone sounded forced. "You came."

"Sounds like a bad name for a band," Jet said.

"We ain't singing no duets, I can tell you that." Tucker smiled. "Gracie, you look like stink."

"Why, thank you, sweetie. I can always count on you to call it like you see it."

"Have they found out who did this?" Tekowski got down to business as usual. "Or why?"

"I have no idea, Tea. Jet was there but didn't get a look at who did it."

"Busy week for you, huh, Jet?" Tekowski said.

Jet had been focused on Gracie, but he jerked his head around and frowned. "What's that supposed to mean?"

"Just seems like a lot of drama, and you're the common denominator. You tell me what it means."

Jet opened his mouth to protest, but Tucker reached out and put a hand over his chest, "Hang on there, Tea. Jet ain't done nothing to you. Let's give him the benefit of the doubt, huh?" He looked back to Gracie. "Did they take anything?"

"I had a little cash on me, but they didn't bother it."

"Robbery had nothing to do with it." A voice boomed from the doorway behind Jet. He had not heard Gutierrez open the door. The policemen stepped into the room and walked to the bedside opposite Professor Winscote. "We're still sorting out the motive, but we have some ideas. Are you feeling better, miss?"

"A little. I'll be better when I can get home."

"Anything come back to you since we talked earlier?"

"Nothing. Still can't remember."

The officer turned to Jet. "I understand you and Ms. Tollison were arguing last night in the anatomy lab?"

Jet appeared puzzled. "Arguing? Not exactly. What does that have to do with anything? Who told you that?"

"Mind telling me what you were fighting about?"

"We weren't fighting," Gracie said weakly. "Jet's been under a lot of stress lately. We, uh, all have."

"Sure, sure. I'm sure you have."

Jet was flabbergasted. What did this have to do with what happened at the park? Had someone mentioned to the officer the events of the week and Jet's suspicions about his brother? He tried to read Gutierrez's face but made no progress. "Who told you we were fighting?"

"Are you denying it?"

"It was a misunderstanding, that's all."

"Okay, so you are confirming what I was told. You were having a disagreement."

"Who told you that?"

"Anonymous call." Gutierrez looked at Gracie. "Ms. Tollison, I'm here to give you some good and bad news both. The good news is, we have a real good lead on your attacker. Judge

Snyder owed me a favor, so we've already executed a search warrant."

"Search warrant?" Gracie said. "Of what? Who is it?"

"I'm getting to that." The officer took a step back and to the side. Before Jet knew what was happening, he felt a wrenching pain like a vise tightening on his right wrist, and it was only when he heard the click of metal on metal that he knew what had happened. "John Edward Townsend, you are under arrest for the assault and attempted murder of Gracie Tollison."

PART TWO

"Envy wounds with false accusations, that is

with detraction, a thing which scares virtue."

— Leonardo da Vinci

TWENTY-SIX

J ET had always wondered if cops really informed criminals of all their rights when they were arrested, or if that was just for television and movies. He knew they were supposed to. He had read about Miranda v. Arizona and knew the background behind the practice. He just figured they didn't really do it. After all, it was the criminal's word against the cop's, right? He certainly never expected to find out firsthand that policemen—or, at least the one who arrested him—really do follow the practice.

Before he had been led across the parking lot and entered the fourth precinct police station, he had already been informed that he had the right to remain silent, what he said could be used against him in court, and he had the right to an attorney, whether he could afford one or not.

It was all surreal. An utter nightmare that he couldn't escape. Gracie had started screaming when Gutierrez had handcuffed him, saying that it wasn't Jet, it wasn't Jet!

The officer had stopped and asked her to clarify, since she had told him minutes before that she couldn't remember a thing and had suggested at the scene that Jet had done something to her.

Gracie grew silent and started sobbing, with Professor Winscote doing her best to console her while the officer pushed Jet out the door.

Tucker had mumbled an encouragement about staying tough, while Tekowski had milked a silent smirk. It got worse when Jet, being pushed from behind by Gutierrez, nearly collided with Sterling Virchow lurking just outside the door.

"What are you doing here?" Jet had asked over his shoulder as he passed. "Shouldn't you be scrubbing the brown off your nose?"

"Med school isn't for everyone, Townsend," Virchow sneered.

Jet caught a glimpse of Gutierrez frowning and shaking his head at Virchow. He suspected they had been talking. In fact, he suddenly believed he knew where the so-called anonymous call came from.

Virchow rolled his eyes and stepped into Gracie's room, and Gutierrez prodded Jet down the hall toward the exit. There, Jet's demands for explanations were met with cold silence as a second officer—presumably Gutierrez's partner—politely opened the door of the patrol car so Gutierrez could fold Jet into the back seat. Jet didn't catch her name, but she was a large, black woman with broad shoulders and thick hips. She was a couple inches taller than her partner, and although she had a pleasant demeanor, her physique suggested she could more than hold her own in a scrap.

Aside from being a little smaller than he'd seen on TV, the interrogation room's layout offered Jet no surprises. A navy vinyl table, four plastic chairs, bare gray walls. He had anticipated a disinfectant smell, a sort of first step toward cleaning up the mess some criminal had made of things. Instead, he smelled cigarettes, which on second thought made more sense anyway. He saw no one-way mirror either, only a camera perched in the corner, spying on him like the eye of Orwell's Big Brother. He tried not to look up at the camera while he waited. He was not a particularly prideful person by nature, but he had enough self-esteem that he didn't want to reveal the fear in his eyes until he had no choice. The shaking was embarrassing enough.

"Can I get you anything, Mr. Townsend?" It was the second officer, head poked through the door. "Coffee?"

"I could really use a Coke."

"Coke it is. Did you get your lawyer on the phone?"

"I don't have an attorney. Called my mom to work on it."

"Good. Be back in a second," the lady said.

The door had barely closed when it opened again. This time it was Gutierrez. He sauntered in and sat down across from Jet, tilting his chair back and folding his arms across his chest. "What's it gonna be? Wonder all night in a cold jail cell what's going on until your lawyer gets here, all the while the suspicion growing that you have something to hide or otherwise you'd be talking to us, or assert your innocence and answer a few simple questions to clear your name so this thing doesn't drag out forever?"

"You think I'm innocent?"

"Doesn't matter what I think. Only matters whether the evidence says. But I'll go ahead and ask. Are you?"

"Of course I am." Jet brought both hands to his head then dropped them emphatically onto the table with closed fists. "This is insanity. Someone's trying to frame me."

"And why would they want to do that?"

"I don't know. Same reason they switched cadavers and put my brother's body at my table."

Gutierrez whistled—high-pitched, drawn out, sarcastic. "Now we're getting somewhere. You may be right. Insanity may be the operative word."

Jet scowled at the man across from him. He looked to be mid-thirties, his features even and well proportioned, not the kind of face that immediately suggested malice. The eyes held a particular darkness though, certainly in color but maybe in disposition, too. It was hard to tell if it was genuine hostility or just part of the job. Whatever the motive, Jet didn't like the way this was going. "I'm not crazy, and I resent you insinuating that I am."

Gutierrez nodded and pursed his lips matter-of-factly. "Fair enough."

The door opened, and the female officer stepped in before Gutierrez could continue. She put an opened Coke can and a chocolate bar on the table. Gutierrez slid them closer to his prisoner. "I see you've met my partner, Officer Weatherspoon. If you think I'm tough, you ain't seen nothing. I'm a gerbil compared to this wolverine."

"Shut up, Sambo." She half-smiled. "Are you harassing this boy?"

"Naw, we're just shooting the breeze. He's trying to decide whether to talk to us now and get it over with or wait who-knows-how-long for his momma to get a lawyer down here."

Jet gulped down the drink while he studied his captors, then brought the empty can hard down on the table and watched it teeter until it settled without tipping over. "I'll talk a little." He knew he should keep quiet but couldn't bear not knowing what was going on. He figured he was smart enough not to walk into a trap.

"Okay, then," Gutierrez said.

"Just know we're not for you or against you," Weatherspoon said. "The only side we take is that of the truth. Now, can you tell us what you were doing at the Palmer Ridge walking track today?"

"I went to talk to Gracie."

"About what?"

Jet contemplated his answer. Some things were best left unsaid at this juncture. "About the usual things friends talk about. I was bored."

"Did you follow her?" Gutierrez asked.

"No, I just figured she'd be there. She's walked there every day this week."

"How long have you two known each other?" he continued.

"A week. We're Gross Anatomy partners. But you already know that, don't you?"

Gutierrez ignored the last part. "And how would you characterize your relationship?"

"I'd say we're becoming friends."

"Is that it? Pretty intense argument last night for two friends, I'm told."

This was the part where Jet wanted to spill his guts and tell about his brother. About what was surely Adam's murder and now a conspiracy to ruin his own life for reasons he couldn't fathom.

But he had seen the look on Gutierrez's face when he mentioned it earlier, and he knew further discussion of such a farfetched tale would only engender suspicion at this point. He had no evidence. But he would get it if he could get out of this new mess. So he chose not to comment on Gutierrez's characterization of his and Gracie's meeting at the anatomy lab the night before.

Maybe if he could figure out where the information came from it would help him make sense of it all. He suspected Virchow, but maybe it wasn't. Either way, he wouldn't get that answer here. So he stared straight ahead. Jaw set, silent.

"Let me jump in here." Weatherspoon reached out her hand and tapped the table between them. "Why were you running across the park toward Ms. Tollison?"

"Because I saw that something had happened to her."

"Oh, that's great." Gutierrez slapped his open hand on his thigh and rocked back in his chair. "You saw it? You can just tell us who did it, and we can all go home."

Jet sighed, impatient with the policemen's exercises in sarcasm.

Weatherspoon frowned and waved the back of her hand at her partner. Whether annoyed herself or just playing her role as good cop in this charade, Jet couldn't tell.

"I just knew she had disappeared. So I ran to where I had last seen her. And I was trying to figure out what happened when the other guy, Ridley, showed up."

"Okay, okay," Weatherspoon said. "You were being a good friend and coming to help her?"

"Exactly."

"What made you automatically think something bad had happened?" she continued.

Jet paused, gathering his thoughts. He wanted to ask why wouldn't he think something bad had happened? After all, his whole first week of medical school had been nothing short of a horror show.

But instead, he changed courses entirely. He sighed and slumped his shoulders, not in an obvious way but just enough for his captors to see him as more deferent than they had first realized. Then he eased into a subtle country drawl so natural it appeared to have always been there. "Y'all know I'm just a small-town boy from Amberton. Ever heard of it? About six thousand folks, but I lived out on the edge, so I'm really just a country boy at heart. All I ever heard about was how much crime there is in the big city, so I've been a little nervous ever since I moved here. Jumpin' at my own shadow. Whole time I was runnin' I was tellin' myself I was overreactin', but looks like maybe not."

Jet went on to explain exactly what had happened—from the moment he found Gracie's CD player to the instant they had heard her whimpering and exactly how they had found her. And how Amos Ridley had held him at bay with a stick while using his cell phone to call for help.

Gutierrez, who had been rocked back in his chair the whole time, slammed it to the floor. "That's poetic right there. Bless your scared little heart. Maybe I'm overreacting, but let me tell you what bothers me, what would keep me awake at night if not for the fact that we have you here in front of us so you can't hurt anyone else. It bothers me that you have Ms. Tollison's blood all over your shirt, that you have dirt and leaves all over your shirt, and that you have scratches on your arms. All the sorts of things one would get dragging a woman through the bushes. It bothers me that you were seen running in a rage toward Ms. Tollison just before she was assaulted. It bothers me that you were found holding her damaged CD player, which suggests you knew your fingerprints were on it. It bothers me that you tried to get the man who came upon the scene to leave instead of asking him to help you find your supposedly missing friend."

Jet weighed Gutierrez's words carefully before speaking. The humble, country boy approach had been a tactical error. It seemed like a good idea at the time, but he had underestimated Gutierrez, who had seen right through it. It made him look deceptive, but there was nothing he could do about it now. "You know as well as I do that Amos Ridley has already told you he remembers me wiping Gracie's face with my shirt. The fact that he can't remember if my shirt was dirty when he first saw me probably indicates that it wasn't, or he would have noticed. And if you've done your job properly, you've found the place where I entered the bushes and was met with a wall of briars that explains the scratches on me. I'm sure there are some broken branches and my footprints there, and I'll bet they're in a different place than where the evidence shows Gracie was dragged into the woods. And I'm sure you've checked around to ascertain that I'm no idiot, so it should come as no surprise when I tell you that if I was going to go assault Gracie in broad daylight with joggers and walkers all around, I would most certainly not run back into said broad daylight to fiddle with a CD player that would in no way incriminate me if found. My fingerprints on it? Considering I've been with Gracie all week and we came to the track yesterday, I'd say that yeah, there's a good chance my fingerprints were on that CD player somewhere."

Jet had never touched the CD player before to the best of his recollection, but they didn't have to know that. "And last but not least, if you search my truck as thoroughly as you've searched me, you'll find that I don't have my cell phone with me. So I had no way to call for help. And since I am a certified CPR instructor and had no way to know that Mr. Ridley had a cell phone, I thought it made the most sense for me to stay with Gracie while he went for help."

Gutierrez tried to hide his surprise, but Jet knew his words had found their mark. His eyes had widened a millimeter or two with each point Jet made, then narrowed back each time to their baseline squint.

Weatherspoon looked amused, turning to Gutierrez with a hint of a grin suggesting she was ready for round two. Bring out the popcorn. Jet knew a second round was coming, too, he just didn't know how to prepare for it. He remembered Gutierrez's conversation with the physician in the ER, how shortly thereafter things had gone from a business card and "call me if you think of anything" to "you're under arrest." And what had Gutierrez meant with his comment about a search warrant?

A knock on the door interrupted Jet's thoughts as a round man in a gray suit stepped in. He wore an untucked, white polo shirt beneath his jacket, black shoes with white socks. His gray beard was reasonably well-groomed, in stark contrast to a wild mop of darker hair and bushy eyebrows that curled up on the ends like wisps of smoke, all overshadowed by a globular nose with a violet gray hue that, under the fluorescent lighting, appeared to match his suit.

"Albert!" Gutierrez said. "What a nice surprise! This keeps getting better and better!"

"Save it, Sam," Albert replied. "Why are you questioning my client without me here?"

Gutierrez gestured toward Jet. "Ask him. His choice."

Albert looked to Weatherspoon, who nodded. "He speaks the truth, Albert. Good to see you, by the way."

Albert turned to Jet and reached out a hand. "Albert Roesink, attorney. Your mom called. I'll be your legal counsel."

"I'm sorry, I've never heard her mention you." Jet reluctantly shook the man's sweaty hand. It reminded him of moist pizza dough.

"That's because she's never called me before. Guess she didn't have an attorney she trusted. Or wanted. Plus, I'm easy to find. You may have seen my ads. 'If you're in the clink, call Roesink.'"

Jet didn't know whether to laugh or cry. He thought he saw Weatherspoon fight back a snicker. The look on her face resembled a snapshot of someone witnessing a car wreck they feel guilty about wanting to watch.

"I need to catch up to speed here," Roesink said. "I need a word with my client." He pointed to the door. "In private."

"No, I'm good," Jet said. "Let's get this over with."

"Hmmph." The attorney was visibly displeased but not enough to press the issue on a Sunday night. "That's your call. Okay, John, you don't say a word without my approval, okay?"

"Okay. But it's Jet."

"Pardon?"

"Jet. Everyone calls me Jet."

"Enough of the pleasantries," Gutierrez said. "Your client was just explaining to me how I should conduct my investigation. And I was about to explain to him how suspicious it is that the victim was injected with—hold on." He reached into his shirt pocket and pulled out a scrap of paper. "Injected with a drug called midazolam. It is a sedative that apparently causes amnesia. Funny thing is, they use it to sedate patients for procedures for that very reason. So they can't remember what happened to them."

"So?" Roesink said.

"So, Mr. Townsend, why don't you tell your attorney where you've been volunteering in the weeks prior to starting med school?"

Jet looked at Roesink, who nodded. "In the ER at the university hospital. It's no big deal. A lot of people do it before they start medical school. My lab partner, Tucker Oliver, told me he worked some in the surgery department. I think Gracie said she volunteered at the children's cancer center. So what?"

Gutierrez dangled the piece of paper between two fingers. "And Albert, you'll be mortified to know that midazolam is commonly used in ERs all over the country to sedate patients for procedures and such. Seems like more than just a coincidence, don't you think?"

"No, I don't think," Roesink said. "I mean, I do think, but I don't think that. You know what I mean."

Jet cocked his head slightly in disbelief. "That's not evidence."

Roesink gently grabbed Jet's arm and tried to whisper something in his ear, but Jet was having none of it.

"I've got this." He waved his attorney away. "Let me work through what you're suggesting. I was about seventy-five yards away when I saw Gracie disappear. Now I'm really slow on a good day, and severely hobbled on a bad one, somewhere north of seven seconds in the forty-yard dash I'd say, and the terrain wasn't flat, so it took me at least fifteen seconds to get there, probably more. But we'll say fifteen. That helps your case.

"Amos Ridley said he was a hundred yards farther back on the track, and he was jogging. So let's say Amos runs a fifteen-minute mile. It might be faster. He'd probably tell you it is, but we'll say a fifteen-minute mile, because that helps your case, okay? At that pace he'll cover two yards per second, which means he'll cover a hundred yards in fifty seconds. Okay? And we'll say he didn't speed up when he saw me take off running, because that helps your case again, and because, well, have you seen his spare tire? Bigger than mine. Looks like it would fit a Mack truck. And he looked like he needed oxygen when he got to the scene, so I'm not sure speed up is in his repertoire.

"So anyway, he sees me take off running, it takes me fifteen seconds to get there, him fifty seconds. Now do your math—that leaves thirty-five seconds for me to make this happen. Now, remember, she was found about fifty feet back in the bushes. If you figure someone could drag a person three feet per second—and I'm not sure I could do it that fast, by the way—it would take at least fifteen seconds just to get her to the spot where she was found. Now remember, I've only got thirty-five seconds. Have you seen me walk? It's not like I limp this way because I think it looks sexy.

"Yet you're saying that while short of breath from running full speed for a distance equivalent to three fourths of a football field, I could overpower Gracie without her screaming for help, drag her into the bushes, inject her with midazolam, walk out of the bushes, and be standing there inspecting a CD player, all in thirty-five seconds? Is that what you're telling me?"

No one said a word for several seconds. Jet could see the officers trying to do the math in their heads. He glanced over at his attorney, who didn't look like he was doing anything in his head.

"My thoughts exactly," Roesink said finally. "If there's nothing more, we'll be going now."

Gutierrez held up his pointer finger. "Hang on there. That's some fancy finagling of some figures, but you forgot one thing. What's to say you didn't attack her some time earlier, then came back and staged it, pretending you were watching her, that you ran over to try to save her. Put her CD player out like it had just happened."

Roesink coughed. "You don't have to answer that, John. I think you've said enough."

Jet waved his attorney back again. "Tell you what. I know ol' Amos isn't going to be able to help you much on this one, but have you interviewed the other folks who were using the park today?"

"Yes, we did. If you'll recall, while the ambulance was loading Ms. Tollison, we asked if anyone had seen what happened. Mr. Ridley was the only one who said he had."

Jet rubbed his chin while he thought a moment. "You asked the wrong question."

"Excuse me?" Gutierrez glared at Jet.

"You asked if anyone had seen what happened to Gracie. You didn't ask if anyone had seen Gracie."

Gutierrez huffed and turned to look at Weatherspoon for her input. "He has a point." She turned to Jet. "But it might take a long time to figure out who was there. A lot of people use that park."

"Not hard at all," Jet said. "Two mothers pushing fancy strollers. No doubt drove the Volvo that was parked beside my truck. Sign in the back window said Baby on Board. Gracie passed them on her first lap. I know they noticed her, because they whispered something as she passed. You know, how women will do. No offense."

"None taken," Weatherspoon said. "But do you expect us to comb the city of Jackson looking for mothers with Volvos just because you suggested it?"

"No, I don't. Just look up license plate MK5U48."

Gutierrez threw up his hands with a you-gotta-be-kidding expression. Weatherspoon gave the bring-out-the-popcorn look again.

Jet shrugged. "I have a good memory."

Roesink jutted his thumb toward Jet. "He has a good memory."

Gutierrez glowered at Jet for a moment, saying nothing. Then he broke into a mocking smile. "You're pretty sharp, I'll give you that. But not that smart. There's evidence you don't know about."

Jet didn't know what the evidence was, but he knew where it had come from. Or, he had an idea how it had been obtained; Gutierrez had mentioned something about a search warrant. He lacked even a vague notion of what could have been found linking him to Gracie's attack, but nothing would surprise him at this point. "I'm listening."

"We searched your house," Gutierrez said. "Just a couple of hours ago. And guess what we found?"

"Quit your games, Sambo, he ain't guessing. Just spit it out," Roesink said.

"Your client is the one with the games." Gutierrez picked up something from behind him and set it on the table between them.

"A box of garbage bags?" Jet said.

"Not just any garbage bags. Heavy duty contractor bags, a full three millimeters thick, a nice greenish-black color that I've never seen before. And guess what? This box here is missing exactly one bag."

Gutierrez stood up, pulling one folded bag from the box and opening it up while he talked. "And we just happened to find an exact match for that bag near the crime scene. Isn't that nice? A perfect tool for draping over someone's head to suffocate them and keep them silent all at the same time while drawing the opening tight around their neck for an added effect."

He pulled the bag over the back of his chair in one fell swoop, crossed his hands to grab the plastic flaps, and then yanked his hands apart with a slashing motion to close the mouth of the bag around the chair. He tipped the chair over backward with a jerk and suddenly backpedaled across the small room, dragging it, helpless, with him. "Very effective, don't you think?"

Jet tried to process the demonstration he'd just seen and the significance of the officer's accusation. "Those aren't my trash bags. Never seen them before in my life."

"Don't say another word, John. Sambo, that's circumstantial at best," Roesink said.

"Circumstantial, huh? Well, what about this?" Gutierrez pulled a clear plastic bag from his pocket and slapped it on the table. It contained a vial of midazolam, a syringe, and two or three needles. "As your client has pointed out, I'm just a little slow on my arithmetic sometimes. So maybe he can help me calculate this: what are the odds—and I'd love a number if you want to do the fancy math—that we would just randomly find these at his house immediately after finding an exact match near the crime scene?"

TWENTY-SEVEN

wasn't sure what I was seeking or what he would tell me, but I had to talk to someone. The walk from the school's main complex where my classroom was to Coach Marchianti's office in the football field house was a quarter of a mile, down a gravel drive that fanned out like a rocky delta into a sprawling parking lot behind the visitor's bleachers. I could have driven, but the walk was therapeutic—I needed to blow off some steam by either burning calories or screaming. The former was better for job security. I tossed rocks as I walked, watching them skip erratically as they collided with their resting cohorts.

Coach's office was the command center from which he pretended to launch ride-alongs with drivers' education students, but where he mostly had them drive around the parking lot while he watched film or talked football on the phone or discussed schemes and alignments with the assistant coaches who wandered in and out. Football at South Rankin High was king, and whatever Coach decided to do during the day would be his business, as long as he won.

I was teaching a full load with six English classes, so unlike many of the other coaches, I stayed in my classroom during my planning period most days. But today was not most days. I had to get out. I had to talk to Coach, and not about football. Jet was in jail, and Judge Aycock had denied the exhumation request. I wasn't sure how the two were tied together, but they seemed inextricably related, and receiving the two phone calls less than twelve hours apart had been disconcerting to say the least. Toxic to my idea of justice's place in the world.

I didn't know what I expected from Coach Marchianti, but I respected him as much as any man I had ever known. Second only to my father, I supposed. Coach knew a lot about football and a little about everything else. Maybe he could help me make sense of things. Or just listen while I vented.

Unfortunately, Dad hadn't offered much in the way of advice, or even consolation. He was at least respectful enough of my concern for my friend to call me as soon as he talked to the judge, but beyond that, he was not much help other than to tell me to let the professionals handle things. Whatever he meant by professionals. I suspected he was as concerned as I was about Jet but even more worried about me sticking my nose into places I shouldn't. His apprehension regarding the latter was justified.

The smell of the field house was a familiar welcome. Jet once told me that about a quarter of the population finds the odor of a skunk to actually be appealing, and I supposed the aroma of sweaty equipment and soured shoes has a similar effect for some folks. I am one of them. Whether it is the associated memories overpowering the nose's natural aversion or it is a genetic variant like that of skunk-likers, I'm not sure. But as I walked in the front door, I took a deep breath as I always do.

I thought it odd that the head coach's office was so close to the front, but there it was, first door on the left. Perhaps some former coach wanted to be the sentry, screening all comers before they wandered through his castle. Or maybe that's just the way it fell on the blueprint and nobody questioned it. Either way, Coach Marchianti didn't seem to mind.

"You know how to do it. Circle the football field a few times, then hit several loops around the back of the bus shop and come back and check in with me before you go back." A skinny teenage boy with a mop of black hair and scraggly excuse for a goatee emerged from the office doorway, nodded, and caught the keys tossed to him. "And don't hit nothin' or you'll wish you'd never even thought about ever tryin' to drive."

"You're supposed to be teaching them how to drive." I tried to sound carefree as I entered and spun around the doorframe into Coach's office. Legal pads and stacks of VCR tapes, neatly arranged by team and season, covered a cherry desk. One wall sported a collection of various coaching awards, framed and arranged just so by Coach's wife despite his protests. A chalkboard covered with X's and O's and lines with arrows hid the opposite wall.

Perched lonely over his desk was a single framed print, a faded caricature of all the original mascots of the Southeastern Conference, posed as if for a family photo. I remembered him having that print in his office at Amberton and had wondered several times why he brought it with him. One day I would ask. Today, though, I had more pressing questions running through my head.

"Driving a car is like riding a horse," Coach growled, crossing his massive forearms across his chest as he leaned back in his leather chair. "I can tell you all day long how to do it, but you just gotta saddle up and climb on if you really wanna learn how to ride."

I smiled. His gruff demeanor masked a heart of gold. He would accompany the boy on the road once he had the parking lots mastered, intimidate and distract him at every opportunity to make sure he could handle himself under duress, then only when the boy had demonstrated himself to be a more-than-capable driver would he pat him on the back with his mitt-sized paw, wink and grin, and insist that even though he was likely to wrap his vehicle around a tree or flip it into a pond, further instruction would make no difference. And the boy would love him for it. He treated girls the same, and they loved him, too.

"What you doin' down here, Coach Reynolds? Ran out of books to read? Or write?"

"Ha ha. You'll see my books on the shelf one day."

"You're prolly right. You usually keep shootin' until you hit where you're aimin'. Seriously, though, I can read it in your eyes. Got somethin' on your mind." He pointed at a cracked leather couch against one cinder block wall.

I sat, knowing it hadn't been a request. "Just had to get out and walk a little is all."

Coach Marchianti uncrossed his arms and leaned forward in his chair. His royal blue polo shirt with the interlocking SR on the chest stretched over his bowling ball deltoids. He wrinkled his brow, pursed his lips, and gestured in the air between us with the curl of two fingers and a wrist. I knew what he meant. *Spit it out.*

"You know me too well."

He didn't answer. Waiting. Coach wasn't a small talk kind of guy.

"Something funky is going on with Jet, and I can't figure out how to help him."

"Never knew that boy to need much help. Smarter than all Amberton combined."

"I know. Started medical school a week ago. But some things have happened, and nobody can explain them." I paused, but he only nodded. "You know Adam was killed in that bad wreck last October. Remember, the Friday night of homecoming? Burned up in Jet's truck."

He grimaced and shook his head. "Yep, that was horrible. Thought an awful lot of that boy. Darn good linebacker in his day."

"Well, Jet is convinced that somehow Adam's body found its way to his cadaver tank." I went on to tell him what Jet had told us, how we went to the anatomy lab and found no sign of Adam, how Jet's classmates acted as if nothing had happened. I explained how I'd secretly hoped to settle it by exhuming Adam's body if it was there but struck out with the judge.

I expected Coach's reaction to resemble mine and everyone else's in one form or another—incredulity mixed with pity. He showed neither. "You sound skeptical."

"Coach, who wouldn't be? I want to believe Jet, but there's no evidence of it, and it seems impossible."

He palmed his square chin, pondering, and I could hear the rustle of thick black whiskers from his half-day beard as he rubbed it. It was a slow, contemplative rub, much different from the frenetic ones I'd seen so many times on the sideline as he deliberated a play call. "You know, my daddy was a state senator once upon a time. I never was interested in going into politics myself, but I got just enough of his blood in my veins that I always kept up with it a little bit."

"Okay."

"So, I know you were just a baby in the early seventies, but what do you know about Watergate?"

I raised my eyebrows, trying to recall what I knew, skeptical about its relevance. "It was the scandal where President Nixon resigned just before he would have been impeached. For his staff breaking in and bugging the offices of his political opponents, that type of thing, then trying to cover it up. I think there were some tape recordings that proved it?"

"Yep. Ever heard of Martha Mitchell?"

The name was only vaguely familiar. "Heard of her. Can't remember why."

"Martha Mitchell was the wife of Nixon's attorney general. She was a big personality at the time. Southern loudmouth from Arkansas or Alabama or somewhere. Pretty likable but rumored to sip the sauce a bit too much." He simulated a drinking motion with one hand. "She tried to tell the media and others what was going on, even claimed that she was drugged and locked in a hotel during the Watergate break-in so's she wouldn't spill the beans. But no one believed her. No one. Even her shrink thought she was mental, a real head case. And guess what?"

"She was telling the truth."

"Yep. Later was proven right about most of it. What's the word? Vindicated? No one's been able to prove the part about her being drugged, but many think there's a lot more reason to believe it than not. Anyway, I read somewhere a few years back that some psych doctor described what he called the Martha Mitchell effect, where a person's shrink don't bother to look for the truth and just assumes a person is crazy because what they're saying don't make sense."

Coach's eyes searched me for a response, measuring my take on what he'd said in the same way he might size up a player's mental toughness or will to win. I wasn't feeling mentally tough and had no idea what winning even meant for this event. "I don't think Jet is delusional," I said finally.

"So he's telling the truth?"

"I didn't say that."

"Well there ain't much middle ground, son. Either he's delusional or he's mistaken or he's right. And I'd leave out the middle one, cuz I'd bet dollars to donuts he ain't forgot what his brother looked like. Plus, he ain't been mistaken too many times in his life that I've heard of."

"What are you saying?"

"Mitchell was a loudmouth and a drunk. Is Jet?" The implication was clear. She had reason for others to doubt the veracity of her claims. Yet she was telling the truth. Did I have any reason to doubt Jet? Before I could respond, he stood up, crossed the office, and grabbed a Bible from a stubby bookcase in the corner. "You still read it?"

"Less than I should."

"Proverbs 18:24." He tossed the Bible to me. "Read it."

"'A man of many companions may come to ruin, but there is a friend who sticks closer than a brother.'"

Before I could comment, he continued. "You remember homecoming, when y'all came home, right?"

I nodded. "That was the night Adam was killed."

"Yep, I guess it was. Remember the story I told about my father in the war?"

I nodded again. I remembered it vividly. He had spoken of his father's friends in World War Two who had sneaked back against orders into enemy territory to rescue him—wounded and bloody and nearly frozen, but alive—despite the fact most thought him likely to be dead.

"Now, let me ask you this? Did his buddies have any guarantees that he was alive?"

"No sir."

"Yet they were willing to deal with the consequences, whatever they turned out to be, because they thought that much of their friend. Case, you remember the red circle I asked Slim to paint on the floor that night?" I nodded again as Coach continued. "Well, I distinctly remember you and Jack and your other buddies and my whole team crammed into it. Why did y'all do that?"

"You said get in the circle if we were willing to fight for our brothers and friends."

"Exactly. So now you gotta decide if you're gonna stay in the red circle."

I studied the floor between my shoes as if it held the clarity I sought. A warm flood of doubt and shame and confusion crept up my neck and face. And anger, too. Coach was right. I had been asking the wrong question. The question wasn't whether to believe Jet or not. The question was what was required to be in the circle with him. Sure, Jack and I had been trying to help. We had even driven to the coast to search a storage room and question total strangers. But when the mystery didn't immediately solve itself, I had stepped back out of the circle without even realizing it.

Still, even if I now knew what the question was, I did not know the answer. "Coach." I looked him in the eye. "I get your point. But I don't know what to do to help him now."

He rolled his chair over and grabbed the Bible from my hands. "For starters, you can be his friend and believe him until you have a bona fide reason not to." He licked a finger and flipped some pages again. "Now look at Luke 24." He handed the book back to me and directed me to read the first several verses. "Don't read more into this than I'm intending," he said as I scanned the text, "but when Mary Magdalene and her friends saw Jesus after the resurrection, what did the apostles think when they were told about it?"

"They thought it was nonsense."

"And what did Peter do?"

I stared at nothing in particular on the wall until the answer came to me. "He went to look at the tomb for himself."

Coach shrugged matter-of-factly and turned away to plug a game film into his VCR. "The bell is about to ring. You better get on back to your class." He didn't look up. "See you at practice later."

TWENTY-EIGHT

N a simple world, life's journey would be mapped by expectations and appraised entirely by the degree of their fulfillment. In reality, the sculpture of a life is quite often molded, not by the outcome as it relates to what was planned, but by the response to the unexpected, the never considered. At least, that was the conclusion Jet had reached. He had dreamed of going to medical school for as long as he could remember, and the expectation of that had determined his path ever since. Read insatiably, become high school valedictorian, make Phi Beta Kappa in college, ace the MCAT, apply to medical school early. That should have been enough.

But somehow the unexpected events in his life had more forcibly defined him, where he would go, who he would become. He never expected as a fourteen-year-old to save the life of a friend and nearly die in the process. He never expected to wind up semi-handicapped and in pain more days than not before the age of twenty. He never expected for his mother to get cancer or for his brother to be killed in a horrific accident.

And if that wasn't enough, he certainly could never have fathomed the possibility his brother's body would find its way to his cadaver tank ten months after his death, then disappear with no trace and no one to believe him. And to top it off, Jet had never, ever expected to spend a night in jail, much less do it while charged with the violent attack of a friend. Attempted murder, no less.

Black, lonely nights behind bars lend themselves to all sorts of crazy conjectures and wanderings of the mind. It had been impossible to sleep, less because of the musty spring-loaded cot and snoring inmate next door than because of his tangled thoughts. Like a snarl of line on a backlashed fishing reel, the events of the past week taunted him, daring him to try to continue fishing for the truth without first unraveling the mess already in his hands. He had scoured every recess of his mind, searching for clues to explain the insanity—the insanity others wanted to pin on him but that he knew was not his. It belonged to something else, some confluence of forces around him. To someone else.

He sat up and swung his legs off the edge of the bed, hoping a new position would help him concentrate. The springs squeaked in protest, but the snoring next door didn't miss a beat. Jet tried to think back to what he knew about Adam. According to Anniston, he had been working on a side job, some type of water testing, independent of his work with the DEQ. She didn't know who Adam was working for, much less what the results were, but that must be the key.

Whatever Adam had been doing, somebody didn't like it. Didn't like it enough to ransack his apartment while he was out collecting samples and then to destroy the specimens. Based on the photos from the storage shed, Adam's hard drive was missing for one reason. It had been stolen. So the motive of the break-in and restaurant encounter had been more than just a scare tactic. The perpetrators were looking for something, almost certainly the test results.

Since the hard drive was missing, the question became where else Adam might have stored any test results, if he kept them at all. Maybe the thugs had found what they were looking for on the first pass, but Adam wound up dead, so maybe not. To find the answer, Jet had called and spoken with one of Adam's friends from the DEQ whom he had met at Adam's funeral. It turned out that several files had been stolen from Adam's desk there. The man said Adam had tried to blow it off like it was no big deal, like maybe he had lost them himself, but in what seemed like a slip of the tongue, Adam had mentioned that his apartment had been broken into two days earlier. That confirmed that the thugs hadn't found what they were looking for the first time. Jet asked if a police report had been filed, but Adam had begged his friend not to say anything. He wouldn't say why, other than he was certain he would lose his job if his boss found out.

So who was Adam working for? The answer would surely lead to who had been harassing him. But how would it tie into what was going on now, so many months later? Had someone wanted to halt Adam's testing badly enough to kill him for it? And if so, how could anyone reconcile the nature of his death— a fiery crash—with his intact body showing up a hundred miles away almost a year later?

Fiery crash. Adam had been driving Jet's truck, and a gas can in the back had fueled the inferno that engulfed the vehicle and destroyed its contents, including the driver's body. But Jet didn't have a gas can, and Adam had no reason to put one in the truck. The second call Jet had made after reviewing the storage shed photos was to Adam's hunting buddy, Tuba Hansen.

"Tuba! Hey, this is Jet Townsend."

"Jet, my boy!" The voice was deep, with a resonating, musical quality. Jet had always assumed Tuba was so named because of his body shape or instrument inclinations, but suddenly a more likely explanation was the timbre of his voice. "You doing okay? Med school, I hear?"

"That's it, yep," Jet answered. "Listen, we are just following up on some insurance stuff from Adam's death, and I needed to ask you something." The big voice seemed to have vanished. "Tuba, you still there?"

"Go ahead, man. It's jus' hard to think about is all."

"Us too. Trying to put it behind us. We're trying to figure out why Adam had a gas can in my truck the day he died. You know, he had left his boat and four-wheeler back home in Ocean Springs. I guess maybe it was for your or Rob's four-wheeler?"

Tuba was quiet again for a moment. "You know, it's funny you mention that. My four-wheeler was in the shop that weekend, and Rob didn't have one. I remember because Adam and I had a laugh about how we was gonna get a deer out of that big holler he always liked to hunt in. We always rode the four-wheeler in. Ain't no way to get a truck back in there." His voice tapered off. "Reckon that was the last time I spoke to him. Anyway, I thought about that, just figured it was your gas can. You know how folks just keep 'em in the back of their truck sometimes."

Jet wiped a tear from the corner of his eye. "Thanks, Tuba. It may have been mine, I can't remember. No big deal. Just insurance red tape is all."

Jet had hung up and stared at the phone for several minutes, heart pounding. Someone had set the truck on fire. He had no doubt. He didn't know who or why, but he was certain that Adam had been killed. He just had to prove it. He planned to tell Gracie about it. She would have to believe him and help him understand what was going on. But he had never had the chance.

Jet stood and paced the small cell, trying to keep his bare feet from slapping the tile floor noisily. Another question had crept into his mind, one he couldn't avoid. Back to the break-in of Adam's apartment and the attack at the restaurant. What were the odds that someone had time to wait on Adam to leave, ransack and search his apartment, then figure out that he had gone out into the Gulf to collect samples, and still intercept him at the restaurant to destroy what he had collected?

The answer seemed to be only one of two scenarios. One possibility was that more than one person was involved, so one could take care of the search while the other followed Adam. That certainly made sense, but some things about the other possibility made it seem at least as likely and much more concerning.

First, Jet had difficulty imagining that a team of men was trying to stop Adam—a kid just out of college, certainly no master of the clandestine, taking some water samples for some project nobody had ever heard of. Plus, the whole thing seemed a bit amateur and goonish. There would be better ways for a professional to get the information needed and send a warning other than tossing furniture, stealing hard drives, and carving up dressers, not to mention assaulting Adam and Anniston in broad daylight at the restaurant.

No, Jet knew something about his brother that might be the very explanation for how it had been accomplished. Adam was a creature of habit. Always had been. While he liked to portray himself as wild and carefree, he had always been one to adhere to rigid schedules and routines. Get up the same time every day, work out the same time, eat the same food at the same restaurant on the same day he had last time, that type thing. Jet remembered tagging along with Adam when he had gone for orthodontist appointments in Tupelo as a teenager and making fun of him for insisting on the same appointment time so he could stop at L. Bow's Burger Bar each and every trip.

"Don't you get tired of the same thing every time?" Jet remembered asking.

"If it ain't broke, don't fix it," Adam had replied. "I like what I like the way I like when I like it."

Jet rolled his eyes and appealed to his mother for intervention, but she told Jet that when his teeth were the ones getting twisted and tugged and cemented and wired, he could pick where to eat.

He grabbed the bars of his cell, tightening his grip, embracing the cold of the metal against his sweating palms, welcoming the dispersion of heat from his hands to match that of his feet into the cool floor tiles. Jet figured that if he knew his brother like he thought he did, Adam had probably collected samples at the same time, on the same day of the week, each time—and probably always stopped to eat at the same place. So it wouldn't be hard for someone to pattern him, and thus be able to toss his apartment before waiting for him at the restaurant with near certainty that he would soon arrive.

And that is exactly what bothered Jet. That, and snarky aunts with gambling problems. He needed to talk to Anniston Lewis.

He had some very pointed questions for her, if he could find his way out into the free world again.

TWENTY-NINE

"THIS may be the worst idea you've ever had."

I studied the entrance to Havenrest Cemetery. Wrought iron words arched between two stone columns, suspended above a cracked asphalt drive. The path was blocked from automobile traffic by a steel cable. "That's my line. I suppose you want to propose a better plan?"

Jack killed the engine as he rolled down both of our windows. The hum of a thousand crickets and frogs carried on the thick, sweltering, night air. "No. I personally think this is a great idea, which makes me worry. Yours are usually much better than mine."

I chuckled. "I hear ya. Wasn't totally my idea, you know."

"So Coach Marchianti quoted Scripture to motivate you to break the law?"

"Noooo, he didn't exactly suggest I do this, but he sure put the idea in my head. Point was that I should have faith in my friend and find a way to get to the truth, I guess. It's not like we're gonna hurt anybody, right?"

"I'm with you, man. If this is what we gotta do, this is what we gotta do."

"I have to admit, I have a bad feeling about this."

Jack smiled. "Our history sneaking around in cemeteries together ain't too spectacular. You remember that night over in Point City with Ada Hunsecker and her friend?"

"Hey, don't blame that on me. Ada was supposed to be my date, but you fouled it up."

"Well, what do you expect? You were busy with her friend. What was her name? Suzy? Lecturing her about some nearby Civil War battle or the history of marble or something. And Ada was scared of the Point City Pirate. Remember? Legend was, he wandered the cemetery during full moons, looking for gold buried with the dead."

"One of the dumber stories you ever made up. So you protected her by covering her face with your mouth?"

"Something like that." Jack grinned impishly.

"Her dad didn't appreciate the protection you were offering."

"Yeah, he about ripped my head off my neck before I could get away."

I chuckled at the memory. That was the last time we had hung out with Ada. Her father and his very large friend carrying a baseball bat had strongly suggested we did not want to return to Point City. The feeling had been mutual.

"Just for the record," I said, "that was Jet lecturing Suzy about the history of cemeteries or whatever. I was looking for the ol' pirate's tombstone to satisfy you so we could get out of there."

"Hope you're a better football coach than you were tour guide." Jack turned to lean out his open window. The sounds of the night rose up as if the volume had been turned down before. He looked up and down the dark street.

"I'm glad Jet isn't here tonight."

"Yeah, it'd be too much," Jack agreed. "Hey, it looks all clear. Are we gonna do it or just sit here yapping?"

"Pull around to the back side, and let's jump the fence there. There's an old road behind it where nobody will see your truck."

Jack cranked the truck and repositioned it as planned. A row of cedars along the cemetery's back fence blanketed the vehicle in shadow from the glow of the gibbous moon.

I grabbed two shovels from the back and tossed one to Jack. "Got something to put it in?" Jack whispered.

I produced a gallon-sized zip lock bag from my back pocket.

"Good grief. How much you planning to take?"

"Better too big than not enough."

I think Jack shook his head, but it was hard to tell in the dark. "Let's go. Don't use your light unless you have to."

Jack scaled the chain link fence first, and I tossed our tools to him before following. A swell of clouds crossed the face of the moon as a flicker of breeze cooled my skin. The growing darkness and hint of wind were both welcome changes, the former to hide our movements and the latter to temper both the heat and mosquitoes. "You think Old Man Hunsecker will be here?" Jack whispered.

"I hope your ugly face is the only other one I see here."

"You remember that time we took that tour here in elementary school or something? They told us about that girl who died in a house fire. Legend was she could be seen here at night sometimes, wandering around with her hair on fire, searching for her baby doll."

I shuddered. I had grown to hope that night in Point City was the last time I'd be in a cemetery after dark. Lurking around tombstones to impress girls with our bravado seemed like a ploy from another lifetime to me. "Dude, you're giving me the creeps. Let's just get this over with."

I palmed a shovel and picked my way around several grave markers toward the center of the property to get my bearings. I had not been back since Adam's funeral almost a year before, but I remembered exactly where he had been laid to rest. I had noted that day what an idyllic site it was, near the eastern edge where several ancient oaks just beyond the fence spread their arms across it, hovering over those plots nearest to them in a protective stance while still allowing the afternoon sun to sneak its warming rays beneath them. I could tell Jack remembered, too, as he began walking on a line toward the spot even before I did.

"This is it." Jack flicked his flashlight on and off a couple of times to show the markings on a stone at his feet. "Adam Wilder Townsend. 1967-1993. He won the race way too soon. 2 Timothy 4:7." Jack left the flashlight off and looked up at me. "What verse is that?"

"The apostle Paul said he had fought the good fight, finished the race, kept the faith."

"That's a good one. Adam was a tough hombre but a good guy, too."

"What would he say to us right now? You know, if he could?"

Jack looked off into the moonlit distance for a moment before speaking. "Remember the story Jet told us at the funeral about the time Adam pounded Murphy McElwain for picking on Jet at the swimming pool?"

I nodded.

"So what do you think Adam would say?"

"He'd tell us to do whatever we have to do to help his little brother."

Jack started digging before I finished my sentence.

The execution of the plan proved much more difficult than the idea of it had sounded. We battled stifling summer heat only marginally attenuated by the intermittent breeze, hordes of mosquitoes undeterred by swatting hands, the sting of perspiration dripping into our eyes, and the burn of protesting muscles. Shovelful by diminutive shovelful, pried from the red clay earth by force of foot and back and biceps, struggling to move that originally displaced and replaced by the bucket of a Bobcat excavator and its two and a half tons of digging force.

Even though we had minimal roots to contend with and the soil was likely infinitely softer than it had been when first disturbed ten months before, what I had estimated to take about an hour took us almost three. Three long hours of furious digging, taking turns to rest our aching muscles, catch our breath, and maintain a vigilant watch for unwelcome guests.

Three or four cars passed on the road near the front entrance, each's headlights casting a fleeting revelation across the grounds, causing our hearts to skip a turn as we crouched, muscles taut, primed to flee if so called for. But no one came. The rustle of a coon or cat in the weeds along the fence line, the persistent onomatopoeia of a whippoorwill, and the drone of insects were the only signs suggesting we were not alone amongst the dead.

"I hit something," Jack finally whispered as his shovel met a new resistance. "I think we're there."

My heart rate quickened. We were upon the point of no return. I jumped in beside him and shoveled hastily. The clang against the shovel was surprising until I remembered that Adam's coffin had been steel instead of wood. "We should only have to fully uncover one end of it, right? Don't most have a seam in the middle so we can open just half?"

"It's called a half couch or full couch," Jack said. "Adam's was a half."

I paused to process the information, shaking my head. "And you know this how?"

"Which part?"

"The sofa part."

"Couch. His was a half couch, like most are, so you can open just the end where the head is. It's a standard term. Believe it or not, I actually did learn a thing or two during my stint at Restor's."

Right. This night would not be our first run-in with a corpse. As ironic and unlikely as it would seem, Jack and I both had been in trouble as teenagers for our actions after finding a dead body on a neighborhood farm. We had not only hidden it, but we moved it and kept it secret for much longer than we should have.

I had not forgotten that, nor most of the ensuing consequences, including our date in front of Judge Aycock. Because of extenuating circumstances, he had only assigned us community service, to "foster a more robust empathy for the dying and the dead," he had said. My sixty hours volunteering at a nursing home had been more than a little enlightening, but what had slipped my thoughts was that Jack had been assigned his time at Restor and Sons Funeral Home. I never thought much about it, figured he swept floors and took out the garbage and such, but evidently he had learned a bit of the lingo as a bonus.

"Okay. Half couch." I tried not to think about what Judge Aycock would say should we meet again. And even worse than that, what my father the sheriff would say. I dropped to a knee in the hole to brush dirt away and try to find the edge to pull open. "Gimme a little light." The casket's regal bronze luster had disappeared under the tarnish of time and moisture and red clay, making it difficult to discern with the eye where earth ended and casket began, but I soon had enough soil cleared away to be able to pull open the right side, where I knew the lower half of the body—if there was one—would be. I couldn't bear the thought of seeing any part of Adam's remains after months of decomposition—the thought was already turning my stomach—but I had to believe the lower half would surely be more bearable than the upper.

The eerie amber glow of the hole with its dirt walls and similarly hued metal floor suddenly turned pitch black, with me inside it. The moon was not only too low in the sky for its glow to reach inside the hole, but was now covered by clouds as well, so I could not even see my hand in front of my face. "C'mon, stop goofing around! Gimme some light!" I growled. We had been there way too long, and I was getting more nervous by the second.

I could hear Jack fiddling with the flashlight switch then pounding the metal casing against his open palm. "It died."

"Died? You put new batteries, right?"

"Thought you did."

I moaned. "C'mon, Jack! That was the one thing I asked you to do. What kind of imbecile doesn't put new batteries in the flashlight before digging up a grave?"

"I don't know, why don't you tell me since you're such an expert on this kind of thing?" His voice dripped acid.

I regretted my choice of words and knew they had stung, but I had no time for apologies. I ignored him and dropped to my knees in the blackness of the grave, temporarily joining the light-less gloom of the perished. I shuddered and my heart raced, a surge of what I knew to be one of mankind's primal instincts, a natural fear of one day awakening in a tomb assigned prematurely.

The sudden clamminess of my sweat-soaked shirt and shorts clinging to my skin like a blanket of cold guilt matched the spreading decay in my disposition. Cremation never seemed so appealing as it did at that moment. *I've got to get out of here.* Irrational thoughts of the walls falling in and the hole becoming mine overwhelmed me. I repositioned my feet toward the left end while bending to grab the front right corner of the casket.

"Case, wait," Jack said, as I gave the corner a vigorous tug.

Nothing happened. I grabbed and pulled again, more forcefully, gathering my legs beneath me and wedging my feet against the walls for leverage this time. Again, nothing budged.

"Case! Stop!" The tone of Jack's anxious hiss stopped me cold. "Blue lights!"

I stood up atop the casket, but my heart plummeted as if swallowed up by the dark pit around me. I was tall enough to see out and confirm what Jack was telling me. Blue lights at the front entrance could only mean one thing.

We had been discovered.

Three long hours of hard digging and sweating, and now, just as we had the casket exposed, we were going to get busted. "Help me pull it open. It's not budging."

"Dude, we've got to go. They're coming!"

I peered into the darkness to see if I could spot someone walking our way. I doubted whomever was in the patrol car had a key to the locked cable blocking the road. "We've got time. I just need help pulling it open."

Jack sighed and dropped into the hole beside me. "The problem is, you don't know what you're doing. Even an imbecile knows you need this." He crammed a slender metal object into my hand then pulled it out before I could tell what it was.

"What the—?"

Jack crouched at the right end of the casket, frantically scooping loose soil with his hands and fumbling with something on the edge of the box. "A five-sixteenths hex wrench. Only way to unlock it."

It was my turn to be the imbecile. It had never occurred to me the casket might be locked, but of course it was. Common sense should have told me that. Or at least told me to find out. Apparently, Jack had known it all along and come prepared, but it was too late now. Peeking over the edge of the hole, I could see the beam from a flashlight bouncing across the tombstones, pausing intermittently for closer inspection. I could barely see the silhouette of the person behind it, moving cautiously in our general direction. "There's no time. We've got to get out of here!"

It seemed logical to split up. No sense in both of us getting caught. I hopped out of the hole and sprinted directly toward the light, hoping desperately that the person who held it was neither fleet footed nor trigger happy. Either way, I had no intentions of getting anywhere close enough to get shot. Or caught, for that matter.

I just figured if I had gotten Jack into this mess, the least I could do was lead the law away from him. I put a tree between myself and the light and ran as rapidly toward the person as I could manage in the dark without tripping over unseen obstacles. I could tell by the way the light stopped moving that my footfalls had been heard. Then the light beam jerked suddenly and pointed straight toward me, making a kind of vertical halo around the shadow of the tree. Knowing I had been located, I turned and angled toward the fence that ran along the property's edge.

"Hey! You stop!" a man's voice whom I did not recognize called out. "Sheriff's department! Stop!"

Well, that answered that question. As suspected, this was a deputy with the McKinley County Sheriff's Department. A deputy who reported directly to my father.

I jumped halfway up the fence, grabbing the chain links with fingers like claws, then searching and finding a toehold for my tennis shoes to push and hurl my body over the six-foot structure, my feet never touching the top bar. I dropped lightly to the ground on the other side and melted twenty feet into the dark woods beyond.

Instinct told me one of two things would happen. The deputy would follow, in which case I might be in trouble since he had a light and I did not. Or he would stop at the fence, believing I was headed to the gravel road I knew to be less than a quarter mile through the woods, in which case he would hurry back to his patrol car and try to circle around to cut me off.

I tried to control my labored breathing, hoping the rustle of summer foliage in the after-midnight breeze would cover the sound of it and my heart pounding like a drum against my sternum. I hid behind the trunk of a large hickory and peeked around it, trying to see but listening for the telltale sound of a man scaling the fence.

"This is Unit Four. The suspect has crossed the fence on the west side, likely heading toward Muscadine Road. Will pursue on foot from this side." No! Not what I needed! Someone would be coming for backup. Soon.

I weighed my options. Hunker down and hide, hoping he would pass me by despite him having a light. Make a break for it now and try to get to the truck before he could catch me, hoping my face didn't flatten against an unseen tree on the way, also risking the chance he was some cowboy itching to sling some lead or that he would get close enough to identify the vehicle. Neither option sounded the least bit appealing.

The fence rattled, harsh as if a T-Rex was trying to shred it, but I couldn't make out through the brambles what exactly was happening. I coiled to make a run for it when I heard radio static again. "Scratch that. Will pursue by car." I breathed a sigh of relief and eased out of the cover when I was certain the deputy was sufficiently far away, wondering why he'd had the sudden change of heart.

I carefully but quickly skirted the outside of the fence, circling around the backside of Havenrest to get to Jack's truck. The quickest way for the deputy to get over to Muscadine Road was the opposite direction, but I feared the worst, that he might instead choose to go the other way, bringing him by our parking spot on the access road. As I walked within sight of the truck, I breathed another sigh of relief when I caught a glimpse across the cemetery of the flashing blue receding, then speeding away.

Now I just hoped Jack was okay and not headed straight into trouble himself, wherever he was. I scanned what I could see of the cemetery. Adam's grave was just over a rise and out of sight. I contemplated making a run back to it but figured—and hoped—Jack had long since gone. I hated that he had not made it to the truck himself.

I reached for the door handle, hoping Jack had left it unlocked as we had discussed, in case we had to leave in a hurry and every second mattered. I would just have to drive around as inconspicuously as possible until I found him.

"So, Mr. Reynolds, did that go as you had planned?" A growling, angry voice, dripping with sarcasm.

I jumped and then froze, fighting the feeling of dread that enveloped me.

THIRTY

"THERE'S a funny thing about being Sheriff. You can't help but lose a little faith in people. In humanity in general, really. Listening to that police scanner, day in, day out, all sorts of crazies wreaking havoc in ways that most of us would like to think ain't normal. A daddy beating his kids. Teenager high on crack setting cats on fire. A woman running her momma off the road for sleeping with her boyfriend. And that was all before lunch today, right? What you think about that?"

I stepped away from the truck but said nothing, feeling a sudden urge to toe the loose gravel along the side of the road.

"Answer me!"

"That's weird stuff," I mumbled.

"Makes you wonder if anybody's truly normal." My father's voice grew closer. "But then you think about friends and family and how, for the most part, they rise above that kind of nonsense. They ain't perfect, but if they get in trouble, it's not crazy stuff, you know? But now here's the ironic thing about it all. A couple of weeks ago, if I'd heard my Deputy Turnip call in that someone saw a flashlight out amongst the Havenrest tombstones, I woulda thought it was either a kid goofing around or some weirdo getting his kicks looking for ghosts or something. But not tonight, right? Tonight I knew exactly who it was. Not some kids sippin' Pabst Blue Ribbon they stole from Daddy's fridge or poppin' pills from Momma's medicine cabinet, not even a real-life grave robber hopin' to steal a suit of clothes or Papaw's watch. No, this time I knew it was going to be my son. My grown son. An English teacher and football coach, in the middle of somethin' he's got no business in."

He was beside me now, looking down with me, twisting his boot in the dirt of the access road as if squashing a bug. I hadn't turned to fully look at him yet, but now I could tell he was in familiar civilian clothes. Dark polo shirt, Levi's, his scuffed ropers. Dad raised his head and turned to face me, arms crossed. Two inches taller than me and forty pounds of muscle stouter, he would have been intimidating even without the memories of his belt to my backside. I forced myself to square my shoulders and look him in the eye. "And author."

"What?"

"I'm an author too. You left that one out."

Dad huffed. "Oh, is that what this is? Solve the crime and write, what do they call it, an exposé? Like your first bestseller?" His voice was thick with sarcasm.

I fought to control my tongue. I loved my father, but he had told me more than once I should be focused on real objectives that would pay the bills instead of wasting time writing. The fact that I had never gotten the nerve to try and publish my first novel only reinforced his position. I wanted to shout in his face that yeah, that's exactly what I was doing. That Jet had convinced me to write his story, against my better judgment. That I still hadn't been sure, but now that I knew what I knew, and especially because my father doubted me, Armageddon was about the only thing that would stop me.

I wanted to shout, but I didn't. It wouldn't help matters, and Dad had the high ground. I was at his mercy at the moment. "It was more of an expository narrative. Not an exposé. I'm not a journalist."

Dad grabbed my shoulder. Not a sign of force but a gesture to emphasize the importance of his words. "I want an explanation. What did you hope to accomplish here?"

I shook his hand away and stepped back. "You know the answer to that. Jet's in trouble, and the judge wouldn't give an order to exhume—"

"There's a reason for that." He cut me off. It was dark, but his voice revealed the details of the scowl on his face. "You don't just go digging up bodies—legally—unless you have an airtight reason to. And you don't do it illegal, period. Do you know you can actually go to the penitentiary for disinterment? For up to five years. Do you understand that?"

I nodded, a white lie. I actually had no idea what the punishment was. But knowing wouldn't have changed anything. "Remember that story I told you about Coach Marchianti's father in World War Two? His buddies broke orders to go save him, remember?"

"That's what this about? Trying to prove something, be a hero?"

"No." I took a breath to cool the anger rousing in my gut. Losing my temper with my father had never served me well. "I'm saying you don't understand what is happening with Jet, and his friends may be the only ones willing to help him. He's in jail right now, you know."

"Yeah." Dad's voice softened slightly. "I heard. Makes no sense. But you've got to let that all work itself out, son. The truth will come out."

"Will it? There's no time for that. They're about to kick him out of medical school, may have already. And nobody believes his side of things."

"Do you?"

"I want to." I dropped my head, ashamed to reveal my own doubts. "That's why I'm here, I guess."

"And what did you find out there?" He nodded toward the cemetery.

"Nothing. Got run off before I finished." I deliberately omitted saying "we" but figured it was futile. We were, after all, standing beside Jack's truck.

A voice crackled at Dad's belt. "Sheriff, this is Turnip. Over."

Dad grabbed his radio and answered. "What you got?"

"Suspect escaped, sir. Hopped the fence and headed toward Muscadine. I drove over with a blue light special but got nothing. Headed back to see if he circled the other direction. Over."

"No, Turnip. I've already looked here. You go back to your patrol."

"What's your twenty, Sheriff? Over."

"I'm here at the cemetery. I'm taking care of things here. Go back to your patrol. Got it?"

"Ten-four. Copy that." Dad held the radio at arm's length, shaking his head at it. It crackled again, and he nodded knowingly. "Sheriff, there's a big hole there. Over."

"I said I'll take care of it, Turnip." Dad dropped the radio to his side but quickly brought it back to his mouth before it had a chance to speak again. "And Turnip. I've told you, we're not truckers. It's just you and me. Talk normal."

Silence for several seconds, then the radio crackled again. "Ten-four, Sheriff."

Dad grumbled something unintelligible. Then he surprised me. He laughed. Not a big laugh, just a short chuckle of amused frustration. "Know why the boys call him Turnip?"

"No sir."

"They tell me it's because he's round and turns purple when he runs. Didn't help that his last name is Green. He's a good kid, though."

I wondered what Turnip thought about his handle, and it was my turn to chuckle. "You knew he wouldn't catch me, didn't you?"

"Let's just say chasin' folks down isn't Turnip's forte."

I smiled, but then my thoughts turned to more serious matters. "What happens now?"

He said nothing for several seconds. Weighing his words or a decision, I knew not which. "Case, you remember Stimpy Riggins?"

"Sure. Stimpy worked at the funeral home way back, when Jack did his time there. Was also the McKinley County Coroner, right? Kind of a strange dude, but always nice to me."

"Yes, and still is on all counts."

"We considered questioning him about Adam but haven't yet."

Dad shot me a stern look as he lowered the tailgate on Jack's truck and sat down. "Well, Stimpy has got himself in some trouble. Wife caught him messing with some girl he met at the video store. The missus got mad and aired her dirty laundry.

Word got out, got back to the girl's father, who tried to ram his fist through Stimpy's skull. Stimpy's fine, got a big shiner and a cracked cheekbone, but that's how we got involved."

"Sorry to hear that." I wasn't much interested in the plot of any Amberton soap operas. "Not sure what that has to do with this."

"I'm not either, but I'm not finished telling you. So in the process of figuring out if we could charge Stimpy with statutory rape or whatever, we found more than we bargained for. Some improper visual aids, let's just say."

I hopped on the tailgate beside Dad, intrigued but confused. "Underage?"

"Yep. Now this isn't out in the public domain yet, so I'm trusting you to keep quiet. I'm telling you only because of extenuating circumstances."

"Yes sir." I nodded. No idea where it was going. "Understood."

"Here's where it gets interesting. Stimpy wants to make a plea bargain with the prosecutor, so he spilled his guts, told us all about the girl, but also about something else he hoped might get him leniency. Last September, about a month before Adam died, Stimpy got called out on coroner duty for some homeless guy by the tracks. Wanderer by the name of Belue. Just passing through. Looked like he died of natural causes or maybe a drug OD."

"Okay. And?"

"And his death certificate says he died of cardiac arrest, but no autopsy was done."

"Y'all didn't do an autopsy? So how could Stimpy have known the cause of death without it?"

"He couldn't. Stimpy was blackmailed and paid to leave me out of the loop and to falsify the death cert."

I whistled out loud. "Wow, Dad. That's bad. You think it's related to the death of that other hitchhiker? You know, the one we talked about that was in the papers a couple weeks back?"

"Maybe, Case, but I hope not."

"That would make it, like, a serial killer or something. Did they figure out what they drugged the guy with? You know, the one the other day."

Dad hesitated, but I knew he would tell me. "Between you and me, looks like some kind of souped-up morphine or something. Like a tranquilizer."

"Wow, that's odd. So, back to Stimpy. Who was doing the blackmailing?"

"We don't know. Stimpy never got a look at him. Guy held a gun from behind and threatened to expose Stimpy, maybe even kill him, but paid him five hundred dollars for good measure."

"So it's somebody he knows?"

"Maybe. We're checking every angle. But this is why I'm telling you. The victim was a body donor. His body was sent to the university. To the anatomy department."

"I don't understand. The guy with the gun wanted to make sure the body got sent to Jackson instead of being autopsied?"

Dad shook his head. "Don't think so. Stimpy says he never told the guy that. He just agreed to make the cause of death look like natural causes."

"Did you called the medical school to track it down for an autopsy?"

"I'm working on it. Believe it or not, this just happened Friday. I called today, and they're looking into it, but nothing yet."

"Wow." My head was spinning. I wanted to see how this could all be connected, but it made no sense. "So why are you telling me this?"

"Because I care about Jet, too. I have no idea if this is in any way connected or not. I don't see how it would be, but I've learned over my years in law enforcement that you need to assume nothing is coincidence until proven otherwise. So I'm telling you to be calm, quit doing stupid stuff, and let me sort this out."

A wave of relief washed over me. Finally, someone on Jet's side. If there was a link, my father would find it. Of that, I had no doubt. "What happens now?"

"You hightail it out of here right now. Your only crime so far is digging a hole. It isn't good, but no real harm done. For all the thankless crap I go through in this job, I'll give my son one stupid pass. But that's it. Quit trying to be a cop before you ruin your real career."

"I'm not trying to be a cop. Just a friend."

Dad ignored me. "I'll take care of things there." He nodded again toward the cemetery. "Turnip and I both need some exercise anyway."

"Dad, we really need to know if there's a body in that casket or not."

"Case, stop it. I told you I'm going to look into things, but I'm going to do it the right way. The legal way. Depending on what I find out, I might be able to talk to the judge again."

My mind was spinning, trying to connect the dots. How in the world would this be anything other than coincidence? Or would coincidence be even more unlikely? "Dad, I appreciate this. More than you'll ever know. But you've got to work fast. Jet is in jail and is about to be kicked out of school."

"I know. He'll have his arraignment tomorrow, I'm sure." He paused and looked at his watch. "Later this morning, actually. Judge will set bail, and they'll figure out a way to get him out."

"But they told him he had one more strike and he was out. It won't matter if he's out of jail."

"I can't help that, son. Look, I'll do all I can, but I can't promise anything. It may all be unrelated. First thing next week, I'm going to Jackson to talk to some folks."

I twisted my body toward him. "What? Next week?"

"Yeah, remember, I promised your mother two years ago we'd go on a cruise for our twenty-fifth. She's been a patient woman with me and my job all these years. I owe that to her. It's gonna be awful, but there's no way out of it."

I hopped off the tailgate with an exasperated sigh. "Can't you send someone else?"

"On the cruise with your mother? I'm open to suggestions."

I elbowed him. "C'mon, Dad."

"Not really. Johnston is in the hospital with his gallbladder. Wofford quit last week to take a job with Hackford County. That leaves me with Turnip and Ernie Leaks. And trust me, Turnip is Sherlock Holmes compared to Ernie."

This was terrible. Next week would be too late. My emotions pivoted once again. From being at the cusp of opening the casket and finally answering the question of whether Adam was there or not, to being run off and not only failing the mission but likely getting arrested. Then being given a pass by my father, who even offered to help, to now realizing it might all be futile, at least in terms of saving Jet from expulsion. And there was one more thing. "The press will go nuts if this gets out while you're gone."

"It's not gonna get out. I know, and the district attorney knows. I'll only be gone four days, and she would rather me work the case when I get back than have someone else fouling it up while I'm gone. Stimpy may be lying for all we know. And he knows to keep his mouth shut if he wants any chance of a deal. And now you know."

"So what if it is a serial killer and he's getting ready to strike again? Time may be of the essence."

"If—let me say again—if the two cases are related, it was ten months between them." Dad stood and closed the tailgate. He turned and pointed his finger at my chest. "Don't you get any crazy thoughts, Case. You hear me?"

"Yessir."

"Now go find Jack—I know he's with you—and get out of here. I'll sort this out when I get back."

I found the keys under the floor mat and climbed in the truck. Now to find Jack. We had four days.

THIRTY-ONE

never was much of a Boy Scout. Made it to the rank of First Class or so, got a few merit badges along the way, but never bought in to the whole Boy Scout concept. I fell in somewhere between Jack, who quit after two weeks, and Jet, who became an Eagle Scout. It had nothing to do with the fun parts like camping, hiking, rappelling, canoeing. I actually excelled in those skills. I just had trouble following the hierarchy model, obeying rules set by patrol leaders who weren't much older than me, who sometimes took themselves and their seniority much too seriously.

I'd like to say I completely outgrew my immature resistance to authority, but the fact that I found myself digging up a grave in the middle of the night in direct defiance of a judge's decision not to grant a warrant for exhumation might suggest otherwise. Either way, even though I failed the Scouts, the Scouts didn't completely fail me. My Scoutmaster was a red-faced German named Weisenberg with a spitting jackhammer for a tongue that slipped into his native language when his temper flared, but who nevertheless taught me many things, among them his favorite phrase and the importance of abiding by it. *"Allzeit bereit!"* If I heard him say it once, he said it a hundred times. Always ready! Another way to say, "Be Prepared," the official Scout motto. For whatever reason, the little voice in my head always spoke German when it reminded me to expect the unexpected.

So even though Jack and I were confident we wouldn't be discovered, we were prepared with a backup plan. Now, maybe our plan wasn't MacGyver-esque because we weren't able to make bazookas or time machines out of shovels and bubble gum, but we didn't mind leaving the shovels behind since they were the same kinds as those found at Walmarts everywhere, and untraceable to us. And we had designated a meeting place.

I drove away from Havenrest at a normal pace, trying not to appear suspicious, which of course was superfluous since I'd already been caught. I followed the access road to the back of the cemetery and took a right on Randall Road, a narrow but paved two-lane. A half-mile farther, I let off the accelerator in anticipation of slowing to a stop until I saw flashing blue lights rapidly approaching. *You've got to be kidding.*

As I teetered on the edge of the critical decision of whether to pull over or hit the gas, the deputy's car whizzed past, doing at least eighty. Turnip and his blue light special. I couldn't help but chuckle. Would he be going that fast if he knew my father was about to put him to work with one of those shovels? I would have to make it up to him one day.

I turned around and retraced my path. It was difficult to see the fence line, but the fire lane cut alongside it by the timber company a year or so earlier was easy enough to discern, emerging from the wooded area to my left. Here the road rose several feet above the land on each side, making it impossible from a vehicle to see a human figure snuggled against either embankment. Before my wheels had even stopped rolling, the passenger door opened, and Jack jumped in.

"Took you long enough. Mosquitoes big as vampire bats about sucked me dry."

"Dude, it didn't go well."

"I know you've slowed down in your old age, but tell me you didn't let big boy catch you."

"Naw, worse than that." I paused, dreading to tell what had happened. I could feel Jack's stare on locked on me like a heat-seeking missile.

"Spit it out."

"My father."

"Aww, no. No way. That ain't good. Not good at all."

"Tell me about it. He was waiting at your truck. Turnip, the deputy, he was just a flushing dog. Busted us up so Dad could shoot us down."

"So why ain't you sitting in his patrol car telling them where to pick me up before I get chewed up by the cottonmouths and alligators?"

"There's no alligators this far from the river bottom."

"Whatever. Pretty sure an eight-footer was stalking me. Are you gonna tell me what's up or not?"

"He let me go, believe it or not. Both of us."

"Let us go? Why? Your Dad's pretty reasonable, but you and I both know he don't cut corners much, family or not." Jack didn't have to remind me. The vivid memory of my father diligently but fairly handling the front end of the case when Jack and I had our trouble as teenagers was always close at hand.

I expected Jack to insist I pull over so he could drive his own vehicle, but he didn't. I turned the truck just outside the Amberton city limits and pointed southwest, toward Jackson. A car fell in behind me, and I watched it for several seconds, hoping to satisfy myself that it wasn't a patrol car.

My thoughts swirled as I deliberated on whether to reveal what Dad had told me, but only briefly. Jack had his shortcomings like anyone else, but divulging secrets was never one of them. If I asked him to keep something confidential, it might as well be sealed behind the walls of Fort Knox. "Stimpy Riggins has found himself in some trouble. And it may tie into Jet's situation."

"Holy smokes," Jack said after I had relayed what Dad had shared. "So Stimpy gets caught messing with underage girls and just happens to suddenly remember that someone blackmailed him to cover up a murder ten, eleven months earlier?"

"We don't know it was a murder."

"What else would it be? Guy points a gun at him, threatens to ruin him, and pays him? Somebody's desperate. Had to be a murder."

"Maybe, who knows? And then the body got donated to the medical school. It's just bizarre."

"And doesn't sound like a coincidence. But that doesn't explain why your dad let us go."

"I think he has been thinking this whole time that Jet was having a breakdown or something."

"Sounds like somebody else I know."

I slapped at him with the back of my hand. "You know you thought it, too. But now even Dad's not so sure. Too much of a coincidence, like you said. So he's gonna look into it. As far as the grave digging goes, since we couldn't open the casket, our only crime was digging a hole. So he cut us some slack. Getting soft in his old age, I guess."

"Not entirely true."

"Which part?" I cut my eyes toward him. He was digging in the pocket of his cargo shorts.

"The part about our only crime being digging a hole." Jack produced a wadded-up zip lock bag and smiled triumphantly.

"What's in the bag?"

"No idea. Don't know, don't wanna know. First piece of something I could grab in the dark."

I nearly ran off the road. "Wait. You got it open?"

"Wasn't hard, just gotta know where to stick the hex key. When Rosco P. Coltrane took off after you, I had time to get it open, reach in and get what we needed, lock it back, and hightail it out of there."

"Gimme that." I grabbed the plastic bag from him. Holding it up over the steering wheel with my right hand while I drove with my left, I examined the bag's silhouette against the glow of the truck's headlights. "Looks like a glove."

"Yeah. Dropped my glove and the, uh, specimen, both in there. Wasn't gonna touch either one with my bare hand."

I reached over to turn on the overhead light but thought better of it. Some things are better left unseen. I dropped the bag on the seat between us, fighting a twinge of nausea.

"I know. It's rough. I left my supper back there on the grass. I won't be eating fish anytime soon."

I cringed. "Turnip's day just keeps getting better and better. Dad's too."

"Hey, we all do what we gotta do."

Do what we gotta do. Yeah, I guess that was the truth. I found myself almost disappointed, though, that Jack had succeeded in opening that casket. Five minutes earlier I couldn't help but be relieved. We had tried our best and fallen short but walked away with no repercussions for our actions.

Now the stakes had gone up again. The proverbial Pandora's box—in this case Adam's box—had been opened, and who knew what the consequences would be. One plus was that my father didn't know we had removed anything from the casket. But how to use what we had taken without him finding out? My plan had been to convince Abi to surreptitiously analyze it at the crime lab for DNA, toxins, or whatever it is they do. Anything to help resolve the issue for Jet. But once armed with the results, how would we use them? Maybe I hadn't absorbed Scoutmaster Weisenberger's *allzeit bereit* as deeply as I thought. We hadn't really prepared a plan that far out.

"At least now we know the casket isn't empty," I said.

"It was most definitely not empty."

"You think it's Adam?"

"Gotta be Adam, right?" Jack paused, and the plastic crackled as he fiddled with the bag. "Or maybe not. Truth is, Case, I don't know what to think anymore. I like your plan, though. Get it to Abi, let's see what she finds. DNA will tell if it's Adam, and if it is, case closed. Jet is delusional, poor guy. If DNA doesn't match, then who knows what happens? Abi or Jet will know what to do, don't you think?"

I didn't answer. I was preoccupied with a pair of headlights in my rearview mirror. "That car behind us sure seems close. Been behind us since we left Amberton."

"Don't be so paranoid. You drive like a grandmaw anyway. Prolly just wants to pass."

I slowed down on a straightaway with a broken yellow center line. The headlights behind me slowed as well, with no obvious effort to come around us. "So much for your theory."

"Whatever. Hey, just pull over at that truck stop ahead. I gotta take a leak anyway. If the dude wants to speak to me, I'd welcome the opportunity."

"You know, they probably sell fried fish strips."

Jack faked a gag and laughed. "I'll hold my nose."

I blinkered right and eased onto the brake, coasting into the brightly lit establishment. The car trailing us slowed as if it might turn also, then waited until I had turned fully perpendicular to the road to accelerate and speed on past. It was impossible to tell a make or model on the dark highway, even with the glow cast by the truck stop. Seemed pointless to try, anyhow. "Told you they didn't want us," Jack said, and I nodded.

The sign across the awning read 24-Hour Power. I always thought it sounded like a chain, although this was the only one I knew of. A man replacing the nozzle after filling up the tanks on his fishing boat was the only patron. Who would be going fishing at this hour? Then I glanced at the clock on the radio. It was pushing four a.m. The sun would start peeking over the horizon soon. I had classes to teach and football practice after. It was gonna be a long day.

"Make it fast," I said as we both climbed out of the truck. "I need to get an hour or two of shut-eye before school."

"You getting old, man. All-nighters used to be no big deal."

"By the way," I said, "you had it wrong earlier. Rosco was the sheriff." Jack frowned at me, puzzled. "Rosco P. Coltrane was the sheriff of Hazzard County, not the deputy. Enos was the deputy."

Jack nodded and smiled as he swung open the door to the quick stop. A loud bell sounded to announce our presence, and a welcoming wave of cool air hit us full in the face. "You're right," he said. "Enos. But remember he moved away and the bigger guy—was it Cletus? Yeah, Cletus took his place. I think Cletus was chasing you tonight."

Jack mumbled, "Ros-co-P-Col-trane," exaggerating each syllable as he walked toward the bathroom in the back of the store, inspecting bags of chips and candy along the way. I browsed a minute under the disinterested gaze of the hefty he-woman behind the counter before grabbing a candy bar and a Mountain Dew for myself. I pulled out my wallet to pay while waiting on Jack to finish his business.

The woman yawned through rows of broken teeth, and I asked if she'd had a long night. She returned her cigarette to her mouth with one hand and adjusted the Rebel Rouser bandana on her head with the other. "Ain't they all?"

I shrugged. "I reckon so." I tried to suppress a smile. Turnip might be a Cletus, but this woman was no Daisy Duke. I couldn't see her bottom half but tried not to imagine her in short-short cutoff jeans.

"What you grinning about?" Jack poked me in the ribs as he slid a root beer onto the counter. "He's got mine too." He took a few steps back to avoid any chance of being confused with someone intending to participate in the payment process.

I shook my head and turned back to pay, but the woman was suddenly distracted. She hurried toward the front window and leaned forward on her tiptoes, craning her neck to look down the side of the store. "That y'all's truck down there at the end?" She pointed with a thumb. "Somebody's messin' with it."

"What in the—" Jack was halfway to the entrance before I got turned around. "Hey!" He burst through the swinging glass door. "Hey!" He yelled louder as he erupted into a run and disappeared from view.

I followed, but Jack had a head start. He was shouting, turning the corner around the store by the time I got out the door. My heart sank when I saw the shattered driver's side window. I paused to peer inside the truck, knowing what I would see—or more precisely, what I would not see—even before I got there. As suspected, the plastic bag and its grisly contents were gone. "Jack, get him! He's got the bag!" I screamed as I pushed away from the truck to join the pursuit.

That awful, distinct sound of a hard object colliding with human flesh stopped Jack's shouting and the crunch of his footfalls on the gravel. I almost tripped over him as I rounded the rear corner of the store on a dead run. A turbocharged roar exploded from around the next corner, and I could make out a spray of gravel as an unseen vehicle sped away into the last darkness of the balmy night.

Jack was sprawled face-first on the dusty rocks. He did not move or make a sound.

THIRTY-TWO

"CASE number MS-305H-709, The People of Mississippi versus John Edward Townsend. We are here for arraignment, Your Honor."

The judge nodded at the court clerk who obligingly took her seat.

The man across the aisle to Jet's right buttoned his suit coat and cleared his throat. "Assistant District Attorney Boyd Moten for the State, Your Honor."

The judge nodded again, this time at the prosecutor, and then turned to Jet. "Mr. Townsend, please step up to the podium."

Albert Roesink nudged Jet, as if the judge's instruction wasn't simple enough. Jet looked straight ahead and complied, trying to look confident for the benefit of his worried mother in the audience behind him, without appearing smug to the judge. He suspected, though, that his trembling hands revealed his true state of mind to anyone observant enough to notice.

The judge had a certain matter-of-fact demeanor about him—stone-faced without appearing disagreeable—with a square jaw, shaved head, and thin lips hidden within a full but neatly trimmed gray beard. He intertwined his fingers and rested them on the bench in front of him. "My name is Judge James Gilreath. I am a United States magistrate judge for the Second

District here in Hinds County, Mississippi. You understand that you are here because of criminal charges brought against you?"

"Yes sir."

"Please state your full name for the court."

"John Edward Townsend."

"Now, Mr. Townsend, I need to inform you of some items as required by Rule 5.2(b) of the Mississippi Rules of Criminal Procedure. First, as I know you have already been informed, you have the right to remain silent, and any statements you make may be used against you. You have the right to representation by an attorney, and if you are unable to afford an attorney, one will be appointed as required by law. Do you understand?"

Jet nodded.

"I need you to voice your answer, son."

"Yes sir," Jet said loudly, hoping he didn't overcompensate and sound surly.

The judge studied Jet a moment without changing his expression, then slipped on rimless reading glasses and looked down to peruse a document on his desk. "Now, Mr. Townsend, have you secured, and are you able to afford, legal representation?"

Jet opened his mouth to answer but was cut off. "Albert Roesink here, Your Honor. I'll be representing Mr. Townsend."

The judge cocked his head to the side and sighed, glaring irritably at the man with tousled hair and the rumpled suit to Jet's left. "Mr. Roesink, I know that you and I have not previously crossed paths in this capacity, but let me make one thing abundantly clear. If I, as the interrogator in my courtroom, preface a question with the name of the interrogee, then I fully expect the interrogee to answer the question, unless he or she is struck with a sudden muteness of biblical-plague-like proportions. Are we clear?"

Jet didn't remember a plague of muteness from the Bible, but he got the point.

Roesink appeared to as well, but he just nodded vigorously. Judge Gilreath raised his eyebrows, waiting on an answer. "Uh, crystal clear, Your Honor, sir," the attorney blurted finally.

"Mr. Townsend?"

"Yes, Your Honor, Mr. Roesink is my attorney. For the time being."

"At last, we're getting somewhere." The judge turned his attention to the prosecutor. "Mr. Moten?"

Boyd Moten looked to be mid-thirties, average height and build. His black hair was combed straight back, with a prominent widow's peak hovering over thick eyebrows and a five o'clock shadow that might have been the vestige of a long night drinking with friends but was more than likely intentional. Despite resembling a grown-up Eddie Munster, he was sharply dressed, with a gray suit, light-gray button-down, lavender tie and polished brown shoes. "Thank you, Your Honor."

The judge raised an index finger. "The short version, please." He waived the file folder in his other hand. "I can read."

"Yes, sir. Two days ago, on Sunday, August 14, Grace Tollison was jogging at Palmer Ridge Park when she was brutally attacked. She was jerked into the bushes, choked, and injected with a sedative called midazolam. We have witnesses who observed an argument between Mr. Townsend and the victim the night before and will also testify that the two had a very close relationship. We have witnesses who saw Mr. Townsend at the scene, racing angrily toward the victim in the moments before she disappeared. We also found, at the home of the accused via a legal warrant, drug paraphernalia and other items consistent with those both used in the crime and found at the crime scene. There was no evidence of forced entry, Your Honor, and the items were found in his dresser."

"And the attempted kidnapping charge?"

"We believe Mr. Townsend's intent was to kidnap her, but it took him longer than he expected, and he had to abandon it because of fear of discovery by other park patrons. *Mens rea,* Your Honor."

Roesink leaned toward Jet and whispered, "That means—"

"Criminal intent without completion of the guilty act." Jet saw that they had caught the judge's glare and tried to finish his thought through the corner of his mouth. "*Mens rea* without *actus reus.*"

"Mr. Townsend, are we bothering you? Are we distracting you from your private discussion over there?"

"No sir, Your Honor. I apologize. I'm pretty good at science, but these legal terms are just way over my head."

Roesink coughed beside him.

"Well I suggest you pay attention. Your attorney can explain later. Mr. Moten was just explaining that it is the State's opinion that you intended to kidnap Ms. Tollison. Now, let me explain what we have." He glanced at the paperwork before him once more. "You are alleged to have committed several very serious crimes. They include the following: stalking, domestic violence, aggravated assault, attempted kidnapping, and attempted murder. These are punishable by up to twenty years in prison. Do you understand?"

Jet reflected on what little Roesink had told him earlier that morning about the arraignment, that there would be no pleas, no testimony, no witnesses, no cross-examination. The judge would just get the basic facts and set bail. Jet knew a few legal terms and principles but not much about legal procedure, so he took his attorney's word for it. Yet here the judge was, asking him if he understood these ludicrous allegations. "No sir, I don't. I didn't do any of those things, and I would like a moment to refute them. Somehow—"

"That's enough, Mr. Townsend. You'll have time for your side of the story at a later date."

Jet wanted to scream but instead held his tongue and clenched his fists in silent protest.

"I have informed you of the charges," the judge continued. "Now I need to ask you some questions in order to set bail. Where do you live?"

"I grew up in Amberton, Mississippi, but I have lived here in Jackson for two weeks. My address is 47 Aikay Drive."

"Do you own property here?"

"No sir, I rent."

"I see. And why did you move to Jackson?"

"I am a medical student. First year."

The judge separated his hands and reunited them beneath his chin, appearing to ponder the implications of that. He looked from Moten to Roesink then back to Jet. "Are you currently attending medical school?"

"Yes, Your Honor. I was. I mean, I am." Jet thought back to Professor Cronin's admonition about him having one more chance. He knew that unless his fortunes turned around very quickly, in all likelihood his medical school days were now over.

"I hope I am." He tried to hold the judge's gaze but couldn't help looking down as he finished his sentence.

"I understand," the judge said. "Have you ever been arrested or convicted of a crime?"

"No, I have not."

"Have you ever received treatment for substance abuse or mental illness?"

"No sir."

"I see. And where is your family?"

"Your Honor, my father is working overseas. My mother is here today, but she lives in Amberton, in McKinley County. That's it."

"Your father—is he in the military?"

"No sir, not exactly. He's a civilian contractor. Works for an engineering firm."

Judge Gilreath stroked his chin briefly before turning to Boyd Moten. "And what is the State's recommendation regarding bail for the accused?"

"Your Honor, due to the heinous nature of the crime, both in terms of its brutality and premeditation, as well as the intent to do even more harm, we believe the accused to be a continued threat to society and the victim. He has no permanent ties to this community, is a man with significant resources, and poses a flight risk. The State requests that he be remanded into custody."

Jet almost swallowed his tongue.

"I object," Roesink said.

Judge Gilreath glared at him. "Mr. Roesink, I am soliciting opinions on appropriate bail amounts for your client, not hearing testimony. So now it's your turn to speak for your client." He gestured toward Jet.

"Thank you, Your Honor." Roesink pointed with his pen at some notes scribbled on a legal pad before him as he spoke. "Mr. Townsend is an upstanding citizen with no criminal history. No, um, arrests or warrants of any kind. He is tied to this community by virtue of his, uhhh, ongoing medical school training. His mother, who has been ill with cancer, is here today in support. My client's assistance with her care over the past few years has been vital to her survival, a fact that is unlikely to change. We request that he be released on his own recognizance."

The bailiff handed Roesink a sheet of paper.

The attorney read it and glanced back over his shoulder toward the audience. "May I approach the bench, Your Honor?"

Judge Roesink waved the attorneys toward him. "Both of you. Please hurry, I have a full docket today."

The three men huddled out of earshot of Jet and the court audience. Moten shook his head while Roesink spoke. Moten and the judge discussed something a moment, then Moten shrugged and shook his head again, and the two attorneys returned to their original positions.

Roesink winked at Jet as he took his place beside him. "You're gonna like this," he muttered.

"Mr. Roesink, get on with it. You would like the court to hear from a character reference?"

Jet was confused. They had discussed earlier whether to ask Jet's mother to speak, but Jet had insisted she not. She would be more than willing, but he wanted to spare her the stress of it.

No matter how eloquent and persuasive she was, she would blame herself if anything short of immediate acquittal occurred.

"The defense would like to call Marta Winscote," Roesink said.

Jet whirled to see the anatomy professor striding down the aisle to the front of the courtroom. She smiled at him as she passed by and stepped to the lectern, front and center. She wore a nondescript brown pants suit and flats. Her straight hair and thick glasses were unchanged. She tucked her hair behind her ears more than once.

"Please state your name," the judge said.

"Doctor Marta Davis Winscote."

"And what is your relationship to the defendant?"

"I am one of his Gross Anatomy professors, and I am a mentor, tutor, and friend to the victim in this case, Gracie Tollison."

The judge leaned forward. "And what would you like to say to the court?"

Jet half expected her, in a twist fit for a movie, to erupt on a rant about the absurdity that bail would even be considered for someone so depraved as to assault a jewel of humanity such as her pupil Gracie Tollison.

She spoke in a soft but clear voice. "Your Honor, I'll be brief. John Edward Townsend, or Jet, as his friends affectionately call him, is one of the brightest minds I have ever known. But that's not why I'm here." She paused, glancing at her hands crossed at her waist before continuing, louder and more confident now. "I'm here because you need to know some other things about him. Things I've learned about him through observation and because I've grown close to his friend Gracie, the victim in this case—bless her heart—who has shared with me some things about Jet that I want to tell you.

"He would never mention this, but less than a year ago, his brother, who was his mentor and biggest fan, was killed in a horrible accident on the very night that Jet proudly told him he had been admitted to medical school. That was bad enough, but he had already been dealing with almost losing his sweet mother to cancer. Now don't count this a negative against him—I'm just being honest—but Jet has had a tough time with all that. I've seen it, and Gracie has told me some things.

"However, despite tragedy and sickness and the awful mental parallels that surely arise unavoidably while dissecting cadavers as part of the anatomy curriculum, Jet has been a bright light in what is often a dark time for many medical students—the first days of Gross Anatomy. Despite battling his own demons, he has selflessly helped other students, including the victim, Gracie Tollison.

"Gracie has told me all about Jet's history and their friendship." Winscote's voice cracked, and she paused to wipe a tear from her cheek. "And she would give anything to be here today. Unfortunately, she is still recovering from her injuries, having headaches and dizziness, but she asked me to tell the court she doubts seriously that Jet had anything to do with her assault."

The judge turned to Boyd Moten. "I assume you've interviewed the victim? What does she say about her attacker?"

"She can't remember much, Your Honor. A plastic bag was pulled over her head from behind, then she was choked and drugged."

"I see. Dr. Winscote, is there anything else?"

Marta Winscote looked back over her shoulder toward Jet. "Yes. I would like the court to know that I'm so confident he will return for his court date, I'll personally back his bail bond, unless of course you—what's the term? Remand? Yes, unless you remand him into custody."

"Thank you, Professor Winscote, but how or whether the defendant posts bail is not my concern. You may take a seat in the audience."

Jet was stunned. He didn't know whether to smile or cry. He was ecstatic to have a friend on his side, a respected professional, no less, and that she thought enough of him to not only speak on his behalf, but to help him post bail. Most of that came at Gracie's insistence, he suspected, but whatever the motive, he was glad. He had already begun to worry what his mother would do. He certainly had no cash, and he doubted she had enough money to cover the required 10% of anything but the most nominal bail amount.

On the other hand, was he just paranoid, or had the professor inadvertently portrayed him as an unstable basket case battling unseen demons? Yeah, everyone knows those types of people hardly ever commit violent crimes of passion. And her statement that Gracie "doubts seriously" that he had anything to do with her attack hadn't exactly been a glowing endorsement, either.

His mother used to tell him never to look a gift horse in the mouth. He had never owned a horse, much less been given one, but he understood the concept. Accept a gift and be glad you got it. He just hoped this particular one wasn't going to kick him in his teeth.

Judge Gilreath watched Professor Winscote work her way to her seat on the back row before looking down to make some notes on the papers before him. "After careful consideration of both positions," he said finally, "including the support of the character witness, I will set bail at \$100,000."

Jet breathed a sigh of relief. His gift horse turned out to be an asset after all. The judge continued with instructions on the process for posting bail and discussed future court dates with both attorneys, but Jet didn't hear a word. He was preoccupied with wondering who was so determined to destroy him.

And how to stop them before it was too late.

THIRTY-THREE

"WHAT are you doing here?" Abi rubbed her eyes. "You know it's five in the morning?" Her tone was one of protest, but she opened the door to her apartment anyway and stepped back to let Jack and me in. She stopped mid-step, pointing and gaping at Jack. "What happened?"

He moaned but said nothing.

"Took a two-by-four to the head." I reached out to steady him as he wavered. "I'm worried about him."

"Well, yeah. Take him to the ER." She reached up and gently inspected the bloody knot on his forehead. "Who hit him? Aren't y'all a bit old for high school bar fights?"

"No hospitals. He made me promise."

"I hate needles." Jack moaned again.

"And we don't know who hit him. Long story. But this was the only place I could think of to take him. You know, since Jet is in jail."

Abi was barefoot, with gym shorts and a faded sorority T-shirt. Her black curls were disheveled, but she was beautiful even without makeup. She gave me a hard look with piercing blue eyes I knew all too well. "I'm a forensic scientist, not a doctor."

I shrugged sheepishly and turned to Jack, who was staggering to the couch and mumbling something about being just fine.

"Good grief." Abi sighed. "Grab a bag of peas from the freezer, and I'll scrounge up something to clean it up with."

She disappeared down the hall, and I stepped into the small kitchen. A coffee maker gurgled on the counter, and I wondered if she had turned it on as she walked by to answer the door or if it had one of those preset timers to start automatically. I turned and grasped the handle of the top freezer but never opened it. The front of the refrigerator below it had caught my eye, just like it always did.

For as long as I could remember, Abi's refrigerator had been a virtual scrapbook, ever changing and evolving in step with the pace of her life. She covered it with crayon drawings and photos of puppies and A+ smiley face book reports when we were kids, then photos of friends and boy bands and bucket list destinations as a teenager.

Now it was a collage of photographs, a visual catalog of her twenty-two years. There she was, sitting on her father's lap while playing with his stethoscope, holding her mother's hand as she tested the ocean's edge with her toes, holding a softball bat with a gap-toothed smile. I smiled at one of her sitting on Jack's three-wheeler, covered in mud and scowling while Jack and I, complete with mullets and fuzz for facial hair, laughed in the background. Another one, from what must have been a year or two later, showed Abi and me together at a junior high dance. Her hair, teased and cemented with hairspray in fine 80s style, made her look as tall as I was. She had a photo of her high school basketball team, holding a state championship trophy, then several of various girlfriends and sorority sisters, wearing silly hats and making goofy faces and kissing the cheeks of fraternity boys. A photo of her pushing Jet in his wheelchair, another of them at senior prom. There they were again, in caps and gowns at their college graduation, smiling happily and standing with their parents. And then there she was with Lane, standing close against each other on the shore of an emerald lake, cheeks and noses rosy from a cold wind that tossed her hair wildly behind her.

"Did you get the peas?"

I startled then recovered to open the freezer and find the sack of frozen peas without glancing back at Abi. "Just looking at all your pics. Seems like they're different every time I come."

"You haven't been here, Case."

I turned to read her expression but couldn't tell if there was a hidden meaning or not. "True. Guess the last time I saw your fridge was your apartment up at MTSU when Jack and I rode up to hang with y'all."

"That was a ways back."

I nodded. Almost three years. I pointed at the photo of her and Lane together. "Where is that? Pretty water."

"Lane's father's place. He's got a little lake house east of Sandy Hollow, towards the Alabama line."

"Father's place, huh? What about his mother?"

Abi shrugged. "Never knew much about her. Lane says she left when he was a little kid."

"Looks like you got all your ex-boyfriends represented there."

She gave me a smirk. "Makes sense. After all, supposedly we *are* Generation 'Ex.'"

"Well look at that. I fully expected to get a rise out of you and instead you made a funny."

She grinned halfheartedly. "Might as well laugh about it. Seems like I've had trouble settling on the right guy. Anyway, it's my life. I won't hide it or apologize for it." She cocked her head to the side and raised an eyebrow. "But if you think it's too many, I can remove the one of us."

I felt a rush of warmth across my face. "That would be a shame." I tapped the photo. "We were quite the pair." I hadn't seen pictures from that dance in years. How odd that a memory could seem to be both from another lifetime and only yesterday. I could still smell her perfume from that night, yet somehow the idea of it was blurry enough to be only a dream. So long ago.

I realized I was staring at the photo, harder than I intended, and that Abi was watching me. Had she commented and I missed it? I sensed my temperature rising again in the awkwardness of the moment, but a voice interjecting from the other room saved me from saying something I'd be embarrassed about later.

"Are y'all making out or having a class reunion in there or what?"

Abi and I shared a fleeting grin before the moment passed. "Sorry Jack," she said. "We're coming." She took the frozen peas from my hand, and I followed her into the other room.

"Good thing I'm not bleeding out in here." Jack held a pillow over his face.

"Don't be such a drama queen," I said.

"Let me smack you with a two-by-four and see if bright light don't split your skull wide open."

"You've got a concussion." Abi pulled the pillow away and began cleaning the wound. "Barely broke the skin. But quite an impressive goose egg. So which of you boys is gonna tell me what happened? Or am I gonna have to start swinging some lumber around myself?"

"Oh no, please no." Jack winced. "Tell her, Case. Hurts me to talk."

I paused to gather my thoughts. "We went to Amberton, Abi. To Havenrest."

Her eyes darted to meet Jack's, but she looked away too quickly, and I understood.

"Jack told you?"

She avoided my gaze. "I knew you would go. Probably knew it before either of you did."

I glanced at Jack who shrugged matter-of-factly but said nothing, watching Abi.

"And what did you find?"

"Casket wasn't empty. I thought it might be." I watched her reaction, but she was stoic. "You're not surprised."

"I told you all along, if Jet says something, I believe it."

"We were going to bring a sample for you to get analyzed. DNA or whatever you can do."

"And?"

I told her about the attack on Jack and the theft of the tissue sample. The color drained from Abi's face. She stood and walked to the window. She parted the blinds and craned her neck to look both directions. "That's scary, guys." Her voice quivered. "Really scary. Somebody followed you? Did you call the police?"

"And tell them what?" Jack said. "That somebody whacked me so they could lift a sandwich bag containing the finger of a corpse, and oh, by the way, the sheriff of the county next door, who just happens to be Case's father, chose to let us go after he caught us grave robbing?"

"I don't like this. This is getting out of hand." She paced and glanced nervously out the window again.

"Abi, there's nobody there." I stood and looked out the window myself then shook my head and turned away. I grabbed Abi's hands in mine. "There's nothing to be afraid of. Whoever he is, he got what he wanted. And you have nothing to do with it anyway."

Abi forced a smile, but it was short lived. An expression of alarm took its place.

Someone was pounding on the front door and shouting her name.

THIRTY-FOUR

JET had difficulty determining the timing of it. He first thought he might just show up on the sixth floor the same time everyone else did and integrate himself into the parade of preoccupied students in stained white coats pouring into the Gross Anatomy lab. But that might be too chaotic, and depending on what had been told about him, he might get held up and never make it into the class at all.

Another option was to let everyone get in and get started before coming through the doors himself, but a grand entrance was the last thing he wanted. Plus, within five minutes or so, the professors would all be making rounds, table to table, and they would immediately notice him.

So instead, Jet arrived at the Gross Anatomy lab early, hoping none of the professors were there already. He was relieved when his code still worked on the keypad and mused that if Cronin had anything to do with it, tomorrow would be a different story. Jet eased the door open and stepped inside the expansive room where he was met with a blast of cool air carrying the pungent, increasingly familiar odor of preservative.

The room was devoid of the living, as best he could tell. And the dead weren't up yet, as each stainless steel tank was closed, per protocol. *Remember, they each gave themselves to you, so give them the respect they deserve in return. Anything less will be an injustice. Now, unlike me, you will never know their stories, how they lived or how they died. Yet you should treat them with the dignity you would give a family member.* Cronin's words from the first day of Gross Anatomy echoed in Jet's head, and as he thought about his brother, an irrepressible chill slithered up his back before spreading across the nape of his neck.

With ten minutes to spare, Jet opened the door off the back corner of the huge dissection room and was surprised to find a space not much larger than a closet. He had only given the spot a passing glance before. It was just an open door into which the professors occasionally disappeared to retrieve some type of dissection tool or one of the elusive 60cc syringes used to douse the cadaver tissues in preservative, lest they dry out. Whatever its usual purpose, today it was a perfect place to be inconspicuous for a moment.

Jet looked at his watch. They'd be here any minute now. Why had he felt compelled to come? Why did he have to see the body once more? Why did he have to see them, his partners, gathered around the body? He couldn't answer those questions with any precision. Maybe he just wanted to read their faces when they saw him. Maybe he just wanted to be there, in the Gross Anatomy lab, as a medical student, one last time. Before the dream of becoming a physician came to an end for good.

He peeked around the corner to see the predictable barrage of students streaming in. Most with strained looks and quick steps, anxious to get going, get a head start on the day's exhausting dissection assignment before grabbing a quick bite of supper and returning to resume the never-ending review process. A few strolled in, talking and laughing, carefree, typically either thankful to be of the pure genius variety or content to finish near the bottom of the class.

Craig Tekowski was the first in among Jet's group. Jaw clenched, brow furrowed, head locked in forward gear like a thoroughbred with blinders, he marched toward his table.

Gracie wasn't far behind, but she had circles beneath her eyes, and she was pale, the kind of paleness manifesting fatigue and headache and fear more than lack of sunshine.

Jet caught a glimpse of Tucker cutting up with another student as he came through the door, but Jet didn't wait. He stepped out, wanting to run to Gracie, but instead he strode toward his group's dissection table just as Tekowski was turning the final cranks on the lever to lift the body out of the liquid.

"Long time no see, Tea," Jet said from behind his partner.

Tekowski whirled. "What are you doing here?"

"Surprised to see me out of jail? Pretty good motive you gave them, Gracie and me arguing in here the night before."

Tekowski's mouth dropped open then closed as his eyes narrowed. "That wasn't me. I'm curious though, what happens to the dynamics of an anatomy group when one member tries to kill another?"

"Stop it, Tea." Gracie walked up. "Jet hasn't done anything of the sort."

It was the first time Jet had seen Gracie since the hospital. He stepped toward her, wanting to hug her, knowing he shouldn't, still wanting to make sure she was alright.

Gracie withdrew. Not an overt back away, but an unquestionable flinch. Instinctive.

"Sure about that?" Tekowski said snidely, eyeing Gracie as he adjusted his glasses. "Funny how they aren't dropping the charges." He turned to Jet. "Surely there's a restraining order or something making it illegal for you to be here, huh?"

"Judge didn't issue one since I didn't request it," Gracie retorted.

"Jet! My main man!" Tucker had arrived. He slapped Jet playfully on the back. "Cool cat with the perfect MCAT." He dropped his voice an octave and held a pencil up to Jet's mouth. "Tell us, doctor, how did it feel to be the guest of honor in the Hotel Cali–po-po?"

Jet wasn't in the mood for levity and didn't really have time for it, but he couldn't help but smile. He opened his mouth to speak, but Tekowski interrupted. "Restraining order or not, we don't have time for this. Good luck, Jet. We'll catch you later." He pulled the sheet back from the cadaver and picked up a pair of forceps.

"You don't seriously think he did it, do you?" Tucker stepped on a stool and leaned across the dissection table to force Tekowski to look at him.

"Doesn't matter what any of us think." Another voice broke in. Sterling Virchow sauntered up and pretended to lean forward and peer at the cadaver before crossing his arms as he stood erect, glaring down at Jet. "He's been charged with a felony and doesn't need to be here distracting us until he's proven innocent. Cronin has said so himself."

"Thank you for that vote of confidence." It was Jet's turn to peer at the body lying in the tank. Unlike Virchow's, his inspection was legitimate. He blinked and breathed deeply through a wave of nausea, conflating the view of the stranger before him with the image, seared into his memory like the cut of a laser, of his brother Adam.

And then suddenly, he knew why he had come. *How did I miss it before?* He frowned, both at what he was seeing—or not seeing—and his failure to catch it earlier. He exaggerated a look of puzzlement. "I know it was last week, but it seems so long ago. Remember Tea, when we were joking about his crack attack? Remember, the scar right here?" Jet pointed at the top of the intergluteal fold. "Wait, what happened? Sterling, I do believe my anatomy group has done plastic surgery in my absence. This gentleman had a scar here just a few short days ago."

Tekowski and Tucker both looked away. Gracie held Jet's gaze through a film of new tears. "You're not helping yourself."

Sterling Virchow had not flinched. "I guess you'll tell us now that your brother had a scar there too?"

Jet felt the blood rush to his face. "Maybe," was all he could say. He saw that most eyes in the room were focused on him now.

Virchow burst into a hateful laugh. "Oh, this is priceless!" His voice rose several decibels. "Priceless! What's your point? You allege your brother was here." He curled his upper lip and pointed at the body. "But now he's not, and your case for this conspiracy theory is centered on this body missing a scar that your brother didn't have either?"

"His name was Adam, and you know it's more than that."

"I'll tell you what I do know. You've been acting like you're insane since day one, and it's not getting any better." He looked around the room. "You all know what they say. If it walks like a duck and quacks like a duck..."

"It might be a two-legged jackass with its snout buried up Cronin's butt," Gracie chimed in. She snatched a scalpel and waved it in Virchow's general direction. "It's time for you to shut up and get back to your table."

Virchow and the gawkers around him stiffened and slowly backed away. Gracie's threat may have had its intended effect, but an unmistakable voice behind her changed that.

"Ms. Tollison, I can't tell you how much it disturbs me to hear my name and a reference to my posterior uttered by someone waving a scalpel around in a threatening manner." Professor Cronin shook his head in disgust. "Everybody get back to work!" Students scurried to their tables like scolded dogs to their kennels. "Now, I'm not going to ask what's going on here, because I know. I'm sorry, Mr. Townsend, but you obviously did not get my message. I suspect you probably came here straight from your bond hearing. At any rate, until the matter of your alleged assault is adjudicated or otherwise settled, you will not be able to participate in this class." He cut his eyes at Gracie, who was gently setting the scalpel on the edge of the table, then narrowed his eyes at Jet again. "You can leave of your own accord, or I'll have you escorted out by security. Your choice."

Jet wanted to protest, but he had prepared himself for this. He expected nothing less. He nodded deferentially. The collective downward gazes of Tea, Tucker, and Gracie told him he could expect no help from them.

He turned to leave then stopped and pointed at the body. "Looks like some powder burns there around the bullet wound, too. Gracie, better make a note of that. Guarantee you didn't before, because they weren't there. And Tucker, why don't you get some calipers and measure that hole. Remember I told ya'll it was at least a .35 caliber? Guarantee that's no larger than .32."

"Get out!" Cronin spat. "Get out of my lab, and don't come back."

Jet turned again, but this time he didn't look back. He stopped in the hallway for a moment, trembling all over, legs suddenly like jello. His breath came in shallow gasps, as if his lungs were fighting for space to expand between galloping heartbeats.

A hand touched Jet's shoulder from behind. He spun and jumped at the same time, drawing back a fist.

"Hold on, there, Mr. Townsend!" Soap, the elderly janitor he had met the night he searched all the tanks for his brother, stood wide-eyed, the whites glowing almost fluorescent against his dark skin. He held his hand up in a defensive position. "It's jus' me. I jus' seein' if you was okay."

Jet took several deep breaths and turned, staring down the hall toward the elevators. "I'm sorry, Mr. Soap. I'm fine. Just getting ready to head on home. Looks like it's the end of the road for me."

"Sorry to hear that, Mr. Townsend. I think you'd be a mighty fine doctor." He paused and looked in both directions. "You know, I usually tell folks to keep they head up, but sometimes it's just better to look down. The Good Book says to humble yo'self and the Lord will lift you up." The gentle, white-haired man turned and shuffled in the opposite direction, pushing his cart full of cleaning supplies, whistling.

Jet stood for a moment, trying to understand the odd little man's point. He turned away to leave, and something brushed against his foot. He stopped and toed the wadded piece of paper. It had probably fallen out of the cleaning cart. Not in the mood to search for a garbage can, he kicked it down the hall, watching it roll and settle against a locker. Jet trudged down the hall and had just punched the elevator button when it hit him. *Sometimes it's just better to look down.*

He hurried back to pick up the ball of paper. Maybe he was as crazy as everyone thought. The elevator door opened, and he stepped in, letting it close before carefully spreading open the paper, half expecting to see someone's discarded anatomy notes.

It took him a moment to understand what he was seeing. Lines and boxes and numbers and letters in blue ink, with nothing to orient him. Then all at once it made sense, like the blurry view through a camera lens suddenly twisted into sharp focus. It was a map. A map of the sixth floor, where he had just been. The Anatomy Department. An 'X' marked one of the offices, with a set of five numbers below it. The combination to the keypad on the door.

THIRTY-FIVE

"ABI!" Someone hammered on the front door. "Abi! Let me in!"

I didn't immediately recognize the frantic voice, but Abi did. She yanked the door open with a heavy sigh.

Lane Buckley stood at the threshold, eyes wide. "What's going on in here?" He did not wait for an invitation to march into the room. After three steps, he stopped in his tracks, eyes searching from Jack to me and back again.

"Jack was attacked this morning," Abi said. "And he won't go to the doctor. Why are you in such a tizzy?"

Lane presented a bloodied paper towel, pinched between two fingers. It was from the 24-Hour Power truck stop. "Strange truck outside, this near the door, heard voices inside." He shrugged. "It's a crazy world." He looked at Jack. "Tell me again why he came here?"

"Forget why I'm here." Jack frowned. "Why are you here? Did you follow us or something?"

Abi waved her hand in the air, like an elementary teacher silencing a rowdy class. "Lane was invited. He comes over for coffee sometimes after he gets off work. Before I go to work."

"Coffee? Sounds lovely," Jack said.

Lane ignored the sarcasm. "So, what about this attack?"

"Long story." I glanced at Jack, who shook his head, just barely. "Some punk hit him in the head at a quick stop. Probably looking for drug money."

"Looks like a pretty bad lick," Lane said as Jack settled back into a chair. "Good thing bone is stronger than wood."

Jack frowned. "Who said anything about wood?"

Lane blinked and shook his head. "Nobody, but what else would it be? I don't figure anybody could put you down with one blow from a fist. If you remember, I learned that the hard way back in the day." He pointed at Jack's head. "Plus, there's a straight line across your forehead. But now that you say that, a metal bat, maybe?"

Jack gave a twisted grin. "Naw, you're right, Sherlock. It was a wooden board. But it ain't nothing." He gingerly patted the knot on his head. "A little headache is all."

"Nothing, my foot," Abi said. "If you won't go to the ER, you'll have to rest today."

"Ain't going to no ER. Don't need any Doogie Howser wannabe to tell me I got a goose egg on my head. No offense to Jet, but I know how they send kid doctors in to experiment on people in those big city hospitals."

Abi sighed and rolled her eyes. "So stubborn. I don't mind you staying here, but you don't need to be alone. I'll call in sick and stay with you."

"No way," I said. "He was with me when it happened. I got this."

"Case, buddy, you got football, and I don't need no babysitter, especially one as ugly as you." Jack smirked at me.

"Let me do it," Lane chimed in. "Seriously." He continued in response to our surprised frowns. "I'm off today, so why not?"

"I'm good," Jack said. "Don't need company making my headache worse than it already is."

"C'mon, Jack," Lane pleaded. He sounded sincere. "I'm happy to help."

"So it's settled." Abi pointed at Jack. "Lane will stay. He's off, so no point in Case or me missing work when we don't have to."

Jack opened his mouth to complain, but I cut him off. "Just do it, unless you want me to take you to the ER. Because you ain't driving." I dangled his keys on my index finger. "I'm taking your truck to school."

He huffed and slumped into the couch, smothering his forehead with the frozen peas again.

Lane stood and clapped his hands together. "Coffee time!" He brushed against Abi and patted her affectionately on top of the head on his way toward the kitchen. "Might as well cook some breakfast too, huh?" He gestured to me. "What you hungry for, Case? Jack?"

I shook my head. "Nope, I gotta motor if I'm gonna be on time. Thanks for hanging with Jack."

Lane nodded but said nothing as I moved to leave.

"I'll walk you out," Abi said. "Gotta ask you something."

Lane mumbled something I couldn't understand, and Abi turned back to answer in a terse whisper. I left them to it and waited out front at the sidewalk, inhaling the heavy morning air. It was still relatively cool but wouldn't be for long. The swelter of a Mississippi August was never far away.

The door closed. She was there, but I didn't look. "Got you a regular Emeril Lagasse, huh?"

"He likes to cook a little, but I don't have him. And vice versa."

I didn't want to think about them eating together regardless of who had who, so I changed the subject. "You think it was Adam?"

"I want to, don't you?"

It was a rhetorical question, so I instead chose to toss other questions around. So many answers still eluded me. If it was Adam on that table, that was one thing. But if it wasn't, did that mean Jet was simply mistaken or outright delusional? And what else? Why would somebody follow us from a cemetery in Amberton and steal our tissue sample? Why had Adam been under attack in Biloxi before he died, and by whom? Who had attacked Jet's friend Gracie and framed him for it?

"What if it's not?" Abi interrupted my thoughts. "Kinda scary, you know? I mean, if Jet can lose it, who's to say that we won't?"

I shook my head. No answers for any of those questions. And try as I might, I couldn't get Lane and Abi's relationship out of my head, either. "Lane mad that you've been trying to help Jet?"

"Nah, he doesn't feel threatened by Jet. Not anymore."

I got the sense that Abi wanted me to ask more, but I didn't. After a moment, I turned to look her in the eyes. Deep blue, alive like a kaleidoscope of cracked glass. First time in a long time I'd really looked into them that way, but I could pick those irises out of a lineup of a thousand.

She looked away. "He's a good guy."

"Didn't say he wasn't." I shrugged. "I know he must be, or you wouldn't be going out with him."

"I told you, we're not together. We dated in college. Broke up. Now we're just friends who have coffee some mornings before work."

"Yeah, I have regular coffee dates with a couple of old girlfriends myself." I smiled, aiming for sarcasm without patronization.

It must have worked. Abi made a face, half grimace, half grin. "I guess it is a little weird. But he just shows up two or three days a week. We're friends, big deal. It's not like you've been coming by."

"What's that supposed to mean?" My tone was more abrupt than I intended.

Abi looked down at her toes curling in the grass at the edge of the concrete. "Nothing. Just don't get to see you guys much anymore, I guess. Thought I might, now that we're living in the same city, but maybe not."

I took a deep breath. "Can I?"

"Can you what?"

"See you more."

She smiled. "You don't like coffee."

I laughed. "That's true. How about I bring a movie and pizza sometime? Remember when we used to do that? Mom would bring me over."

"Good times. I may not be as cheap a date as I was back then. You might have to throw in some slice-and-bake cookies."

I laughed. "I'm on a teacher's salary, but I think I can swing that." I jerked my head toward her apartment. "What about him?"

"What about him? He knows we're just friends. Just friends. Been that way quite a while."

"Uh, huh." I nodded. I liked what I was hearing but did not at all understand the complexities of it. "Gotta figure out what to do about Jet. But I'll call you, Abi. I'll call you."

As I turned to head to my truck, I caught a glimpse of Lane peering out the window.

THIRTY-SIX

JACK watched the activity in the tiny kitchen through one open eye. Something ran down his face and he wiped it away, hoping it wasn't blood, relieved to see it was just water from the condensation on the bag of peas. He pulled the bag away and tossed it on the glass coffee table, then wiped his head with his shirt.

"Abi doesn't have a lot to choose from. Hope you like omelets," Lane called over his shoulder as he pulled slices of bread from the toaster with one hand while deftly flipping his egg concoction from the skillet to a plate with the other. "Found some ham and cheese and a bell pepper. Added some steak seasoning too. You won't believe how a pinch gives it a pop of flavor."

"Whatever, man. It's fine. I told you I'm not very hungry."

Lane slid a plate and a glass of orange juice onto the coffee table before Jack. "Got to have protein to heal. And they say vitamin C helps fight infection."

Jack reluctantly picked up a fork and took a bite, eyeing Lane as he chewed. He gave an approving nod, took another bite, bigger this time, and pointed his fork at Lane. "Pretty good, I have to admit. I don't get you, though. Why are you here?"

"What you mean?"

"I mean just that. Why are you here? It's not like you and me are tight. Don't you have something better to do?"

Lane smiled. "I know we've had our differences. But I care about Abi. And I want her friends to be my friends."

Jack was quiet while he attacked his food. Then he stopped and wiped his mouth with the back of his hand. "Abi says y'all aren't dating. But I know you ain't over here sharing morning coffee or whatever because you just want to be her friend. So what's the truth?"

"She's telling the truth. But I'd be lying if I said I didn't want it to be more. We had a good thing, but I just pushed too hard, wanting to get married and all. So I'm not going to make that mistake again. She'll come around."

"Yeah, okay." Jack scraped up the last bite. "Don't hold your breath."

Lane picked up the empty plate and walked to the kitchen. "How's the head feeling? Abi's probably got some ibuprofen in a cabinet here."

"I don't need no nurse. If you'll just drive me home, you can go do your thing, whatever that is."

Lane sank into the couch opposite Jack and rested one foot on his opposite knee. "Yeah, I can do that. But tell me first. Why do you dislike me so much?"

Jack shrugged. How could Lane not know the answer to that question? "What's that saying about judging a man by the company he keeps? Last time you and I had any real dealings we were fighting in the street, then your buddy VJ MacIntosh ran Jet over and nearly killed him. Tried to kill him."

"That was a long time ago, and you know we were just stupid kids then. I never meant for anything like that to happen." He sat upright and studied the floor, resting his elbows on his knees. "Abi thought I deserved a second chance."

Jack sighed and shook his head. "I'm sorry, dude. I'm not too good at letting go of grudges." He chuckled. "But you do cook a mean omelet. And I reckon I need people to forgive and forget some of the dumb stuff I did as a teenager."

Lane smiled and nodded but said nothing.

Jack rubbed the knot on his head, gathering his thoughts. "So, what happened to you after Jet got hurt? I know VJ went to juvie, but you disappeared. Next thing I know—what, seven years later? You walk in the door with Abi that night at Jet's house."

Lane looked at the floor again. "Bad times. Dad packed us up and moved us up to Murfreesboro. He was doing regional sales, so he could pretty much live where he wanted. He thought I needed a change of scenery, a different school." He snapped his fingers. "And just like that, I went from having friends and being the up-and-coming starting quarterback at a small school to being a nobody at a big one."

"Little fish in a big sea."

"Yeah. So I quit football, staggered through high school in a stoned haze, and went to community college only because my father knew someone on the admissions committee and made me go."

"Ouch. How could he make you?"

"I was lost but not stupid. I could either stay in college on his dime and get into the trust he had set up for me when I graduated or drop out and be broke. He didn't give me a third choice." Lane's eyes flattened into narrow slits, and he met Jack's gaze for a second before looking away. He took a deep breath. "I did consider a third choice, though, to just cash in my chips and check on out. But I changed my mind, thank God. I transferred to Middle Tennessee State, ran into Abi, and suddenly I was alive again."

Jack let out a low whistle. "We all figured Abi was the reason you went there."

"Nope. Pure serendipity."

"Serendipity, huh. That's a Jet word right there. And now your plan is to win her back and ride off into the sunset together?"

"Maybe."

"Look, you asked me why I don't like you. So let me ask you something. Why did you always hang out with VJ? That guy was—is, I guess—nothing but snake spawn."

Lane fidgeted with his fingers. "VJ, huh? Well, when he moved to Amberton, we wound up in the same class. I was a jock, he was a guy who hated sports and talked funny. But we had one thing in common."

"Spiderman underwear?"

Lane didn't flinch. "No. Our mothers."

"Mothers? I was always told VJ didn't even know who his was."

"That's just it. I lived with my father, and he did too. My mom was a drunk, so Dad divorced her and got custody when I was a little kid. I never saw her after that. VJ and I understood each other a little."

Jack felt a twinge of guilt. His own father had been killed in Vietnam when he was two, and his stepfather had died when he was a teenager. "I'm sorry, man. I didn't know. Guess we have more in common than I thought."

Lane shrugged. "You never know, do you? But don't be sorry. It is what it is. Anyway, VJ was the only one from Amberton who kept in touch after I moved. Nobody else seemed to care.

"You still talk to him?"

"From time to time."

"Where is he now, anyway? Figured he'd be the mascot for the state penitentiary by now."

"He's back in Amberton, believe it or not. Living off his family's money. You know they made a pretty penny selling his granddaddy's farm to the government for the highway."

"Back in Amberton, huh? I'll have to look him up sometime."

"It's not worth it, Jack. Let it go."

"Let bygones be bygones."

"Exactly." Lane reached out his hand, offering to help Jack up. But it was more than that. A peace offering. "Come on, knot-head. I'll drive you home."

Jack grabbed the hand and pulled himself up. "Sounds like a plan." He offered a conciliatory smile and pointed at the coffee table. "Hope Abi didn't plan to eat those peas."

THIRTY-SEVEN

wanted to sleep for a week when I got home, but the messages on my machine wouldn't let me. Either Jet couldn't contain his excitement, or he didn't even try. While I was at school and football practice, he had left me four messages, each sounding more urgent than the one before, urging me to come to his apartment as soon as possible. He had a break in the case. He was sure of it. I considered calling him, but a call with Jet and his racing mind could send one's mind into a tailspin. And after our all-nighter, I was too tired.

The other message was a little more straightforward. Jack said that Lane had taken him home, which was perfect for me, since that's where my truck was parked anyway. I decided to start there. Jack's lights were off when I arrived, and I couldn't help but smile. I was craving sleep myself, and I hadn't even been bludgeoned with a piece of lumber. I hid Jack's keys and took my truck, planning to call him later.

A few minutes later, Jet barely let me get in his door before he bubbled over with details of what he had found.

"A map? You really think that's what it is?" I eyed the crinkled sheet of notebook paper spread on his kitchen counter with more than a little skepticism.

Jet nodded. "Yep. The janitor dropped it for me. On purpose. Now don't repeat that to anybody, ever. I don't want the old man to get in trouble, no matter what happens to me. But it's a map." He pointed at some numbers scrawled on the paper. "See that? It's the combination for a door lock. I'm sure of it. Five numbers, just like on the door to the anatomy lab."

"Why would the old man give you this?"

"I don't know. But he wants me to find something in there. I'm sure of it."

"Jet, I got to tell you—"

"Remember that night we all three went to the anatomy lab and Soap stopped us and ..." He had a puzzled look. "Wait. What about Jack? I called him, too. Have you heard from him? Kinda thought he might come over with you."

"Jack, he, uh, he ..." Suddenly I saw no reason to add to Jet's worries by telling him the whole truth about Jack's injury. "He's down with a migraine, I think. So it's just me."

Jet nodded. "That's cool. You and I can do it. You know Jack, he can be a hothead sometimes, so maybe it's for the better, you know, in case we do run into trouble."

"Jet, listen to me—"

"I'm sorry, Case, you're right. That's not fair to ask you to do this. I've got nothing to lose at this point—not really—and you've got everything to lose. I'm just getting excited, I guess. I really believe this is the break I've been looking for."

"No, that's fine. I'm happy to help. But there's something else I need to tell you." I swallowed hard. I wasn't sure how he was going to take what I had to tell him next. "Please don't be mad, but Jack and I went to Adam's grave."

"Went to his grave? I don't understand."

"I'm sorry, but I knew there was only one way to find out if Adam's body had been removed." I explained what Jack and I had done, right up to the part about getting caught by my father, which I omitted. Maybe because I thought the fewer who knew the better, maybe because Jet had enough on his plate to worry about already, and the worst part of the story was yet to come.

"Tell me what you found in the casket." Jet was teary-eyed but firm.

I took a deep breath. "There was a body in there. It was dark, our light gave out, but there was a body. We, uh, Jack, um, took a piece of tissue—"

"So Abi can run DNA on it."

"Yes. Well, no, not exactly. Not anymore." I explained how the sample had been stolen, again leaving out the part about Jack's head getting belted like a high fastball.

Jet blinked hard twice but showed no emotion. He stepped toward me, and I recoiled, wondering if he was about to lose his composure and do something unpredictable. But he reached past my head and calmly removed a glass from the cabinet above me. He filled it with ice and poured a glass of sweet tea from the fridge, then drank it slowly, staring out the window over the sink.

I couldn't stand the silence for very long. "Jet, talk to me, man."

"You know, that night you and Jack came with me to the dissection lab, I thought about stealing a lab jacket from one of my lab partners' lockers. Try to run DNA on some of the tissue stuck to it. Then I remembered that formaldehyde destroys DNA." He shook his glass back and forth and watched the ice settle before taking another sip, then he turned to me with a somber smile. "So, no DNA. I suppose the plot thickens."

"Say what?"

"Your book. I told you this would make a good story, didn't I? It's getting better and better. Now, not only did someone switch Adam's body out, but they trailed you all the way to Amberton to keep you from getting DNA evidence. That means they know that who is in Adam's grave can prove it. Not to mention they've also framed me for attacking Gracie. Like I said, the plot thickens."

"You're right, Jet, it's gotten interesting. And I've been writing it all down, just like you asked me to. Everything I've seen and everything you've told me. But you know some would say there's another strong possibility for what's happening."

He snorted. "If you're suggesting there's a chance that I'm crazy or blind, then no. I admit, there's been a time or two I questioned myself, but not anymore." He locked his eyes on mine and spoke with an emphasis on every syllable. "I'm telling you, my brother's body was in that tank." He pointed to the crinkled notebook paper. "And this is going to help me find out why."

———————

"3-2-5—." Jet entered the code as I called out the numbers, and it suddenly occurred to me that he was just humoring me. "You know them already, don't you?"

Jet smiled flatly and punched the last two numbers. He grasped the doorknob and held it tight, as if willing the code to work while fighting a part of him that hoped it wouldn't. Then he turned it slowly. It relented, and the door cracked open.

Jet held it there and looked at me. "You don't have to do this."

"Shut up," I whispered. "I'm here now. Let's hurry."

He nodded and looked up and down the hall before stepping into the room, closing the door behind me. The darkness was intense, but I found the light switch and flipped it quickly. The space at first appeared tiny, but further inspection showed that was an illusion created by the congested arrangement of the furnishings. A wood laminate corner desk with a towering hutch on one side guarded entry into the office, a series of metal file cabinets lined the wall behind the desk, and another row of file cabinets along the adjacent wall to the right closed the loop. The only personal touches were a few potted plants atop the file cabinets, a framed aerial photo on one wall of the medical center from its infancy in 1956, and a single-family photo on the desk. The middle-aged woman in a homely floral dress, posing stiffly beside her husband and two teenage daughters, confirmed my mental image of a stern secretary adept at deflecting requests for meetings with anatomy professors and demanding prompt return of borrowed files.

"I don't think *feng shui* is her thing." Jet gestured from the photo to the furniture crammed around it.

I nodded. "What exactly are we looking for?"

"Not sure, but from the looks of this room, I'd say a file of some sort."

"Well that narrows it down," I mumbled.

"You start on the other end, and we'll meet in the middle." Jet opened one of the file drawers in the corner. He shook his head. "It'd be nice if the drawers were labeled."

"I'll bet Mrs. Shui there can tell you what's in every drawer." I nodded toward the empty chair at the desk. "How do I know what I'm looking for?"

"You'll know it when you see it."

Jet thumbed past some personnel files going back at least twenty years, while I glossed over some financial documents I did not understand. Budgets and expense reports and files of purchase orders. Then there was a cabinet filled with folders of anatomy notes, many of them old typewritten notes on Courier 10-point, a few of them ancient master copies for ditto machines from over a decade before.

"You have to learn all these words?" I flipped through a few pages. "Flexor digitorum brevis muscle? Interosseous talocalcaneal ligament? What the heck?"

"Nah, learning the proper names for the parts of the body is completely optional." Jet's voice was laced with sarcasm. "We can just call them whatever we want. Focus, please."

"I'm just saying, I think they need some better names than those."

Jet didn't respond. He was locked in on the contents of a different drawer. "Jackpot!" A quiver crept into his voice. "These files are for the body donation program."

"That's got to be it."

"They're labeled by year. 1988, 1989." He pointed at another drawer. "Check that one."

I opened the next file cabinet and saw the files organized by year there as well. "Here it is. 1994."

"Uh uh." Jet shook his head. "Go back. Adam died last year. 1993. That's where we need to go."

The section for 1993 consisted of about forty or fifty hanging file folders. None were labeled, so I slid them out, careful to keep them in order, and transferred them to the desk behind us. "What are we looking at?"

"Chain of custody records for donated bodies. Look, each one has been assigned a number. No names."

"There's got to be a master list with the names and number assignments somewhere."

"Maybe. But there's useful information here. It shows the date of death, county of origin, the coroner's name, the cause of death, and where the body was assigned here in the department."

Jet and I divided the folders in half and worked through them. I called out the first one. "14288. Alcorn County. Myocardial Infarction. Coroner Albert Gruley. Dental Gross Anatomy." I paused and glanced at Jet. "Dentists take Gross Anatomy?"

Jet never looked up. "They do. Don't cover as much as we do, but they have the class." Without pausing, he read the details of the next record out loud as I had done, but soon we each grew silent as we hurriedly scanned them for anything recognizable or useful.

I skipped through several diagnoses—some with which I was familiar, such as pneumonia and motor vehicle collision, and others I had never heard of, such as amyotrophic lateral sclerosis—wondering if I was missing something. The counties seemed to be randomly distributed, although I was not sure exactly where a few of them were. Then something caught my eye. "Jet. Look at this. This one was from last September. What was that, a month before Adam died?"

"I'm sure a lot of people died in Mississippi a month before Adam."

"Maybe. But how many donated their bodies to science? And in McKinley County?"

Jet grabbed the folder from me. "September 10, 1993. McKinley County. Drug overdose. Coroner Buford S. Riggins. Orthopedic Surgery."

"So, Stimpy's real name is Buford."

Jet sighed. "Who cares. This is the guy your dad told you about. The one Stimpy was blackmailed to cover up. Whoever he was, he likely didn't die of an overdose. That murderer didn't want him having an autopsy but apparently had no idea he was coming here. So let's think." He stared at the document for several seconds. "First, we have this body donated to Anatomy from McKinley County. Then a month later Adam appears to die in a wreck, but he didn't, because he shows up almost a year later in Anatomy with a gunshot wound, meaning that somebody else was put in his coffin. What are the odds this is coincidence?"

"I'd say next to zero, but there's no gunshot wound mentioned as cause of death for any of these. And this guy was assigned to orthopedics."

"True. And look here, did you see this?" Jet pointed at a box with a check mark in blue ink, in the bottom right corner of the document. "This is where they indicate when the cadaver has been destroyed and disposed of. We need to keep looking."

We rolled through the remainder of the records without noting anything significant. "What now?" I asked. "Is that what the old janitor thought we needed to find?"

"I don't know, but I'm getting nervous. We've been in here for a long time. If I get caught, they'll lock me up, bond or no bond."

"Wait. I've got an idea. What county did Adam live in?"

"Jackson County, in Ocean Springs, but he worked a lot in Biloxi, which is Harrison County."

"Give me a minute." I picked through the folders again while Jet peeked out the door and then paced. I looked up. "Nothing here from either of those counties."

"Okay." Jet shrugged. "That may or may not mean anything."

"You're right, but at least now we know. Now, how many dissection groups do you have in your Medical Gross Anatomy class? How many cadavers?"

"Well, we have 103 students. 102 now since I'm out. But we had four per cadaver, and one group started with three. So twenty-six cadavers."

"Okay then, the key may not be what's in here. The key may be what's not in here. Jet, there's only twenty-five cadavers assigned here to Medical Gross Anatomy. One folder is missing."

"That could be important," Jet whispered, "but we have a more immediate problem."

Someone was punching the keypad at the door. We were about to have company.

"Thank goodness you're here!"

The elderly security guard eyed me suspiciously as I closed the door behind me, stepping into the hall. "What are you doing in there?" The alarmed flare of his eyelids made his eyes appear at least twice their normal size behind the thick tinted lenses of his glasses. A lock of dingy gray hair looped down on his forehead, and he flicked it back in place. "No one is supposed to be in there. These offices all stay locked."

"I figured that, Officer…" I glanced down at the plastic badge hanging from his shirt pocket. "Officer Melbrook. But you're just in time. You must have a knack for this type of thing. I'm worried sick. See, here's the deal. I'm over there in the hospital, visiting my dear old grandmother. Sick in the ICU with uh, a case of the, uh, emphysema. Smoked all her life, bless her soul. So we're waiting through the night, hoping she'll live through it, right? Then I look up and my daughter is gone."

"You have your daughter here with you at two in the morning?"

"Well, um, yeah. My wife ran off with her boss, so it's just me and my daughter." I put my hand over my mouth, trying to produce a tear. "And so she's been there with me, right by my side. But she wandered off."

"The ICU is on the fourth floor." Melbrook punched the code into the lock again. "Let's see what's going on in here."

"Fourth floor, yes. But last time she was in the hospital, Grandma was on the sixth floor, so I thought my daughter, Abi, might have gone to the bathroom, then got confused coming back. Fourth floor bathroom's been out of service all day, so we had to go down one floor."

The guard turned the knob and opened the door. "And what made you think she wandered down here? And how did you get into this room?" He flipped on the light and scanned his surroundings, squinting in the brighter fluorescent light.

"Well, I went up to the sixth floor of the hospital and didn't see her. And I remembered that the hospital connects to the medical school on the third floor, so I went down there and came this way, thinking she might have gotten confused, like I said. So I came up to the sixth floor, like I told you. Grandma's old floor."

"What's your name, son?" He held out his hand. "Let me see some ID. And you didn't tell me what you were doing in this room."

"Sir, we're running out of time! Hurry! Please!" I pointed at the radio on his belt. "Can't you call someone on that thing? What do you call it, an APB? My daughter is wandering around here, lost and scared, I'm sure. Abi is her name. Abi Marchianti." I wrung my hands together. "I'm so worried. There's so many freaks out there. Do you think some weirdo took her?"

The old man's look softened. He stood a little straighter and poked out his chest, just slightly. "Calm down, there, son. I'm sure she's fine." He pulled the radio to his mouth and turned his back, speaking in hushed tones. I couldn't make out every word but could hear enough to tell he was buying my story. He turned back to me. "It's not exactly an all-points bulletin, but they'll call the operator. She can make an overhead announcement. We'll find her. I know this place like the curves of my wife's back."

I thought I heard a snicker under the desk but ignored it. The old man didn't seem to notice. "Mind if I make a call?" I pointed to the phone on the desk.

"Go ahead."

I picked up the receiver and adjusted my position just slightly so he couldn't see what numbers I pushed. "Yes, this is Joe Marchianti. I was just checking to see if there had been any word on my daughter, Abi?" I paused and pretended to listen. "You found her? She's back?" I raised my voice an excited half-octave higher. "Thank you. Thank you! I'll be right there." Another necessary pause. "Pediatric ER? Why?" I softened my voice. Subdued and worried now. "Okay. I'll head down there."

"What happened?" Melbrook asked.

"They found her, but she's so upset she's just frantic. Won't stop crying and screaming. So they're having her checked out."

"I'm sorry. Bet they can give her a sleeping pill or something to calm her down."

"Yeah, maybe. Listen, I appreciate all you've done. You clearly know how to handle these situations. But I need one more favor."

"What's that?"

"I have no idea where the Pediatric ER is. Can you take me down there?"

"Absolutely. This place is impossible to navigate 'less you've been around it a lot. But like I told you, I know it like—" He paused, and I cringed, hoping not to hear another simile about some part of his wife's body. "Well, let's just say I know it well." Melbrook patted me on the back as I turned to walk toward the door. "Lost my granddaughter in Walmart one time, prolly twenty years ago. Scared the willies out of me. No feeling of relief like when you find them."

"Ain't that the truth? Let's hurry, please."

The old man had a bit of a limp. He bustled down the hall ahead of me as best he could but still slower than I would have liked. I wanted to put as much distance between us and the anatomy offices as I could, as quickly as possible. "How long you been here?" I was trying to distract. Jet needed time to get the files back in their places, as I figured Melbrook would be back.

"Oh, 'bout ten years, give or take. Used to do security for a trucking company. Night shift. Pretty good pay, and nobody bothers you." He punched the elevator button for the third floor.

"Had any child abductions?" I asked.

"Nah, nothing like that."

"Probably see some strange stuff though, huh?"

"Usually pretty quiet on this end. Now the ER, where we're headed, it gets crazy. Like the wild, wild West sometimes."

I thought I'd take a stab for the heck of it. "What was that you said was on the sixth floor? Anatomy? Is that where they have the dead bodies? Ever see any weird stuff there?"

His gait slowed slightly as we crossed the threshold from the medical school into the main hospital. "Usually pretty quiet there, too. Seen them moving them bodies in and out at strange times in the middle of the night, though. I try not to pay no attention. None of my business." His gait slowed even more, and I knew he was going to stop. "Say, you never told me what you were doing in that room when I found you."

I suppose he probably turned around as he finished the sentence, but I had already rounded the corner and was moving into a full sprint before the last word evaporated from his lips.

THIRTY-EIGHT

J ET was sleep deprived. And that was before he spent a whole night sneaking into the anatomy office, evading detection, and mulling over the findings afterward. But instead of needing to pull over for a power nap during the three-hour drive to Ocean Springs, he remained alert. His mind spun and twirled like a majorette's baton in a college football halftime show.

Who could have wanted to harm Adam? Clearly, someone was out to get him. His apartment had been ransacked, his hard disk drive stolen, samples from some of his research destroyed. The timeline was interesting, though. As best Jet could tell, Adam had met Anniston Lewis at roughly the same time his troubles began. And according to his best friends, Anniston had acted oddly on the day they interviewed her, becoming indignant, racing to the casino afterward. All particularly suspicious since Anniston's aunt, the one-and-hopefully-only F. Liona Broom, appeared to have gambling debts up to her bloodshot eyeballs. Jet's preacher had always told him that money wasn't the root of all evil, the love of it was. Jet was learning that maybe owing money spawned plenty of evil of its own. In this case, he just had to figure out how. And prove it.

What made no sense to him, though, was how Anniston Lewis was connected to Sylvester Cronin. Clearly, there was some collaboration between whoever was after Adam—and evidently killed him—and the professor who apparently coordinated the cover-up afterward.

Jet suddenly had an idea, but he needed to make a call. He veered off the highway at the first gas station he saw, confirming the presence of a pay phone out front and lamenting the fact he had not invested in one of those car phones.

He knew the number by heart, as he did most numbers after he'd called them at least once. "Abi, are you busy?"

"Steady. Are you okay? You usually don't call me at work."

"I need some help."

"Jet, where are you?"

"Out and about. But I need a favor. You still keep in touch with Samantha?"

"Sam, my old roommate?"

"Yeah, didn't you tell me she got a job in DC?"

"Well yeah, we still talk. She went to work for USIS. I think it stands for US Investigative Services. She says they're contracted to do the background checks for government employees."

"Exactly. So, I need someone to find out if my anatomy professor, Sylvester Cronin, has gambling debts or any ties to the Gulf Coast. Business, family, whatever."

"What are you talking about?"

"Well, Abi, I'm headed to Ocean Springs right now. Much to my surprise, Adam's old girlfriend, Anniston, has agreed to meet me. I think she's somehow tied to Adam's death, or at least she knows what happened. But Cronin has to be involved, too, and I can't figure out how. Nothing happens in that anatomy department without him knowing. So there has to be a connection."

"Jet, those government background checks take months to complete, at least."

"Just because they have so many and there's a backlog. Sam can sneak one to the front of the line, I bet. I'm sure she owes you a favor for something. Surely you pulled her away from some loser at a party or two over the years, huh? Plus, I don't need the whole thing. Ask her to just skim the surface. I'll bet it pops out. Please?"

The voice from the pay phone told Jet he'd have to deposit more coins to continue talking. But he was out of both coins and time.

"Please, Abi. I need it ASAP. My future depends on it."

"Jet, I'm not sure—"

"I'll call you later. Thanks!"

The Fat Daddy Lounge was nestled between a rundown gas station and a used car lot, one block north of Highway 90. It wasn't hard to find if you knew where to look, but nothing about the one-story cinder block building and faded sign over the door suggested it was a destination for anyone other than the locals. The two Harleys in front fit the profile. Jet wouldn't have been surprised to see a whole gang of bikers roll up from the looks of the place.

He took a deep breath and entered, hoping for the best. The darkness was intimidating, its contrast to the dazzling brightness just outside the door magnified by the surprise of it. Jet wondered for a second if the restaurant had any lighting whatsoever, but as his pupils finally accommodated the change, he got his bearings. A bar extended down the length of the room to his left. Bearded men in denim and leather occupied two of the dozen or so red vinyl stools set before the bar. They rested their elbows on the polyurethane-coated wood, quietly nursing beers in clear mugs. They both glanced in his direction, but neither acknowledged him further. The place was empty otherwise. Jet zigzagged between the round tables and metal chairs and took a seat in one of the booths against the wall opposite the bar.

He faced the front door. It was a matter of habit, for whatever reason. No paranoia. He just always liked to see who entered and left. On the wall was a collection, if one could call it that, of prints and posters of women in Mardi Gras costumes, complete with Venetian and carnival masks, rich headdresses, colorful makeup and beads, each of them eyeing the patrons. A huge charcoal print of a male lion sprawled over the doorway, his eyes also alert, as if lording over his domain. *Panthera leo.* Jet loved the regalness of the scientific name.

"Louis," a voice said.

Jet turned to the waitress standing beside him, also looking at the print. "I call him Louis. Not sure why. A tribute to Louis Armstrong, I guess. Or maybe King Louis the Thirteenth. I dunno." She set two plates down on the table and slid into the seat across from Jet. "Fat Daddy's famous ribeye steak sandwich or the award-winning boast of the coast burger?"

Jet hadn't really thought about food, which was unusual for him, but his mouth watered at the aroma. Thin-sliced steak dripped au jus down the edges of a French roll, and a two-inch thick burger bubbled with natural juices and was topped with melted cheddar and a pile of onion strings.

Jet pulled the burger to him. "You must be Anniston."

"Wow. Adam always said you were smart." She gave a jesting smile as she pulled the steak dish to her. The smile disappeared, and she covered her mouth. "Oh gosh, I'm sorry. I don't really know you. I hope that's not disrespectful. But I don't see the point of pretending people never existed after they're gone. Right?"

Jet liked her immediately but had no intentions of that getting in the way of what he had to do. "No offense taken." He smiled and continued to size her up.

Anniston Lewis was striking. Hazel eyes, square chin with a hint of a point at the bottom, high cheekbones. An easy beauty, his mother might say. The kind of girl who was a pleasure to look at any time but might be magazine-cover material after an hour with a makeup artist. He suspected she didn't spend much time with makeup artists. Her hair was pulled back in a ponytail, and an even tan on her face and neck suggested she kept it that way most of the time.

She nodded at the food as Jet took a bite of the burger. "Sorry about choosing the meal. Only get a thirty-minute lunch break, and that's only if it's not busy, so I figured I'd save time. Plus, these are the best we've got." She took a bite of the steak sandwich.

"No, you did just fine." Jet wiped the corner of his mouth with a napkin. "Thanks for agreeing to meet with me. Listen, I'll get right to it."

Anniston held up her hand. "Look, Jet, before you go too far with this, I gotta tell you. Two of your friends already came down here and had this same talk with me."

"Case and Jack. Yeah, I know. I asked them to. And they filled me in afterward. But they didn't tell you everything."

"What do you mean?"

"I'll get to that. Give me a minute. First off, I know what you told them about Adam working for the Gulf Seafood Consortium on the side. What exactly is that? I tried to look it up but came up with nothing."

"Honestly, I don't know whether it's a real organization or just a name made up by the companies that got together and hired Adam. He never really said."

"Okay, I'll chase that rabbit later if I have to. I know about someone breaking into his apartment and carving STOP into the furniture. Could have been related to his DEQ job or something else, but since he was testing for pollution, it seems like the likely suspect would be something related to that job. But there's a few things that bother me about all that. Wanna hear?"

"Please."

Jet held up an index finger. "I'll list them for you. One, what are the odds that his apartment gets broken into on the very day you two meet? Two, what are the odds that you and Adam rush to his office after the first break-in, then two days later his office is broken into as well? Three, why did Case and Jack's questions prompt you to race down to the casino, the very same casino where your Aunt Fly-On-A-Broom was in debt out the wazoo, to meet with the casino boss?" He dangled his three fingers in the air for effect before dropping his hand to the table, tapping it with clenched fist softly, methodically.

Anniston glared at him before she spoke. "Jet, I cared about Adam, too, and I'd love to help, but I don't have to listen to this." She rose, jarring the table and rattling the silverware against the plates. "Besides, who cares? He's gone, and we can't get him back." She wiped a tear from the corner of one eye.

Jet reached across the table and grabbed her hand. "Please, Anniston. Sit down." He said it louder than he'd anticipated. Maybe he'd even yelled, but he didn't regret it. "I'm sorry."

She pulled her hand away and held it to her chest, posture rigid, full of uncertainty.

Before Anniston could make her decision, a man with a giant paw lightly touched her shoulder. Someone was standing beside him as well. "You havin' trouble with this guy, Annie?" the first biker said. He glared at Jet. "Need me to toss him?"

"Please, Anniston." Jet pleaded in the calmest voice he could muster. "Hear me out, and then I'll leave."

Anniston sighed heavily and sat back down. "Thanks, Bohannon. You, too, Rabbit." She blew both men a kiss. "I'm fine."

"She's family," Rabbit said. He patted Jet on the shoulder brusquely as both men turned to move back to the bar. "Better be cool."

"If that's the rabbit, I don't want to see the wolf." Jet smiled as the men retook their seats.

"They're regulars in here. Look like grizzlies but really just koalas when you get to know them." Anniston twirled the straw in her drink between her thumb and middle finger. "Enough animal metaphors. Let's cut the crap. Spit out whatever it is you've got to say. Why are you here?"

Jet took a deep breath. "Did you truly care about my brother?"

Anniston's eyes narrowed. "I told you I did."

"Then I'm gonna choose to believe you. Ever play much poker?"

"I'm a slot girl myself, but yeah, I've played a little. Your point?"

"Okay, then you'll understand this. I'm going all in with you. Betting every chip I've got then showing all my cards. I don't have time for anything else."

She nodded but said nothing.

"But you've got to promise me the same in return. If you cared about Adam like you say."

"I'm listening."

"I loved my brother. Looked up to him my whole life. We weren't much alike, but we each admired what the other didn't have. If his death was nothing more than a horrible random tragedy on a cold country road, then I could deal with that. No choice. But there's more to it than that." He was trembling now. His heart beat in his vocal cords. He stared at her hard. No bluffs, no games. "Anniston, my brother Adam's body was on my dissection table the first day of Gross Anatomy. Not a burn mark in sight. Took me a couple days to figure it out, but when I did, somebody moved it. Doesn't take a genius to connect the dots that his death was no accident. And I think you know what happened."

Anniston Lewis's jaw dropped as if it had come unhinged. She shook her head violently. "No way, no way. Impossible. There was a fire. What about the fire?"

"You tell me about the fire. Adam's gas can was in his storage shed in Ocean Springs along with his four-wheeler. And his hunting buddy didn't have his four-wheeler, either. So what, Adam bought a gas can, moved it to my truck when he borrowed it, and was taking it to his hunting camp, even though he knew neither he nor anybody there would need it? Does that make sense?" He paused and watched for a reaction, but she didn't budge. "Somebody staged that fire. That was somebody else's body in that truck, and somehow Adam wound up on my dissection table." Jet slammed his fist down on the table. "Now, seeing as how you came along just about the time he started getting harassed, I'm betting dollars to donuts he got killed somewhere else and you know what happened to him. Now tell me."

Anniston held up her hand and cut her eyes toward the bar. Rabbit and Bohannon were up out of their stools again. She shook her head and waved them off, and both men eased back down.

She turned back to Jet, teary-eyed. Her voice quivered when she spoke. "Jet, please believe me. I had no idea. Your friends told me you were having a hard time with Adam's death, but they said nothing about his, his body…" Her voice broke completely, and she covered her trembling lips as the tears broke free.

His instinct was to give her a napkin, but he might regret it later if she was indeed complicit in this nightmare. He didn't move, and she pulled one from the dispenser herself.

She smeared what little mascara she wore across her cheeks and spoke softly, deliberately, staring at the table. "My Aunt Elfie—F. Liona Broom, as you know her—had a gambling problem. Thirty-two thousand dollars in debt. Not a lot to some folks, but a fortune to her. She was about to lose her car, her trailer. Then one day late last summer, a man came to me. Said he had a proposition, a way to clear her debt." Anniston paused and crushed the napkin in her fist, but she didn't look up.

Jet's anger simmered, coming to a boil, and he fought to contain it. He had often seen his mother take the top off a saucepan on the stove to release the heat, lower the pressure, keep it from boiling over. He had no top to remove and feared he might explode if this story ended where he thought it would. But his only choice was to endure the heat. "Go on," he managed to mumble.

She took in a deep breath and released it slowly. "Adam was working for that seafood group."

"Gulf Seafood Consortium, whatever that is."

"Yeah, GSC. When dockside gaming was legalized in 1992, Biloxi's commercial fishing industry took a dive. Employees left to go work for casinos, most seafood processing plants sold their property to gaming interests, and whole fishing fleets were sold. Everybody knows the casinos we have now aren't going anywhere. I mean, Harrison County's unemployment rate has dropped fifty percent in two years, and there is no end in sight. New casino projects are either popping up or are being discussed in every direction. Adam said GSC wants to stop the growth and save what's left of their industry here."

"So what's that got to do with Adam?"

"Some people have been concerned about the environmental impact of the casinos."

"Seems like I've read about that. Wastewater treatment, water runoff, impacts from dredging, encroachment on existing wetlands, that type thing?"

She shrugged. "I suppose. He said GSC figured that if they could show a negative impact from the casinos in place already, it wouldn't take much to make an argument that further waterfront development should be halted or at least delayed until more testing can be done."

"The government hasn't already sorted all that out?"

Anniston's face twisted into a frown. "Really? The governor and legislature pushed the gaming laws through without blinking an eye. Last year the state made ninety-five million dollars from the casino industry and this year is projected to clear 130 million. They'll be the first to look the other way."

"So they hired an inside guy sympathetic to their cause, from the DEQ, to run the testing for them."

"Yep. That was Adam."

"And you know all this information how, exactly?"

Anniston shrugged. "From Adam. He was a believer. He talked, I listened."

"You still haven't told me how this fits with what happened."

"Like I told you, my aunt owed a small fortune of gambling debts, mostly at the Double Luck. So this guy Bobby Meyerling, the son of the owner, offered me a deal. He said he'd cancel my aunt's debt. All I had to do was get close to Adam and find out where he had the test results. They were gonna try to scare him into stopping the testing, and I would help steal the results if necessary. Then Aunt Elfie would be debt free.

Jet wanted to choke her. But he couldn't do that. For one, he didn't want to go to jail, but more than that, he didn't want to get decapitated by her bosom buddy bikers. "So it was you," he growled. "It went too far, and they killed him."

"Jet, listen to me. Please. Just stay calm and listen." She reached out to touch his arm, but he tensed and clenched his fist, and she withdrew. "The day I met Adam, at the restaurant. It went as planned. I distracted him, one of Bobby's men destroyed the vials in his truck, and they tossed his apartment. They stole his computer drive and carved a threat into his furniture. Adam acted like he knew right away what it was about, but he didn't tell me much at first. He insisted we go to his office, though, where he looked through some files. I knew then that's where the data was stored. Two days later, Bobby's people broke into his office and stole the documents. I was supposed to be done at that point, but by then I was hooked."

"Hooked? Drugs?"

"No, no. On Adam."

"Oh. Didn't he suspect you? I mean, that's quite a coincidence."

"I don't think so. He never acted like it. We, we just fit, and he trusted me. We couldn't stay away from each other." She wiped another round of tears away with her wadded napkin. "I felt so bad about what I'd done, I cried myself to sleep every night for a week. But I couldn't tell him."

"How'd you feel a month later when they killed him?" Jet sneered. "Cry about that?"

"No, Jet. That's not it. You don't understand."

"Well make me understand, Anniston. Help me understand how you're not responsible for the death of my brother."

"You know what Adam did when he found out the files had been stolen from his office?"

"Knowing him, he wanted to kill somebody. Sounds like he should have."

"He laughed."

"Laughed? What are you talking about?"

"He laughed. He was mad, sure, but he laughed about somebody going to all that trouble to find test results showing that the water quality was perfectly normal."

Jet leaned back and folded his arms over his chest, considering the implications. It didn't make sense. "Normal? How could he be sure?" He shifted positions and put his elbows on the table, focusing on Anniston's reaction as he spoke. "Some of the samples were destroyed that day before they could be tested."

She didn't flinch. "True, but he'd been testing for months, over and over. Said he knew that last one would be normal too, but the people paying him insisted he get one more round. He didn't care. Easy money. He wasn't sure whether he was glad the water was clean or sad he didn't find a way to slow down the waterfront development."

Her demeanor suggested she was telling the truth, but she had conned Adam. Jet was determined not to follow suit. "Why, then, did you race to the casino to meet Bobby Meyerling when Case and Jack told you that foul play was suspected in Adam's death?"

She nodded. "My aunt went right back to gambling after I got her cleared. That's why I moved out. I was fed up with her. But I thought she was doing it at a different casino. When those two came to me, it put some crazy doubts in my mind. What if? So I confronted Bobby. And you know what he told me?"

"That if he wanted to kill somebody to tie up loose ends, you'd be first up?"

She paused and blinked twice, taken aback. "Yes, that's exactly what he said. Then he laughed and asked me why he'd want to kill somebody for proving that the casinos weren't polluting the water."

Jet had to admit, even if the tests were abnormal, it made no sense to kill Adam over that, a month later, no less, and let Anniston stay off the hook. Not unless she was an ongoing accomplice. And if that was the case, she wouldn't be confessing right now. She was telling the truth. He knew it as well as he knew his own name. "Can I borrow a phone?"

Anniston nodded. "Sure, at the left end of the bar. If you're calling long distance, better use a card. Boss'll have my head."

Rabbit and Bohannon scowled at Jet but said nothing as he picked up the phone and dialed. Two rings and she picked up. "Abi." He cupped his hand over the handset's microphone and spoke in muffled tones. "What did you find out?"

"On Cronin? Not much. No connection to the coast or anyone on it, and Sam said she checked everything. Grew up in Indiana, college at IU, med school in Ohio, worked in Washington State ten years before coming to Mississippi. Family ties, including his wife, all north of the Mason Dixon Line."

"I owe you."

"More than you know." Abi hung up.

He fished in his pocket for the photo as he returned to his seat under the watchful eye of Rabbit, Bohannon, Louis the Lion, and the Mardis Gras ladies. "One last thing, Anniston." He slid one of the photos taken from the storage shed across to her. "I had three questions about this photo. Where the computer hard drive was, why the gas can was there, and why Adam had all these medical supplies. You told me Adam's hard drive was stolen, and I'm inclined to believe you. I'm still working on the gas can. But the other? Tape and gauze and ointments? Adam hated the sight of blood, so I know this wasn't left over from a Boy Scout first aid merit badge or a second career as a medic. Any ideas?"

Anniston sighed and gave a sad grin. "Oh yeah. Adam didn't want anyone to know. He was embarrassed about it, but I helped him with it a few times. He had a pilonidal cyst."

"Pilonidal cyst?" One of the very few things Jet had not read about at some point in time.

"I have no idea what caused it, but it just appeared right at the top of his butt crack. Had to be cut out and left open to heal over time. It had just healed a week or two before he died."

Jet sucked in a breath and nodded. Some things were beginning to make sense. Perhaps the trouble Adam was in on the coast fizzled out on its own and had nothing to do with his death, after all. But the clues they found investigating it might be important in proving what did happen to him.

Abi's eyes widened, and she held up her index finger. "Hold on, you won't believe this." She heaved her purse on the table and dug through it. "It's silly, but I just couldn't get rid of these." Anniston pulled out a small stack of photos of her own, five or six of them. She teared up again as she flipped through, smiling and then cringing at the end. Jet reached out, and she laid them in his palm before snatching back the one on top. It was of her and Adam, leaning against the railing of some rickety dock jutting into a backwater channel, smiling like they'd just shared an inside joke. "Let me keep this one. I don't need the others."

He perused the four-by-six photos. Random snaps with mostly poor focus or lighting or both, one or two with some other acquaintances he would never know. The last one, though, was different. It was just what he needed.

"I used it to blackmail him," she said.

He dropped his chin and gave her a serious look beneath raised eyebrows.

"Not like that. I took it when he wasn't looking and told him I'd show everybody if he ever did me wrong. He could have taken it from me, but he didn't. I think he thought it was funny himself. Sort of this little game we played." She stood abruptly, looking at her watch. "I've got to get back to work." She grabbed her purse and stopped mid-pivot. "I hope you find out what happened, Jet. I never would have hurt him."

"I think I believe you."

He turned to leave, but she stopped him. "Jet? I don't know how in the world Adam's body got switched like you're saying it did or whatever. That doesn't make sense to me. But I promise if I had known that I would have already told you everything."

"Can I call you later? May have some more questions." Anniston nodded, and he turned and walked out the door.

THIRTY-NINE

"YOU know I could get in big trouble."

"How?"

"Fraud or false pretenses or something."

I smiled into the phone. "Yeah Abi, I bet they'll lock you up if they find out. I think impersonating a newspaper clerk is a felony."

"Very funny. Your boy Jet is already using up my favors for the day. He's on a crusade of his own."

"I know. Our plan is multifaceted."

Abi snickered. "Mmm hmm, I'm sure."

"So, did you make the call or not?"

"Your appointment is at ten fifteen."

"That's in an hour!"

"Good luck with that. He had a cancellation. It was that or two weeks."

"It's perfect. I called in sick today anyway. You're the best."

"And tell me again why you couldn't make the call yourself?"

"Because a pretty voice like yours is much more persuasive than my rough country drawl."

"Ahh. I don't think the prude who answered was into my voice too much. You'd better find your sophisticated journalist voice. Anyway, aren't you worried you'll be recognized? You were just caught breaking in there last night."

"I was a frantic father looking for my lost daughter. I doubt the old man gave it a second thought after I disappeared. Plus, we didn't take anything."

"Why don't you just wait on your dad to get home and handle this? You said he's suspicious now. It's just what, two more days until he gets back?"

"First off, he's not entirely convinced about what happened. Second, it will take too long for him to dig to the bottom, if he's able to at all. Jet's been kicked out of school, and if he doesn't get back soon, even he will be too far behind to catch up this year."

"You be careful, Case. I worry about you. Jet's in this whether he likes it or not, but you don't have to get yourself in trouble."

"You know me better than that, Abi. Speaking of Jet, what did you hear from him?"

"Called me about an hour ago. He's on his way to the coast. He's convinced that girl had something to do with Adam's death."

"Maybe so. It's certainly fishy, but somebody had to work from this end, too. What about Jack? He feeling any better?"

"Haven't heard today. But Lane said they got along real well yesterday. Tore down some rotten bridges to the past, maybe."

"That's good, I think."

"Yeah, I'm hoping Lane will branch out a bit and make some new friends. He needs a new coffee partner."

I paused, not sure how to respond. Might as well be honest. "I wholeheartedly agree. Not sure Jack's your guy, though. What about your roommate? Rylee?"

"She hates him. Why you think she never came out of her room yesterday morning?"

I wanted to say Rylee was a smart girl, but I didn't. I really didn't have anything against Lane now other than the fact I was falling for Abi again, and he was bribing her with Folgers and gourmet cooking and who knew what else. "Hey, I gotta hurry, but I'll call you later." I started to hang up but held on. "Abi?"

"Yeah?"

"I'm glad you're here."

"Here?"

"You know, in Jackson. So we can hang out some."

She laughed. "Hang out? Is that what we're going to do?"

I knew she was giving me a hard time. "Don't be a smarty. You know what I'm talking about. I told you I wanted to see you more."

"I know. That sounds good, Case. I have missed you. Got a lot to catch up on."

Music to my ears. "Amen to that. I'll call you later."

———

"Have a seat, Mr. Reynolds. Professor Cronin will be with you in just a moment. What newspaper did you say you were with?"

"The *Amberton Advocate*." I held up my badge as I sank into a burgundy leather chair, glad the identification didn't include a photo. I'd gained quite a few pounds since starting at the *Advocate* as a skinny summer intern five years earlier. "Up in McKinley County."

The secretary tapped a pen against her temple, precariously close to a bouffant that surely could collapse if disturbed. "Oh yes, Amberton." Her voice was loud and nasal. "I knew a girl from there back in junior college. You ever know any Carnathans? I think her name was Celia. Or maybe Celeste?"

The chestnut hair color wasn't fooling anyone. I suspected the secretary's junior college days were somewhere north of forty years prior. I shook my head and smiled. "No, ma'am, I don't."

"Ah, maybe a year or two before your time." A red light blinked on her telephone, and she picked it up, listening briefly. "He will see you now." She nodded toward the closed door to her right.

I turned the handle and stepped into the office, trying to take everything in. Professor Sylvester Cronin was just as Jet had described him. About an inch shorter than me, rotund, wearing a white starched shirt bought twenty pounds ago and blue tie with a perfect dimple at the top just below the knot. Neatly trimmed hair, seamless into a groomed beard, gray at the edges matching that of the temples. He sat behind a mahogany desk and did not rise to shake my hand. "What can I help you with, Mr. Reynolds?"

"I'm with the *Amberton Advocate*. Wanted to ask you a few questions."

The anatomy professor removed his glasses and pinched the bridge of his nose. "Aw, no. A newspaper reporter? Missed that when Alice told me." He sighed and narrowed his eyes into a suspicious glare. "Questions about what?"

"This won't take long, sir. My paper is doing a series of feature stories on different professions. Between you and me, my editor's daughter is a high school senior with the motivation of a mushroom, and I think she hopes it will inspire her. Not sure why she would think her daughter will actually read the paper, much less use it to decide she wants to be something more than a mooch. Anyway, physician is one of the featured professions. So I thought, why not begin with the legendary travails of Gross Anatomy?"

Cronin gave a patronizing smile and looked at his watch but did seem to relax a bit. "And so what do you need from me?"

I measured my words carefully. *Get to the point without raising suspicion.* "I'm going to interview some doctors for information about the level of difficulty of the material, that type thing, from their point of view. I'd like to hear your perspective, though. How do the students cope with the course emotionally? You know, mountains of material, cadavers, that type thing."

"Cadavers?"

"Well, yeah. You know, if I see a dead possum in the road it turns my stomach. I can't imagine looking at a dead human being, much less cutting on one."

"We don't just cut haphazardly, Mr. Reynolds. We dissect, carefully and with a purpose. Are you trying to convince readers to go into medicine or scare them away?"

"Neither, sir. Just hoping to present the facts."

"Our students do just fine. We are very deliberate in our selection process. Our selection committee prides itself in choosing only those students who are properly prepared for our program, both academically and psychologically."

I nodded and pretended to scribble some notes. "Let me ask you this. Where do the cadavers come from? I think our readers might find that interesting."

"Come from? They come from everyday people. Just like you and me. People who want to serve the greater good by donating their body to science."

"All of them?"

"Occasionally we get an unclaimed John or Jane Doe, but most are voluntarily donated."

"And how does that process work? Donating, I mean."

"It's very simple, actually. The donor notifies our program of his or her intentions, there is some paperwork, and upon the death, our people are notified and take care of the rest."

"And what happens to the body once it is brought here?"

"The body is preserved by a special embalming process and stored until it is needed."

"Is that something you supervise, Professor Cronin? I imagine that's quite a responsibility, overseeing such a delicate operation."

He folded his hands together and rested them on his desk as he leaned toward me. "I supervise everything."

I waited for him to elaborate, but he didn't. He just watched me. "And? You didn't answer my question."

Cronin repeated his patronizing smile and settled back into his chair. He stroked his beard a few times before he finally spoke. "Dr. Marta Winscote is the director of the body donor program. She handles the day-to-day operations. Now, Mr. Reynolds, I thought this feature was about becoming a physician. You seem disproportionately interested in our body donation program. Where did you say you were from again?"

"I'm sorry, it's just fascinating to me. Let me get back to the Gross Anatomy aspect. You said you are careful to pick the right students. What does it take? You know, to survive the course?"

"Well, it takes dedication, discipline, persistence. And of course, a high acumen as a foundation. But most of my students don't just survive, Mr. Reynolds. They thrive."

"I'm sure they do. But there must be exceptions. How many students drop out during this course each year?"

"It varies. Usually five to ten."

"Any so far this year?"

Cronin watched me intently while I again pretended to scratch important information on my notepad. "We've had a casualty or two."

I wanted to ask him who had dropped out and why but didn't. I did lock my eyes on his. "The material just too difficult, I suppose?"

"One could say that." He looked away and blinked then turned back. His demeanor had changed, the way a cloudy day darkens to signal an imminent storm. "I'm going to ask you again, Mr. Reynolds. What newspaper are you working with?"

I knew it was a rhetorical question but answered anyway. "The *Amberton Advocate*, sir."

"Mmm hmm. Amberton. Friends with John Edward Townsend, I imagine."

I felt a twinge of panic but recovered quickly. "John Edward? Is that Jet? You know, I never even knew his real name. We're about the same age, but we never really hung out together. Supposedly, he's a smart guy. Rumor back home, though, is he's run into some problems. Gone mental or something?"

Cronin shook his head. "I'm afraid I can't comment on my students' performances. Let me just say some students have more difficulty with the emotional aspect than others."

"Yes, sir. Bless his heart. I always thought Jet was a little flaky. Hey, maybe my article will inspire someone from back home who's a bit better prepared. We need good doctors. National shortage, you know."

The professor stood and looked toward the door. "I have a meeting. Thank you for your interest."

Ending the interview suited me just fine. It seemed he wasn't the person I needed to talk to anyway, and his belief in my charade seemed to be fading. I reached out to shake his hand. "Thank you, professor. Good luck with the remainder of the year."

Cronin ignored my attempted handshake and escorted me out of his office. I paused at the desk of Secretary Alice of the Bouffant to thank her for her assistance.

I waited for Cronin to disappear back into his office, then smiled at Alice and whispered. "Can you tell me where Dr. Marta Winscote's office is?"

"Dr. Winscote?" she bellowed. "Why, of course! Two doors down the hall to the left."

"Is there something I can help you with?" A tall woman with glasses and a lab coat stood in the doorway, smiling.

"Dr. Winscote!" Alice's face erupted into a huge smile. "What delightful timing. This gentleman wanted to speak with you."

"Let's hold on just one second there, folks." Cronin's voice behind me was clear, his annoyance even clearer. "I'd like to verify that you are who you say you are, Mr. Reynolds."

I reached for my badge and moved to pull out my wallet, but Cronin waved a hand dismissively. "Alice, I'd like you to call the *Amberton Advocate* and ask about Mr. Reynolds here, whether or not he's actually working on an article as he claims."

"Sir?"

"Just what I said. *Amberton Advocate*. Dial it and I'll talk." He turned to me. "I'm assuming you know the number, Mr. Reynolds? Surely you don't mind me verifying, do you? Can't be too careful these days."

I had no idea what to do. So much for *allzeit bereit*. Be prepared. My old German scoutmaster would not be impressed. I had not considered the possibility that Cronin would call my bluff this way. The best-case scenario seemed to be that he would discover the fraud and ask me to leave, but I would have no opportunity to talk to Dr. Winscote. Worst case, he would have me escorted out by security and possibly call the police. Was it a crime to impersonate a member of the media?

He might also notify my actual employer, in which case I was likely to get fired. And because it would almost certainly appear I was in collusion with Jet, it would nullify whatever meager chance he had of returning to medical school. I'm not sure why I didn't just walk out the door. Instead, I froze and blurted out the phone number, still familiar from my days as a summer intern. "I, uh, will, uh, do you want me to talk to them?"

Cronin shook his head and waited on Alice to dial the number before taking the phone. "Your editor's name?" he asked me.

"Rooker. Ethel Rooker." I resigned myself to my pending destruction. If nothing else, I could read the reaction of the professor as the truth came out and do my best to castigate Cronin before he gave me the boot. What difference would it make now?

Cronin asked for Ethel Rooker and paused, tapping his pen on Alice's desk while someone on the other end located the editor. It wasn't hard to get through to upper management at a small-town newspaper with four employees. "Hello, Ms. Rooker." He introduced himself. "I have a young man here who states he is one of your employees and that he's doing a story for your newspaper on a career in medicine. I'm just calling to verify." Cronin paused and listened. "No, ma'am. Yes, his name is Reynolds. No, there is no problem. Yes, we are very happy to help inspire future physicians. Ma'am?" Cronin appeared confused. "Yes, I'll tell him. Happy to help, Ms. Rooker. You have a nice day also."

I wondered if the stunned look on my face matched that of the professor. "Well, Professor?"

"Well, you appear to be telling the truth, Mr. Reynolds. I won't apologize for checking to verify, but I will apologize for not having done that before your arrival, so as not to waste your time." Cronin frowned at Alice, whose bouffant seemed to wilt.

"Sounded like there was something she wanted you to tell me?" I asked.

"Hmm, oh yeah. Said to remind you she gets a copy of your book when it gets published. I thought you said this was for a newspaper article?"

"Uh, yes sir, it is. That's an entirely different project."

Dr. Winscote had been patiently waiting near the door. "Mind telling me what's going on here?"

I stepped over, reached out and shook her hand. It was cool but her grip was solid. "Case Reynolds with the *Amberton Advo-*

cate. Small town paper. Just doing a little personal interest story and wondered if I could ask you some questions."

She glanced at Cronin, whose shrug suggested she could take it or leave it. Winscote studied me head to toe before she answered. "Amberton, huh?"

"You know it?"

"Hernando County, right?"

"McKinley."

She nodded. "Come on down to my office, Mr. Reynolds, and we'll talk."

––––––––––––––––

Marta Winscote's office was a cluttered mess. Stacks of several different scientific journals rose from the floor in no particular arrangement. Notebooks and file folders loaded two bookshelves, and textbooks that could have filled the shelves were instead scattered on the floor, a metal desk, and the chairs in front of it. Three or four framed photos stood on a single shelf suspended on the wall behind the desk.

"Have a seat." She cleared several books from one of the chairs. "Pardon the mess. Teaching three classes and conducting my research don't leave much time for housekeeping."

"Thanks for seeing me. So, what is your area of research?"

"The role of glycoprotein expression in the extracellular matrix of embryonic hearts to stimulate the formation of mesenchyme."

My vacant expression must not have been hard to interpret.

"I'm sorry. Heart development in the fetus. Now, what can I do for you?"

"We're doing a series of stories on different professions. I'm working on one about the practice of medicine. I thought it would be interesting to take a look at Gross Anatomy. After all, it's the foundation upon which everything else is built, is it not? Learn everything there is to know about the human body in order to take care of the human body, huh? I'd like to know all about it. How hard it is. What it's like to dissect a human being. How the students handle it."

"Dr. Cronin is the director. I would expect he could give you all you need." She smiled stiffly. "If I know him, I would guess he gave you more than you asked for."

I smiled back at her joke. "Yeah, he's pretty intense. But he tells me you are the director of the body donor program."

"That's true, yes."

"So I guess that's what I'd like to ask you about. Is it tough to get enough donors for the medical students to work on?"

"It can be at times. But you'd be surprised. People are more generous than you might think."

"Bet you get them from all over the state, huh?"

"We do. More come from around Jackson, I guess. And the coast. More heavily populated."

"You know, I heard a rumor there was a guy from McKinley County who did that. Year or so ago." I watched her closely, but she didn't flinch.

"Maybe so," she said matter-of-factly. "Hard to keep up with them all." The phone rang, and she held up a finger while she answered. "Yes Maurice. How many of the samples? Did you check the controls? Did Sterling look at it? Okay, just run it again." She sighed as she hung up the phone. "One of the grad students in my lab." She stared past me for a few seconds, saying nothing, preoccupied. "I'm sorry, I'll be right back." She stood and strode past me out of the room.

I sat in my chair, feeling awkward. Would she even return? So far, I had learned nothing from my conversation with Cronin or her that I thought might help Jet, although maybe the Sterling she referred to on the phone was the same obnoxious medical student we had run into in the hall outside the anatomy lab that night. Jet seemed convinced he was out to get him in some way. Was there a connection?

I stood to leave but paused when the small group of photos behind her desk caught my eye. One was of her in cap and gown, flanked by an older man and woman, presumably her parents. Another showed her in long white lab coat holding a plaque, surrounded by a similarly attired group of men and women. But the third photo is what grabbed my attention. Dr. Winscote in a loose, bright orange sweater, bellbottom polyester pants, dark round glasses and headband, cradling a laughing baby in her arms. Orange against a bluebird sky and a background of brilliant aquamarine water popped from the paper despite the photo clearly being taken many years ago.

The trees in the background were deep green evergreens fronted by a huge sycamore, easily identified by its characteristic white bark and golden fall foliage. Sycamores had been one of my favorite trees since I was a small child and heard Bible stories of Zacchaeus, a "wee little man" who climbed one to get a glimpse of Jesus. My father enjoyed pointing them out to me, and I enjoyed picking which ones I thought I had low enough limbs to climb.

I startled at the man's voice behind me. "What are you doing?" I replaced the photo on its shelf and turned. Sterling Virchow stood in the doorway. Yep, that answered that question.

"I'm sorry. Beautiful picture there. It just caught my eye. Her child?"

"Not that it's any of your business, but I believe so, yes. I remember you. You were with Jet Townsend that night."

"My name is Case Reynolds." I stepped to him and began extending my hand but dropped it when I realized he had no intention of reciprocating. "And yes, I am a friend of Jet's, but I'm here with the newspaper." Less a lie than when I arrived, apparently, since my old editor had somehow endorsed my presence there. "Learning about Gross Anatomy for a story I'm doing."

"I'm sure. It's a shame about your friend, Jet. Bright guy, just couldn't cut it. You know, history is full of tortured geniuses like Van Gogh, Hemingway, and Poe. Ever heard of Kurt Gödel? Genius mathematician who became delusional that people were trying to poison him, so he would only eat food his wife cooked. Poor guy actually starved to death when she was in the hospital for several months. Weighed sixty-five pounds when he died."

"Yeah, and Abraham Lincoln and Winston Churchill both supposedly needed shrinks, and look where that got them. Since we're playing the ever-heard-of game, you ever heard of the Sword of Damocles?"

Virchow stiffened, somewhat taken aback by my turning the tables on him. "Sounds familiar."

I smiled. He was in my wheelhouse now. I didn't know a lot of science, but history and literature were a different story. "Guess you don't take a lot of history classes over in the School of Biological Sciences. Anyway, Damocles was a brown-noser who wanted to see what it was like to be king. King Dionysius traded places with him for a day but didn't tell him he had hung a sword by a single horsehair right over the throne, pointed at his head. When Damocles saw it, he tucked tail and got out of there."

"Your point?" Virchow snarled.

I smiled. "Nice pun. The point is that those who would seek power better be prepared to accept the danger that comes with it."

"Are you threatening me, Reynolds?"

I poked his chest. "I'm not sure what your angle is, but I'm telling you that when I find out you had something to do with what's happened to Jet, I'll make sure justice comes down on your head, sword tip first."

Virchow turned pale, but the blood rushed back and his face became crimson. He opened his mouth to speak but was interrupted by Dr. Winscote's voice behind him.

"Sterling. I've been looking for you."

He glared at me for an instant before forcing a smile and turning around. "Sorry, Doc. We got our wires crossed, I guess. I've just been talking to your reporter friend."

"Okay, I showed Maurice what we need to do. Give me a second to finish here, and I'll be right down."

Virchow walked out without acknowledging me further.

Dr. Winscote watched him leave then turned back to me. "Listen, I'm sorry, but there's a problem in my lab. I've got to get in there and straighten things out. Good luck with your article, okay?"

"Thank you. Can I ask you one more question?" Time to sink or swim.

"Quickly."

"What would you do if one of your cadavers turned out to be the murdered family member of a student? Would you be the one to handle that type of thing?"

Her eyelids flared before she looked away quickly then back at me. Was it my imagination or had she glanced at the photos behind her desk? "I'm sorry about Mr. Townsend." She looked away, but in the opposite direction. "Apparently you do work for the paper, but I assume you are here to some extent because of him?"

There was no point in lying to her. Virchow would tell her later anyway. "I would like to know why the smartest and toughest person I know is convinced of a conspiracy about his cadaver. The thing is, I think you believe him, too. Jet told me you're the only professor he trusts."

She removed her glasses and rubbed her eyes. "I'll tell you what I believe. I believe Jet is a brilliant mind and a good person, but unfortunately, neither guarantee success in medical school. I believe it highly unlikely he assaulted Gracie Tollison, and I believe he deserves his day in court to prove it. I believe Professor Cronin can be difficult and is overly intolerant of weakness of any sort. And I believe any far flung what-ifs about murdered brothers showing up in our anatomy lab are more fodder for tabloids than material for what I am sure is a reputable newspaper such as yours." She replaced her glasses and reached out her hand. "Good day, Mr. Reynolds. I need to get down to my lab."

FORTY

THE note read: *Edward T. Johnson. 1638 Atterberry Lane. Jackson. It's the turn just past Hideaway Rd.*

Dr. Winscote's secretary had given me the name and address as I was leaving. Someone from the newspaper had called saying that Mr. Johnson would meet me at that address for my next interview, but I didn't spend much time wondering who the message was from. Edward T. Johnson was a code. For all intents and purposes a rearrangement of John Edward Townsend. The reference to our favorite neighborhood hangout as kids, the Hideaway, removed any doubt. Jet wanted to meet. The question was, where? And why?

I drove to a quick stop to get a Jackson street map and found Atterberry Lane to be less than five minutes away, in a part of northeast Jackson with which I was actually somewhat familiar. The house was a quaint, red-brick bungalow design, subtly out of place among the predominance of ranch-style homes in the area. Jet's red F-150 sat in the driveway.

He was smiling when he opened the door, before I even had a chance to knock. "Case, come on in. You got my message."

I followed Jet in through a living room into the kitchen. "Pretty clever, there, Mr. Johnson. Why didn't you just leave a message for me to call you?"

He twisted his mouth into an incredulous frown and huffed. "How much fun would that be?"

A woman and two men sat at the kitchen table. Before I could ask whose place it was, the pretty redhead arose to greet me, reaching out with a handshake.

"Case Reynolds, meet Gracie Tollison," Jet said. "One of my anatomy partners. Or, well, she used to be."

"Met her at the hospital briefly," I replied. "She brought me your keys."

"I've heard a lot about you, Case," Gracie said.

"Same here." I winked at Jet. She was just as lovely as he had told me. "But don't believe everything you hear about me. Nice place you've got here."

"It's fine." She shrugged. "Close to the med school, which is the most important thing."

Jet motioned to the other two men. "Case, I'd like you to meet my other lab partners."

Both men were just as Jet had described. Craig Tekowski, stiff and bespectacled, pale skin and perfect hair. Tucker Oliver, small and wiry, easy smile, tousled hair. Tekowski nodded with a tight half-smile, but Oliver slid around the table to shake my hand. "Glad you showed. My man Jet insisted you'd wanna be here." He hopped backward to sit on the kitchen table, which didn't look particularly sturdy but nevertheless didn't flinch under his slight frame.

I searched the faces in the room. "He knows me well, but someone want to tell me what I'm here for?"

"We asked Jet to come over so we could talk to him about what happened in Gross Anatomy," Gracie said. "There are some things he needs to know."

Anger surged within me. "I don't know you guys, but if you have information about what's going on, it's high time you 'fess up. Or maybe you hadn't noticed that Jet's been kicked out of school?"

Jet held up both hands to calm me. "It's okay, Case. They couldn't help it. Let Gracie explain." He spun a high-backed wooden chair toward me.

I grabbed the back with both hands and shook my head. "I think I'll stand. Couldn't help what?"

Gracie put her hands together as one might to say a prayer. "Put yourself in our shoes. Most everybody in the class had heard about Jet, either before he got here or shortly after school started. Superstar brain, 4.0 GPA in engineering, perfect MCAT, that type thing. And because folks are nosy, especially about people who intimidate them, rumors about his story got around. You know, survived a murder attempt, his mother had cancer, father shipped overseas, brother died unexpectedly, all that. So it's natural to wonder about somebody like that. Can he handle it? Will he crack? Med school is cutthroat. Some hope others fail so they can take their place in the pecking order."

"Jet can handle it, I assure you." I said. "Question is, where do you guys fit? You know, in the hoping-others-fail part."

"Case," Jet said. "Dude, just listen."

"So," Gracie continued, "the second day of class, Jet, bless his heart, he just freaks out, nearly passes out for no apparent reason. Everybody thinks hey, there it goes, the tower is crumbling."

"Nobody has ever confused me with a tower." Jet smiled. "Maybe an igloo."

If Jet's intention was to lighten the mood, it worked. Tucker burst out laughing, and I couldn't help but chuckle. Gracie smiled and patted Jet on the hand. Even Tekowski grinned.

"So anyway," Gracie said, "the second day of Gross, Igloo has a spell again and actually passes out, hits his head, all that."

"Hammered that head, let me tell you." Tucker pounded his fist into the palm of his other hand. "Thought it might've killed him."

"It was bad," Gracie said. "Scared me to death. Anyway, next thing we know, Professor Cronin asks to meet the three of us in the lab early the next morning. When we get there, he has replaced our cadaver with another one."

"Not just any cadaver," Tucker said. "One with a hole in it, just like our first one."

"And you didn't go to the Dean right then and there?" I said.

"For what? Case, remember, we didn't really know Jet. So here we are, Cronin telling us that he's trying to save Jet. That Jet is having some psychiatric issues, PTSD-type stuff, that apparently the cadaver we had was similar in age and appearance to Jet's brother, and if he replaces it with another one who doesn't have that resemblance, Jet will realize it was all in his mind, and he'll be fine."

"But why fake a bullet hole?"

Tekowski spoke for the first time. "He said if Jet knew the cadaver was switched, it would just feed his delusion and paranoia. It made sense at the time."

"That's utterly ridiculous," I said. "So you took the bait. Hook, line, and sinker."

"It made as much sense as anything," Gracie said. "He said he was trying to protect Jet. Plus, he talked about how the lawyers could swoop in and make a mess of the whole operation for discrimination if they had to dismiss him. Just a big distraction for everyone, and we barely had time to eat and go pee, much less be hassled by interviews with lawyers."

"And it didn't seem a little fishy?" I looked back and forth between Jet's three partners. "To any of you?"

Gracie pointed at Tucker. "To be honest, he didn't buy it, and I just wasn't sure. But we had other reasons to hide it."

"He threatened you, didn't he?"

"Not exactly." Gracie grimaced. "Well, sort of. How'd he put it, Tea?"

Tekowski shrugged and folded his arms over his chest. "He said he'd be worried about students who weren't willing to stretch the rules just a little to protect their partner, that medical school could be harder for those type people. He didn't threaten us, but we knew what he meant."

Now we were getting somewhere. "Jet, this is it. It's what you need to get at Cronin and get back in school."

Jet shook his head. "What does this prove? That the anatomy director decided a cadaver was needed in some other capacity, so he switched them out? I don't think that's illegal."

"Aw, come on. He didn't just switch them. It was clearly some sort of deception. I mean, he dissected the second one to match the original. Mutilated it even, with a fake bullet hole."

"Whatever, Case. It's thin at best, and I'm sure he's fabricated some explanation. But you're missing the point. It explains nothing about my brother. Nothing about what happened to Adam."

Gracie patted Jet's hand. "Jet, baby, we just thought you needed to know what happened with the switch. We're risking a lot to tell you. But we don't know anything about Adam. We just don't see how that's possible. You told me his body burned up in the wreck."

Jet jerked his hand back. "It was Adam, I'm telling you."

"Hey, man, we heard you dug up Adam's grave." Tucker was looking at me. "What did you find? If it was empty, that would be suspicious."

"Oh, come on," Tekowski said. "You believe in UFOs and chupacabras, too?"

"Shut up, Tea." Tucker reached across the table to swat at his detractor. "I saw a UFO once. And I'm not sure about chupacabras, but I do think Bigfoot is a possibility."

I sighed. "To answer your question, no, it was not empty. But get this. We took a tissue sample, and it got stolen from us on the way to the lab."

"Wow, that's heavy," Tucker said. "But you can't report it because you obtained it illegally, huh?"

"That about sums it up."

Jet turned to Gracie. "Can you go get your Gross notebook? You know, the one where you make your diagrams and notes?"

"Jet, honey, I'm not sure—"

"I want to show Case something."

Gracie nodded and left the room but returned in less than a minute with a three-ring binder.

"Turn to the first day," Jet said.

She flipped a few pages and slid it across to him.

Jet studied Gracie's diagrams for a moment then tapped the page and motioned for me to look. "Gracie takes immaculate notes. Drew this the first day."

I peered over his shoulder. "Remember, I'm not a medical guy."

"Don't have to be to recognize this." He pointed to a crude penciled diagram of the backside of a human. "Right there."

"That's the butt."

"But look at that line right above it."

"It was a scar right at the top of his intergluteal fold," Gracie said. "The new cadaver didn't have one."

Jet smiled. "It was, and I had never seen that before." He reached in his pocket and held up a photo for me to see from behind him then spun it onto the table. "Until I found this."

Tucker grabbed the photo. "What's this?" His eyes widened as he examined it.

"That is my brother Adam."

I couldn't believe my eyes. It was a snap of Adam laid out across a bedspread, shorts partially pulled down, with a piece of gauze jutting from a wound at the top of his butt crack. The intergluteal fold, as I had just learned from Gracie. "Where'd you get this?"

"Anniston had it." He looked at the others around the table. "My brother's girlfriend. Adam had what's called a pilonidal cyst, basically a pocket of infection that just appears right over the tailbone. He had to have surgery to cut it out, and she actually helped him change the dressings." He chuckled. "She took a pic when he wasn't looking, just messing with him. I bet Adam had a fit."

"And he never told you about it?" I said.

Jet shook his head. "Nope. Didn't want Mom to worry, I'm sure. And didn't want me to know he had a physical flaw." He grinned somberly, blinking to contain the moisture forming in his eyes. "Always was kind of vain about his appearance."

"Wait a minute," Tekowski said. "So you're telling me…"

"The same thing he's been telling you all along." I patted my friend on the back. "That was his brother on that table."

Gracie was at Jet's side before I finished my sentence. She wrapped her arms around him and buried her face into his neck. "Oh, Jet, honey. I'm so sorry. I'm so sorry."

An expression of relief washed over Jet's face. He shot me a look, and I returned a somber smile. Finally, someone outside his old circle of friends believed him. "It's okay," he said. "I almost didn't believe it myself."

While Jet entertained apologies from his other shocked lab partners, I decided to call my apartment and check my answering machine.

"HEY, Case, uh, just checking in, uh, to see if y'all found out anything. I'm uh, gonna stay in today. I called Jet, too, but no answer, really need to talk to him. Got a bad feeling. Umm, yeah, just call me."

My frown deepened as I listened to the message a second time. What was Jack talking about? I hit the end button on Gracie's cordless phone. "Jet, you gotta listen to this. He must've called right after I left this morning." I redialed the number, waited for the answering machine to pick up, and entered the code to replay the message. I held the phone to Jet's ear and leaned in so I could hear the message a third time.

Jet handed the phone back to Gracie and turned to me with a worried look. "So why isn't he answering his phone? Surely he didn't try to go out."

I tried not to reciprocate his look of concern. "Sleeping, maybe?"

Tucker slid off the kitchen table and stood. He pointed at the phone, now resting on its receiver. "Who are y'all talking about?"

I shrugged. Nonchalant. "Our friend Jack. He's been under the weather."

"Back to your bigger problem," Tekowski said. He was on his feet now. "Don't mess around. You've got to go to the cops or something. You're being set up. In more ways than one."

Jet shook his head. "I'd like to talk to the police, but my evidence is circumstantial. I'm sure it's not a crime for a professor to change cadavers for whatever reason, and I can't prove it was Adam, at least not in a way that will hold up in some legal sense."

"And proving it was Adam is just the tip of the iceberg," I said. "How did he die and how did he wind up in the anatomy lab? Whose body actually was in his truck that night? Who is trying to cover it all up, and why?" I didn't feel like delving into it with Jet's medical student friends, but I was skeptical about Anniston Lewis's story and planned to grill Jet about it some more later.

Tucker paced the small room, pounding his fist in the opposite palm. "No doubt Cronin is involved. But I also think that troglodyte Sterling Virchow has something to do with all this. He's been after you from the start, Jet."

"You gonna beat some sense in to him, big man?" It was the first time I'd seen Tekowski smile. He seemed genuinely amused by the idea of Tucker getting violent.

"You'd be surprised what I can do, Teacakes. Just try me."

Jet laughed and gave Tucker a high-five. "Maybe Sterling is in on it, but Cronin sure doesn't seem to like him much. I just don't know."

Gracie huffed and crossed her arms. "Jet, I just can't stand the thought of going back in that lab, knowing what I know."

"You've got to, though. Tucker, you and Tea, too. Just keep doing what you're doing. Don't let my predicament jeopardize your status. Case and I are gonna figure something out."

I appreciated his confidence, but I didn't exactly share it. For the first time, I wished my father wasn't out on that cruise. As reluctant as he had been to help, he was still infinitely more likely to be able to pull the right strings than we were. But we didn't have time to wait. I knew it, and Jet did, too. "I'm guessing Jack has a whopper of a headache," he said. "Let's go check on him."

That sounded like as good an idea as any.

"You love her, don't you?"

I braked, spun the steering wheel, and turned to face forward as I finished backing out of Gracie's driveway. "Who?"

"Don't play dumb. The same girl it seems like we've all been in love with at one time or another."

"Not Jack. He's always been more interested in the chase than the catch."

"True. But I wouldn't doubt it either. She has that effect on people."

I gave an acknowledging nod. "That she does. I guess I've never stopped loving her. Just seemed like it wasn't meant to be, so I put it out of my mind and moved on."

"Well, she's here now. Same town as you. Don't let your chance slip away."

I tried to read the look on Jet's face as I turned onto the I-55 access ramp and headed south, but he was looking away, out the window. "I thought for the longest time that you guys would get married," I said. "You don't think about it?"

"I've told you. We were good together for a time. Finally figured out we were better just as friends. I'd still like to see her happy, though. Besides, I think I may focus on that redhead back there."

"Gracie is pretty cute."

Jet grinned like I hadn't seen him do in quite some time. He had smiled or laughed a time or two lately, but those had been fleeting looks linked only to a singular vanishing moment, with no sense of permanence or foundation. This was different somehow, the kind of grin rooted in a greater expressive whole. Yep, that was it. He had a new glimmer in his eyes. A glimmer of hope.

"And as a bonus, she now officially believes you might actually be sane."

"That's bound to help." His grin widened.

———————

Jack didn't answer the door when we knocked and rang the doorbell. Jet tried to peek in a window. "Maybe he's sleeping, like you said."

"Yeah, his truck is here. Could be in the shower."

"Let him rest?"

"If he's sacked out, he'll wanna kill us if we wake him up." I grinned. "So let's go wake him up." The key was in its usual spot under a terra cotta pot in the corner of the carport. I tossed it to Jet.

Jet shook his head. "Clever hiding spot there." He turned the key and swung the door open into the kitchen.

"Shhh." I held my index finger to my lips and slipped into the room. I removed a glass from a cabinet and filled it with water, topped it off with a few cubes of ice, and tiptoed down the hall.

"He's gonna kill you," Jet whispered, "not to mention it might not be a good idea for his concussion."

I ignored him and suppressed a laugh as I pictured cold water being poured on either Jack's snoring face or his unsuspecting naked body on the other side of a shower curtain. The back of the house was quiet, though. No music playing, no water running, no snores of deep slumber. Jack was not there.

"Maybe he went for a walk," Jet said.

I gave him an incredulous look. "Jack Masterson on a neighborhood walk?"

"If a hot girl asked him."

I nodded. That was plausible. The starter homes on his street were crammed shoulder-to-shoulder, full of young couples and singles sharing rent. Jack had never been shy, especially around the female species. No doubt he could be hanging out any number of places. I took a quick detour through the living room as I made my way to the front door, but I didn't like what I saw. An overturned can of soda saturated a *Sports Illustrated* magazine on the coffee table. Jack's recliner sat at an awkward angle, as if it had been abruptly moved, and the TV tray that seemed to be a permanent fixture in front of the recliner was sprawled on its side on the floor. I called Jet into the room. "What do you make of this? Doesn't look good to me."

"Looks like Jack was playing football with himself."

"Seriously. This is odd."

"Left in a hurry, I'd say. Why don't you call Abi? Maybe she knows something."

I grabbed Jack's phone and dialed. She didn't answer, either.

FORTY-ONE

ABI's car was not in front of her apartment, but Lane's car was. Her door was unlocked, so we walked straight in without knocking. Lane was sitting on a stool in the compact kitchen, absently spinning a quarter on the Formica.

"Not home yet?" Jet asked.

"Should be any minute." Lane gave only a cursory glance toward Jet and me before resuming his activity. "Might have stopped at the grocery store or something." Then he looked up abruptly, suddenly distracted by something other than the spinning coin. "How's Jack today? I meant to call and check on him this morning but got tied up at work."

"Was just about to ask you if you'd heard from him," I said. "He wasn't at home when we just went by there. His truck was, though."

Lane frowned and then shrugged it off. "That's odd. But he was feeling a lot better when I left yesterday."

Odd. A good word for Jack. Or unpredictable. Yes, that was better. Nothing if not unpredictable. I had a lifetime of memories to attest to it. Whatever caused him to leave his apartment in such a mess, I suspected it was somehow tied to a girl. I looked forward to hearing the story.

"Where's Rylee?" Jet peered down the hall toward her room.

A floral duffle bag protruding from Abi's bedroom door partway into the hall caught my attention.

"Out of town. Something with her job. I think that's what Abi said."

"Abi going somewhere?" I nodded at the bag.

Lane barely looked. "You'll have to ask her."

I took a seat on one of the barstools. "So you guys doing more than breakfast now or what?"

I expected Lane to bristle or tense at my provocation, but he did neither. He spun the quarter again. "Nah, nothing like that. Just had to ask her something." He watched the coin spin and meander around the counter for several seconds then slammed his palm down, flattening the quarter beneath it. "Never gets old." He stood and brushed past me to look out the front window. "Sometimes she dillydallies around after work. Might be an hour or so before she gets home."

"I'm sure she'll be here in a few," I said. "Maybe it's none of my business, but really, what's the deal with y'all? You datin'? If we're interfering with something…"

Lane stepped back from the glass. "I just need to talk to her." He sighed and ran both hands through his hair. "Okay, I'll tell you, because I'm sure she will. Yesterday she asked me to stop coming by so much, since we're not together anymore. I just need to talk to her about it in person."

Jet glanced my way with a raised eyebrow and shook his head. "Dude, I can tell you. If Abi has her mind made up about something, you can forget it."

I suddenly felt uncomfortable. For one thing, it was more than a little weird for Abi's three ex-boyfriends to be waiting on her in her apartment. And yes, I was ecstatic that Abi was sending Lane packing, but still I was empathetic, despite our past. If he was going to get dumped once and for all, I was sure he would prefer it to be in private. More than that, I was certain Abi wouldn't do it with us around. And I certainly didn't want anything to interfere with that. I pulled my keys out of my pocket. "C'mon Jet, let's go find Jack. Lane, tell Abi I'll call her later. We've got some news about Jet."

"Whoa." Lane perked up. "Hang on. You've had a break in the case?"

"A break of sorts," Jet said. "Evidence that Adam's body actually was in that anatomy lab."

"Wow. That's huge. What did you find?"

"Adam had a unique scar. It was on the first cadaver but not the one they have now," I said.

Lane turned to Jet. "So you've got a photo or something to prove it?"

Jet shook his head. "I wish. No photos allowed in the Gross lab. Just some crude notes and eyewitnesses. So that's why we can't call the police. It's circumstantial evidence right now, and it sounds outrageous if you think about it. I mean, how did Adam die, how did his body get there, and what would be the motive for whoever did it?"

"We're close, though," I said. "C'mon, Jet, let's go."

I've read, or maybe Jet told me, about the butterfly effect, how according to chaos theory the single flutter of a butterfly wing can set in motion a series of events that causes a tornado weeks later. I'm no physicist, but it always sounded ludicrous to me, at least in terms of the physical world. What I have since learned, though, is that in the world of human interaction, of human discovery, the butterfly effect is very much a real entity.

Except the flutter that causes the chaos doesn't have to come from a butterfly.

In one of his many ramblings, Jet once told me the average human eye moves over 100,000 times per day. That it's a common misconception that humans can scan their surroundings like the lens of a camera by moving their eyes around, seeing everything at once as the eye passes over it, like a hand feeling the entire surface of an object as it glides over it. Apparently, it just doesn't work that way. The eyes can track up and down, back and forth, but they do so in small increments, moving a few degrees at a time, focusing, processing the information gathered during the microsecond of a pause, then moving on.

So, my eyes moved just a few degrees. A flutter like a butterfly. A random movement, I think. Or maybe it was a subconscious thing I already knew, somewhere deep down, that just needed an excuse to emerge.

The color of the water in the photo on Abi's refrigerator caught my eye. The photo was the one I'd noticed before of her and Lane, pressed close because of the winter cold, smiling happily (him more so than her, in my opinion) on a beautiful lakeshore, the water shimmering a brilliant, blue-green behind them. The word turquoise came to mind, but whatever the proper designation for the water's color, its chroma was too intense, too rich, to be typical for northeast Mississippi bodies of water.

The trees in the background looked familiar. A row of pines, their evergreen contrasted by the silvery-white bark of a lone hardwood patriarch looming before them, barren and leafless but standing proud. Without question a sycamore.

A sycamore I had seen before, though it had been clothed in golden fall foliage the first time.

I jerked the photo off the refrigerator and held it up for Lane to see. "Tell me about this."

"What about it? Took that close to my Dad's lake house. That's not where we boat and fish, but it's close by. Makes better photos."

"Abi told me that. What about the water? Why is it that color?"

Lane smiled, but Jet spoke first. "Bentonite."

"Ben what?"

"Bentonite," Jet said again. "It's a clay, used for face washes and kitty litter, I think. Mined pretty commonly all over the world, but there are deposits in Alabama and Mississippi."

Lane nodded. "Dad's place is close to an old bentonite quarry. Abandoned twenty years ago. The stuff is usually gray, I think, but right there in that corner of the county it's a greenish gray. Under a blue sky it makes the water almost glow. Beautiful, huh? Great for a backdrop."

"Yeah, it's beautiful. Never seen anything quite like it." I paused, studying Lane carefully. I wanted to measure his reaction to what I said next to the fullest, so there would be no uncertainty in my mind. "Only place I've ever seen freshwater that color with a sycamore like that is in a photo behind Dr. Winscote's desk at the anatomy department."

If I thought Lane Buckley's reaction might be subtle, if even present at all, I was dead wrong. His eyes widened, the color drained from his face, and his lips parted as his jaw dropped just enough.

Jet was watching me and missed all the fireworks in Lane's expression. "What are you talking about, Case?"

"I'm talking about that lake right there. It was just a hunch, but from the look on Lane's face, I'm relatively certain your anatomy professor has a picture of it in her office."

Lane tensed, indignant now. "Don't be ridiculous, Case. You're talking crazy."

I had questioned whether I was crazy or not a few times in my life. But this wasn't one of them. I couldn't connect all the dots, but I could link enough to know things were about to get very interesting. "Aw, come on, Lane. Jet, bear with me here. You've been trying to figure out what the connection was between Adam's death and the anatomy department, and you thought there might be a link between Professor Cronin and whoever was threatening Adam down on the coast in the weeks before his accident. But that was a dead end, right?"

"Seems to be." Jet's eyes went wide.

"Lane, you said something very interesting to me at Adam's funeral. It bothered me then, but I blew it off. But now it really bothers me. You told me the gas can that crashed into Adam's cab was metal. But the gas can he had in storage was plastic. So how did you know that? I didn't know that. Jet, did you know that?"

Jet shook his head. "Never asked."

"Metal, plastic, who cares?" Lane said. "I don't even remember that conversation."

"I do. It was odd to me that you specified, but I thought maybe it was a guess on your part. It did make sense, and you're a smart guy, so no big deal. But then when Jack got hit on the head, you said something about him getting hit with wood even before we told you that. Again, maybe just an accurate assumption. That's what I thought. Again, no big deal."

Lane was ashen again, but now his jaw was set, and he glared at me. "Case, I know you're in love with Abi. It's been written all over your face. But I told you, she broke it off with me. But she and I are still friends, so making ridiculous accusations against me isn't going to get you brownie points in her book."

I nodded. "Fair enough. I admit, those two things are circumstantial at best. In fact, I barely gave either blunder a thought. Until now. Until I saw this picture of you at your Dad's lake, standing in the exact same spot as one of Marta Winscote, who happens to be the program director for the body donor program. Is Jet supposed to believe that is a coincidence?"

Lane had started inching toward the front door, ever so subtly, but Jet repositioned himself to intercept him.

Jet's face was blood red now. "Lane, what is he talking about?"

"Who is Dr. Winscote to you, Lane?" I insisted. "What's the connection? And what's it got to do with Adam?"

Lane pounded his fist against the wall to his back. "This is ridiculous! You two are crazy. I'm outta here."

He tried to step past Jet, but my friend didn't budge. He backed against the front door, arms crossed, fists closed. "You answer Case's questions," he growled, red-faced and tense as an oak post.

I couldn't help but think of my favorite part of the classic Kenny Rogers song, "Coward of the County," when the oppressed protagonist Tommy has had all he can take, and "stops and locks the door" of the bar before singlehandedly wiping out the evil Gatlin brothers' gang. My buddy Jet was by nature a docile person, but his expression and posture told me he had reached his threshold, and for all intents and purposes, had stopped and locked the door.

I suddenly feared for Lane's safety, mostly because of what a serious violation of it might mean for Jet's future. "Lane, back away and sit down." I pointed at the couch. "Right now."

Lane complied, watching Jet like a deer in a tiger cage as he sat down. "Settle down, guys. Let's talk this out. Jet, I'm truly sorry about Adam. It was a terrible thing. And I don't know anything about your anatomy class and what you saw. But I can tell you, I didn't have anything to do with anything you're talking about."

"You were there that night," Jet said. "In Amberton. You and Abi came to my house that homecoming night, when I announced about medical school. You guys left, Adam left, and by morning, he was dead."

"If you remember correctly, I was with Abi that night."

"So she can vouch for you for the whole night?" I asked.

Lane gave me a smirk, a look I hadn't seen from him in a long time but one that seemed too easily resurrected. "Yeah, she'd be able to do that."

"That's odd." My tone was equally smug. "Because she told me you proposed to her that night, she turned you down, and you got mad and drove off."

His sneer melted as quickly as it had appeared into a look of pained doubt and disheartenment. "Okay, you're right. I didn't know anyone knew that. It's embarrassing. I got upset. I mean, who wouldn't? So I dropped her off and just drove around."

"Abi told me you never came back that night. You were supposed to be staying with her at her parents'. Where did you go?"

"I hooked up with an old friend, alright? If you want, I'll give you her number. She'll be mad at me, because I'm sure she's not proud of it, either. But if that's what it takes, then fine. But I'm telling you, I didn't hurt Adam. Look, I'm not sure why you're trying to tie me to this. I mean, random comments about gas cans and wooden sticks or whatever? And the color of some water? Dad says there are dozens of bentonite quarries all over the state and in Alabama, too. Case, you are really grasping at straws here."

His tone softened, and he took a deep breath. "But I understand. Case, I know you'll do anything to help your friend. And Jet, I think you've gotten a raw deal somehow. Please, just tell me how I can help you, and I'll do whatever I need to do. I still love her, but I can see it's not going to work out with Abi. But I told you guys, I just want to be friends."

I felt sorry for the guy and guilty for my accusations. He was right. Maybe I was willing to find clues and make connections where none existed.

Jet sat down in one of the chairs, still tense. I had too much nervous energy to sit.

"What now?" Jet looked up at me.

"Well, I think I can talk to ol' Stimpy Riggins the coroner, pick his brain for clues since he was the one at the scene of Adam's accident and got the death threats on the other body."

"I just know Sterling Virchow is involved somehow," Jet said. "Had it out for me from day one. I've just got to prove it."

"You know, he's working with Dr. Winscote," I said. "Ran into him that day I went up there to see her and Cronin."

"Yeah, but that makes no sense. For her to be involved, I mean. She's the professor who's helped me the most. Gotta be Cronin."

"Sounds like you're right," Lane chimed in. "I wouldn't think the one who helped bail you out of jail would have anything to do with it."

Jet inched to his feet and reached toward the end table between the couch and his chair. Before I knew what was happening, he had grabbed one of Abi's brass lamps and yanked it from the table, ripping its cord from the electrical outlet. Jet has always had a long and slow fuse, and I've only seen him truly angry a handful of times.

This was not one of those times.

This was different. Nearly a year of inexplicable sorrow replaced by a week of objectless anger now had a target, and death burned in Jet Townsend's eyes.

Lane's eyes widened and he cowered, collapsing onto the couch to mitigate the force of the impending blow, but I leapt to cover the short space separating me from Jet and grabbed his arm. "What the heck are you doing?"

Jet did not answer. "Tell me how you knew that!" he screamed at Lane.

"Knew what, Jet? Knew what?" Lane screeched, shrinking back and holding his hands near his head in a defensive position.

Jet dislodged my hand from his arm with a jerk and brought his own hand, lamp and all, to his side. "I never told anyone that."

"Told what?"

"That Marta Winscote bailed me out of jail. Other than Gracie and Mom, I never told a soul. Not you, not Jack, not Abi. It was too embarrassing." He nodded at Lane, still recoiled on the couch, and pointed the lamp at him. "Somehow, this loser knows Professor Winscote. You were right. It's him."

I turned to Lane, my pulse quickening. The tears in his eyes and defeat in his posture told me all I needed to know. Whatever doubt I had let creep in was gone for good. I didn't feel sorry for him, though. I was willing to do anything to find out the truth.

"Tell us, Lane. Tell us right now, or I'll watch Jet work you over like a sweet-toothed fat kid on a piñata." I patted Jet on the shoulder. "No offense, man."

Lane sat up, rubbing his hands back and forth over his knees. "Jet is right. I know Marta Winscote."

"Know her?" Jet exclaimed. "How? What does that mean? What did y'all do? Why?"

Lane stood and looked at his watch, but I put my hand out to let him know he wasn't going anywhere. "Jet, it wasn't supposed to happen." His voice quivered. "It was an accident."

"What do you mean, an accident?" I pushed him, and he took a step back. "Quit beating around the bush and tell us what you're talking about!"

"It's a long story, guys." He wrung his hands. "But I'm worried."

"Worried? You're worried?" Jet said. He lifted the lamp. "We don't give a crap about your feelings right now. I swear, you tell me what you know, or I'll bash your head in."

"It's Abi. She should have been home."

A wave of nausea overtook me. "Lane." I spoke slowly for emphasis. "What is going on with Abi?"

Lane looked back and forth from me to Jet. "You guys know I love her, right? I would never hurt her."

"Tell me!" I shouted, balling up my fist.

"I'm afraid he took her."

"Took her? Who? What are you talking about?"

"He said he might do it, just trying to help, some ridiculous ideas about talking some sense into her for me, as a friend. I really thought he was joking."

I started to ask again who he was talking about. Then it hit me. I suppose it could have been any one of a dozen people, but somehow I knew who it was as well as I knew my own name. Quite possibly the only person I ever truly hated, despite my best efforts to forgive and forget, the way my upbringing in church had taught me. The person who had antagonized me from the first time we met just as Abi and I were attempting to hold hands for the first time, to the ensuing fist fight, to the last time I had seen him, behind the wheel of a black Camaro doing his best to ram the life out of my best friend Jack, and almost killing Jet instead.

I looked at Jet. "VJ?" I muttered slowly, in disbelief and utter disgust.

Jet's eyes widened, and his jaw dropped. "VJ MacIntosh had something to do with this? You and VJ killed my brother?" Jet screamed and raised the lamp again, intending to decapitate Lane, judging by the fury in his voice.

I ducked under Jet's raised arm and hooked my right arm in his, stopping him from swinging while pivoting my body at the same time to remain facing Lane in case he made a move. I fully expected him to either be on the attack or for me to have to chase him out the front door.

Lane did neither. He stood stock still, arms at his side, facing us stoically, only closing his eyes.

"Put the lamp down! That's assault with a deadly weapon!" I said to Jet. "Just what you need right now—a felony. Plus, we've got to get information from him. So Lane, where is VJ? Where would he have taken Abi?"

"I'm not sure. He doesn't have a place around here, as far as I know. I told you, he's been staying somewhere in Amberton, I just don't know where. He said if he saw a cop, he'd just end it all, whatever that means. It was strange, but he's like that sometimes. I swear I thought he was joking."

I nodded, balled my fist, and hammered Lane in the jaw with a left hook before he had time to flinch. He collapsed back onto the couch, unconscious.

"Holy..." Jet's voice trailed off.

"That's only a misdemeanor." I shook my hand to ease the pain in my knuckles. "You'll have your chance, but the last thing we needed was for you to kill him. C'mon, let's get him in the truck. I need to make a couple of phone calls, and then we're going to Amberton to find Abi."

PART THREE

"Hate is a bottomless cup. I will pour and pour."

— Euripides, *Medea*

FORTY-TWO

"HE'S moaning," Jet said. "You think these stockings will hold him?"

I looked back at Lane, wedged into the compact back seat of my extended cab Tacoma, hands and feet tied together in front of him, another stocking over his mouth. "You'd think Abi or Rylee would have some duct tape or rope or something besides panty hose. But I think they'll hold."

"He may go nuts when we wake him up."

"Nah, I think ol' Lane is about broken. Got the ice water?"

Jet nodded. "Yep. Just tell me when to hit him with it. We need some answers."

"Speaking of answers, I called 4-1-1. Nothing. No listing for VJ MacIntosh."

Jet made a grumbling sound. "And what about the sheriff's department?"

"You won't believe this. Of course, Dad won't be back for two more days. But the dispatch likes me, so she gave me a little info. Turnip and the other deputy are both out on a call. Another body turned up. East side of the county, in Gunner's Run."

Jet scowled and jerked his head back toward our prisoner. "So I guess we're stuck with our other killer back there?"

I shrugged. "At least for a while, I guess."

"We could take him to the police here in Jackson."

I shook my head. "I'm not sure we should have told the cops anyway. You heard what VJ said about ending it all. You want to take that chance with Abi's life? Plus, who's gonna believe us? He's knocked cold with a swollen face, and you're out on bond for assault already. They'll arrest us instead."

Lane moaned again. His eyelids were fluttering, but he wasn't awake yet.

Jet sighed. "The other murder back home. How many is that now?"

"Well, there was the hitchhiker the month before Adam died. The one that Stimpy got blackmailed to cover up. Then one a couple of weeks back. And I read where they're looking at two other cases around the state that were similar. Now this one. All seemed to be wanderers or homeless men. Drugged or something before they were killed."

"Drugged?" Jet cocked his head to the side. "With what?"

"Dad told me not to tell, but I guess it won't matter. Said it was some kind of animal tranquilizer, kin to morphine." I looked hard at Jet beside me. "You think VJ is capable?"

Jet sat more erect and pointed ahead. "Take this exit. We've got to find Abi, and I've got an idea."

I slapped the blinker upward and turned the steering wheel at the same time. "What you thinking?"

"Let me run in to University Hospital and make sure Abi's not there. I can get one of my buddies in the ER to call the other area ERs real quick and make sure, too, before we leave town."

"Atta boy. Use that genius brain." I smiled.

Lane's groaning took on a different tone. I didn't have to look to know he would be fully awake any second now.

"What about him?" Jet asked.

I turned in to the Jackson University Hospital emergency department entrance. "Go do your thing. I'll watch him." I eased my truck past the ambulance bays and parked in a corner spot, in one of the fifteen-minute parking slots intended for patient drop-off and pick-up, careful to position the truck so Lane's side was against the brick wall of the building.

The bustle of activity outside my window astounded me. Ambulatory patients and their families poured in and out of the double doors to the emergency department, making me wonder if a revolving door might be more appropriate. A security guard manned the entrance like a hotel doorman, and ambulances moved in and out as casually as taxis at a downtown hotel.

I kept expecting a team of physicians to race out and climb in the back of one of the ambulances like I'd seen on TV, but it didn't happen. That, despite at least one of them bringing in an apparent trauma victim, based on the urgency in the paramedics' movements and the profuse amount of blood on the patient lying on the stretcher.

Lane kicked the seat in front of him, and his muffled sounds took on a different urgency.

I jerked around and showed him my fist. "Stop, or I'll hit you again."

He nodded, eyes wide, and attempted to speak through the gag.

"You gonna be cool? If you do, I'll take that gag off."

Lane nodded again.

I gestured for him lean forward and pulled the stocking over his head.

He touched his face where a bruise was already forming. "You hit me."

"I saved Jet from killing you. Now shut up."

He took a deep breath and peered out the window. "Where are we?"

"Looking for Abi." I glanced around to make sure no one was watching and then craned my neck to glare at him eye to eye. "And there's nothing I won't do to save her. Nothing. Now stay put and don't make a scene, if you know what's good for you."

"Why would Abi be here? Did something happen?"

"Be quiet." I turned around and took a sip of the ice water Jet had brought, hoping to gather my thoughts, wishing Jet would hurry up.

"Can I have a sip? That gag sucked me dry."

I nodded, lifted the cup and turned as if to pass it back over the seat, and instead rolled down my window and tossed the contents out without looking.

"Excuse me?" The voice was gruff, loud, and close, and I must have jumped three inches in my seat. The wet uniform at my window was not a welcome sight.

"Officer." I offered a weak smile. "Please tell me I didn't pour that on you."

The policeman leaned down and peered in my window. "I'm afraid you did, son. Can I ask what you think you're doing?"

I was going to jail. No doubt about it. I might not have to stay there, but technically this was kidnapping, whether Lane was an accomplice to murder or not. It suddenly dawned on me that he hadn't actually even confessed to a crime. What if he and VJ hadn't done it? I dared not look over my shoulder but knew

Lane must be showing the officer his bound wrists and legs. In seconds I would be dragged from my truck and frisked face-down on the pavement. My father would be so proud.

"Waiting on a friend, sir," Lane said. "He ran in to check on someone."

I pivoted in slow motion, still expecting some sort of ruse, but Lane had somehow maneuvered his body to hide his bindings from the officer's line of sight. He smiled. "If he doesn't hurry up, I'm gonna get his seat. Pretty cramped back here."

The officer frowned, either because he sensed something wasn't quite right or because it was his natural response. He opened his mouth to speak but was interrupted.

"Officer Gutierrez?" Jet's voice.

The policeman stood upright and found the source of the question. I could then see Jet in my side mirror, standing at the back of the truck. "Mr. Townsend, hello. What brings you back to these parts? I thought you'd have crawled back home by now."

"Very funny, sir. You know that would violate the terms of my bond. But I'm glad to see you." Jet motioned toward us. "You met my friends, there, I see. Look, somebody called and left a voicemail saying that my friend Gracie had been attacked again. I raced up here, all in a panic, figuring the SOB who did it the first time had done it again. But she's not in there, not in any of the local ERs. So somebody is messing with me, and I don't think it's funny. Isn't that a crime? I'd like them to be prosecuted."

Gutierrez chuckled, amused by Jet's agitation. "No that's not a crime. It's called a joke." He looked back at me again. "Not sure you want to be hanging out with this guy. He's going to be indicted for kidnapping and assault, you know."

Lane kicked the back of my seat again. "Maybe not," I said. "Kidnapping is a horrible thing to do." Another kick. "But I believe my friend will be able to prove his innocence."

"Maybe so, maybe so." Gutierrez peeked back at Lane again as Jet climbed into the truck. "Missed your shot for a better seat."

"That's an understatement," Lane said. "Have a nice day."

I raised the window rapidly as I backed out but tried to leave as nonchalantly as possible, fighting the urge to gun it. "Wow that was close. How do you know him?"

"That's the guy who arrested me. What are the odds?"

"Surprises everywhere today. Lane, why'd you do that?"

"I told you, I'm worried about Abi. Getting delayed here in Jackson for hours just puts her in more danger, and I won't do it."

"Well she's not in any of the Jackson ERs," Jet said, "so we're going to Amberton unless you have a better idea."

Lane shook his head.

"Okay, then," I said. "It will take us awhile to get there. Lane, start talking. Every last detail, down to the color of your underwear and what brand tampon you used."

I watched Lane's response through my rearview mirror. He nodded without looking up. "Okay, I'll tell you everything. Like you said, it was the night we came back for homecoming, last fall…"

FORTY-THREE

Ten months earlier

"HOLD on, give me a second," Abi said.

Lane waited and watched Abi as she paused in the threshold then turned and half-trotted back inside Jet's house to speak to him once more. She moved like she was almost giddy, a departure from her usual even keel. She hugged Jet again, congratulating him. Lane couldn't hear the words, but from the way they looked at each other, the emotion shared between them was clear.

Lane was silent until they got to the car. He frowned while he held the door open for her. "What was that, back there?"

"What do you mean? I'm happy for him. I knew he would have no trouble getting into medical school, but I'm excited he's staying close."

"Excited he's going to be close to home or close to you?" Lane slammed the door and marched around to the driver's side.

Abi glared at him for a second before speaking. "Don't be ridiculous. It's both, but not for the reasons you want to believe. We've been over this. Jet and I fit better as friends. That's it."

"Just the perfect fit, huh?"

"Ugh!" Abi folder her arms and turned away. "Why do you have to be this way, twisting my words to fit your jealous paranoia?"

Lane cranked the car and said nothing for a time, measuring his words, turning the small box in his coat pocket over and over as they rode in silence. They rolled to a stop at the curb in front of Abi's parents' home. He put the car in park but kept it running since the October night was cool. "You're a once-in-a-lifetime type girl, Abi. A thousand guys would fight each other just to have you notice them. And somehow you noticed me. Pulled me from rock bottom and saved my life. Seriously, I was ready to call it quits until I found you again. You know that. I'm desperately in love with you. I'm sorry I'm such a jealous nut sometimes."

Abi's posture softened, and she reached over and grabbed his hand. "C'mon, Lane, you don't have to be that way. I may be a lot of things, but sneaky isn't one of them. I'm always honest with you."

"I know. Deep down, I know. Although, in my defense, you were sneaking around with Case the first time we dated."

Abi rolled her eyes and gave a half grin. "We were fourteen, and I didn't even kiss him. I'd say I've matured a bit since then." She pulled her left hand away from his and reached for the door handle with the other. "Let's go inside. You know Dad will want to hear about the game." She gave him a stern look. "And about Jet, too. Like it or not, since I decided not to follow in the old man's footsteps, Dad thinks Jet going to med school is the next best thing."

Lane reached out and grabbed her hand again. "Hang on. I've got to ask you something."

Abi let go of the door and settled back into her seat. "Okay, babe, what is it?"

"I want us to be together."

"We are together."

"Forever."

"Forever is a long time, Lane. But okay."

Before she could say another word, he slid a ring onto her finger. "Abi, will you marry me?"

Abi jerked her hand back like it had been snakebit and flung open her door to turn on the cabin light. "What is this?" She examined the huge diamond set in white gold.

"What do you think it is, darling? It's an engagement ring!"

Abi closed the door. "What have you done? It's, it's beautiful! It really is. But, but…"

The cabin light snapped off, and they were in the dark again.

"But what? I said forever, and you said okay. That's what marriage is. Forever."

Abi held her hands in her lap and peered toward them in the dark. "I was saying okay, like, it's okay for us to think about those kinds of things. I wasn't expecting a proposal."

"Well, I wanted it to be a surprise. Come on, let's go tell your parents. That's a lot better story than a football game or some old boyfriend's career plans."

"Wait, Lane." Now it was her turn to reach out and play the hand grabbing game. She held his wrist with one hand and slipped the ring into his palm with the other. "I can't take this."

"What do you mean?"

"I'm just not ready. That's a huge commitment, and I don't plan on messing it up. I'm just not ready. I care about you, I really do. But, I, I told you I'd always be honest with you. And I am."

Lane stared at her. "Get out." He shook as he reached across her to open her door. "Get out."

"Lane, don't be that way. Let's talk about it. Just give me some time."

"Get out of my car! Right now!"

Tears welled in Abi's eyes as she stepped out. "Where are you going?"

Lane said nothing, just stared straight ahead as he waited on her to move away from the open door.

She watched him for a few seconds, then nodded. "I understand," she said softly. "I'm sorry. We'll talk about it in the morning. You know where the key is. I'll have the guest room ready for you." Abi stepped onto the curb, and Lane gunned the car in reverse, slammed the brakes to close the passenger door, then screeched into drive and sped into the night.

VJ MacIntosh popped the top on a Miller Lite and chugged several gulps before slapping the dashboard of Lane's car. "Boy, I'm glad you came by! The ol' Southern 8's ain't what it used to be. Boys in there can't play a lick of pool, which would be okay 'cept they won't come off no money either."

"Glad I could be of service," Lane answered flatly.

"I can't believe the heifer said no."

"Don't call her a heifer, VJ. She didn't say no as in never. Just not right now."

"That's a no in my book." VJ sneered. "And any chick that messes over my best friend is a heifer in that same book. Why you think she snubbed you? You told me you had her all wrapped up."

"I never said that. I said I thought she was the one. She'll come around. It's complicated. Let's just ride awhile, let me clear my head."

"Complicated? It ain't rocket science. She either wants you or she don't." He gave a haughty laugh. "And it looks like she don't."

Lane shot VJ an angry look. He wanted to hit him but thought better of it. He didn't have many friends, and this one was better than none at all. "I don't want to talk about it."

"Bull. If that was so, you wouldna come got me. Hey look, I've got an idea. Let me drive. You sit over here and drown your sorrows. Mr. Miller makes everything feel better. I got a whole case."

Lane narrowed his eyes. "How many have you had?"

VJ held up his hands. "This is the second one. I swear. I don't drink when I shoot pool. Messes up my a-lign-ment." He pointed toward the shoulder of the road. "Pull over right here."

Lane let off the gas pedal and eased to a stop. A few beers did sound like a pretty good idea, after all. Abi would be mad if she found out, but she'd be asleep when he got in later anyway.

VJ was talking before his butt hit the seat on the driver's side. "So, it seems to me that punk Jet—'bout the stupidest name I've ever heard, 'specially for a fat boy—may be behind Abi giving you the cold shoulder, huh?"

"I don't know. Maybe. She just found out he's gonna be in Jackson near her, instead of some Ivy League or California school or something. So maybe."

"Maybe, nothing. There's no doubt. Don't he know he's had his chance?"

"Just drive. Got a full tank of gas and nowhere to be. Thanks for the beer."

They spent an hour riding backroads and the Amberton loop, from Walmart to Hardee's, past the Junior Food Mart and back again, with VJ talking nonstop about nothing in particular while Lane tried to drown his sorrows. VJ finally decided he had had enough. "Okay, dude, time to drop your sorry carcass off somewhere. I'm gonna either find some action or go get flat, or both, but this ain't getting me anywhere."

"Ride by there first," Lane said, eight beers in and thick-tongued.

"By where?"

"By Jet's house. Sorrrry scummbag."

VJ nodded and showed his teeth in a vicious smile. "Now you're talking. What you gonna do?"

"I dunnnno. Might bust him up or somethin'."

VJ laughed. "I hear ya." He made a quick U-turn and was idling by the Townsend house in less than five minutes. "Well, lookee there. We timed this just right. Isn't that Jet's truck backing out?"

"Yeah, that's the punk," Lane said.

VJ turned into a driveway two houses down and waited for Jet's truck to pull out. "Let's see where he goes." He backed out to fall in behind the red F-150 as it shot past. It turned out of the neighborhood and onto the highway but headed away from town. "Uh, oh, thought he might be having a late-night rendez-vous with Queen Abi, but I guess not."

Lane drank and VJ rambled on about loyalty and justice as the miles passed and they followed the taillights, just far enough back so as not to be suspicious. Jet's truck turned off the main highway and headed south. "Let's get on back," Lane slurred. "He's goin' somewhere out in the boonies."

"Didn't come this far to turn tail and run on home. He needs to be sent a message." VJ stomped the gas pedal and let out a loud whoop when the engine roared its approval and the truck lurched forward. He barely slowed down as he veered sharply off the highway and gained ground on Jet's truck, careening through each turn and accelerating with each downslope of the winding, hilly road.

"You gonna get us killed!" Lane sat erect in his seat for the first time.

Jet's truck disappeared just beyond a rise in the road, and VJ hit the gas again. "Yeah, well, what a way to go!"

Lane's stomach dropped and reeled as tires cleared the pavement then bounced hard on inadequate shock absorbers. He was so preoccupied with the landing after VJ's assault of the small hill that he didn't notice Jet's truck looming only feet ahead until they were almost on top of it. "Whoa!"

If it alarmed VJ, he didn't show it. He flipped the headlights to bright and swerved left to come alongside the braking truck. "Get you some of this!" He laid on the horn.

"Stop it, VJ! Stop!" Lane cried "You're nuts!"

To Lane's relief, VJ tapped the brakes, enough for the other truck to pull ahead again, but the feeling was fleeting. Just as Jet's taillights came into view alongside Lane's window, VJ swerved again, this time to the right. Whether he thought Jet's truck had cleared enough for him to fall in behind him, or whether he intentionally bumped the left side panel behind the rear tire was not clear, but the result certainly was. The F-150 spun 360 degrees, its headlights blinding for a millisecond before they blazed on past with the rotation.

Lane thought by some miracle it was actually going to reorient into its original direction, but most likely due to Jet's overcorrection, it veered to the right and skidded into a ditch. VJ sped on by.

Lane jerked around in his seat, expecting to see Jet's truck flip or explode, or both. "What was that? You ran him off the road!"

"It appears so. Bad night for Jet lag."

Lane turned forward and tapped VJ's shoulder with his beer can. "We've got to go back. He may need help."

VJ huffed. "Are you crazy? Why don't you just call the sheriff and have him meet us so we can tell him what happened, and he can arrest us, all easy-like!"

"Dude, turn around. At least make sure we don't need to call 911 for him. You don't have to stop."

"He'll recognize us," VJ scoffed in a nasal, sing-song voice. He eased the car to a stop on the shoulder of the road.

"Just do it, VJ."

"I'm not driving back there. But it's your car. If you want to go back, you drive."

"Fine!" Lane got out, slid in behind the wheel, and tapped it impatiently while VJ sauntered to the passenger's side as leisurely as a walk on the beach.

"Lead on, Mr. Boy Scout." VJ chuckled as he climbed in.

Lane wheeled the car around before VJ even closed the door. "You can't just leave him. It's probably too dark to see the car good, so he'll never know it was us." He fully intended to backtrack, make sure Jet was okay, and drive back to Amberton. He wasn't thinking very clearly, but he had enough of his senses to begin wondering whether any evidence of the collision was left on his right front fender.

Suddenly, everything changed.

Adam Townsend, not Jet, was standing in the middle of the road. He was shouldering a rifle and taking dead aim at the driver's side of the oncoming vehicle.

Lane slammed on the brakes and tried to throw the car into reverse, but before he could change directions, Adam was at his window screaming and hitting the window with the barrel of his gun.

"Roll down the window or I'll blow your brains out! Right now!"

"Get out of here!" VJ yelled. "Now!"

Easy for him to say. The gun wasn't pointed at his head. He lowered the window slowly.

Adam's mouth dropped when he recognized who was driving. "Lane? What are you doing? You almost got me killed!"

"Adam? We were, uh, confused … thought you were…"

"Thought I was Jet? Trying to get him killed, then?"

Lane waved a hand at Adam. "No, no. Just old friends horsing around, trying to scare him. As a joke. Really stupid. Just got too close, you know? Didn't mean to clip you. That's why we came back."

"Are you drunk?" Adam leaned down to peer in the window. "Who's in there with you?" His eyes widened even further when he saw who was there. "VJ?" He raised the gun to his shoulder and shoved the barrel in the window. "I ought to end you right here!"

Lane was afraid he might do just that. VJ had already almost killed Jet one time. Adam wasn't likely to buy that the second time was an accident. Lane put his hand over the end of the barrel. "It's not his fault. It was me. Yes, I've been drinking. Just goofin' off, didn't mean to hit your truck. Stupid. VJ's been yelling at me to pull over for the last five miles."

"Yeah, sorry, there Adam," VJ said. "I don't want no trouble. Tried to stop this idiot. Can we help you with your truck?"

Adam stared them both down. He dropped the rifle to his side. "If my truck is messed up, your bank is gonna fix it. Let's go look. Pull around here and give me some light."

Adam turned back toward his truck, and before he even took a step a shot exploded. He collapsed to the ground and never flinched. The only thing that moved was the blood pooling beneath him on the asphalt.

FORTY-FOUR

ET whirled with a yell and lunged toward the back seat like he'd been shot from a catapult. He flailed wildly at Lane. "You just shot him? You coward! You shot him in cold blood!"

Lane covered his head with his bound hands to deflect the blows. "I didn't do it, Jet! I swear. VJ shot right across me. Thought it blew my eardrums out!"

I grabbed at Jet's shirt and fought to pull him back into his seat without running off the road. "Stop!"

Jet spun back around and slammed himself into his seat. He punched the dashboard and spoke between heaving breaths. "Why … can't … I … beat the crap out of him?"

I spoke without turning my head. "Because someone will see you, and we'll get stopped, and we've got to find Abi."

Jet flipped the sun visor down and glared at Lane in the mirror. "Why would VJ do that?"

"Because VJ is nuts. It just took me too long to figure it out, and I'm so sorry for it. He said he did it for me because if Adam went back and told Jet we had run him off the road thinking he was Jet, then any chance I had with Abi would surely be ruined forever."

"VJ is a lunatic of the highest order," I said. I adjusted the rearview mirror so I, too, could glare more easily at our captive.

"Most deranged individual I've ever met. But why didn't you turn him in after you got home safe?"

"Part of me wanted to believe he was on my side. And I knew if he went down, I'd go with him. It was my word against his. We were in my car, I was drunk, and VJ shot him with the pistol I kept in the glove box. Plus, I had a lot stronger motive than he did. Jilted lover and all."

"It was a murder." I said.

"I told you, I don't have any excuse. I was in shock, confused. I messed up, Jet, and I know I can never make it up to you. I never knew it would go this far. But I'm willing to tell everything. I can't stand the guilt anymore, and I'll accept the consequences if it means we can save Abi."

Jet was seething. He spoke through gritted teeth. "We should throw you in jail the minute we get to Amberton."

"No time for that," I said. "Unless you're willing to drop him off at the door and trust him to turn himself in. If we go in, we'll have to answer a thousand questions, and that will just delay us."

"I'll do it if you want me to," Lane said.

"Not a chance," Jet growled. "You're staying with us. Now tell me how Adam wound up in the anatomy lab, you gutless piece of garbage."

Lane scrambled out of his car, screaming. "Oh, no. No, no, no! What have you done?"

VJ strolled up calmly, wiping the Glock 9mm down with the front of his shirt. "You mean, what have *you* done?" He tossed the gun to Lane, who caught it by reflex.

"Oh, no. You're not pinning this on me."

"We're not pinning this on anyone. Listen to me, though, and we'll get out of this. For now, we have to pretend you did this."

"What are you talking about?" Panic filled Lane's voice.

"Help me pick him up and get him in the trunk. Quick, before anyone comes by!"

Lane obeyed, wide-eyed and confused. VJ grabbed the shirt collar and Lane the ankles, and they tossed Adam's lifeless body in with no small effort. "Solid, ain't he?" VJ commented as they strained.

Lane turned and vomited.

"Now," VJ said, "follow me. There's an old logging road a half mile back. I'll leave Adam's—well, Jet's—truck there. We're headed to Jackson. But we gotta hurry. It'll be morning before we know it."

———

"I'm telling you, she's not gonna do it," Lane said.

VJ bobbed his head up and down. "She absolutely will. Trust me. You're in trouble, and she won't be able to resist."

"The only trouble I'm in is because of what you did."

"You'll thank me later. C'mon." VJ parked the truck at the curb.

One generation prior, the Highland Colony apartments had been in a posh neighborhood, but the area had suffered from a migration of upper-class residents to the suburbs, and the three-story complex had succumbed to partial neglect like many others around it. The wrought-iron fence surrounding the painted white brick was rusting, and the automatic gate looked as if it hadn't closed in years. In the dimness, Lane could make out dark shutters hanging at odd angles from some of the windows, and the shadows in the corners were darker than they should have been, probably from mildew.

"Nice place," VJ quipped.

Lane noted the empty swimming pool in the courtyard. Why didn't she move somewhere nicer? And safer. He had only been there once, and that had been low on the list of things to discuss. Maybe he would ask her one day, but not now. "Here," he said softly. "9B."

VJ rapped on the door.

"Shh. Don't wake up the neighbors."

"Folks don't open their doors to see what's going on with the neighbors in places like this," VJ said. "Good way to get shot."

A rustling came from the other side of the door, and an overhead light flickered on. A pause while she looked through the peephole was followed by the distinct click of two deadbolts turning and the metallic slide of a chain lock. The wooden door cracked open. "Lane?"

"It's me," Lane whispered. "It's okay."

The door opened wider, and an inside light came on. Marta Winscote peeked out and eyed VJ, looked in both directions, then motioned for them to come in. The apartment's furnishings were humble, appointed for function over style. A glass-top table and four chairs to the left toward the kitchen. Living room to the right with a cornflower-blue couch and matching armchair, a coffee table, and a squatty oak entertainment center overwhelmed by the wall behind it. "What are you doing here? And who's your friend?"

"This is VJ MacIntosh," Lane said. "We need your help."

"At two in the morning?" She covered a yawn with a fist.

Lane looked nervously toward VJ. "I, uh, well, we…"

VJ rested his hand on Lane's shoulder and patted it. "Let me explain. He's too traumatized. Bless his heart, it's just awful. He and this guy, they were just messing around. Having a few drinks, playing cards, you know? Then the dude just goes nuts on Lane. Pulls a gun, starts waving it around. Right, Lane?"

"Said he was gonna kill me," Lane said weakly.

"So Lane knows he's got to do something, or this idiot was gonna kill him. So he grabs the gun, it goes off."

"Oh, no!" Marta grabbed Lane with both hands, looking him up and down. "Are you hurt?"

"No, I'm fine."

"But the other guy…" VJ said.

"You shot him?"

"I was just trying to get the gun away."

Marta put her hands to her face in horror. "Where is he? Did you call the police?"

"No, he panicked," VJ said. "Ran off and called me. So I'm thinking, this doesn't look good. Lane's been drinking, other guy is dead, Lane's got gunpowder on his hands, left the scene. No way this doesn't get pinned on him."

Marta frowned at Lane through eyes filling with tears. "What is he talking about?"

"I've never asked you for anything," Lane said. "But I need your help now."

The anatomy professor turned and walked toward the kitchen. Her fingers trembled as she grasped the phone. "I'm calling the police right now. Lane, you just, just tell them the truth, and everything will be fine."

"Put the phone down," VJ said in a forceful monotone. "Your son needs your help, and if you ever want to see him again, put the phone down right now."

———————

Jet's jaw dropped. He spun toward their captive in the back seat. "Dr. Winscote is your mother?"

Lane nodded but didn't look up. "She left us when I was little. Dad says she was a drunk; I dunno. Didn't hear from her for years, then somehow she got herself together, went back to school, all that. Out of the blue, she contacted me about a year ago, just a few months before what happened."

"I don't understand," I said. "What did you and VJ get her to do?"

"VJ was right. I was in too much shock to think. But he convinced her to let us swap Adam's body with one in the anatomy lab."

"Why would she do that?" I asked.

"Guilt, I guess. I had told VJ about how desperate she was to get back into my life, so he saw an opportunity."

"But why such an elaborate scheme?" Jet said. "Why do that to Adam? To me?"

"I'm sorry. It just got out of hand. With the gunshot wound, there was no way to make it look like an accident. VJ said if we hid the body, there would be a huge missing persons investigation, and if we didn't, then it was clearly a murder. Either way, it might wind up back on us. On me."

"It *was* a murder, you scumbag," Jet growled.

"I know it was, and I'll never forgive myself for not stepping up and putting a stop to what happened after it."

"So you swapped Adam's body with one in the lab and faked the crash and fire," I said.

"Had to rush like crazy to get it all done before morning. I just knew the cops would stop us any minute, but we never saw one. Marta—Mom—opened the door to the lab for us and showed us where to find a stretcher, but she wouldn't watch. Like it made her less guilty or something. So we made the switch, raced back with the new body, put Adam's belongings on him, found that gorge farther down the road, and drove the truck in it. Wouldn't have thought it, but it took four or five drops to get even that heavy metal gas can to bust the window. But it finally worked."

"And you burned my brother up, like a piece of dirty charcoal."

"It wasn't like that, Jet. I was in shock, I swear. It's been eating me up. Now I just want to find Abi and put an end to this before VJ hurts someone else. I can't take it anymore."

"You knew I was going to med school. You knew I'd be in that anatomy lab."

"I never even thought about it. Not then, at least. Maybe VJ already had it on his mind, I don't know. I, I was in shock."

"You can't tell me it was an accident."

"It's VJ, I'm telling you. He's evil. A few weeks later, he somehow got the codes and snuck in and switched things around. He thought it was funny. Then he blackmailed Mom to switch the body out as soon as you figured it out, said he'd turn her in if she didn't and I'd get blamed for the murder."

"What if I'd called the cops that very first day instead of freaking out like I did?"

"VJ was sure Mom would take the fall for me, if necessary. She had nothing to gain by all three of us getting caught, and there was nothing to link her to me or VJ. Plus, there was a chance it would look like some kind of mixup by an idiot coroner and Podunk sheriff—no offense, Case—back in Amberton. As it turned out, it was even better than VJ hoped. Jet, you looked like you were crazy, and all the students believed it and weren't suspicious when they switched to another body to protect you."

"And the attack on Gracie, where Jet got arrested?"

"VJ again. Wanted to keep making Jet look like some kind of psychopath. Broke in your house, put the midazolam syringes there, the whole nine yards."

"One thing makes no sense," I said. "Why would Marta appear in court as an advocate for Jet if she was in on it?"

"I can answer that." The disgust was thick in Jet's voice. "What better way to divert attention from herself? Brilliant."

We drove in silence for a time. Jet said nothing more, fidgeting with his fingers in his lap. He hid it as best he could, but he wiped his eyes periodically as he stared at the floor. It was just too much for him, and my friend's anguish made me want to kill VJ MacIntosh, or at least see to it that he found himself on death row where he belonged. Lane rotting behind bars seemed appropriate, too, and what minimal consolation I could find at the moment came from the idea that Lane himself appeared resigned to that fate, as long as we found Abi. And as much as I hated to admit it, I agreed with him on that. I would do anything to save her.

The familiar Amberton city limit sign was both a welcome and an unsettling sight. What were we going to find, if anything? What if we were too late, or what if we were in the wrong place? The decision to bring Lane and not go immediately to the police in Jackson suddenly seemed silly. But then I thought of Jet's pending indictment and its effect on his credibility, and I knew we had no choice. If only Dad wasn't on that stupid cruise. What was left of the McKinley County Sheriff's department was all wrapped up in that other murder case.

I pulled the truck onto the packed gravel of a used car lot and shifted into park. I turned in the seat and glared at Lane. "Where to? We need a plan. Where would VJ go?"

"I don't know for sure. There is one place, out where his family farm used to be."

"You said you didn't know!" Jet erupted.

Lane cowered in his seat. "I thought if I told you, then you wouldn't bring me along.

"So you just thought you'd lie again," I said.

Lane grimaced. "I just want to help fix what I've messed up. I don't know if he's there, but it's worth a look."

"That doesn't even make sense," Jet said. "Four-lane highway took that farm out years ago. There's got to be somewhere else."

"Jet, I've got an idea," I said. "Can you borrow your dad's truck?"

"I'm sure. Mom might ask a few questions, but I can make something up."

"I think you need to ride out to where they found the body and talk to Turnip. Tell him what's happened. If we don't find Abi right away, we're going to need help."

"No," Jet protested. "It's too risky. One of us needs to watch Lane while the other takes care of Abi."

"I wish Jack was here. Then he could help me do that, but he's not. We've just gotta do the best we can." I nodded toward Lane in the back. "But he'll help me. He's not gonna do anything to hurt Abi."

"No," Jet said. "We need to stick together. Besides, you know the deputies better than I do."

"And you know your story better than I do." I reached over and put my hand on Jet's shoulder. "I've got to do this, Jet. I've got to find Abi."

Jet nodded. He understood the recent swell in my affection toward her, and I think he had sensed her reciprocation toward me. Besides, he knew the plan made sense. Lane's feelings for Abi would keep him from jeopardizing her safety, but who knew if he could lead us to VJ or not? If we failed to find her, we needed help casting a wider net. And time would be of the essence.

"Jet, going out to Gunner's Run is a bad idea," Lane said. "We need to stick together. VJ is crazy and capable of anything. It may take three of us."

Jet whirled in his seat. "Shut up, you've got no say-so in the matter."

Lane threw up his hands, still bound by the stocking. "Okay, okay. Just trying to help."

Jet rolled his eyes. "Some help. Take me to my house."

No one spoke until I pulled into Jet's driveway five minutes later.

"Tell your mom I said hello." I tried to sound calm and un-worried.

Jet stared out the window at nothing in particular. "Hey, Case?"

"Yeah?"

"You still been keeping notes for your book?"

"Every day."

"Good. Me too." He got out of the truck and paused, hold-ing the top of the door with his hand. This time, he looked hard at me. "What if something happens to one of us? How will the other one know what happened? You know, how to finish it?"

"Don't be ridiculous."

Jet kept staring at me, saying nothing. Insisting on an answer.

I sighed. "The other one just embellishes to finish it as he sees fit. Isn't that what you told me before?"

Jet nodded and closed my door, satisfied with the answer.

FORTY-FIVE

EVERYONE in Amberton knew Gary Higginbotham. He wasn't the only postman, but he was the one who had been doing it the longest, for as long as Jet could remember, and probably his parents too. But it was more than his longevity that made him such a familiar fixture in the community. Sure, the energy and enthusiasm with which he performed his job was remarkable, but the way he related to his customers was even more so. He could discuss the finer points of throwing curveballs with Little Leaguers and with equal ease appear to be interested in the intricacies of knitting with little old ladies.

But he had always made a special point to spend even more time with Jet when he ran into him, asking with fascination what he had been reading about lately. From quantum mechanics to geopolitics, Gary always wanted to hear. He didn't always understand the answer, but he usually researched it enough to discuss the next time they met.

The number was listed in the phone book, and he answered on the first ring.

"Mr. Higginbotham?" Jet asked.

"That's me. Unless you didn't get your mail, in which case my name is Snuffleupagus."

Jet normally would have chuckled at the reference to the beloved Sesame Street character, but not today. He was reassured, though, that his old friend hadn't changed.

"This is Jet Townsend. 1933 Northside Drive. John Edward."

"Jet. I know who you are. How are you? Hey, what about Schrödinger's cat? You know, the one locked in the box with the poison? Dead or alive?"

Jet was amazed. Their last conversation about the famous theoretical experiment in quantum physics had probably been five years earlier. "Both, until you open the box. But look, I've got a big problem, and I hate to bother you, and I'll never ask anything like this again, but I have a question. Could be life or death."

"Wow, now that's a coincidence. Like the cat. But Jet, I'm just a lowly postman. I don't do life or death much."

"I know, but you can help me this time. I'm looking for an address. Doesn't have to be exact, just ballpark. I'm trying to find VJ MacIntosh."

The other end of the line was silent for an uncomfortable few seconds. "I'm really not supposed to give out that kind of information."

"I know, and I promise I'll never bother you again. Please, Mr. Gary. I'll explain everything later. Please just help me."

"VJ MacIntosh. I knew a Paul MacIntosh back in the day. Fine fellow, Paul was. Lived over off of Bellevue Circle at the edge of town, but they sold that place after he died. Don't know a VJ though. What about Vance?"

Jet's pulse quickened. "Vance. Yessir, that's it. Vance was Paul's son. Vance Jr. is his grandson. VJ. That's who I need to find."

"Okay, I'd hate to lose my pension, so if you care anything about me, please don't tell anyone I told you. But I trust you. I recognize that name. Off the top of my head, there are two places I can think of where he gets mail."

———————

Jet was thankful his mother hadn't been home. He always loved seeing her, but he never had been good at hiding things, and she would pick up on his angst. His father's keys were hanging on the nail in the pantry where they always were, so he left his mother a note saying he needed the truck for a bit so she wouldn't worry. He was pleased to find a half tank of gas, and in no time was headed toward the murder scene to find the sheriff's deputies.

Gunner's Run was just a small community about ten miles out of Amberton. When he was younger, Jet had thought it a cool name for a place, invoking images of Civil War battles or gangsters with machine guns. Turned out he was partially right. It had been named after a Prohibition-era moonshine route for a man named Gunner. Not quite as glamorous, but still kind of neat. Some guns had surely been involved either way.

Thoughts of county history and illegal alcohol didn't ease Jet's troubled mind, though. What Gary Higginbotham had told him made no sense. Pulling out an old map of the county had provided no reassurance. In fact, it deepened his confusion. Why would Vance MacIntosh Jr.—VJ—be receiving mail at the lake house near the old bentonite quarry? That was the lake house belonging to Lane's father, the one where Lane and Abi had posed for the photo, and the one where Lane's mother had posed so many years before, holding her son. What was the connection?

Jet's unease grew as he drove. What kind of monster had VJ MacIntosh become, and what might he do to Abi? What were the odds that the death of the hitchhiker, whose body was donated to the Medical Center a month before Adam was killed, and the fact that the coroner, Stimpy Riggins, had been blackmailed not to perform an autopsy, were a coincidence? And what about the other recent deaths around McKinley County, all male, all wanderers, all drugged and killed? Clearly, VJ was adept at using drugs on his victims, as evidenced by what happened to Gracie. Could he really be behind it all?

Jet had read case studies of serial killers for a psychology course in college and knew that many were masters of manipulation. VJ clearly had manipulated Lane to cover up Adam's murder, but it seemed unlikely Lane knew anything about other killings. After all, when his connection to Adam's death had finally been suspected, guilt had quickly overtaken him, and he had folded. Yes, part of that may have been his concern for Abi, but either way, he had confessed everything when expanding the lie would surely have been easier.

Still, manipulation or not, it boggled the mind that Lane would even associate with that kind of sociopath. Jet remembered profiles of killers completely void of a moral compass or social conscience, the kind of evil beings who tortured pets for sport. Psychopaths. Was that what VJ was? Whatever he was, he had Abi, and time was surely running out.

Jet shuddered against the chill that ran down his spine. He stepped on the gas.

FORTY-SIX

AFTER I dropped Jet off at his house, I pulled in the driveway of an abandoned trailer a mile down the road and got out of the truck.

"What are you doing?" Lane asked as I slammed the door behind me.

I circled around to the passenger's side, checked to make sure no vehicles were coming from either direction, and flipped open my pocketknife.

"What are you doing?" His eyes widened in alarm as I opened the door and flipped the seat forward.

"Shut up and hold your arms out." I pretended not to see the ligature marks on his wrists as I cut the nylon stockings away. I motioned toward his lower half. "Legs now."

"Whew, that's a relief." Lane rubbed his wrists and ankles. "Talk about uncomfortable."

I motioned to the front passenger door. "Get in."

"Why'd you cut me loose?" Lane stretched his arms and legs as he sprawled in the front seat. "Don't get me wrong, I'm glad you did. Just surprised me, is all."

"I'd have done it a long time ago, but I didn't feel like arguing with Jet. His emotions are running high."

"So you trust me?"

"That's a stretch, but I think you got caught up in a bad situation. VJ is the murderer. Still, I'd keep you tied up if I didn't suspect I'll need your help if we find Abi. Now, where are we going?"

"I told you. VJ's old family farm. His grandfather's place."

"And I'm telling you, not Papa Mac's. That was our hangout back in the day. I knew that farm like the back of my hand. But then VJ moved to town, Papa Mac died, and they sold that land to the government for the highway. There's nothing left."

"Have you looked?"

I jerked my head around and stared at Lane while I considered what he was suggesting. "Well, no, not exactly. I know my first year of college they cut the trees, dug it up for dirt for the highway. I had no reason to."

"I'll show you." Lane pointed in the direction he wanted me to drive.

It was impossible. I shook my head and huffed. "We've got no time to waste."

"I know, believe me." Lane pointed again.

A few minutes later, we turned onto a narrow, overgrown gravel road I had once been quite familiar with. "This used to be MacIntosh Road. Ran through the middle of the MacIntosh Plantation once upon a time. Dead ends at the overpass now."

At one point, the plans had been for the old plantation road to be paved and extended several miles to connect with Highway 23, a sort of rural expressway. At least, that's how the county supervisor who lived and owned a section of property along Highway 23 had pitched it when he convinced the state to elevate the four-lane over the county road. Some savvy taxpayers had caught on, though, the program got nixed, and that supervisor was not doing any more supervising.

As far as I ever knew, the area under the highway overpass had just become a destination for neophyte graffiti artists and teenagers looking for backseat romance.

"Look." Lane pointed to his right as we passed under the shadow of the highway and reached the end of the gravel road. A battered black metal mailbox and its overgrown driveway hunkered in the shadow of the highway's raised shoulder.

"What in the world?"

"Right there." Lane pointed down the path of packed earth. "Think about where you are on the old farm."

I closed my eyes, trying to remember the old place. So many years had passed, so different now. The familiar landmarks all destroyed. All except the old gravel road. "How far down there?" I tried to resurrect the faded images.

"Couple hundred yards."

"But there never was a house on this farm. At least, not in my lifetime. Just an old barn."

Lane nodded. "That's it. VJ sold everything but this after his father died. You can't see it from the highway because of the trees grown up along the edge. Never would even know it's there, but he built a house where the old barn was. Even used some of the cedar and cypress timber from it."

I couldn't believe it. Made me hate VJ even more. As teenagers, we had found a body in that dilapidated barn, a story that led to Jack and Lane squaring off in a legendary street fight and VJ almost killing Jet. I had enough bad memories from that place already, and here we were again. Were there more bad memories to come? I had to think VJ relished the irony in his twisted mind. He was just evil enough to have somehow planned it all this way.

I wished again that Jack was with me. Never saw him back away from a scrap. Never saw him lose one, either. The only consolation to his absence was the thought of telling him about it later. He would turn green with disappointment that he missed the action.

"What?" Lane noticed my expression.

"Nothing." My tone turned serious. "You really think he's got Abi there?"

"I'm guessing so. It makes sense. No reason not to. Even if folks knew she was missing, no one would suspect VJ. I'm the only one that knows he's been anywhere near Jackson, much less Abi. And VJ trusts me."

"How do we do this?"

"If I had to guess, she'll be in the back room. I'll go knock in front. VJ won't suspect anything, and he'll let me in. I'll see if I can sneak back and unlock the back door, then you can ease in and get Abi while I distract him."

"What if she's in not in the back?"

"Then we'll just have to wing it. I'll go in, and you wait."

"I ain't waiting long." I slid my Springfield 9 mm out from the space between the seats and chambered a round.

"Hang on there, what's that for?"

"That's for me doing whatever I gotta do to save Abi Rossini. Problem?"

Lane shook his head. "Didn't know you were packing. Not a big fan of guns is all."

"Dad taught me never to bring a knife to a gunfight. And who knows what VJ's got in there. I've got a permit."

Lane gave a slow nod. "Okay, whatever. Let's go."

The sun had already dropped behind the rise of the highway above us, and hosts of hidden critters were warming up their voices for their evening performance as the shadows lengthened. "It'll be dark soon," I said. "Got a light?"

"Sorry, I forgot to pack that as you were knocking me unconscious and tying me up."

"Yeah, guess not."

The driveway seemed longer than two hundred yards, but maybe it was because we inched along. I held my pistol, not risking tucking it away, half expecting VJ to jump out of the bushes any moment. For all I knew, he had a rifle—or worse, a 12-gauge full of 00 buckshot—drawn down on us. I wanted to approach the house from a different, less predictable direction, but there was no other option. The driveway and the lot where the house stood appeared to be the only oases of cover around. Open fields stood in one direction and the raised highway in the other.

We pressed on, my only reassurance being what Lane had said about no one suspecting VJ. With any luck, maybe that meant he didn't suspect anyone would be coming for him, either.

It was almost dark by the time the horizontal roofline of the house loomed ahead. It was a tiny structure, no more than two bedrooms or so, weathered wooden siding and a rusty tin roof, not unlike the exterior of the old barn from my past.

Yellow light emanated from a single window, casting a glow across the ground beneath it. I was reminded of a Thomas Kinkade painting I had once seen of a cottage with a welcoming glow in the window and was struck by the stark contrast of emotions invoked. There was nothing welcoming about this light. If one looked into hell it would probably have a glow, too.

"Go slow and give me a few minutes," I whispered, motioning for Lane to continue on the path to the front door while I detoured to the side. I skirted along the edge of the trees, working my way toward the back of the house. The edge of the yard, if it could be called that, was littered with old farm implements, pieces of discarded tin, old paint cans and other junk, creating a veritable obstacle course for me in the sparse light. The house had no exterior light, which explained why I had never noticed it before. The trees shielded it from view during the day, and the light from the windows was too scant to bring attention to it after dark. What kind of weirdo doesn't have outside lights? The answer came easy. The kind who didn't want to be noticed.

I fought the urge to inch closer to the house, to peek in one of the small windows, hoping desperately to see Abi. To crash the glass, firing on anyone who dared come at me, grabbing Abi and shielding her and yanking her from the would-be clutches of a monster. I knew it was too risky, though. Just follow the plan. Give Lane credit. His plan made sense. Don't get stupid and rush into disaster.

What would my father think of me? He had chastised me for playing detective before, and this particular stunt might send him over the edge. I think he trusted my natural instincts and my abilities, but in his admonishment, he was basically right on all counts. I had no formal training, I was risking losing my real job, and I was putting myself in unnecessary danger.

Well, he was right on almost all counts. I had thought this through and saw no other options. The danger for the girl I now realized I had loved since I was fourteen years old was real, and so the danger in which I placed myself was entirely necessary.

I watched the back door from the shelter of the trees for ten or fifteen seconds before inching up to it in the dark, trying not to step on anything that might sound an alarm. The back had no windows, so I found myself staring at the rusty doorknob. How would I know when to open it? Had Lane already gone inside and unlocked it? Not likely. I had gone slow, but Lane would have to be nonchalant and take his time so as not to seem suspicious.

But would I hear him when he unlocked it? What if VJ was standing there with him? We should have worked out the details better. I needed a signal that all was clear. Why were there no windows back here?

I fingered the gun in my hand, both reassured and unnerved by the cool, hard steel against my palm. I had never fired at a human before, and a wave of doubt about the legalities of the matter washed over me. Sure, I had a permit to be packing, as Lane had called it, but I was standing with a drawn weapon at the door of another man's house. Even if I did rescue Abi, if I had to shoot VJ, would I still go to jail? What if Lane had us on a goose chase of paranoia, Abi wasn't even here, and VJ suddenly came out shooting at an intruder?

I took a deep breath. I was in the right place. She had to be here.

A word rose up in my head. Spoke to me. *Packing.* Such an odd way to describe carrying a weapon, if you think about it. Yet somehow, in that moment, I knew it also connected me to Abi. The answer to my questions, whether or not she might be in the house, how she got there. A flashback to her apartment earlier that day. Lane spinning a quarter on the counter, waiting for Abi. Her bag lying in the hall. Packing. Packed. Packed for what? Why had she packed her bag?

I stared at the doorknob, my heart galloping across my sternum. I begged God for a click from the other side. Something to tell me that the plan was working, that my paranoia was unfounded.

Unlock it.

Unlock!

My breath came in heaves, my chest tightening. *Calm down, Case! You can't figure this out if you panic!* Then I heard it. Just as I'd imagined, the click of the door being unlocked from the inside. *There it is!* No need for baseless hysteria. The plan was working.

I hoped she was close when I got in. Get in, get out, run for the truck. I hoped Lane could figure out a way to escape, but he had helped create this mess, and I would not wait on him. Getting Abi out of harm's way was my sole concern.

I reached for the doorknob and turned it, holding my breath, hoping it didn't creak. The cool of the metal was not unlike that of the weapon in my other hand. *Packing.* Abi's bag had been packed. Ready to travel. Ready to ride. Why? Was Abi going to stay with a friend?

Wait. Why was there no vehicle here?

My heart sank, and I recoiled. Oh, no. No, no. I stepped back and looked both ways, trying to focus, pull it together. I wasn't sure exactly what was going on, but I wasn't going in the back door like someone inside expected me to. Part of me wanted to run. Into the trees, toward the truck, go find help.

But I couldn't do that and be able to live with myself later if the worst happened, as I feared it would. If more people died.

I grabbed the pistol in both hands and crept to my right, inching along the outside wall of the house, my shoulder scraping the rough-hewn wood as I slid along, trying to even my breathing.

I yearned to leave the darkness of the back of the house, to reach the light, scarce as it was, that leaked from the paltry window on the side.

I paused at the corner, trying to remember what obstacles I might encounter as I made my way toward the window, toward something that might help me see what I needed to do. I would have to hurry, but the corner was dangerous, an easy place for an ambush. I squatted low and tried to be as quiet as possible so as not to give away my arrival, then I whirled, trigger finger poised and ready.

Nothing. No movement, no sound other than night critters. No light either, now. I stood and crept along again, straining for any unwelcome sound or movement, focused on the dark window situated just past the air conditioner unit. I searched for a sign of movement in the window, a weapon pointed at me from beyond it, waiting for me to pass through a shooting lane as I detoured off the wall and around the unit, but I wouldn't be able to see anything inside. It was too dark. I was careful to plan my step around a shovel leaning against the unit, afraid to try to move it for fear of making noise.

All at once, the shovel came alive, leaping from the ground. It made no sense to shoot a shovel, but instinct told my hand otherwise. A shot rang out just as the flat of the blade centered my forehead, and all went to black.

FORTY-SEVEN

THE rain started slowly. Just a drop at a time, like when it's barely cloudy and you feel something hit your head and look up into the sky to see if it's raining, and then another drop hits you square in the forehead. Except these drops burned. Barely at first, then more. They kept coming in the same spot. Drip, drip, drip. I tried to see the sky, but it was black.

Then the black faded into a deep crimson, gradually so it was impossible to tell the moment the red took over from the black, and I knew it wasn't rain like I thought. Drops of blood, but somehow cool, not warm like blood should be. Whose blood, though? It couldn't be mine, could it? Abi's? She was calling me, but her voice was so far away, too far.

I tried to fend off the blood but couldn't move my arms. The crimson fog cleared, and a hazy figure emerged, standing over me, leaning down, maybe trying to help me see. I cried out when I realized it was Adam, blood dripping from a hole in his chest, yet smiling, strangely enjoying my revulsion. "Come on, Case, it's show time!" Adam sneered. Then his chest exploded, and an ocean of ice-cold fluid poured upon my face.

"Ah!" I lurched to the side, coughing and sputtering, trying to reach my face to wipe the ice water away. Then I realized my hands were bound behind me.

"He's alive!" Lane Buckley stood over me, holding an empty plastic pitcher, his face twisted into a smirk. "The mighty Case Reynolds lives. Gonna pour ice water on me, were you? Well, how's it feel?"

I blinked hard to clear the water and assess my situation. Vertical cypress planks for the walls, terra cotta tiled floor, some sort of corrugated tin between cedar beams for the ceiling. I was sitting against one of two cedar posts in a transition point between a small kitchen to my right and living area to my left. My feet were free, but my hands were bound behind me and tied to the post.

"Case, are you okay?" My heart leapt as I strained to turn, recognizing Abi's voice before I could clearly see her. *She's okay!* But something didn't make sense. She was sitting on a sofa. Why wasn't she tied up like me? Ecstasy upon realizing she was alive was instantly replaced by devastating doubt. Abi? It couldn't be!

"Of course he's okay!" Lane pranced across the space in front of me, mocking me. "Right, Case? You've been hit harder than that on the football field, right? Wait, let me guess, the star quarterback was too quick to get hit like that. Well, tonight you ain't no star. You gettin' old, man." He stopped over me again, leaning forward with hands behind his back, jeering. Peering at my head. "I must say, VJ's old shovel put quite a knot on your head. Thought you outsmarted me, didn't you? I knew when you didn't come right in, something was up. Reckon any of the manure from that shovel got in that wound on your head? Could cause quite an infection, I suppose."

I was so confused. "Abi?"

She looked terrible. The red of her bloodshot eyes against her brilliant blue irises was unnerving. Her hair was disheveled, and she had obviously been crying.

"Abi isn't the one you need to be talking to," Lane said. "I've got the answers. Might not be the ones you're looking for, though." He held up my pistol and waved it in front of him. "Thanks for the pistol. Had to dump mine."

"Where's VJ?" I fought against my splitting headache as I looked from Lane to Abi.

Lane burst out laughing. "What'd I tell you, Abi? Told you! I told you I'd bet a thousand dollars that was his first question. VJ, VJ, VJ. Where's VJ? What is it with him, anyway? Jack the Ripper would be jealous of the fascination with VJ."

"Lane!" I yelled. "Untie me right now and tell me what is going on!"

"Who are you to make demands?" He waved the gun again. "Look, if you've got questions, you better be asking." He looked at his watch. "We gotta get this show on the road. Abi and I got places to be."

My fingers frantically searched the bindings that held my hands behind me. It was nylon rope, looped around each wrist and tied in the middle, as best I could tell. Somehow it was all connected to the post, but I couldn't make out the mechanism. I leaned hard against the post to see if it would give, but it did not budge.

"Don't bother," Lane said. "Posts are cemented in. You're stuck."

"And you're bleeding." I nodded at a stain on his blue jeans.

Lane touched his hand to his left thigh and wiped the blood on his shirt. "Yeah. Ricocheted off that shovel, I think. Maybe you're luckier than I thought."

"You didn't answer my question. Where's VJ? Abi, what's going on here?"

"VJ MacIntosh," Lane said. "Villain of all villains. You seen that movie that just came out, *The Usual Suspects?*"

"Don't guess I have," I said.

"I'm not gonna ruin it for Abi, but the whole movie everybody's trying to figure out where the vicious mastermind is. 'Where's Keyser Söze?' Just like 'Where's VJ?' Well, in the end, Keyser Söze wasn't who they thought he was at all. Quite a twist, I must say, sure fooled me. I was watching it last week, stunned how much the whole thing reminded me of everyone's obsession with VJ. Guess what, Case?"

He stepped toward me and bent down slightly. "VJ ain't here!" he screamed. "VJ MacIntosh wasn't ever any criminal mastermind. He came out of juvie, got locked up again, and came out a broken-down wuss of a half man. Couldn't find his place." He made a sweeping hand motion. "Just look at how he decorated. Built a house like a barn and put ships and flowers on the walls. Lost."

I had noticed an ocean scene on one wall and some sort of floral print on another, but I didn't care and didn't look again. "What are you talking about? You told us what happened. You and Abi fought, you picked up VJ, he killed Adam and talked you and your mother into helping him cover it up."

Lane dismissed my summary with a wave of his hand and a smug smile. "Pretty good story, huh? You and Jet swallowed it. Hook, line, and sinker. Yeah, Abi and I had a spat that night.

And I got mad and picked up VJ. But he was just there for moral support after that. That pantywaist was all talk, no action."

"So you killed Adam?"

Lane shrugged. "He was in Jet's truck, and I was mad. Everybody knows Jet decided to go to med school in Jackson to try to get back with Abi. She didn't see it, but I did. I wasn't really trying to run him off the road, just mess with him and burn off some steam. But then we rode back by and there was Adam, drawn down on us like Rambo or something. He was hot, threatened to tell Jet everything when we got back. I couldn't let that happen." Lane looked at Abi. "You understand, don't you baby? Keeping us together was all that ever mattered."

Tears streamed down Abi's cheeks. She nodded and looked down.

"See, Case? Abi knows we're supposed to be together." He rubbed his thigh and winced in pain.

"Abi, talk to me!" I begged. "What are you doing?"

She shook her head. "No, Case, just listen to Lane, and it'll work out."

"Work out? What's working out? This lunatic has me tied up, and you're okay with that? Tell me you're not in on this."

"Shut up!" Lane growled. "I told you to leave her out of this." He thumped his chest with his fist. "I'm the one with the answers you want."

I stared at Abi while Lane ranted, trying to find a modicum of clarity in her expression. She shook her head almost imperceptibly and raised one shirt sleeve a few inches. The bruises and ligature marks on her wrist were unmistakable.

I turned back to Lane, trying not to give away what I had learned. "So that was you who attacked Gracie Tollison at the walking track, tried to make it look like Jet? And you followed us to the cemetery that night and hit Jack with the two-by-four?"

Lane spread his arms wide and poked out his chest. "Me. In the flesh."

"And you switched the bodies to make sure Jet got his brother in anatomy."

"Wasn't that hard with the right plan. Genius, I'd say." He smiled at Abi. "Baby, next time you see your old flame Jet… Wait, I don't think you will. Anyway, maybe we'll call him one day to tell him he failed. I bet he's good at anatomy, but dissecting the truth? Failed."

He waited for her to respond but she did not. "Get it, babe? Dissect, like in anatomy? Failed?" He waved a hand at her and chuckled. A weird, awkward chuckle, like a man accustomed to telling bad jokes and then plotting his revenge when no one laughs.

I kicked my legs in frustration. "You're insane. But why do that to Jet? Wasn't killing his brother enough?"

"Come on, Case. That didn't accomplish a thing. Jet was marching on, gonna be a big-shot doctor. I saw an opportunity and I took it. Ruin Jet and get rid of evidence too. You know, kill two birds with one stone."

"What evidence?"

"Have you ever thought about that phrase? Two birds with one stone? Who kills birds with stones nowadays anyway? Kinda silly if you think about it. Ah, but saying two birds with one shot doesn't have the same effect, though, does it?"

"What evidence? You said get rid of the evidence."

"You think you're so smart. Figure it out."

Talking to a maniac was exasperating. "Whatever. How did you get your mother in on it too?"

Lane cackled. "My mother had nothing to do with this."

I wrestled with the rope around my wrists while I also struggled to untangle his words. "Lane, enough with the lies. I saw the photo of Marta Winscote at your lake house. Holding you in her arms, I'm fairly certain. Same place as you and Abi in that photo on her fridge. I know she's your mother. You had to have help to get access to the anatomy lab."

"You know nothing about my mother. Nothing!" he bellowed. "My mother was killed when I was six!" He began to pace, limping, the bloodstain larger. He took a breath and spoke more softly. "She had a big heart, kinda like Abi here. Picked up a hitchhiker one afternoon, trying to be a Good Samaritan. You know, just help the guy get a few miles up the road. To thank her, he murdered her with a rusty hunting knife and dumped her in a ditch. Really hit the jackpot with the fifteen bucks she had in her purse."

Killed by a hitchhiker while doing a good deed. It was a terrible injustice, but that was no excuse. "Lane, I'm sorry about your mother." I tried to sound empathetic. "But hurting me isn't going to bring her back, even if you and Abi live happily ever after."

He grinned and winked at Abi, who feigned a half-smile of her own. "That's what Abi said." His smile evaporated into a wild-eyed scowl. "But I know you don't think Abi and I should be together." Lane brought up the gun and leveled it at me with both hands, peering down the barrel with me in his sights.

I turned my head and body to the side with my eyes closed tight, feeling even more vulnerable since I couldn't hold up my hands. "Hang on, Lane. Hang on! I know you want to tell me the rest of the story. What about VJ? Where is he?"

Lane dropped the gun to his side. He took a few steps, grabbed a wooden chair and sat down in front of me, leaning forward with the gun between his legs. "VJ! Yes, VJ. I do want you to hear about the mighty VJ MacIntosh. His fall from the imaginary throne, built in the minds of old friends."

"He's never been my friend."

"Well, he's never gonna be, either. Bless his heart, he just couldn't get right. He left us permanently last year. November, maybe? Coupla months after all that happened."

"You killed him."

"No, I did not. Don't you say that." He held the gun sideways and waved it in my general direction again. "VJ was messed up, but he was my friend, and I did not kill him. He got himself hooked on crack somewhere along the way. I found him dead in a puddle of his own vomit back there in the back." He pinched his nose and frowned. "He'd been there a few days. It was rough."

Abi inched forward in her seat, leaning.

"Why should I believe you?" I said. "All you've done is lie."

"I don't really care if you believe me or not. But hold on." He stood and spun the chair away from him across the hard floor, walked over to a small table against the wall, and opened a drawer.

Abi reached and grabbed something off the coffee table in front of her while he searched.

"Yeah, here it is," Lane said. "Abi, come here. Show this to wannabe detective Reynolds." He patted the gun. "And remember what we talked about, baby."

It sickened me to hear him call her "baby." I wasn't sure what they had "talked about," but I suspected Lane had threatened her to keep her mouth closed or watch me suffer the consequences. I wasn't naïve enough to think he had any intention of letting me live, though, and I hoped she knew it, too, no matter what he might have promised.

Abi stood and moved toward Lane. She didn't look at me. She hung her head at first, but about halfway to him her posture changed. She stood taller, almost defiant. Proud, as was her nature. There was my girl. "What you got there, honey?"

"Show him." Lane placed the object in her hand.

Abi stepped slowly to me, her back to Lane. Her eyes held some fear and uncertainty, but more than that, I saw resolve. She squatted down and held the object for me to see. It was a driver's license. Issued by the State of Mississippi, for one Vance MacIntosh Jr.

But the face in the photo was not VJ.

It was Lane Buckley.

FORTY-EIGHT

BI palmed the license and stood, but her gaze diverted toward the floor and she nodded. I followed and saw it. A set of fingernail clippers in front of her foot. She tapped it toward me as she stood.

"That's right," Lane said. "VJ died, but who knew it? All his family is dead. I was his only friend. He had this house here, a lake house, a fairly fat bank account, and some dividend checks. Why let all that go to waste?"

"So you took over his identity?" I tried to maneuver the clippers toward my body with my heel.

"It wasn't hard to be VJ MacIntosh and Lane Buckley at the same time. Just get an ID made, master his signature, keep his bills paid, use an out-of-town bank branch where they knew neither of us. Easy. Gradually, through small transfers so as not to draw attention, Vance MacIntosh Jr.'s money has been becoming Lane E. Buckley's money."

I had the clippers in my hand now and was thankful Lane hadn't bound my hands behind the post. As they were, in front of it, I had some room to work. His treachery was impressive, but master of kidnapping perhaps he was not. I had no intentions of him having future chances to work on it. "You weasel. He was your friend."

"Yes, and as a true friend, I knew he would want me to have his money."

The clippers were working. A strand or two at a time, but they were working. "What about Marta Winscote? If she's not your mother, why did she help you?"

"Well, maybe I wasn't totally honest about VJ's family. Marta was his mother, not mine. But she had disappeared when he was a baby. A drunk, I think. That part was true. Tried to get back in VJ's life for several years after she moved back. He didn't want to have nothing to do with her, though, until toward the end. She was willing to do anything to get him back."

I clipped another strand. "So you told her VJ killed Adam, didn't you?"

"I'll give you credit, you ain't no dummy. That's the gist of it, yeah. And she didn't pay close enough attention. I found a way to get in the lab, went back a couple weeks later, made sure ol' Jet had a present waiting for him when he opened his tank."

"How'd you know which tank was going to be Jet's?"

"Wasn't hard to find a list."

"You're a sicko." I jerked at my bindings and pretended to be panicked by the futility of trying to escape, but I was making progress with my clippers.

He rubbed his hands together. "No, just a man who appreciates good entertainment. And it has been priceless."

"Where does VJ's mother think he is now?"

"Well, her dear, kind son VJ mailed her a very nice handwritten letter a few weeks after she hadn't heard from him. Said he had gone to Oregon to live with a friend for a few months. You know, to try to get himself straightened out. No doubt she understood the importance of that."

"And let me guess, his good friend Lane Buckley was gonna look over this place for him while he was gone."

Lane pointed at me and winked. "Bingo. Plus, she knows VJ's good friend Lane wouldn't hesitate to implicate her in the Gross Anatomy fiasco she participated in, if necessary, to protect himself and her beloved son."

"You're bleeding more, honey," Abi said sweetly. "If we're going to get on the road, we need to get that stopped."

Lane glanced at his leg, where the entire front of the thigh was stained now.

I clipped as fast as I could.

"I'm okay. We'll look at it in a minute."

Abi moved toward Lane. "C'mon, it could be dangerous. You've got to save your strength. Let me put a dressing on it and get you some clean clothes."

I held my breath, hoping he'd let her leave the room. Instead, he stopped her with a motion of his hand.

"I told you I'm fine." He gestured at me with a jerk of his thumb. "I've got to finish with him."

Something about the sideways jerk of his thumb popped a word into my head. *Hitchhiker.* "Does Abi know what else you've been up to?"

Lane's eyes narrowed, wild and lupine. "What are you talking about?"

"You know what I mean. It's no coincidence that four hitchhikers have turned up dead in the past year around here. I'm just wondering, did you think that would bring your momma back?"

"You shut up. Shut up about her!"

"Does Abi know she'll be with a serial killer if she sticks with you?"

He took three steps toward me, teeth gritted, and raised the gun again. "I told you to shut up."

"Lane, calm down. We can work through it. What is he talking about?" Abi moved behind him to get in my line of sight. Her eyes widened, inquiring.

I wanted to nod to tell her that yes, I had cut the rope, that I would pounce on Lane and fight for both our lives if he would only get close enough to me. But that wasn't true. Not yet.

"Tell me something." I lowered my voice, trying to appear calm. Hoping to buy more time. "What about the hitchhiker at the railroad yard? How did he tie in to all this?"

Lane shot a glance toward Abi before he answered. Not really ready to confess just yet. But not able to resist. "I'm telling you, the gods have been smiling on me." He spread his arms wide, like he was celebrating reaching the crest of a mountain. "I mean, I thought I was going to have to kill that moron Stimpy Riggins when he finally told me he'd sent that body to Jackson. But something held me back. It intrigued me, for some reason."

He held one hand to his face, like he was pondering, then he pointed at me. "Then, sure enough, bam. Not long after that Adam was dead, I remembered what happened to the last body, and I knew it was meant to be. VJ's momma was large and in charge, ready to help us, whether she knew it or not. Don't that sound like the gods working to you?" He used his arms again to emphasize his point, but this time he raised them toward the ceiling, as if calling his imaginary higher power.

I ignored his theatrics. "How did you do it? None of the hitchhikers had bullet wounds."

Lane's smile was the embodiment of evil. If he had wanted to keep his extracurricular activities hidden from Abi at first, he was way past that now. The temptation to brag even more was just too much. He glanced at her again as he turned away from me, but it didn't stop him. "I'm glad you asked. I think I'll show you." He opened the drawer again, this time producing a syringe. "Beautiful stuff right here. VJ actually told me about it, learned it from a guy in prison. Four thousand times more potent than morphine. Two milligrams will take out a wildebeest. One hundredth of that can kill a human in twenty minutes. Gotta use more than that, though if you want it to work quick."

"Lane, is that true?" Abi asked. "Killing Adam, uh, you know, to keep us together, that's one thing, but a serial killer?"

"We'll talk about that later, babe. I think we're about done here."

I was afraid if I continued to provoke Lane that he'd pop off and shoot me, but what choice did I have? I was running out of time before he was going to do it anyway, and I needed him to do something stupid. "Ask him about the newest one, Abi. Sheriff's department is out at Gunner's Run right now working a murder scene. Another innocent hitchhiker, I'm sure. That's where Jet is. He'll be back with help soon."

Lane looked at his watch. "You think you're so smart." He smirked. "He's still ten minutes away from there, clear across the county. Then ten more minutes to get the attention of whatever cops are there and explain himself, then however long it takes somebody to finally ride out here. We'll be long gone."

"They'll shut down every road out of the county."

"No they won't," Lane said. "Dumb VJ left a receipt in the garbage for his and Lane's plane ticket out of Memphis. So an A.P.B. will go out to find VJ and Lane somewhere between here and there, the cops will root around here trying to see if Abi and Case are left lying in a shallow grave, and Lane and Abi will be long gone in the opposite direction in a car nobody knows I own. It's in an old barn a half-mile from here. By the time they find your truck, it'll be too late."

"And me?"

"Lying in a shallow grave, of course. What do you think the shovel was for?"

A chill ran down my spine. "It'll never work."

Lane smiled. "You know that part will, but you're right, my plan didn't work quite to perfection. I thought Jet would be here with us. Two out of three ain't bad, though."

"Do not hurt Abi."

"Oh, I would never do that. I'm not talking about her."

I frowned. "What then? Who?"

"Nobody but you ever said it was a hitchhiker at Gunner's Run."

My heart sank. "What are you talking about, you weirdo?" I yelled, trying to unscramble my thoughts and process what he was saying.

"I certainly never said it was a hitchhiker there."

"Tell me right now. What have you done?"

Lane methodically marched back to the table and placed the syringe in the drawer. He closed it slowly, precisely, appearing to savor the tension suspended in the triangle between us. He turned back, shaking his head, feigning sincere disappointment. "And it seemed like Jack and I were getting along so well."

Abi shrieked and collapsed to her knees.

The color of the room turned blood red, and a blitz of thoughts and images scrolled across my mind in an instant. Jack's longstanding distrust of Lane, ever since their fight years back, Lane surely holding a grudge for the beating he took. Lane insisting on staying with Jack and taking him home. Surveying, planning, plotting his revenge. Jack calling and leaving a message that he desperately needed to talk to Jet earlier, then his apartment in a mess with a spilled can of soda, a chair moved out of place, a TV tray overturned. Jack's vehicle parked outside his home with no sign of him anywhere.

"No!" It couldn't be. Impossible. Not Jack, my oldest friend in the world! For an instant, the moment overwhelmed me. I wanted to collapse in a heap and cry, beg for a minute to mourn my friend before the inevitable happened to me. I had managed to finally cut through with my clippers, but for some reason my hands were still bound and not budging. There was no more time for me to try a different part of the rope. I was doomed. But maybe it was better that way, since I had failed everyone I cared about. Maybe I didn't deserve to live myself.

But the moment passed just as quickly as it had come. I couldn't quit. It just wasn't in me. Maybe Abi would make it and be able to tell that I had gone down fighting. My family would take some solace in that, right? A spark of resurrected fury lit a fuse in my gut, and I welcomed the burn. Whatever happened, my dying breath would be spent trying to get at the wretched, pitiful excuse for a human being before me. The fuse found a powder keg, and I exploded with a scream like a battlefield war cry. "I'll kill you! I'll kill you!" I thrashed and heaved at my bindings like a wounded jungle predator intent on destroying its captor. I lost my balance and lurched onto my side. My shoulder popped. The pain should have been excruciating, but I felt very little.

Lane whooped and jumped around, wild-eyed, now completely unhinged. "Get it, boy. Get it! This is better than I thought. I wanted to watch you die from e-tor-phine like a dirty zoo animal, but this is even better. Like shooting at a cat with his tail on fire!" He raised the gun and fired. The explosion in the confined space was deafening. I spun and recoiled as I the bullet cracked the tile inches away from me. "Jump, boy, jump!" Lane yelled again with delight. "Lemme see some moves!"

As quickly as Lane had raised and fired the weapon, Abi was on her feet. She grabbed the closest thing she could reach—a small lamp from the side table—and lunged at Lane, bringing it down toward his head.

He somehow detected it coming and dodged just enough to miss a knockout blow as he swung the gun toward Abi. Instead of hitting his head, the lamp came down hard on his hand, sending the Springfield spinning under the sofa. Lane froze and eyed the crack where the gun disappeared for a split second. Then he balled his fist and crashed it into Abi's jaw with a roundhouse, sending her to the floor in a crumpled heap.

I lifted my head toward the sky and roared, a primal, anguished howl like a lion who's been defeated but would rather die than give up his pride. I doubt it affected Lane in his state of frenzied psychosis, but it helped me summon the last measure of my strength.

I lunged again with everything I had, straining every sinew, willing them to break if the rope would not. My shoulder popped again, this time with a loud report not unlike a small caliber gunshot. The laser of pain matched the sound, but the gun was under the sofa, and I had not been shot.

Suddenly, somehow, my hands slipped free of the rope. I don't know if it was because of the cut I had made or the change in angle of my wrists from the dislocated shoulder, but I was free.

Lane's expression changed from a sneering type of delirious ecstasy to a gape of confused alarm in an instant. I was on him before he moved an inch, and I caught him with a right hook in the temple. He reeled backward and to my left but did not go down. I couldn't raise my arm to hit him with a hard left, and it cost me. Lane recovered enough to slide a chair between us as he staggered behind it and lunged for the table against the wall.

I charged him again. Lane snatched up the syringe and popped the cap off the needle in one motion. He raised it to stab me as I came at him, but I blocked the blow, a technique my father had shown me for defending against a knife attack.

I failed to account for the fact I only had one functional arm, though. Weakened from blood loss, Lane had trouble keeping his balance on the one leg. We fell to the floor, me with a death grip on his wrist. He twisted his body to switch the syringe to his other hand, which would mean the end for me since I couldn't even feel my left hand anymore.

As he tried to shift his weight, the muscle tension in his right arm relaxed slightly. With all the force I could muster, I pulled his hand down in a swinging motion toward his thigh, plunging the needle deep into the muscle.

Lane just smiled. He froze and relaxed, still conscious, like he was aborting a detox by mainlining his favorite hallucinogenic drug. Why? I tried to pull away. I couldn't.

Then I saw the reason.

Lane had jerked my left hand down to his leg, trying to interpose it between the needle and himself. And it had worked.

Almost. The needle had plunged through the webbing between my thumb and forefinger, pinning my hand to his leg.

Injecting the deadly etorphine into both of us.

I grabbed the syringe. Yanked it out. Tossed it aside.

I tried to stand, but my legs were jello. Lane had received the bulk of the injection, as his eyes were already rolled back and he had gone limp, though the sickening smile remained.

Surely I didn't get a full dose, did I? I tried to call Abi, but only a slurred moan came out. *Get up! Go call for help!* I tried to stand again, but it was impossible.

The floor and ceiling and walls melted into a whirling blur of red, gray, and brown.

It was turning black.

So sleepy.

Abi asleep, too. At least she'd wake up.

Maybe I'd see Jack.

Jet could finish the stor—

FORTY-NINE

Four days later

JET eyed the dumpy man with the rumpled khakis and faded polo shirt who entered the hospital room. "Who are you, and what do you need?"

The man gave a polite nod toward Gracie and then fixed his gaze on Jet. "Name's Clyde Merimore. You're Jet Townsend, right? I was told you'd be here. Wondered if we could talk a few minutes?"

"Someone called from your paper yesterday." Jet shook his head. "And the answer is the same today. I have nothing to say right now. Don't know why you want to talk to me anyway."

Merimore fidgeted with his pen. "Was hoping you might help me with the story." He nodded across the room. "You know, until something changes."

"Give me your card, and maybe – and I stress maybe – if something changes, I'll call you."

The reporter nodded deferentially and backed away two steps. "Give me the first crack at it?"

"Goodbye, Mr. Merimore."

The reporter opened his mouth as if to speak but then closed it and nodded. He clipped his pin on the V of his shirt and left.

"He's just doing his job," Gracie said. "It is a good story. If you're a reporter, I mean."

"There's nothing good about it," Jet said. "And like I said, Case and I had an agreement to write it ourselves."

"Even if Case can't do it?"

"That was our agreement, Gracie."

"I know, baby. I'm sorry, I know this has been hard on you. It's all just too much. Just awful."

"I keep playing it over and over in my mind. Abi said the gun was found right where it slid after she hit Lane. She's positive. But why didn't Case go after it once he got loose? Instead, he attacked Lane hand to hand, with only one good arm, knowing he was likely to get stabbed with the needle. Stupid."

One good arm, needle, stabbed. Lane Buckley reaching in a drawer, trying to kill... Jet's words were like a brisk breeze against a thick morning fog. I licked my lips and tried to find my voice. "We can't all be geniuses, but I thought he might have a gun in the drawer."

"Case!" Jet turned around and clapped his hands once. "Hey boy, you're awake! Gracie, he's awake!"

Gracie and Jet stepped to my bedside. "I do believe he is." She patted my arm warmly, as if we were old friends. "Welcome back, Mr. Reynolds. You were missed."

"Thanks. You seem much nicer than your friend here. He was kinda rough on that reporter." I pointed my thumb toward Jet and realized my hand was shaking.

He grabbed it and shook it hard with both of his. "Ha ha! I knew you'd come back."

"And who are you?"

"Cut it out." Jet grinned. "You're not foolin' me. How long you been listening, you sorry bum?"

I smiled weakly. "Long enough to know there's a lot that I don't know. What happened?" The fog was clearing but I was a still long way from clarity. I wiggled the fingers on my left hand and tested the sensation in them, noting a yellowing bruise between my thumb and first finger. My shoulder was in a sling, but I remembered it being limp and useless before and welcomed the bolt of pain as I tested its function. "Last thing I remember, I was getting ready to walk toward the light."

"Well, Jet moved the proverbial light down the road a ways." Gracie smiled. "You're at University Hospital."

"Your shoulder will be fine. Doc says you dislocated it and impinged the brachial plexus—er, pinched some nerves—in the process, but it's back in place and working. May need some rotator cuff work later, though."

"I don't understand. How did I...? There was no way to survive, right? I mean, Lane, he... I saw him —"

"Yes, Lane is dead," Jet said.

Gracie tapped my arm again. "Jet saved you. He gave you the antidote."

I rubbed my eyes, trying to make sense of things. I didn't even know what day it was, but I'd get to that later. I wanted to know why I was alive. "The antidote?"

"For the etorphine," Gracie continued. "It's a drug called naloxone. Same thing used for morphine and heroin overdoses."

I looked at my old friend. "How?"

Jet nodded toward the door, and Gracie turned and left the room. "Remember when we stopped at the hospital to see if Abi was there? You had just told me about the murder at Gunner's Run and how the killer was using a strong sedative, so on a hunch I lifted some naloxone from the ER. Just in case. After I did it, I thought it was a stupid risk, so I didn't tell you. I was just gonna return it when we got home. Guess it wasn't so stupid after all."

"Wow. But you were all the way at the other side of McKinley County. I should have been dead."

"Lane made a slip. He mentioned Gunner's Run when I said I was going to the murder scene to find Turnip. But if you remember, he was still unconscious in the back of the truck when you named where it was, so how could he have known Gunner's Run unless he was in on it somehow? I didn't catch it until it was almost too late. I turned around when it hit me."

"You could've gone on for help."

"Didn't figure there was time for that, and looks like I was right, eh? Although I expected to find VJ and Lane both trying to do you in."

"Lane wanted you and me both to come to the house."

"Yeah, remember he tried to talk me out of going to Gunner's Run? Abi said he kept ranting about both of us needing to be taught a lesson. I think he saw us as competition for her."

"Abi!" I tried to rise up in the bed.

"Abi is fine. She has hardly left your bedside. Your parents have been here the whole time, too. They just left to go get a bite to eat."

"Where is Abi? I need to see her."

"Gracie went to find her. She's probably down there telling the nurses how to take care of you."

"Abi saved me. He was gonna shoot, and she hit him, then he knocked her out." My voice fell off as if the words rolled over a cliff. I remembered the last thing Lane had told us, the reason I had lost my cool before he had started shooting.

"Jack." I collapsed back on the bed and closed my eyes. I suddenly wanted to vomit.

"Case!" Abi had my hand before I even knew she was there. "You're back." She rubbed my face then leaned down and hugged me cheek to cheek. "It's good to see you awake." She pushed back and studied me, like a parent inspecting a child who's been away at camp for the summer.

"I'm happy to see you too, Abi."

"You came for me. Lane would have killed me."

"Or married you."

She shook her head. "He would have had to kill me." Her expression changed to one of puzzlement. "What's wrong? You look upset. Don't worry, the doctor says you'll be fine."

"No, it's not me. I'm glad you're okay. You know I'd go anywhere and do anything for you. It's just hard to believe what happened, though. How long have I been out? Did I miss the funeral?"

"Lane's funeral? I guess so. Who cares?"

"Don't be ridiculous. I'm talking about Jack."

Abi frowned and looked at Jet, who smiled. "It's the sedatives they had him on. He doesn't remember. Case, my friend, how about I make your day with the best news you've heard in a long time, other than learning that Abi told me she's in love with you. Oops, did I just say that?" He laughed and punched me in my good arm. "Jack's not dead, you old goofball. Jack's doing just fine. Well, almost just fine."

I looked back and forth between them. "Jack's alive? I thought—"

"You've been out of it for four days, Case," Abi said. "You had a respiratory arrest even after the antidote. Jet did CPR, but you were on life support for three days. Had a seizure, so they put you on meds to prevent another one, and you've been loopy for the past two days. We told you when you first woke up, but I guess you don't remember."

"Lane said that was Jack's body they found up at Gunner's Run."

"Lane wished Jack was dead, I'm sure," Abi said. "But it wasn't Jack. He got a bad headache, called 911 himself, and he's been here in the ICU, too."

"Subdural hematoma," Jet said. "A slow bleed around the brain, sometimes takes days to get big enough to cause symptoms, but by the time it does it can be life threatening. It's from the lick he took with the baseball bat. So technically, Lane did almost kill him. Almost."

My heart was racing, like a vise had been removed and it was trying to make up for lost time. "So Jack's okay? He's okay?"

"Needed brain surgery but yeah, he's gonna be just fine."

"Oh, yeah!" I pumped my fist in the air. "That's my boy, Jack."

"Shh." Abi giggled. "Your nurse is a scrooge. She'll make us all leave."

My thoughts turned dark again. "Who was it? At Gunner's Run?"

"A guy from Minnesota," Jet said soberly. "College student thumbing his way across the south for a semester."

I shook my head in disgust and sighed across a heavy silence. I looked at Jet. "I'm sorry about Adam."

Jet patted my shoulder. "He's been gone almost a year, and I've already done my mourning. I'm glad we got closure. I owe you, buddy."

"His body?"

"They had already cremated him." Jet looked away. "But that was probably best."

My thoughts shifted, and I looked at Abi. "What about the other part?" I reached for her hand. "The other good news Jet mentioned."

Abi blushed and her blizzard blue eyes flared. "Jet has a big mouth."

"I'll bet my hair grows back before your shoulder heals." Jack replaced the dressing on his scalp and fell back onto his pillow, pretending to be upset that I had snickered at the fact half his head was shaved.

I kicked Jack's hospital bed from my wheelchair. "Maybe, but at least I look normal. You look like a kid who got into his mother's Nair bottle."

Jack laughed. "Funny. I'm thinking about shaving it and going with the bald look anyway. You know, all Michael Jordan."

"Michael Jordan? Not even close." I thought about the basketball legend's two-word fax earlier in the year. "I'm back." Announcing he was returning to the Chicago Bulls, out of retirement. I held up one finger to emphasize my point. "Although, there could be a symbolic aspect to it. After all, you did have an 'I'm back' moment. Came out of a sort of permanent retirement yesterday, at least from my perspective."

"Okay, Case, you're as bad as Jet sometimes. Overthinking the joke."

I smiled. It *was* good to have him back. I turned to see Jet strolling in. "Speaking of Captain Overthink, there he is."

Jet stopped just inside the doorway and eyed us both. "You two invalids comparing walking canes?"

"Bedpans," Jack quipped. "But hey, I just thought of something. Case, have you thought about how Jet saved you? I seriously think y'all may be legally married now in some states."

"What? He gave me the antidote. A shot."

"Yeah? And what else?"

Jet puckered his lips and faked some chest compressions in the air.

"Aw, man. Mouth to mouth?"

Jet grinned and batted his eyes. "Don't worry, sweetie, I used a breath mint."

I couldn't help but laugh. It was short lived, though. A knock at the door stopped me, and a tall, broad-shouldered woman in in a police uniform entered.

She nodded and surveyed the room. "Ah, I see Mr. Masterson has company. Good morning, gentlemen."

Jet sat on the sofa. "Officer Weatherspoon."

"You two know each other?" I asked.

"Yes, Mr. Townsend and I go way back. Daddy says tell you hello, Jet."

"Officer Weatherspoon's partner is Gutierrez. You know, Case, the one you dumped the water on outside the ER. And if that doesn't make you think it's a small world, you remember the old man we met that night outside the anatomy lab when I was giving you that tour?"

I eyed the large black woman closely, attempting to gauge whether she was friend or foe on this visit. "The janitor, er, custodian, we met?"

"Mr. Soap is Officer Weatherspoon's father, believe it or not," Jet said.

"Been there a hundred years," the officer said. "Maybe that's why my beat includes the hospital. That place is in my blood, I guess."

"Okay, okay." Jack slapped me lightly on the arm with the back of his hand. "Did you knuckleheads forget this is my room? She's obviously here to see me." He looked at the policewoman and smiled. "You obviously know who I am. Now I kinda know who you are, but how can I help you?"

"I'm sorry, Mr. Masterson." She stepped to the bedside and extended her hand to Jack's. "My name is Bianca Weatherspoon. Jackson PD. I've been around the past few days, trying to wrap up this case. You and Mr. Reynolds here have just been too incapacitated to know it."

"Well, quit calling ever'body mister," Jack said. "I'm Jack, he's Case, and you know Jet."

"Case Reynolds." I leaned across Jack for a formal introduction and handshake of my own. "But you already knew that."

"I'm glad to find you both awake and doing well. I came in to get Jack's statement about the night he was assaulted, which led to his hemorrhage. And Case, I'll have to spend some time with you as well. We got a boatload to discuss."

"I suppose I need to get an attorney." I looked to Jet for confirmation.

"Attorney?" Jack said. "What a bunch of nonsense. You're a dang hero. They better not be trying to pin something on you. Jet either."

Weatherspoon laughed. "You can get representation if you want, but I don't see much need. Pretty clear you were trying to save Abi and killed Lane Buckley in that house in self-defense."

That part was certainly true, never mind the fact I actually kidnapped him to get him there. My mind raced down the list of activities I'd participated in in recent days, all illegal to varying degrees. Grave-robbing, false impersonation, breaking and entering, kidnapping. How much of that did she ever have to know? None, if I had my way.

"What about the kidnapping charge?" Jet said.

It was as if he read my mind. My eyes widened and I held my breath. Had they found out we kidnapped Lane? Surely no one cared under the circumstances, right?

"I guess this means the charges against me will be dropped for what happened to Gracie? You were going to check on that."

I exhaled in relief.

Weatherspoon chuckled. "Still pending, but I think you're pretty safe, yeah? That dude used the same drug on Gracie and Abi both. It's called midazolam. He sho' 'nuff tried to nail you with it, huh? You know we traced the bottle we found at your house right after Gracie's assault back to University Hospital. Still haven't figured out where he got the other stuff, though. Etorphine, I think they called it. I never heard of it. Maybe the zoo, who knows?"

This line of conversation also made me nervous. Had they discussed where Jet got the naloxone he saved me with yet?

Surely that had come up. I wasn't sure, but would that be a felony?

The look on Jet's face didn't exactly reassure me. He had something on his mind, yet I doubted he would take this conversation in a precarious direction. He was too smart for that. "Did they happen to say what department it came from?"

"The midazolam? Does it matter?"

Jet shrugged. "Just curious, is all."

Weatherspoon touched her chin. "You know, I think they said surgery maybe? You know they use that when they put people to sleep for surgery. Don't know it makes any difference. That snake probably wandered around until he saw an opening and then swooped in to lift it."

"Yeah, it doesn't matter," Jet said.

I raised my hand. "Officer Weatherspoon, can I ask a question, before we get to all the other stuff?" I hesitated to say too much, because I didn't want to cause trouble for anyone, but I couldn't help myself. "Your father, Mr. Soap. Did he know something was up? Jet said, he, uhh, reached out to him."

Jet and the officer shared a look. "I know Daddy tried to help Jet. We've talked about it. He feels bad, because he did suspect something. He just didn't know what it was or what to do. Been getting paid a lot of years to clean up. Wasn't never his place to butt in others' business."

"Can I tell them what you told me?" Jet asked.

"Go ahead," she said. "Don't see what it matters now."

"Mr. Soap saw two people moving a body in the middle of the night, after I figured out it was Adam in the anatomy lab. It seemed odd, but he didn't think too much about it until later, after he heard about me."

"He wasn't sure of the exact date of it," Weatherspoon said, "but I suspected it was the day you had your spell and passed out. And guess what? I checked our call logs. We had a call about a gunshot at the back of the hospital, outside. But we never found a victim."

"Holy cow," I said. "They actually took the replacement cadaver down there and put a bullet hole in it?"

"Nuts," was all the officer said in response.

"Lane and Dr. Winscote," I said. "Had to be them. Couldn't have been VJ. He was already dead by then."

Weatherspoon nodded. "I guess. He just saw two people, one several inches taller than the other." She chuckled. "Daddy's eyes aren't so good anymore. He actually thought it was two women."

Jet's double blink and subtle, sideways head pivot told me that was the first time he'd heard that last detail.

FIFTY

ET waited until all the other students had taken their places in the anatomy lab before he eased in and slid up to his
table. Perhaps he could slip into the flow of things and go
unnoticed. Aside from the inevitable unpleasantries of whispers
and awkward stares, he had feared that getting acclimated to the
pervasive presence of death would be even more difficult than
before, perhaps even impossible. But before walking through
the door, he had taken on a workman-like mentality. Like a man
faced with a loathsome job he has no choice but to perform to
feed his family.

"Welcome back, Jet. Missed you in biochem this morning."

Jet cringed at the sarcastic voice behind him. Of course. Why
would he expect anything other than immediately having to deal
with Sterling Virchow's nonsense?

Yes, he had missed class. The entirety of the morning had
been occupied by meetings with various medical school administrators and their attorneys, not to mention a number of professors, each of whom felt compelled to stress the importance of
the material he'd missed and the difficulty he would face in
catching up. He had listened patiently to the professors, but the
administrators and the attorneys had been particularly displeased
with what he had to say. What he proposed.

Virchow jabbed a finger in Jet's back. "You hear me? Almost
had to cancel class, everyone was so worried about you."

Jet gritted his teeth and turned to face the imposing figure behind him. "I'm sure you missed me, Sterling, but if you don't mind, I've got a lot of catching up to do."

"Yes, you do. We all may have to start over now that you've run off half the anatomy department."

"That's on them, not me," Jet said. "Hmm, maybe it's on you, too, seeing as how you and Marta Winscote are such big buddies. Research partners and all." He turned back toward his table, but Virchow reached out to stop him.

"Just what are you implying?"

Jet sighed and spoke matter-of-factly. "I'm not implying anything. I've had a long week, a really long week." He jabbed his finger into the center of the lettering on Virchow's lab coat. "And I'm telling you categorically and unequivocally that if you don't shut up and leave me alone, I'm going to pull that pretty monogrammed jacket over your head and give you a much-needed face-lift, all hockey style."

Virchow took a step back. His face twisted into a haughty sneer. "Oh, maybe the rumors of you being violent are true."

"Leave us alone and go back to your table," Tucker Oliver chimed in. "Don't be such an immature prick."

Virchow huffed and spoke over his shoulder as he walked away. "Says the man with the body of a child.

Gracie patted Jet on the back as he took his place back beside her at the dissection table. "Maybe you should've just leveled him."

"Yeah, that's just what I need right now. Get reinstated and expelled the same day."

"He's a punk," Craig Tekowski said. "Good to have you back, Jet."

"Well, Tea." Jet chuckled. "I believe that may be the first nice thing you've ever said to me."

Tekowski suppressed a smile and picked up a scalpel. "Don't get used to it. Can we get started?"

"Where are we now?" Jet peered over at Gracie's notes.

"We are down to the splenius muscles and the erector spinae muscles." Gracie pointed to the corresponding locations on the cadaver. "Here and here." She paused looked at Jet, studying him. "You gonna be okay with this?"

"I'm fine. Just ready to dive in and get it behind me." He looked around the room. "What's the word on the interim director, Professor Osecki? I met her this morning, but it was hard to tell. Don't guess I met her the first two days I was here."

"I don't think she's a hard case like Cronin," Tucker said.

"So Cronin was in on it, too?" Tekowski asked. "You know, the whole, the uh, thing with your brother. Nobody really explained all that. We just know Cronin got canned."

Gracie touched Jet's shoulder. She would answer since he didn't want to talk about it. "Tea, you know Jet doesn't want to talk about all that, and we shouldn't ask him to. But as best they can, tell Dr. Cronin didn't know about the, um, murder and all that. His mistake was in not recognizing what the problem was. He thought Jet was having a breakdown, so he let Winscote convince him to switch the bodies. Seems ludicrous, but it happened."

Tea shrugged. "No offense, Jet, but I hate it for him. Seemed like he really knew his stuff. Probably not a bad guy if you got to know him. Can we get started?"

"Not a bad guy?" Tucker said. "Are you serious? He rode Jet like a pack mule. Me, too, for that matter."

"Honey, I think you brought that on yourself the first day." Gracie laughed. "Had him floundering to figure out whether your last name was Tucker or Oliver. Rubbed him the wrong way from the start."

"Then you had to go trying to flip the body over," Tekowski said. "Your obsession with finding that bullet got us all in trouble. Like you're a forensics expert or something." He tapped the edge of the stainless steel tank with his knuckles like a judge banging a gavel. "Guys, seriously, we need to get going if we're gonna get through today's assignment."

"Whatever." Tucker ignored Tekowski's entreaty. "Good riddance as far as I'm concerned. Right, Jet?"

"Yeah, good riddance. Seems like a popular theme these days. Even from people you least suspect."

"What do you mean?"

"Well here's the thing. Case told me something Lane mentioned to him when he had him tied up. And it's been bothering me, wondering what he meant. I first thought it was random, but the more I thought about it, the more I thought not. He said it for a reason. The question was, why?"

"Jet, baby, what are you talking about?" Gracie asked.

"Lane said the reason he switched the cadaver tanks so we would have Adam's body was to kill two birds with one stone. It was clear he wanted to drive me crazy and make me look that way, too. But that's not two birds. That's kinda the same thing. The more I've thought about it, the more I was sure there was something else."

"What are you doing?" Tekowski asked. "Guys, he's going off the deep end again."

"It's funny you're speaking up there, Tea, because I've wondered if you had it in for me from the beginning. What really bothered me was that somebody told the police Gracie and I had an argument in the anatomy lab the day before she was assaulted. It was an anonymous call, but it still helped the police make their case, because I confirmed it before I knew I was a suspect. The only people who were in here that night were Gracie, me, you, and a couple of students down on the other end. I barely noticed them and can't tell you who they were. I first thought one of them had to have told Virchow." He turned his head slightly and called back over his shoulder. "Hey, Virchow."

Sterling Virchow stepped over. "What do you want?"

"Did you tell the police that Gracie and I got in a fight?"

"What are you talking about? I haven't talked to the police. C'mon now, Jet, don't have another meltdown. It's distracting."

"Watch and see. Did you break into my house and plant evidence for the police to find?"

Virchow shook his head. "You are losing it, ol' boy. I knew it was a mistake for them to let you back in here."

"You might be right. Time will tell."

"Jet, honey." Gracie touched his sleeve. "You need to stop."

"What about you, Gracie? Who did you tell? At least you've seemed to be on my side. You know, the funny thing is, it occurred to me that maybe you're not who I think you are. I mean, what better way to distract from the fact that you're involved somehow than to fake your own attempted kidnapping? After all, Dr. Winscote admitted you guys were friends."

"Jet Townsend." Gracie planted her hands on her hips. "You've gone mad. She helped me study one time. That's it."

Jet noticed some of the students from adjacent tables beginning to gather around. "One thing that's bothered me." He raised his voice. "How did that vial of midazolam get planted in my house? Officer Weatherspoon finally told me where they found it, in the top drawer of my dresser. The thing is, I had just dug through that drawer for a particular pair of socks before I left the house, fifteen minutes before Gracie's attack. And it wasn't in there. There's no way Lane had time to kidnap Gracie and then plant that, because my roommate Sammy had been home for two hours when the cops came with the warrant. And there was no sign of forced entry either. So how did it get there? I'll tell you—somebody had a key."

"This is way more interesting than dissecting," a voice from the crowd said. Several others muttered words of concurrence. One of the associate professors marched toward the gathering group from across the room with a frown of consternation, seemingly determined to disband them. Then Dr. Osecki reached out and stopped him. She shook her head and whispered in his ear. He nodded and stood still with his arms crossed, watching alongside the new course director. Her eyes met and locked with Jet's, but she said nothing, nor did she move.

"So who had a key to my house?" Jet looked around at the faces of those raptly listening. "My roommate Sammy? Yes, but he's not connected to this. Who else? I'll tell you. Nobody. But what about this? Gracie, what happened the day I passed out in here. Did something fall out of my pocket?"

"I can't remember."

"Oh, I think you can. My keys fell out. And who brought them to me in the ER several hours later? Gave them to my friend Case."

"I did, but—"

A string of murmurs and whispers erupted from the by-standers. "He thinks she did it. Gracie? No way, I didn't think she was like that."

"Yes, you brought me my keys that day." Jet glared at Gracie. "With plenty of time beforehand to make a duplicate. You know what else I found interesting?"

"Jet, c'mon, you don't seriously think Gracie did this, do you?" Tekowski said. "You're taking this too far."

"I'm not sure this is the way to go about it," Tucker said softly. "Jet, maybe you need some more time off."

"Leave him alone," Virchow said. "This man has something to say, and I want to hear it."

"What I found interesting," Jet continued, "was what the police told me after it became obvious I was being framed. Late the very night I fell and hit my head, two people were seen up here moving bodies around. The witness said it looked like two females, one taller than the other. Because they had no reason to believe otherwise, the police assumed it was Adam's killer, Lane Buckley, and Dr. Winscote. You know, for whatever reason the witness mistakenly thought Lane was a female. Dim light, poor eyesight, whatever. Two females. Gracie, what do you think about that?"

"Sounds like Gracie has a lot of explaining to do," Virchow said.

Murmurs from the crowd again sounded agreement.

"I agree as well," Jet said. "Gracie, can you explain yourself? Tell me who you told about our disagreement the night before you were attacked."

"I mentioned it to Tucker," she said. "We were talking about what we would do if you had to drop out."

"And Gracie, I'm wondering, how tall are you?"

"Five-eight."

"Five-eight. You've spent time with Dr. Winscote. How tall is she?"

"I'd say she's about five-nine, give or take an inch. You've seen her standing here."

"So why would the witness who saw Winscote moving a body around think he saw two women, one taller than the other?"

"You'll have to ask him that," Gracie said.

"I don't think I do," Jet said. "I've been thinking, what would the motive be? What did Lane mean when he said he was killing two birds with one stone?" Jet moved around the end of the table with the collective eyes of the group following him. He stood behind Tekowski, who was frozen in place while Tucker Oliver had nonchalantly inched away from the table by at least a foot. Jet put his hand on Tekowski's shoulder and patted it. "Tea, you've really hated the distractions I've caused, and I'm sorry for that, but I never took you for someone who would help set me up."

"Glad to hear it," Tekowski said. "Mind if I ask a question or two?"

"Be my guest," Jet said.

Tekowski nodded. "Gracie, the day you brought the keys to Jet, how did you get them?"

"Tucker was the one who picked them up. He brought them to me an hour or so after we finished our lab. Said he forgot to give them to me and figured I'd see Jet before he did."

Tekowski crossed his arms and turned to stare at Tucker. The crowd started rumbling again.

"And Tucker, how tall are you? A few inches shorter than Dr. Winscote?"

"My height has nothing to do with anything," Tucker said scornfully. "You're barking up the wrong tree."

Someone whispered in the background. "I think he means, barking down."

"Jet, dear, can I ask a question now?" Gracie said.

Jet made a sweeping gesture with his hand. "Please."

"Tucker, what did you tell me you liked to do in your spare time?"

"What are you doing, Gracie?" Tucker asked. "You turning on me to deflect attention from yourself?"

"Didn't you tell me you had accumulated some debt? And you were afraid of what would happen if you didn't figure out a way to pay it off?"

"That's nobody's business." Tucker's voice shook.

"Motive," another voice mumbled in the crowd.

"It's my turn." Sterling Virchow stepped up to the table directly across from Tucker. "Where did you say you volunteered this summer? Here in the hospital?"

"What does that have to do anything?"

"Forget it," Virchow said. "Gracie, where did Tucker work this summer?"

"In the surgery department here."

"Jet, where did the officer say the midazolam bottle traced back to?"

"Why Sterling, I do believe it was stolen from the surgery department here. Not the ER, as some assumed."

Virchow nodded. "I thought that's what you told me." He looked around the room, like a seasoned attorney eyeing the jurors in a closing statement. "And does anyone in here know where the surgery residents come in to practice their techniques and learn landmarks for their procedures? They often bring students with them."

Tekowski answered. "I do believe they often come to the anatomy lab to practice."

Jet raised a hand, and Virchow stepped back. "So, one last thing, Tucker. We saw you have a fascination with bullets. You know, trying to dig them out of cadavers."

"You don't know anything." Tucker stepped back again as two students moved out of his way.

"I know enough to know that might kill two birds with one stone," Jet said. "You finding the bullet. You know, it took me awhile, but I figured it out. Why would Lane get someone in here to help him? A student. Wouldn't another person being involved just muddy it up, make it more likely something would slip? Well, in some ways yes, just like today.

"But what about if he needed a way in, someone with the codes to the door? Huh? Who better than a first-year medical student who had access to the lab well before Gross Anatomy started and one with a gambling debt to pay off? Plus, it allowed him to keep an eye on me, know how I was reacting, what I was suspecting. But more than that, if things went badly, it gave him a way to recover some evidence. If the bullet was still in that body, it might somehow be traced back to him."

Jet paused and shook his head in disgust. "Maybe he wanted to hang on to the gun and knew he could if the bullet could be recovered. Maybe he'd used that gun somewhere else that could be linked back to him. We'll never know. But I know this. You were looking for that bullet for a reason. Look around the room. Everybody else knows it, too."

Tucker's face was ashen. Beads of sweat had formed on his forehead, and he looked even smaller than usual. Jet almost felt sorry for him. Almost.

"You don't know anything." Tucker said. "You don't know what it's like. Nobody ever gave me a chance at being anything, but I got in med school anyway. Too many college loans, so I needed to pay a different way. It just backfired." He took two more steps back. "Jet, I didn't mean to hurt you. Lane said it was just a little thing. Nobody would ever know, and my school would be paid for. I didn't kill anyone." Tucker stepped back again, and it reminded Jet of what he must have looked like the day he himself had passed out. Tucker didn't go down, though. He gathered himself and turned to leave.

"Don't you run away, Tucker!" Jet slammed his palm hard against the side of the dissection table.

Tucker jumped at the crash and stopped. He turned back. His eyes roved wildly from the dissection table to Jet to the gawking horde of onlookers. "I sure ain't staying around here." He spun and shoved past two students in his path.

"Get back here!" Jet bellowed. He lunged in Tucker's direction, but there was no point. Tucker was as quick as a cat on a cattle prod, and Jet was handicapped. Tucker bolted toward the door. Before he reached it, though, he disappeared with a thud and a moan.

When Jet rounded the row of dissection tables into the aisle in the center of the room, he saw why. Gracie had him pinned with a knee in his back and one arm twisted behind him. She looked up at Jet with a smug grin. "You need to ask him some more questions?"

Jet was too stunned to answer.

Gracie shrugged. "Woman's intuition told me he'd be headed for the door soon. And then six years of Taekwondo kicked in." Her smile spread across her face. "Literally."

Jet broke into a broad smile himself. He nodded at Tekowski and Virchow. "Nice job. You two should hit the theater circuit if the doctor thing doesn't work out." He turned and fixed his gaze on Gracie. "And I think she's a keeper, don't y'all?"

FIFTY-ONE

THE knock at the door startled me from a restless sleep. I rubbed my eyes and forehead, trying to clear the fog, vowing to call the doctor and ask about cutting back on the seizure medication. Either that or do it myself and take my chances. Not being able to sleep well or stay awake was a bad combination.

I expected another round of knocks since it was taking me so long to get out of my recliner, but whoever was there wasn't knocking again. The knob jiggled, and metal ground against metal within the cylinder. He was picking the lock. A surge of panic enveloped me, but I fought it. *They're all gone. It's supposed to be over.* Still, I jumped up and looked about the room for a weapon as the door moved, angry at myself for leaving my pistol in my bedroom.

The door opened and two men entered, both imposing figures, thick and barrel-chested, one several inches taller than the other. The taller man held something between his fingers. "Need some WD-40 in that lock. Barely could get the key to turn."

I slid my pocketknife back into my pants. "Dad, you scared me half to death."

"Sorry, but you didn't answer the door. I knocked several times."

"It's the medications. I've gotta do something about that." I looked at the other man and smiled. "How are you, Coach Marchianti?" I reached out to shake his massive hand.

"Better than you, I reckon. Just dropping by to check on you and ran into your dad out front. Came by the hospital once but you were in la-la land that day."

"I feel like I'm still there sometimes."

"It'll get better," Coach said. "Rex tells me he's been trying to decide whether to arrest you or deputize you."

"Nope," Dad said, "I've made up my mind. House arrest. I know something else, too. That's my last cruise. Caught some bug, hugged the toilet the whole time. And if that wasn't bad enough, found out Case was playing sheriff and nearly got himself killed. Thought I was gonna have to kill or bribe somebody to get us off that ship." He gave me a hard look. Luckily, he got better fast and no helicopters were needed."

"I've told you I'm sorry, Dad. Jet was in trouble, and we couldn't wait."

"Your investigating had nothing to do with writing another book?"

I smiled. "No, not really."

Dad gave me a frown and incredulous cock of his head.

"Okay, maybe a little at first. But not at the end. Speaking of which, I need to interview Stimpy Riggins sometime so he can give me his version."

Dad rolled his eyes and nodded.

"You know," Coach said, "I feel a little responsible for what happened. Like maybe you took my speech about the red circle a little too far?"

"No sir, I didn't. Jet was in trouble, and we all did what we had to do."

Coach Marchianti gave a knowing look that said he would have done the same. I thought Dad might have smiled. A hint of curl at the corner of his lips but no more. Probably not recognizable by anyone other than a son.

"I was just down at Jackson PD," Dad said, "trying to make sure I got what I need to finish my investigation. Word is they arrested a medical student this afternoon."

"Tucker Oliver, one of Jet's anatomy partners. Jet called me about an hour ago. Turns out this guy was in on it, too. Lane had hired him."

I didn't tell Dad what else Jet had told me, about how things had worked out. In addition to being reinstated, he had two demands in exchange for promising not to file a lawsuit against the medical school, one that he would almost certainly win.

The first condition, which turned out to be the easiest to achieve, was to not be prosecuted for the theft of the naloxone. The second, which was more difficult to negotiate because of skittish attorneys fearing a different lawsuit, was to have fifteen minutes to question Tucker, in class, unimpeded by the instructors.

Marta Winscote had refused to implicate Tucker, but Jet was convinced of his involvement. The most likely reason for Winscote protecting him seemed to be that, since VJ's remains still had not been found, she believed he might still be alive somewhere. And since Lane was dead, the only other witness was Tucker. If he remained protected, then maybe VJ would be, too, if he were ever located.

Jet was certain that Tucker would cave if he worked it right with a little help from a few classmates, and apparently, they choreographed it to perfection. Jet got a full confession right there in front of the entire Gross Anatomy contingent of professors, students, and body donors. The fact that Sterling Virchow helped him was perhaps the greatest surprise, but Jet said Virchow had turned out to be human after all. He had a change of heart when he found out the truth about what happened to Adam and the plot to cover it up.

"You think Jet's gonna be okay?" Dad asked. "He's been through a lot. More than anybody should have to endure."

"Jet's tougher than you think. Mentally tough."

"So are his friends," Coach said. "I saw that years ago on the football field. Hey, I'm glad you're doing okay. I gotta run. Back at school this week?"

"Maybe a half day tomorrow. Thanks for coming by."

Another knock at the door greeted Coach Marchianti just as he reached for the knob. He pulled it open and smiled, stepping back. "Abi Rossini. Speaking of strong-willed people. Come on in. I'm sure Case would rather see your pretty face than my ugly mug."

Abi's laugh was natural and easy as she gave the coach a hug. "I'm sure he was glad to see you. Your pep talks are better than mine any day." She turned to look at my father. "Is everything okay, Mr. Reynolds? Thought you went back to Amberton this morning."

"Just a few loose ends downtown. I'm heading on back." Dad patted me on the shoulder. "Call me if you need anything." He wrapped an arm around Abi's shoulder. "Keep an eye on him for me?"

"Yes sir." Abi grinned and winked at me from beneath Dad's smothering hug. "It won't be easy, though."

My heart fluttered.

She closed the door behind the men, and I tried not to stare. For the life of me, I can't remember what she wore that day, but I'll never forget her face. At first it was the blue of her eyes, the bronze of her skin, the ease with which she wore her beauty that grabbed me, as it always has. But what held me, what made me forget everything else for that instant, was the ever-so-brief way her gaze met mine before she quickly looked me over. Examined me from head to toe in a millisecond, but not like a nurse or a critic or even a friend, but like I belonged to her. The image of the look and the feeling it gave me are indelibly seared in my memory.

I finally managed to speak. "How was your day?"

Abi put her hands on her hips, protesting the question. "The important question is, how was yours?"

"I'm fine. Headache now and then."

"I'm not asking about your headaches. I'm asking, how are you?"

"I'm fine. Or I will be. I just need to get back to work and forget about it all. Same as you. And Jet. Jack, too, I guess."

She came to me, leaned over, and straightened the sling on my shoulder with an empathetic wince when I grimaced in pain. "You can't forget about it totally, you know. Jet's counting on you to write that book. Besides, you don't know how it all ends."

"Don't I?" I sighed. "Maybe I'll just forget about it for a little while."

"Moving on with life doesn't mean forgetting the past. I've been thinking about it all day. Sometimes you've got to go back to where you've been to know where you're going."

I frowned, uncertain of her meaning.

She breezed across the room before stopping at the back door. "Get up, Mr. Lazy Bones. Come out on the porch. Let's talk about the ending."

I found her sitting on the wooden porch swing, pushing it back and forth with her toes as the chains suspending it from the ceiling creaked with their effort. She patted her hand on the open space beside her and smiled. "Remember my fourteenth birthday party?"

I smiled and sat down beside her. "How could I forget it?" The nervous excitement consumed me that night at her pool house, on a similar swing, as I had sat beside her, touching her fingers for the first time in a romantic way, sensing that she finally knew I was in love with her.

VJ and Lane and their cronies had fouled it up, destroying the moment forever. And even though we had later dated, the thrill—the simple but profound ecstasy of that instant—seemed forever lost, at least in my mind. It exhilarated me to think perhaps she remembered the experience with even a fraction of the same fond regret, if there could be such a thing, that I did.

"I think sometimes it's therapeutic to go back to the beginning." She touched the tips of my fingers with hers, then turned and looked into my eyes. Each of us searching for hidden truths, or maybe just confirming them, just as we had that night.

She remembers.

"You know, start over," she said. "Except don't let the distractions of the past get in the way." She didn't have to mention

VJ or Lane or anyone else. Yes it was tragic, but they were gone, and we didn't have to talk about them.

"Start back at the beginning," I said.

She intertwined her fingers in mine and squeezed. I wanted to kiss her, but she put her head on my shoulder instead. The kiss could come later.

I smiled and pushed the swing, calmed by the rhythmic squeaking of its chains.

THE END

ABOUT THE AUTHOR

W. D. "Dwight" McComb earned an engineering degree before deciding that a career in medicine was his true calling. Twelve years after his medical training was complete, he finally made time to also pursue his other lifelong dream, and he hasn't stopped writing since.

From word one, his goal has been to write compelling and clean fiction without sacrificing authenticity. His debut novel, *The Truth That Lies Between,* received widespread praise and was named a Finalist for Serious Writer Book of the Year and the Readers' Favorite Book Award for Southern Fiction.

He continues to practice medicine in northeast Mississippi, where he lives with his wife and three children. After coaching a few hundred of their soccer, baseball, and softball games, his kids recently made him retire his coaching hats for good. He still gets to throw batting practice.